W9-AVO-205

A WANT OF KINDNESS

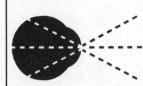

A WANT OF KINDNESS

JOANNE LIMBURG

THORNDIKE PRESS
A part of Gale, Cengage Learning

GALE
CENGAGE Learning·

Farmington Hills, Mich • San Francisco • New York • Waterville, Maine
Meriden, Conn • Mason, Ohio • Chicago

GALE
CENGAGE Learning®

Copyright © 2016 by Joanne Limburg.
Thorndike Press, a part of Gale, Cengage Learning.

ALL RIGHTS RESERVED
Thorndike Press® Large Print Historical Fiction.
The text of this Large Print edition is unabridged.
Other aspects of the book may vary from the original edition.
Set in 16 pt. Plantin.

LIBRARY OF CONGRESS CATALOGING-IN-PUBLICATION DATA

Names: Limburg, Joanne, 1970– author.
Title: A want of kindness / by Joanne Limburg.
Description: Large print edition. | Waterville, Maine : Thorndike Press, 2017. |
  Series: Thorndike Press large print historical fiction
Identifiers: LCCN 2016059169| ISBN 9781410499295 (hardcover) | ISBN 1410499294
  (hardcover)
Subjects: LCSH: Anne, Queen of Great Britain, 1665-1714—Fiction. | Great
  Britain—History—1660-1714—Fiction. | Large type books. | GSAFD: Historical
  fiction. | Biographical fiction.
Classification: LCC PR6062.I443 W36 2017 | DDC 823/.92—dc23
LC record available at https://lccn.loc.gov/2016059169

Published in 2017 by arrangement with Pegasus Books, LLC

In memory of
Ruth Helen Limburg

DRAMATIS PERSONÆ

Lady Anne of York, later Princess of Denmark

Anne's Kin

Lady Mary of York/the Princess of Orange/ Queen Mary II Anne's sister

The Duke of York/King James II Her father

The Duchess of York/Queen Mary Beatrice Her step-mother

King Charles II Her uncle

Queen Catherine Charles II's wife

Ladies Catherine and Isabella Anne's half-sisters

The Duke of Cambridge; James, Prince of Wales Her half-brothers

The Duke of Monmouth Anne's first cousin, Charles II's natural son

The Prince of Orange/King William III Anne's first cousin, later her brother-in-law

Prince George of Denmark Anne's husband

Lady Mary, Lady Anne Sophia Their daughters

William, Duke of Gloucester Their son

The Earls of Clarendon and Rochester Anne's maternal uncles

Lady Rochester Her aunt, later her Governess

Lady Clarendon Her aunt, later her Groom of the Stole

Anne's Household, and her Friends

Lady Frances Villiers Anne's Governess

Elizabeth 'Betty' Villiers, Barbara Villiers/ Berkeley/Fitzharding, Anne Villiers/ Bentinck, Catherine Villiers Lady Frances' daughters

Sarah Jennings/Churchill/Marlborough Anne's dear friend, Maid of Honour to the Duchess of York, later Anne's Lady of the Bedchamber

John Churchill/Lord Churchill/Earl of Marlborough Sarah's husband

Mary Cornwallis Anne's friend

Frances Apsley/Bathurst Friend to Mary and Anne

Sir Benjamin Bathurst Frances' husband, and Comptroller of Anne's household

Beata Danvers Anne's Woman of the Bedchamber

Margery Farthing Anne's nurse

8

Mrs Wanley Nurse to Lady Anne Sophia, later Woman of the Bedchamber to Gloucester

Lady Charlotte Freschville, Lady Anne Spencer, Lady Charlotte Beaverwort Anne's Ladies of the Bedchamber

Mrs Abigail Hill Sarah's cousin, employed as Anne's Woman of the Bedchamber

Henry Compton, Bishop of London Preceptor to Mary and Anne

Dr Lake, Dr Doughty Anne's chaplains

Sir Charles Scarburgh, Dr Radcliffe, Sir Richard Lower Physicians

Mrs Judith Wilkes Midwife to Anne, and to Queen Mary Beatrice

The Duke of Gloucester's Household
Mrs Pack, Mrs Atkinson His nurses
Jenkin Lewis His manservant
Reverend Pratt His tutor
Bishop Gilber Burnet His preceptor

Other Persons at Court, and in Government
Sydney Godolphin/Lord Godolphin A promising man in Government, friend to the Churchills and later to Anne
Margaret Blagge, later Godolphin Former Maid of Honour to Anne's late mother

The Earl of Mulgrave Courtier, soldier, and wit

Lady Peterborough, Lady Sunderland Ladies in Waiting to Queen Mary Beatrice

The Earl of Salisbury, The Earl of Sunderland, The Earl of Nottingham, The Earl of Shrewsbury Statesmen, in and out of office

William Bentinck, later the Earl of Portland, Arnold von Keppel, later the Earl of Albemarle Friends and advisors to William III

Mrs Dawson Woman of the Bedchamber

PART I

CALISTO AND NYPHE

Anne and her sister Mary make their entrance into Court under wooden clouds, that smell a little of distemper. Their bodies are draped in heavy layers of silk and brocade, run through with gold and silver thread, and made heavier still by the many jewels their dressers have attached to them; Anne feels heavy inside too, as if all the months of practice and expectation, the dancing lessons, the acting lessons, the fittings, the conversations overheard, and even her own prayers have all been mixed up and baked together, so that now the whole concoction sits stolidly in her breast, like a pudding on a pantry shelf.

For all this weight, she treads daintily — if not quite as daintily as Mary — her arms outstretched as they have been taught, holding a castanet in each hand. The sisters take their places first, then the other young ladies take their places behind and to either side.

First they curtsy — everything begins with a curtsy — then there is a little pause, a quick burst of applause, and the music starts, half flowing up from the pit, and half down from the clouds, two separate streams of sound that pool together on the stage, exactly where she stands.

Now they begin to trace the steps that they have learned, with the viols and the recorders treading alongside, three slow beats at a time; underneath the music, Anne can hear the heels of their shoes sliding against the baize, the little thuds they make when they all step in time, and the rustling of their skirts whenever, with a pert clicking of castanets, they kick up and show the Court their stockings. It is a pretty song, so the hardest task she has is to keep herself from humming. The Court is watching her, so the Court might well be listening too.

Anne is, for once, grateful that God has given her such bad eyes. From the stage, the Court is no more than a glistening murmur, held at bay by a row of candles. Their flames run together, making a bank of fire. She can see smaller lights flashing on the dancers' costumes and when the dance brings her close enough, she catches a glimpse of a face: Mary's is taut with concentration; the others' are scared or

14

excited or saucy, according to temperament. This is as much as she wishes to see. If she saw anything more, she fears she would not be able to dance at all.

The music stops, the Court applauds, and now Anne can go back to the tiring-room, where Danvers and the other dressers are waiting, and where she can refresh herself from dishes of oranges, olives and almonds. As she steps through the wings, she meets the Duke of Monmouth and his gentlemen on their way to the baize to dance a minuet. Lady Henrietta Wentworth stops suddenly to watch them walking out, and Carey Fraser, who is just behind, nearly trips over her gown — a couple of the other young ladies giggle, and are shushed.

Monmouth is the King's eldest son, but not his heir: that is the King's brother, the Duke of York, Anne's father. Mary's and Anne's places, at Court, and in the succession, are therefore ordained by God, and the masque they are about to perform has been commissioned so that these important truths might be confirmed and demonstrated. Monmouth's place is altogether less certain, but he is handsome and beloved, one of the lights of the Court, so it is only right that he should have his minuet, and lead the dance. Mary says it is to show the world how well the King loves him; Squinting Betty Villiers, who has no part, says it is to show the Court how well his leg is turned.

The masque has been written by a Mr Crowne who, as he writes in his dedication to Mary, has been unexpectedly called out of his obscurity by the command of their step-mother the Duchess, to the glory of serving her fair and excellent Highness. So unexpected was this call, he explains, that he has not had time to ripen his conceptions, and regrets that the words he has found for Mary to say must fall sadly short of the excellence of her thoughts:

> For none can have Angelical thoughts but they who have Angelical virtues; and none do, or ever did, in so much youth, come to so near the perfection of Angels as yourself, and your young Princely Sister, in whom all those excellencies shine, which the best of us can but rudely paint.

Anne is used to hearing Mary's perfections praised: she is quick, she is diligent, beautiful, agreeable, pious; she dances gracefully, draws and paints exquisitely, embroiders charmingly. Conscientious in all things, she read the whole libretto of *Ca-*

listo: the Chaste Nymph as soon as it was put into her hands. Her young Princely Sister has seen only her own parts, because reading makes her eyes water. Mary's view is that Anne could read much more if she wanted to, but as she is herself always just as willing to talk as to read, she has told Anne the whole story, more them once:

'We're to play sisters — Calisto and Nyphe — they're princesses, and nymphs serving Diana. Jupiter and Mercury watch them. Jupiter loves Calisto. She loves only innocence and chastity, but there's a jealous nymph, Psecas, who thinks she's shamming it. Psecas knows Mercury loves her, and means to pretend to love him in return, so her conduct will shame all the rest —'

'How's that?'

'Because if one nymph loses her honour, it throws suspicion on the others. Where was I . . . ? Jupiter tells Mercury how he'll appear to Calisto in Diana's shape, thinking that she cannot mind if her mistress caresses her, so he finds Calisto and embraces her and she thinks he's Diana run mad and calls "Help!" —'

And here Mary strikes the appropriate attitude.

'— so he shows himself in his true shape, but she still won't have him, so he orders

17

the Winds to seize her. Then his jealous Queen, Juno, comes looking for him. In the meantime, Mercury promises to make Psecas a goddess, and they plan to have Calisto shamed, and Nyphe too. Nyphe finds them and — listen, Anne, this is your biggest part — she quarrels with Psecas, who thinks herself above the others now —'

'And I tell her that I am a princess born, but she is only made great by her lover.'

'So you have read *that,* at least — yes, and then Psecas and Mercury plot to show Nyphe with Mercury and Calisto with Jupiter in front of Diana and Juno. Then Juno finds Jupiter and Calisto, and Jupiter tells her he's to have Calisto as well as her. Then Nyphe finds Calisto alone, and they weep together.'

'But then . . . ?'

'Then Mercury finds Psecas and tells how he's roused Juno to punish Calisto, and now they will shame Nyphe. Now the sisters are enchanted and afraid. They see Diana and — no, there's something else: Juno appears and tells Diana she is deceived in Calisto, and — Sister, you do not *listen* —'

'I am. I do. Mary, do please go on.'

'Very well. So now . . . so *now* the sisters come. They think Diana is Jupiter so they strike her with darts, so Diana says they

18

must die. Then Juno says she'll crown Psecas a goddess, but Psecas makes Mercury angry, so he tells all to Diana, and so the sisters' honour is restored. Psecas is banished, and Jupiter sets the sisters in the sky to rule over a star. And that's the end.'

If Mary has told this story more than once, it is because Anne has asked more than once, partly because she is reassured by repetition, but also because the story seems to complicate itself further with every telling. By this time, though, she has grasped the chief point, which is that nobody much cares if she understands, as long as she speaks her lines beautifully, and as she is well able to do this — Mrs Betterton has even commended her voice to the King for its sweetness — she is no longer troubling herself, or Mary, about the intricacies of the plot. After all, Mary is thirteen and it is quite natural that she should comprehend more than Anne, who has only just turned ten.

Anne understands this much: the play is about lovemaking, adultery and attempted ravishment, but it is from the Classics, and all the parts are taken by ladies, so there can be nothing improper in it. The gods Jupiter and Mercury are played, respectively, by Lady Henrietta and Sarah Jennings, while their father the Duke has commanded Margaret Blagge out of retirement from Court to play Diana, and Anne has heard from several reliable sources that Mrs Blagge is so given over to goodness and piety that she has sworn never to say or do one amusing thing ever again. Margaret is sharing a tiring-room with the princesses and other principals, and while they wait between acts she sits on a chair in the corner, reading a book of devotions. When they are called for the first act she puts down the book with conspicuous reluctance, accepts her bow and arrows from her dresser, and takes her place at the head of her train. Mary follows her, then Anne, and then Lady Mary Mordaunt, who is Psecas. A group of lesser ladies, playing lesser nymphs, join them in the wings, and they complete the retinue.

Anne hears Jupiter's last lines —

She swiftly by like some bright meteor shot
Dazzled my eye, and straight she
    disappeared

— and thinks, as she always does, of Mrs Jennings, who leaves the stage as they come on, bright-haired and dashing in her breeches, her smile like a private letter.

After a long evening of pursuing and plotting, resisting and weeping, denunciations and revelations, all interspersed with the affairs of shepherds and shepherdesses from the King's music, and dances of Basques, Cupids, Winds, Satyrs, Bacchuses and, finally, Africans, the sisters make their final entrance under a great canopy, with the Africans supporting it.

Jupiter is to crown them before an assembly of all the gods, so as soon as they reach centre stage, the wings are pulled back, and behind and above them a heaven is revealed in the form of a glory, with the gods and goddesses seated in front of it. The glory is made of a huge back piece with a round hole in the middle of it, taffeta stretched over the hole and many dozens of candles behind. Anne can see nothing of this, but she can feel the heat, which, added to the warmth of the footlights, her heavy costume and the press of bodies on stage for the finale, is suddenly almost too much. But soon enough Lady Henrietta has descended from the glory to speak the epilogue, and it is nearly over.

Jupiter announces a final change of heart: he will not waste their virtue and beauty on a star. That is no way for a king to dispose of princesses: he will keep them to oblige other thrones, to grace some favourite crowns. Having spoken, Lady Henrietta steps forward in her own person and addresses the real King, on the subject of the real princesses:

Two glorious nymphs of your own godlike
    line,
Whose morning rays, like noontide, strike
    and shine
Whom you to suppliant monarchs shall
    dispose,
To bind your friends, and to disarm your
    foes.

THE KING'S DOGS

The tiring-room is suddenly full of dogs, excitable little spaniels; for formality's sake, a footman announces that the King is coming. All the goings-on in the room, the eating and drinking, flirting and gossiping, jokes and congratulations, stop in an instant; for a moment there is nothing to hear but panting and snuffling on one side of the doorway, and well-shod feet approaching from the other. Then Anne's uncle is at the door, and the room lowers itself, bending at the waist and the knee.

The men on either side of him have kept their heads covered, so must be ambassadors, here to examine Mary. The usual pack of courtiers follow the three of them as they approach her, and she greets them all with a perfect curtsy, first taking a step to one side, towards the men, then drawing the foot back so that her heels touch, before making a bend of carefully judged depth, allowing her arms to fall gracefully to her sides. All the men, apart from the King, bow in return, the ambassadors slightly, the courtiers deeply and elaborately.

The King lifts Mary's face by the chin, holds on to it while he praises her dancing, her poise, her height, her fine verse-speaking, her charming yet modest demeanour and, most fulsomely, her beauty. The ambassadors join in with accented compliments. Meanwhile, Anne's favourite spaniel, Hortense, starts sniffing about her skirts, so she bends down to pet her. They are both of them afflicted with a constant watering of the eyes, and Anne believes that this has given them a special understanding.

She is stroking Hortense's ears when a hissed *Your Highness!* from somewhere makes her jump: the King has finished with Mary and is now addressing her. As she straightens up, she feels one of her worst blushes coming, hot and red, spreading out from the sides of her nose all the way to her ears, up to her temples, and down to her neck. Once the blush has started, nothing can go right, and her curtsy is sufficiently unlike Mary's for some of the courtiers to laugh a little into their sleeves. The King, at least, doesn't laugh. She looks straight up at him, at his black intelligent fox face, and waits to hear what he has for her.

'Anne, I think you astonished our Court tonight.'

She sees she is expected to speak.

'How is that, Your Majesty?'

'With your voice. We hear it so seldom, and that is a great pity, for it is a very fine thing, sweet and clear. If you were not a princess, you should have a great career upon the stage. It was a pleasure for us to hear you speak your lines — a great pleasure. We must work upon that voice — I shall have Mrs Barry give you more lessons.'

'Thank you, Sir.'

'But tell me . . .' and he leans towards her, 'which shall you be, do you think? A comedienne or a tragedienne, hmm?'

Anne knows that she should provide an answer, but she has nothing to offer except more blushes. All the same an answer comes:

'Her Highness is too modest to give an answer, for the truth is that she knows she must excel at both.'

But it isn't her voice — it is an older, altogether more confident one, and it comes from behind her, from the same source as the hiss: insolent Mercury, speaking out of turn.

Her uncle's gaze shifts, and a change comes over him, so that he reminds Anne of the way Hortense looks when she thinks she might have caught the scent of something interesting.

'Vivacious Mercury,' and he beckons Sarah Jennings forward. She makes her curtsy a little awkwardly, because she is still in breeches, but a sound performance, all the same.

'So, Mercury, what will you?'

'I, Your Majesty?'

'Yes. The Lady Anne is for the stage, but Mercury?'

Sarah gives the King, the ambassadors and Court gentlemen only the shortest time to watch her thinking before she replies:

'Well, Sir. When Mercury has put off his costume he must become Mrs Sarah Jennings again, a most dutiful Maid of Honour to her Grace of York, and later, if it pleases God, some gentleman's virtuous wife.'

There is a brief silence in which many things Anne does not understand seem to be happening, and then her uncle bursts into laughter, taking his pack of gentlemen with him.

After the King has left, Anne asks Sarah why he laughed. Was it because she was jesting?

'No,' Sarah replies. 'He laughed because I was in earnest.' Then she lowers her voice and adds: 'Your Highness, try not to screw your eyes up so: people are saying it gives you a disagreeable look.'

Anne's Eyes

For as long as Anne can remember, her eyes have caused consternation. It is on account of them and their watering that her earliest memories are all in French.

She is at her grandmother's chateau in Colombes, and one of her grandmother's physicians is dropping something into her eyes. She cries, then her face is wiped, and she is given something to eat. Later, in the nursery, something nasty is spooned into her mouth; she splutters, and cries again, and is given something nicer to console her.

Her grandmother falls ill and takes to her chamber; then she disappears altogether and Anne is taken to another nursery. It belongs to her cousin Marie Louise, who is sometimes kind to her and sometimes a tormentor. Every now and then their play is interrupted for visits from Marie Louise's mother — the kind and pretty aunt whom everyone calls Madame — or from more physicians who come to put drops in her eyes. Sometimes they cut or blister her for good measure. The doctors come and they go, but there are always ladies to wipe her face, to administer nasty spoonfuls, and to feed her sweetmeats afterwards.

Months pass like this, then a day comes when the house is full of people hurrying and hushing and nobody remembers to wipe her eyes. They are all wiping their own, because her aunt Madame is dead. Her uncle, Monsieur, comes to the nursery, puts his hand on her head, and gives her a candied apricot. She does not like Monsieur — maybe it is his smile, or perhaps his smell — so she hides the apricot inside her sleeve and drops it later, in a corner.

On Monsieur's orders, Marie Louise and Anne are dressed in long violet gowns with veils down to their feet, and she is dragged, stumbling, to a chapel where she is upset by overwhelming music, rich scents and too many adults weeping.

Soon after this, she is told the good news — her father has sent for her, and she is to return to London, because her eyes are cured! She is put on a boat with her ladies, and two pearl and gold bracelets, a present from the King of France. They are such beautiful things that she feels compelled to

29

lick them, but as soon as she does so, they are taken away. And then her eyes are wiped again.

MAN OR TREE?

That night they stay at their father's house, at St James's, but next day they are sent straight back upriver to Richmond, where the air is cleaner, and the smell of rut only perceptible when the deer are in season.

Even in a royal barge, with eight strong oarsmen, the journey takes a couple of hours or more, and the first part, from Whitehall Stairs, is never pleasant. The night before, in the prologue to *Calisto,* Thames made her appearance as a beautiful river nymph draped in silks, leaning on an urn, attended by Peace, Plenty and the Four Parts of the World, all come to pay homage and bring her presents of sparkling jewels. In daylight, her character is quite different. Her broad body is pasted all over, in the most ramshackle way, with boats of various sizes and states of repair, which are themselves studded haphazardly with boatmen, passengers, coal, timber, livestock, cabbages, pails of milk, and whatever else London and the Court might consume, or excrete. Her attendants, the watermen, hail her with coarse and violent oaths. One small mercy, as Danvers says, is that it is February, and cold, so the smells are not too bad.

But the cold, like the watermen, is no respecter of rank, and it is pretty bad. The princesses are sitting in the shelter of the tilt with their dressers and Sarah Jennings, they are wrapped up in heavy cloaks, fur boas and fur muffs, but the cold comes to find them all the same, to pinch their royal noses. Anne pulls her hood over her face, as far forward as she can. Mrs Danvers asks if she might not push it back just a little, but Anne says 'No', and this sets Mary off telling Mrs Jennings her favourite story about her sister. Anne supposes Mrs Jennings must be the only one of their step-mother's Maids of Honour not to have heard it already.

'My sister can be so stubborn.'

This is how it always starts.

'She was quite small then — I remember she had not long returned from France — and we were walking in the Park together, out in the open, and we saw something at a great distance. Whatever it was, it was too far away for us to be certain as to what it was — of course we both have our bad eyes, but even if we did not — but we were wondering aloud together what it was, and then a dispute was started between us as to whether this something were a man, as I believed, or, as my sister thought, a tree. After a short while, we came near enough to make out the something's shape, and then, clearly, it was a man, so I said, "Now Sister, are you satisfied that it is a man?" But then Anne, after she saw what it was, turned so that she had her back to him, and cried out, like this — "No, Sister, it is a tree!" '

Sarah laughs obligingly, then turns to Anne and asks her, 'But what were your thoughts?'

Anne pushes her hood back long enough to say, 'Mary tells everyone about this, but I don't recall it,' then having nothing more to add, retracts her head again.

THE RUIN OF WINIFRED WELLS

Anne has been told, many times, that Richmond was a great Palace once, but that was before Cromwell and his traitorous Parliament took possession and sold it. Then the buyers took down the white stones of the State and privy apartments, the Great Hall and the Chapel, leaving only the red-brick buildings that had housed the lesser people, the courtiers and officials. Now Cromwell's head sits justly rotting on a spike above Westminster Hall, while the Duke of York's daughters inhabit these red-brick remains, along with their governess, Lady Frances Villiers, her daughters Betty, Barbara, Anne and Catherine, their chaplains, nurses, footmen, necessary women, laundresses and suchlike, portraits of forgotten courtiers and various pieces of heavy oak furniture no longer wanted at St James's or at Whitehall, where tastes run to more delicate items, fine-legged, inlaid or japanned, and preferably made of walnut.

So when they sit down to dine, it is at a refectory table of quite exemplary sturdiness, the bulbous legs of which, as Sarah Jennings points out, resemble nothing so much as two rows of squabbish frights in farthingales.

Eating dinner is one activity to which Anne always applies herself most diligently. It is not only that she loves it for itself, but also that nobody can reasonably ask her to speak if she's using her mouth to eat with. When at table, the sisters always divide the labour between them: Mary keeps up the flow of conversation, while Anne eats.

In this way, they work together through the first course, and the second. Mary chatters, laughing first, then checking herself, then moralising, then forgetting herself, and laughing again. The Villiers sisters, Betty especially, do nothing but laugh. They find Mrs Jennings particularly amusing; Anne cannot help noticing that her sister does not.

With dinner almost over, the broken meats of the second course not yet removed, Anne pulls a silver dish towards her, and helps herself to a sippet. It is her favourite way to end a meal: first she crams the sodden bread into her mouth, then — and this is the heavenly part — she presses it against her palate with her tongue, forcing the warm gravy out over her tongue and down her throat, waiting until the last, tiniest drop has gone before chewing and swallowing the squeezed-out bread. She has finished one and is reaching for her second, when Mary's brittle voice cuts in:

'Sister, must you always finish every sippet on the table? I fear you will grow as fat as our mother did.'

The word 'mother' to Anne means a richly upholstered lap, and sweet bites offered by sparkling, chubby fingers. Fat or not, the face has long since faded, and she takes the portraits on trust. Now another sippet has arrived in her mouth; she hears her sister huffing through her nose, and glances towards her.

Mary is sitting bolt upright, her face severe, a silver spoon held with conscious delicacy halfway between a bowl of rosewater cream and her perfect mouth. Anne stops, shamed, her mouth full of half-sucked sippet. She can hardly spit it out, but she no longer feels like swallowing. Then Mrs Jennings pushes another dish towards her, saying, 'But such tiny morsels, what difference can they make?'

'Besides,' Betty adds, 'surely it is the duty of every royal person to increase her dignity?'

'My sister needs to learn to moderate her appetites.'

'Quite so,' says Betty, and then, in a voice a little less like her own and a little more like Mary's she adds, 'We might all profit by your example: I have never known Your Highness to sit down more than three hours at the card table, or to write to her dearest dear Mrs Apsley more than twice in one —'

'That's enough, Betty.'

'Yes, Mother. That was too sharp: Madam, forgive me.'

If Betty sounds less than sincere, Mary is gracious enough to accept her apology in the spirit in which it should have been offered. Anne continues with her sippets, and the conversation moves on. Sarah Jennings is asked for her opinion on the Duchess's other Maids of Honour, which she delivers in plain terms.

'Great fools, for the most part, and easy prey. There's hardly one among them who wouldn't exchange her honour for a pair of kid gloves, a fan or two, a handful of compliments and some inferior verses bought off a hack.'

'I heard,' says Barbara, 'that Monmouth and Mulgrave and even —' she stops short and looks at Anne, '*others* are daggers drawn over Mrs Kirk.'

'Mary Kirk is the biggest fool of all of them — and lately most unwell.'

'That I can believe.'

'It was just the same when my sister Frances was at Court. Worse, perhaps — have you heard of Winifred Wells?'

'Winifred Wells?' Betty sits up. 'Wasn't she the one who —'

Sarah, not to be cheated of her story, cuts in again. 'Had a mind to take Lady Castlemaine's place with the King. She was pretty enough, but had no wit to speak of, and surrendered far too readily to hold his interest —'

'There is a verse about her!' Betty again. 'It puns upon her name, like this:

"When the King felt the horrible depth of
    this Well,
Tell me, Progers, cried Charlie, where am
    I? oh tell!
Had I sought the world's centre to find —" '

'Betty! You are quite incorrigible! Remember where you are!'

Sarah takes up the story again.

'So, the affair did not last, and no-one — except I suppose Mrs Wells — thought much more of it, but then some months

38

later, at a ball, in the very midst of the Court, as she was dancing in Cuckolds All Awry, she suddenly stopped, and groaned, and before everyone's eyes she dropped her child!'

Anne clears her throat suddenly, and everybody looks at her.

'What became of the baby?'

'Another dancer, a lady, took it up in a handkerchief —'

'Did it not cry? Had the dancers stepped on it?'

'No, I believe it was . . . it was an abortion, quite dead.'

'Just as well, under the circumstances,' says Barbara.

'Perhaps, but Mrs Wells had to leave Court, all the same.'

Then Lady Frances announces, very firmly, that dinner is over. Anne is glad of this: she has the beginnings of a stomach ache.

A CATECHISM

First, Anne believes in God the Father, who hath made her, and all the world.

Second, in God the Son, who hath redeemed her, and all mankind.

Third, in God the Holy Ghost, who sanctifieth her, and all the elect people of God.

Her duty towards God is to believe in him, to fear him, and to love him, with all her heart, with all her mind, with all her soul, and with all her strength; to worship him, to give him thanks, to put her whole trust in him, to call upon him, to honour his holy Name and his Word, and to serve him truly all the days of her life.

She knows that she is not able to do this of herself, because she is weak, and naturally sinful, and so cannot walk in the Commandments of God, or serve him, without his special grace, which she must at all times call for by diligent prayer.

Every morning and every evening, she says

the Lord's Prayer, and asks him to lead her not into temptation.

She prayed last evening, and again this morning, but she cannot deny that her heart and mind were both times very much taken up with the play, the dancing, the costumes, the Court and Mrs Jennings.

So that there was not enough room in them for God.

So when she prayed, he did not hear her; he caused sippets to appear before her at dinner time, and she ate a surfeit of them.

This surfeit being an offence in his eyes, he has sent her a correction in the form of a stomach ache, so there will be no cards after dinner, and no tea.

But as he is merciful, he has also provided a spoonful of Mrs Danvers' surfeit water, and a soft bed on which she may bear her sickness patiently, and with a contrite heart.

IN THE RUELLE

Anne is the cunningest fox that ever was. She has made a harbour of the ruelle in one of the bedchambers at St James's, and her sister and step-mother may seek as much as they like, but they shall not find.

When Anne was smaller, too small to understand that grown people have different pleasures, she supposed that the Palace was built with hide and seek in mind. Behind the well-ordered state rooms is a ravelled heap of closets, staircases and narrow, curving passages that drop down a step without warning, or run on for miles with nothing in them but bottled ships and dead mice, or end abruptly in sullen, doorless walls. Hiding in the ruelle, Anne sits between the two palaces: to her right, behind the hanging, is the Duchess's Great Bed; on her left is the wall, with a door in it which leads to a closet, which has another door, that leads to a staircase, that might lead to another closet, or the kitchens, or outside, or anywhere.

As far as the game is concerned, it makes no difference where the staircase goes, because neither Mary nor the Duchess will be ascending it to find her. Anne has taken care to put the greatest possible distance between her and her pursuers, and to travel it by the most elaborate route. This is not a stratagem that would ever occur to the other ladies, who are both by nature too obliging to put anybody to the trouble of searching too long or with too much effort. Anne has no such scruples: she likes to know that her absence is felt.

Once she has arranged herself comfortably, and her eyes have accustomed themselves to the darkness, she rummages about under her skirts until she finds her pocket. She has a secret hoard in there, some sugarplums she had from the housekeeper this morning. It is only after she has popped one into her mouth and broken its shell that she remembers she has given them up for Lent.

Anne had her first proper conversation with her step-mother a couple of months after the new Duchess's arrival in England. Her English had already improved greatly by then, and she was crying only every other day, so was a good deal more approachable than she had been. She had come to visit Anne and Mary at Richmond, and, although religion was not to be mentioned, they had come, somehow, to be talking of fast days.

'We had *soupe maigre,*' said the Duchess, 'every fast day the same, and I hated it *so* much, but my mother said I had to have it, she made me and she watched me and I was not allowed to stop until I finished the bowl.'

Anne, so used to parables and homilies, searched for the moral.

'But then you found the soup was tolerable after all?'

The Duchess shook her head. 'No. Never, and every fast day I wept into the soup.'

Anne thought of the Duchess's mother on her visit, insisting that she must have precedence over all the great English ladies, and seating herself in the Queen's presence while other duchesses stood. Mary must have been thinking the same, because she remarked that the Duchess Laura was indeed a most commanding person.

'Commanding, yes. I was scared of the men who cleaned the ashes in my chamber — they had black faces — what do you call them here?'

'Chimney sweepers.'

' "Chimney sweepers" Thank you. They frightened me when they came, and I told my mother, so then she told them to come closer to me: I was of the Este family, and I should not be frightened.'

For a long time, it seemed as if the Duchess was as frightened of the Duke as she had ever been of chimney sweepers, and whenever he came close, she would cry all the harder. Fortunately, however, he fared better with her than fast-day soup: after a while, she came to find him tolerable after all, and a little after that to love him. These days when she cries it is usually because he has been moving in close to some other lady. That said, the Duchess is in excellent spirits today. She has recently come out of her first confinement with a healthy child — a daughter, but never mind — and the Duke, when not out hunting, is most attentive.

Anne becomes aware of busy noises in the closet next door. She wipes her mouth quickly, and straightens her skirts, but when the door opens it is neither Mary nor the Duchess, but only a necessary woman, a very young one, with a fresh chamber pot. Both girls are equally startled; they blush at each other, while the necessary woman hurriedly conceals the chamber pot behind her back. Then she curtsies and mumbles something that might be 'Your Highness'. They blush together for another moment, then Anne whispers, 'Pray don't alarm yourself: it's only a game. I'm hiding.'

When the necessary woman has completed her return journey, and the renewed blush has died down, Anne is returned to darkness and to quiet. Nobody else comes into the chamber or the closet. She hears the clang of the bell in the clock tower, and begins to wonder if Mary and the Duchess are ever going to come. Perhaps they have given up the game altogether, and have sent one of their ladies to look for her. They might have picked up their work again, or started playing cards. The Duchess's card-playing has improved along with her English, and nowadays she plays as often as any other lady at Court; she even plays on Sundays, with the Queen. Dr Doughty has made it clear to the princesses that it would not be expedient for them to join her on these occasions: Sunday card-playing is a sin, and more to the point, a Catholic one.

WHAT A GOOD
ENGLISH PRINCESS
KNOWS ABOUT CATHOLICS

They do not belong to God's Church, but to the Pope's, and he is the Antichrist, the Son of Perdition, who opposes and exalts himself above all that is called God, and sits in the temple, dealing in signs and lying wonders.

Some you meet may be agreeable, even kind, they may do many good works, but nevertheless they shall not be saved. Salvation is the reward of a life lived in the light of God's truth, a truth found only in the Bible, which Catholics do not hear. In the English Church, the Bible is read over to the people once every year, and in their mother tongue, so that they might see for themselves the process, order and meaning of the text and therefore profit by it, but in the Popish Church, such scripture as the people hear is broken up and read to them in Latin, which they do not understand; then the Word is further smothered under a

47

multitude of responds, verses and vain repetitions. If any drops of truth remain, they are quenched by the priests and Jesuits, with sophistry and traditions of their own making, founded without all ground of scripture. Such men can take the text and twist it, and do so with such serpentine subtlety, as to amaze the unlearned, and turn plain truth to riddles. By these means and others, the Popish clergy maintain their abominable mischief and idolatories, and damn their people with them. Any Englishman who chooses such a religion, when the truth is plainly laid before him, has declared himself an enemy of that truth. And if he is not a true Christian, then he is not a true Englishman either, for a man can be loyal only to one prince, and the Catholic looks not to his King, but to the Pope in Rome. His design, and that of Popish kings across the Channel, is to bring England under Catholic tyranny, and to this end they have waged ceaseless war against the English, from without, and from within. Queen Elizabeth's life was often in danger; there was even a plot to kill King James with all his Parliament, which by the grace of God was foiled. Every year the people give thanks for this deliverance, and burn the Pope in effigy, with a cat sewn into his belly to make him scream.

And this was deliverance not only for the King and his Parliament, but for every Englishman, for it is quite certain that under a Catholic prince he would lose his freedom, his religion, his property and the rule of law, and in their stead get persecution, blood and fire. Foxe's *Book of Martyrs,* which is nearly as true as the Bible, shows how this happened in the reign of Queen Mary, when anyone who proclaimed God's word was hunted down, imprisoned, examined, tortured and condemned to die in flames. Anne Askew was so tormented on the rack that she couldn't walk to her own execution; Lawrence Sanders' death was drawn out on purpose, because they burned him with green wood, and other smothering fuel, so put him to much more pain. When the bloody Bishop of London had Thomas Tomkins in his custody, and found that neither by imprisonment, nor beating, nor by shaving off his beard could he persuade him to renounce his faith, he became so vexed against the poor man, that he thought to overthrow him by some forefeeling and terror of death. With this in mind, he took Tomkins by the fingers, and held his hand directly over the flame of a candle, but so rapt up was Tomkins' spirit that he felt no pain, and never shrunk, even when the sinews burst, and the water spurted into Master Harpsfield's face.

No-one was spared in these terrible times, not even princesses. The Queen's own sister, the Lady Elizabeth, suffered terrible persecution, which no-one could have borne more bravely. By the Queen's own orders, she was fetched from her sickbed by a troop of a hundred and fifty horse, put under armed guard, and taken to the Tower, where she was examined, and falsely accused of treason. Then she was imprisoned in Woodstock, still under guard, and in danger from plots to murder her. The Bishop of Winchester even sent a writ for execution while she was there, and it was only by God's Providence that this came to no effect. All the time she was in captivity, guiltless men were racked in the Tower, in the hopes of persuading them to accuse her, and even when she was let out of prison and went to Hatfield, she was closely watched until her sister's death.

The story of Lady Elizabeth and her miraculous preservation is the only one in the book that does not end in death, but that is not to say that the others do not have happy endings, because every martyr in it concludes his or her earthly life by praising

God even in the midst of the flames, and departing to a better place, there to live in joy unspeakable. In the pictures their faces are rapt and beautiful, their arms raised like a preacher's in the pulpit, and words of faith come out of their mouths on long ribbons: 'Welcome lyfe!' says one; 'Lord receive my spirit!' cries another. Every story is beautiful, because it tells that even though there may be persecution and suffering in this life, for those who remain steadfast in their faith there will be a just reward in the next, and for their persecutors, just punishment.

It puzzles Anne very much, knowing all this, that her father should choose to be one of them.

LOVE

'I love my love with an A,' says Mrs Jennings, 'because he is Admirable.'

It is Betty Villiers' turn. 'You would be better, Mrs Jennings, to love him with a B, seeing as he is Betrothed to another.'

'And you with a C,' says her sister Barbara, 'because you are Canker-tongued.'

Betty shrieks with laughter. 'How you cheat, Bab! Canker-tongued! There is no such word!'

Now Sarah declares herself sorry to have ever started the pestilent game, turns her back on the Villiers sisters, who carry on without her, and sits down next to Anne.

It is summer, so the Court has moved to Windsor. The King spends his time fishing, walking, playing tennis and visiting his mistresses in their lodgings, while the Queen holds picnics. Today she and the Duchess have joined their two households together, and there are several dozen women gathered under the shade of the oak trees, ladies and servants seated side by side. Leaves sieve the strong afternoon sunlight, letting through just enough to lend the servants' plain gowns a few hours of sparkle, while protecting the ladies' complexions.

Food and drink are shared along with the sunlight, and everyone has brought a dish: there are chines of beef, venison pasties, several dozen ruffs and reeves, baskets of fruit, all kinds of sweetmeat and several cases of wine. Mary is sitting a little way away, with her friend Frances Apsley, picking delicately at the contents of a fruit basket, so Anne has been able to work her way through the heavier dishes unseen and unrebuked.

The Duke's newest daughter, baby Catherine, has joined them for the meal, and is sitting on her nurse's lap, mumbling a crust of bread. She has a sticky cascade of saliva running down its bed of crumbs from her lower lip onto the lace of her mantle. A few more crumbs come out every time she smiles, but all the same her smile is beautiful, and Anne has a most excellent way to bring it out. If she sounds one pair of strings on her guitar, the corners of Catherine's mouth will begin to turn up; if she thrums all the strings at once, then the baby smile will break out in its full glory. Pushing the experiment a little further, she plays the first few notes of the chaconne that Signor Corbetta has been teaching her this last week, and now the baby is more delighted than ever, crowing and waving her newly unswaddled arms about until the crust flies out of her hand.

Sarah Jennings rushes to pick it up, but Mary Cornwallis gets there first. She is the York sisters' oldest friend, and has been stationed at Anne's side all afternoon, ready to assist. She is unable to get as sure a grip on the crust, however: the baby has mushed it to paste and there is nothing to do but wipe the mess off her hand on the grass.

'Not such a prize after all,' says Mrs Jennings. 'Too bad.' Catherine's nurse reaches into her pocket and produces another crust, which the baby snatches.

Anne can hear her sister Mary, still engaged in her *tête-à-tête* with Mrs Frances Apsley. She is admiring the cornelian ring Mrs Apsley is wearing, saying how well it becomes her, how it draws the eye to her elegant hands. Having Mrs Apsley to love makes Mary happy; if you are to make a proper figure at Court, having someone to love is essential, and there are right and wrong ways to go about it, as there are right and wrong ways to dress, to walk, to dance, and to play. Anne strikes a thoughtful chord, catching first Mrs Jennings's eye, then Mrs Cornwallis's.

'Your Highness.' It is Mrs Jennings. 'Will you play the whole tune, or are you meaning just to thrum at us?'

'Oh yes indeed, do play us the tune!' cries Mrs Cornwallis. 'It's a new one, isn't it? You play so well, it is always such a pleasure to listen!'

So Anne plays the rest of the piece, for the company, and the baby, and for Mary Cornwallis.

FROM LADY ANNE OF YORK TO MRS MARY CORNWALLIS

Wednesday five a clock

I have said that I have gone into my closet to pray but I must write to you my dearest friend, if Mary can write to Mrs Apsley then I do not see why I should not write to you. Fate has cruelly parted us since this morning but in a letter I might yet tell you my heart. I will send this by the hand of Mr Gibson the drawing-master, you must know him, he is a dwarf.

Your affectionate friend,
Anne

THE DUKE'S DOGS

It is an early afternoon in August, nearing the end of another Windsor summer, and Anne is on horseback. She has her usual mount from her father's stables, a roan jennet named Mercy, quiet, comfortable and surefooted, with the character of a perfect lady, in horse form or in human. They have been hunting together since early morning, and in all this time Anne has only persuaded her to canter twice, and to gallop not at all. The truth is that the Duke does not wish her to gallop: that is why he has had her mounted on Mercy, and accompanied at all times by a trusted equerry, a portly older gentleman the Villiers girls call Wheezing Warner. They might laugh as much as they like today: Anne won't hear them, because despite the twin impediments of Mercy and Warner, she has long since left them behind. And Mary too. One of the chief pleasures of riding, for Anne at ten, is in leaving Mary behind.

Another is the knowledge that, even though he has ordered the impediments, her father is proud of her when she joins him in the field, is delighted that one of his children, at least, loves sport as much as he does. He has no living sons, but in her riding habit, with its buttoned-up doublet, long-skirted coat, boots, hats and periwig, Anne could be both son and daughter. Only her petticoat gives her sex away. She doesn't resent it on that account, although she might wish that it weren't so heavy, or so hot.

The sun is at its highest now, and the day is growing overripe. There is a glare about that draws the water from her eyes, and powerful smells are rising off the coats of horses and gentlemen, and — though one should never say so — off the coats of ladies too. Mr Warner is wheezing especially hard, and there is a dampness on Mercy's neck. Anne feels as if her own blood-heat is trying to rise out through her skin to join the heat outside. But they have come to a stop finally, the stag they have pursued for five hours is harboured in a thicket, and they are all gathered outside, waiting for the huntsman to drive him out.

Waiters have jumped down from their wagons and are moving among the riders with refreshments. Mr Warner hands Anne a mug of small beer; she drains it with what Mary, or Lady Frances, would say was unseemly haste.

'The stag is tired, Your Highness,' the equerry says, as he takes the mug back. 'I think we are nearly at the end.'

Anne nods slowly. 'Yes,' she says. 'Besides, he's old. He'll not stand long before the hounds.'

She expects Warner to say at this point that her knowledge puts him to shame, and he does. Then she nudges Mercy forward a little, so as to be nearer to her father, and have a better sight of his dogs.

They have had a hard day of it. The stag's great age has been evident not only in his girth and magnificent crown, but also in his cunning: he has in the course of this one morning's hunting run straight into the middle of three different herds, and on two of those occasions confounded the hounds completely, so that it has taken some time for them to pick up his scent again; too many times to count he has doubled back over his tracks and then back again; once he had even headed straight for the river and it had seemed for a moment that he was about to take soil, but at the last moment, in a move the hunt had come to recognise as his signature, he had doubled back again.

Now they have tracked their quarry to the entry in this thicket, and the scent is strong. They have run up to the entry, and pulled back again, bawling: they believe that the stag is there. The sound of a pack in full cry, each animal barking as if tuned to a different note, all the notes moving with and across and after each other in agitated counterpoint, is Anne's favourite sound, and it charms her further and further forward, until she is close enough to discern each broken bough at the entry, close enough to see the huntsman stop to check the footprints, to make sure that the hounds are baying for the right beast, close enough —

'Anne — get back this instant! Warner! What are you about, man?'

It is the Duke's voice, half-fear, half-rage, and louder even than the hounds. She pulls back at once, and goes to beg her father's pardon, but he has not quite finished being angry yet.

'What did you think you were doing, girl? Have I not taught you better? Do you have a sword now, do you? Do you?'

Anne opens her mouth and shuts it again.

'Well, do you have a sword? A stick?

Anything? Are you armed?'

'No, Sir.'

'No, of course not, so when the stag is unharboured, when he rushes out of that entry, when he comes at you with his great horns, what will you *do*, Anne? What. Will. You. *Do?*'

His face is very red: it might be the heat, or the beer he has been drinking all morning — he is blowing the smell of it into her face as he shouts — or then again perhaps she and her foolishness are the cause of all of it. She finds she cannot say or do anything in response, except turn redder herself.

They hold each other's gaze for a moment, the red-faced Duke and his ruddy daughter, mouths firmly shut, one enraged, one sullen. Then Henry Jermyn, the Duke's Master of the Horse, appears at his side, ready to soothe and to charm. Anne has never understood what is supposed to be so charming about him, but he does amuse her, if only by having ridiculous short legs and an enormous head. Next to her stately father, he always looks especially absurd.

'No harm done, Sir,' he says to the Duke. 'She is in one piece still, and — if you will permit me to say so — Her Highness's spirit and grace in the field, the figure she makes on horseback must be such a source of pride, and were she my daughter —'

'That's enough, Jermyn. You've stuck the point. Anne, I will not send you back for now but you must stay where you are. Warner, mind she goes no further.'

The Duke and Jermyn turn their horses round, and at the very next moment there is a shout from the huntsman: the stag is unharboured.

Anne turns in time to see him take a few, stiff steps forward, then stop and stand, facing the hounds, who know the danger in their well-trained sinews, and hold back. While the hounds and stag face each other, the huntsman runs to the Duke and Jermyn; they put their heads together for what can be no more than a minute but seems much longer, and while they do so nobody else speaks, no animal moves. The huntsman nods, and signals to his men, who in turn call the hounds back softly, and couple them. And as they do so, the Duke is carefully, quietly drawing his sword.

The exhausted stag, whose fear has driven all his cunning out, turns his head at once to flee, but the Duke has galloped up already, and his sword drives home.

Now the Duke dismounts, and the huntsman hands him a shorter blade, a hunting knife. He cuts the stag's throat, then he bloods the youngest hounds. Then the *Mort* sounds, and it is safe for Anne to urge Mercy forward again, and watch as the stag is butchered. Her father looks up and sees her; he laughs and tells her to close her mouth; he tells Warner to help his daughter dismount, and when she has done so, he walks up to her, laughs once more, then, with deftness and some affection, he dabs her nose with blood.

From Lady Anne of York to Mrs Mary Cornwallis

Thursday ten a clock

I trust you are not still vexed that Mrs Jennings walked always at my right hand when we three strolled in the gardens yesterday, it was indeed a little unkind of her but not yet uncivil because it is true what she said as a Maid of Honour she does have precedence. Please believe I shall always be your friend on all accounts, and took up my pen today only to tell you so, and whatever becomes of me, I must not live when I cease to love you and there is no-one I love more than you not even Mrs Jennings.

Your <u>most</u> affectionate friend,
Anne

MARY'S CLOSET

Anne cannot remember having said the prayer for a sick child before. Mary tells her that she has, already, said it over twice, once for Edgar, and then again for the other Catherine; now they are both kneeling in Mary's chamber at St James's with Dr Doughty, saying the prayer for the present Duchess's Catherine, who is in the nursery, fretful and feverish, and suffering convulsions. One way or another, God will soon deliver her from pain.

The words of the prayer are familiar enough — God, mercy, life, death, sickness, salvation, Jesus, soul — but, whatever Mary says, Anne is unfamiliar with the order in which they appear in this instance, and as she very much does not want to make a mistake, she holds her prayer book close to her face, and attends to the printed letters with all her attention. She has no energy left for the production of tears, but Mary has said the same prayer six times at least, and she has tears enough for the both of them. As soon as they have said 'Amen', she cries out 'Oh the poor dear distressed bab!' and doubles her efforts. Anne is no longer distracted by the effort of reading, and joins her lustily. Dr Doughty leaves them to embrace each other, and to soak each other's pinners.

When they have cried as much as they are able, Mrs Langford offers Mary a handkerchief, and Danvers performs the same office for Anne. Then Mary takes a candlestick up in one hand and Anne by the other.

'Come into my closet, with me, Sister,' she says to Anne, and over her shoulder, to the nurses, she adds: 'You may scratch at the door with news.'

This is a surprising invitation. Mary, for all her sociability, guards her closet and her privacy jealously, and has all the more so since her monthly courses began. Anne, whose own closet is so much smaller, is agog to take a look. It is nothing disappointing, full of wonderful gifts from their father, and still more extravagant ones from their uncle. Her cabinet, her table, and the writing-desk that sits on it are all decorated in a beautiful floral pattern, made out of many-coloured woods which Anne supposes to be both rare and precious. Mary has not only the usual cane chair to sit in when she writes or reads at her table, but also a pair of armchairs, upholstered deliciously in velvet, and edged with gilt. The cane chair, the walls, and the work box next to the desk are all covered with needlework — flowers and animals, scenes from the Bible which Anne can recognise, a few other scenes from other kinds of story which mean less. There is more evidence of Mary's wide reading on the hanging shelf above her desk, where her bible and copies of devotional works are placed at one end, and plays, poetry and romances at the other, with a decent space in between. When Mary replaces her prayer book on the shelf, she snatches another book which has been lying open on the table, with a quick glance at Anne, and puts it back on the shelf too, but at the other end. Anne, who does not like it when Mary treats her like a child, is more than a little vexed by this.

'You needn't hide anything. I heard Barbara Villiers say she had lent you *Five loveletters from a nun,* so you see I already know about it.'

Mary blushes. 'Well, even so, it's not the kind of frivolous stuff that should be open today.'

'So were you reading it after you knew Catherine was ill?'

Mary's blush deepens gratifyingly. 'Of course not! But I had it open on the desk before I heard the news, and only happened to leave it there.'

Then she recollects herself, and takes charge again.

'Sit down while I close the door.'

Anne chooses an armchair, hoping as she sinks into it that Mary will not judge it too comfortable for the occasion, and bid her stand up again. Happily, she only sits down in the other armchair. She winds her hands into a tight knot in her lap, and sighs.

'Anne, I don't know what to make of this,' she says at last. 'We're told God-knows-what of Bab, good one day and ill the next, so I kill myself with sighs for her, then I kill myself again with joy, the good and ill is so confounded together in me, it makes me quite mad . . .'

'Me too, me too.'

'. . . but today . . . today . . .' She unknots her hands and places the right one flat on her midriff. '. . . while we were praying just now, I felt the most melancholy qualm come over my stomach.'

Then Mary knots her hands up again, making a period of them. Anne, whose temper is more sanguine, asks if she might not think of taking a cordial.

'Or the surgeon could come in to bleed you, perhaps.'

Mary makes an impatient noise.

'That can hardly help our sister.'

'We've prayed. That will.'

'Yes, yes,' says Mary, but she is shaking her head as she says it. 'But we — the reason why I asked you to come in here . . .'

She leans forward and offers her hands to Anne, who takes them, and as she does so her gaze, which has been wandering and distracted up till now, fixes itself on Anne's face. Her dark eyes take the light from the candles, and hold it.

'Anne, we have prayed just now for Bab, but we must pray again, together, we must offer up our broken hearts to God, for her sake.'

There is something disturbing in the flame-bright eyes, and Mary is holding Anne's hands so tightly now that they are beginning to hurt. The pain makes her feel as if someone, somewhere, might somehow be angry.

'Do you think then that her sickness is a punishment? But she is so innocent!'

'No, not a punishment, or at least, not to her.'

'O Mary, not to us!'

Mary lets Anne's hands go, so that she can knot and unknot them again, and her gaze slides guiltily away.

'Anne, I have sometimes thought that lately — I especially, I have been so much at Court, so taken up with frivolous —'

'O I *wish* you would not —'

'Don't shout at me!'

'So I'll whisper it then: I wish you would not talk such stuff. A punishment to you that Bab is sick? If a sick baby is a correction to anyone, then it must be to the *parents.*'

Mary looks horrified. In her eagerness to show that she can know better than Mary, Anne has said what she should not. She is ashamed of herself, and starts to cry. Mary takes one of her hands again, but gently this time.

'I believe we might fairly say that . . .' She stops. Neither sister can meet the other's eyes. 'I believe that — since it was you and I that spoke for Catherine at her christening — her *proper* christening, where her parents were not — I believe we might speak again for her now.'

Anne still has the handkerchief Danvers gave her, stuffed into her sleeve. She pulls it out and wipes her face with it.

'I understand.'

'I knew you would. So, kneel with me, then.'

They go down onto their knees, face to face, hands together in front of them, in the proper attitude for prayer. Anne waits for Mary to speak, but she is frowning again, looking about her: something is giving her new qualms, is not to her perfect liking.

'Do you think perhaps — the case is so extreme — ought we perhaps to prostrate ourselves before the Lord?'

Anne takes a sceptical look about her.

'In here? How could we? There is scarce room enough for two to kneel.'

It is true: their prayer hands are only a few inches apart, but Mary is pulling her dark brows together, and thinning her lips, trying to think of an argument. She looks as if she might have thought of one, but Anne never finds out what it is, because at the very moment Mary opens her mouth, they hear the sorrowful scratch.

TOM THUMB, HIS LIFE AND DEATH

After Catherine has joined the others in the vault, Mary does indeed prostrate herself. Her melancholy qualms overpower her completely, and she takes to her bed, where she refuses to eat, hardly sleeps at all, and is more often than not in floods of tears. The doctor proclaims it a mother-fit, brought on by grievous passions; she is given violet water, then a purge, and finally bled.

Grief has always made Anne's appetite bigger rather than smaller, so while Mary cries she eats, and she eats to the rhythm of rhyme in her head, that has stolen into the silent days where Mary's voice is not:

His body being so slender small,
The cunning doctor tooke
A fine perspective glasse with which
He did in secret look
Into his sickened body downe
And therein saw the Death

Stood ready in his wasted guts
To sease his vitall breath.

Tom Thumb and the cunning doctor are
there to greet Anne when she wakes up, and
they follow her everywhere till it is time to
say her last prayers, and sleep again. After a
few days, when it is clear that Mary will not
be up and about for at least a week yet, and
that Anne, though eating heartily, is not
quite herself, Mrs Cornwallis is sent for to
bear her company. She brings a new book
with her, a volume of love poems, written
on purpose to be sighed over, and as she
reads them aloud in her sweet voice, all un-
noticed, Tom and the doctor take their leave.

THE DEAN OF THE CHAPELS ROYAL

Some things are not difficult for Anne to grasp: that there is but one living and true God, for example, is as simple a lesson as one could ever wish to learn. Other, more intricate truths, such as the matter of God's being at once of one substance and three Persons, she is content to take on trust, knowing that she will never comprehend them, and that she need never try. Anne does not deal in abstractions, which is why, even though she has to believe in a God without body, parts or passions, she can't help but give him a face. How can God be expected to make his face to shine upon her if he doesn't possess one?

The face of God has many aspects. It shines upon her when she is good. When she feels guilty it darkens; at the worst of times, it is thunderous. When she prays to it, more often than not, it has a deliberate blankness about it, like the face she has

74

sometimes seen on her uncle when someone has approached him with a petition. God has many other expressions which are recognisably the King's: amusement, enjoyment, indulgence, boredom. Like the King, he is very forgiving, but only up to a point, and there is no predicting, on any given day, where that point might be. God is to be feared as much as loved, lest he grow angry, and his face turn stern or red, like the Duke's.

Lately Gods face has also acquired a look of Henry Compton, Bishop of London and, more recently, Dean of the Chapels Royal and the princesses' Preceptor. In the months Anne has spent under Compton's tutelage, God's face has grown square and soldierly, with a nose like a rock on which the true Church might be built, and eyebrows of righteous black ink. He holds a copy of Mr Foxe's book in one hand, and a copy of the Articles of Religion in the other. Those same Articles in which it is said that God has no parts.

Mary and Anne have been studying the Articles in preparation for their joint Confirmation, which they are receiving today at the Bishop's request, and with the King's express authority. They stand side by side in the Chapel at St James, before the Bishop so fearfully splendid in his robes, and agree in their charming voices to renew the vows made for them at their baptisms. Then they kneel, so that the Bishop can lay his hand on their heads, one at a time, and ask their Protestant and English God to defend them with his heavenly grace.

Afterwards, they are each given a copy of *The Whole Duty of Man,* and are much congratulated, though not by their father. They spend the day of their grandfather's martyrdom mourning together with him as they have always done, and at first, so Mary says, it looks as if things may carry on with them much as before. But then, in March, in full sight of the King, the Court, and of all England, the Duke turns back at the Chapel door.

LETTERS FROM LADY ANNE OF YORK TO MARY CORNWALLIS, AUGUST 1676 — OCTOBER 1677

Wednesday three a clock, St James's

I visited the baby Isabella today I am so thankful that she is so strong and like to live. It is true I have been much with Mrs Apsley of late, she has been so kind as to give me the cornelian ring just because I so admired it, Mary is vexed. But do not you be vexed with me, Mrs Apsley is nothing to you, there were never friends like us, I am yours, and will be yours always, say you will come today with us to take the river air, it is the only pleasant place in this heat, I can show you how well the ring looks and we can play cards and besides I must see you else I die.

Your affectionate friend,
Lady Anne

Saturday nine a clock, St James's

I was long in hopes of a visit from you
but you have not come so I see I must
write to beg your company. Mr Gibson
will bring you this not Mrs Jennings she
is quarrelling with her mother who says
two of the Maids have had great bellies
at Court and she will not leave her child
there to have the third but Mrs Jennings
loves Mr Churchill and will not leave
though his family will marry him she
says to a shocking creature. I should
never be false to you like he is to poor
Mrs Jennings. I am yours and will be
yours in despite of fate and fortune.

Your affectionate friend,
Lady Anne

Wednesday ten a clock, St James's

Do not chide me I beg you that I did
not write last night the Duchess had a
great ball my sister and I did not rise till
eleven o'clock this morning Tuesday I
was busy trying on gowns and manteaux
and I played the Duchess at cards and
won Monday I took physic so could not
leave my room to see anyone not even
you. Mrs Jennings has had her mother

banished from Court she said she is a madwoman but still she was crying at the ball. Please come visit me this afternoon that I may be ravished once more by your beauty.

Your affectionate friend,
Lady Anne

Friday eleven a clock, St James's

I said I would write as you see I am as good as my word but I cannot see you till the day after tomorrow as today I have music before dinner then my sister and I must be fitted for all our mourning for tomorrow I must own to my shame I hate to fast but it is for my grandfather who is a martyr so I shall try if I can with a willing heart I shall bear it better in hopes of seeing you so perfect in person and in soul.

Your affectionate friend,
Lady Anne

Thursday ten a clock, Windsor

I have received your letter and kissed it already a hundred times. I am glad so glad the physic has wrought well and to read you are in better spirits. I wish you had been here last night we have been so very gay Mrs Jennings is to marry her Mr Churchill Mary has danced again with my Lord Shrewsbury and reads romances in her closet. Tomorrow I am to go hunting again with father the huntsmen have seen a great stag in the forest it shall be a fine day I hope and all the better because you are not sick anymore if you only knew how I prayed for this you should never doubt me more.

Your affectionate friend,
Lady Anne

Friday eleven a clock, St James's

I wish that I could see you today we are all most melancholy since the Duke spoke to Mary yesterday. She must have the Prince of Orange whether she will or no she weeps in her closet I will weep too to see her go out of England but if I only know that you love me still I can endure even that. My head aches I must take a cordial.

Your affectionate friend
Lady Anne

ANNE IN FLAMES

'Now, Nephew, to your work! Hey! Saint George for England!'

With this, the King draws the bed-curtains, and Mary and her new husband disappear from view. His Majesty has been the most cheerful member of the party from the start, perhaps the only truly cheerful member. The groom is taciturn, the bride distraught. Her father can barely hide his displeasure at giving his daughter away to a Protestant prince, while her step-mother, who looks as though she might give birth before the ceremony has even finished, cries incontinently all the way through. Anne, who is sorry to see her sister unhappy and married to a sour-faced Dutchman who will take her away to Holland, cries a little too. She thinks it must be the crying that is making her head ache so.

But the headache is still with her the following day, and now she has a backache to go with it. She wishes she were not sitting on a stool, but she is in the Banqueting Hall, watching the Prince and Princess of Orange receiving congratulations and compliments upon their marriage, and precedence dictates that a stool it must be. The noise around her is at high tide, with a showy swell of music and compliments from the visitors, and from the courtiers a murmuring, whooshing undercurrent which washes in and out of her head and makes the ache worse. Seated on her stool behind the main players, she can hear exactly what the Court is muttering behind its doffed hats and its fans today: what an ugly brute the Prince of Orange is; what an absurd pair they make, she so tall and stately, he so short and hunched; listen to his asthmatic wheezing; mark his sour face; such a deplorable lack of courtesy towards his bride. Oh, but he is a great General; there will be no more costly wars with the Dutch. Did you see the jewels he gave her? Forty thousand pounds' worth — how well they will become her; such sport it is to watch the maids and mothers pulling hair and clawing eyes to get their places in her Court . . .

The afternoon wears on, the rich colours on the backs of the bowing aldermen shout up to the swirling pigments on the ceiling, which chorus their acknowledgements, while the streams of voices clash together and make whirlpools in Anne's hot head: an honour to present to your Hunchback our gift of asthma; your most gracious sour face; our absurd felicitations. When she arrives back at St James's she is put straight to bed.

Next morning she wakes to a sore throat, a quite unbearable thirst and the news that she has a new brother.

'He is made Duke of Cambridge, Your Highness,' Danvers tells her, as she offers a sip of cordial. 'A fine boy, likely to live —'

'— and the Prince of Orange's face is all the sourer for it,' says Martha Farthing, with satisfaction. She is Anne's old wet-nurse, and a Catholic; she and Danvers disagree about many things. Today they are especially at odds over the question of who should nurse Anne.

When Dr Scarborough arrives, he looks into Anne's face and settles the question with one word: Farthing has already had smallpox and Danvers has not, so it is Danvers who has to withdraw, scattering tears and promises of prayer as she leaves.

The doctor gives other orders: the fire is stoked up as high as it can go, the bed and the windows are dressed in red cloth; sweet handfuls of rosemary are thrown onto the fire and add their flavoured smoke to the sweating air. Swaddled in the heaviest bedclothes the household can muster, Anne is roasted like mutton; tiny new flames erupt all over on her skin. She sleeps when the little fires allow her to; her mouth and throat are now so sore that she cries; she does not wish, for once, to eat anything.

After a while, when candles have been lit and then snuffed, and the thin winter sun has crept around the room, and departed, and the candles have been lit again, Anne wakes from shallow, pimpled sleep to hear raised voices outside the door: Lady Frances, and Dr Lake.

'. . . must attend Her Highness.'

'But Dr Lake, shall you then carry your fever to your other charges, to Lady Isabella and the little Duke?'

'I told you, I am here on Dr Compton's authority. We do not know how busy and zealous your Mrs Farthing has been —'

Anne's nurse, who saw her charge waking and has come over to her with a glass of cordial and a wet cloth, pauses in her ministrations.

'Mrs Farthing has always kept her religion to herself, but if Dr Compton wills it, then . . . only pray keep a prudent distance.'

'Your servant, Madam,' Dr Lake replies,

and, without scratching or knocking, bursts into the room, prayer book first. He and Mrs Farthing stare each other down for a moment, then she drops a curtsy and leaves. Now there are only four in the room: Anne, Dr Lake, smallpox and God. The chaplain's face appears around the corner of a red swathe, like that of some tortured soul bobbing to the surface in a lake of fire. It makes its compliment and says how delighted it is to hear she is a little stronger today.

'Thank you, Dr Lake. My backache is quite gone, thank God, and Farthing says my pox are yet few. I have had a little broth this morning.'

'Splendid! Mrs Farthing is diligent, I am sure . . .'

The face comes a little closer and the voice drops.

'. . . but has she said anything to — discomfort you?'

'No, Sir — only that when I ask for something cool to drink she says I may not.'

'And she is quite correct: you must sweat out the fever, Madam. I meant — has her conversation been such as to make you . . . uneasy?'

'Not at all. She has told me so many droll tales of me and my foster sister as babies, though today she complained of —'

But Dr Lake is not interested: he cuts Anne off, and she is glad in a way, because it hurts so much to talk.

'Have you prayed at all, Madam, since you were ill?'

'I have said the Lord's Prayer twice, and told the Lord in my heart that if I live I shall give to the poor.'

Neither of them speaks for a moment — there is nothing but the crackling of the fire, and a scuffling on the other side of the chamber door — and when the chaplain starts again his voice has lost the urgent edge it had before.

'In that case, Madam, I take it that you understand the danger you are in?'

'Well enough, Sir.'

'I shall kneel now, Your Highness. Pray with me, if you can.'

He begins, 'Remember not, Lord, our iniquities . . .' The words are comforting, familiar. Slowly, her eyes close.

When she opens them again, her first thought is that all Dr Lake's prayers have availed nothing, and she is in Hell. There is nothing to see or feel but flame. She makes as if to scream and no sound comes out, but she has managed to rouse a tormentor, a she-devil, whom the flames part to reveal.

She reaches her terrible hand out towards Anne's face and she screams again. Another tormentor comes, a giant in dark robes, who roars 'PLETHORIC!' and orders one of the lesser fiends who follow him to stab her in the arm, so that more flame pours out of it.

When the fiends have withdrawn, she tries to pray for God to deliver her, and for forgiveness, but instead of sound a ribbon comes out of her mouth with the words on. The tormentors appear again, and now they are also vomiting the printed ribbons that say 'Crisis' and 'Quite disordered'. This is her existence for some portion of eternity: she burns.

Anne's Skin

After several weeks have passed, a miracle occurs, in that Danvers and Farthing finally agree on something: Anne is now fit to leave her chamber. Once the Duke has called Dr Scarborough in, and he has agreed with both women, only in costlier language, the swaddling tedium of the sickroom is at last unwrapped, and she is allowed to visit the Duchess in her lodgings.

Wishing to dress as the occasion deserves, Anne waves away the nightgown that Danvers brings her and orders her to bring the new green skirt and bodice, that has the ribbons down the front. She apprehends her folly as soon as Danvers starts lacing her in, when the stiff material at once begins to chafe at scabs through her chemise, but this is the decision she has made, and she will not allow it to be a wrong one, so she stands up as straight as she can, bites her lip and itches.

Mary has yet to see this new green costume, but she is sure to admire it when she does. Of course she will be there: she sent a message every day that Anne was ill, to ask how she went on, so she must be eager to see her recovered. It is cheering to know that Anne's sickness has not, after all, robbed them of the chance of a proper farewell before Mary leaves for Holland. It is true that nobody has said that Mary will be with the Duchess, but Anne can only assume that this is because it goes without saying.

So when she arrives, and Mary is nowhere to be seen, her disappointment is too great to be hidden.

'Oh, but they told me you were in such good spirits,' said the Duchess, as they sit down at the tea table. 'Whatever is the matter? Does your head ache again?'

'No, Madam, I am quite better — it is only that I was in such great hopes of seeing my sister today.'

The Duchess looks up at Mrs Jennings, who is in attendance, and asks if she might pour the tea.

'You must not vex yourself about your sister, Anne; she escaped the sickness, and is quite well.'

'I know that: I received many kind messages from her.'

The Duchess and Mrs Jennings exchange glances again. Sarah looks a question at the Duchess, who shakes her head and turns back to Anne.

'The Duke will be here soon, Anne,' says the Duchess, and she says it as if it were the answer to the Mary-riddle, so it can make no difference to the conversation that it is not. The subject will be changed. Sarah finishes pouring the tea and the Duchess bids her sit with them. Anne takes her dish up in both hands. Nobody corrects her. She looks up from her first warm sip to see that the Duchess is smiling at her.

'You look so well, Anne . . . hardly any scabs at all, and such as there are on the small side, I think.'

She looks to Mrs Jennings for confirmation.

'Indeed, Your Highness, it could have been very much worse — I think the Lady Anne will quite recover her looks.'

The word 'scabs' has drawn Anne's attention back to a patch of skin just beneath the top of her stomacher, where the itching and chafing are at their worst. There is nothing she can do; she draws the inside of her cheek between her upper and lower teeth, bites down just a little, and holds it there;

the itching starts to fade, which is just as well, as the Duchess and Sarah have not quite done with their scabby discourse.

'I have an excellent receipt from Lady Peterborough,' the Duchess is saying, 'for a water to get away the signs of the pox. It is for lime quenched in white rosewater — you may wash with it at your pleasure, and afterwards anoint your face with pomatum made of spermaceti and oil of almonds. I shall have the Duke's apothecary make up both, Anne, and send them to your rooms.'

'That sounds an excellent remedy, Your Highness,' says Sarah, 'though I believe there is another that might also work very well — I heard one of the Queen's women saying she had used it on her daughter. You take spermaceti, again, and twice so much virgin's wax, then you melt them together, spread them upon a kid's-leather mask. You lay this mask on the face, then keep it on for a night and a day.'

'I do not think,' says the Duchess, looking at Anne's face, 'that you at all like the sound of that, do you Anne?'

'It does not sound . . . *pleasant.*'

'Perhaps not, Your Highness,' says Sarah, her voice pulled a little too tight, 'but it *works.*'

Anne cannot think of a reply, and is

spared the bother of trying, because the Duke is announced. She curtsies, and her convalescent knees complain. Then her father embraces her. There is nobody with him. She hears her voice come out wavering, like an ill-played recorder.

'Sir, I had thought you would have my sister with you. Where is Mary?'

'Let us sit, my dear . . . good . . . I wanted to tell you this myself — I trust you will bear it patiently: your sister Orange is in Holland — she sailed a fortnight ago.'

'Then the messages she sent . . . ?'

'I had them feigned — I hope you can forgive me for that — I did not want you upset while you were still in danger. I thought it best that you should think your sister here.'

'But she was not here.'

'No, she was not.'

Anne's Heart

If Anne could see inside her own heart, she would find that it is, like the Palace of St James's, built for games of hide and seek. That it is to say, at first sight, it might seem to consist solely of its well-appointed public chambers, its State apartments, but were she to look longer, look harder, she would perceive that the greater part of it — privy chambers and passages, staircases and closets — lies behind, and is no less vast for its neglect.

This is what she might see, if she could, or if she chose to. As it is, she sees nothing, so when Mary slips as it were through a ruelle, into some dusty closet, she does so unregarded.

PART II

ANNE'S MATERNAL LINE

Between the smallpox and the Prince of Orange, Anne's old circle is quite broken up. Three of the four Villiers sisters follow Mary to Holland, while their mother Lady Frances succumbs to the fever. A few weeks later, the Duke of Cambridge dies too, so the Prince is once more allied to the heiress apparent of England, and can be the better pleased with his bargain.

The death of Lady Frances has particular evil consequences. The first of these is the Duchess's dream and the muttering that follows it. Her vision, as she repeats it to her Catholic ladies, who repeat it to other, Protestant ladies, one of whom repeats it to Anne, is as follows:

'Oh, such a terrible thing! Lady Frances Villiers appeared to me, in some anguish, and so I heard from her own lips that she was now damned, and suffering in the flames of Hell. Of course I was incredulous at first — such a virtuous and prayerful lady as she was — but then she bid me take her hand, and I did, and — mercy! — it seemed so extremely hot that it was impossible for a body to endure it.'

The second is Lady Harriet Hyde. With Lady Frances dead, and — according to some at Court — consigned to that part of the Inferno which God and the Pope reserve for Protestants, the Duke and Duchess set about appointing a new governess for the Ladies Anne and Isabella. Anne's mother's family, the Hydes, step forward, and push for their interests, as they have been doing most successfully ever since her grandfather Hyde arrived at Court out of Wiltshire, dragging his green lawyer's bag behind him. This most capable man, after many years of graft, was pleased to drag his green bag all the way to the Lord Chancellor's office, before his daughter outdid him, by promoting herself into marriage with the Duke. Now they are both dead, but her Uncle Laurence, envoy to The Hague and very much alive, has spied another vacant office adjacent to royalty, and proposed his wife for it. To Anne's horror, the Duke agrees.

There is no smell of the green bag about Lady Harriet. She is an Earl's daughter, one of the Court beauties whose portraits hang in a succulent row in Windsor, and though it might be fifteen years since Lely painted her, she still knows how to look at a page and make him blush.

It was Anne's own mother, the first Duchess of York, who commissioned the paintings, though she had the good sense not to propose herself as one of the sitters. She knew that she was no beauty. Anne knows how much she resembles her mother in person and habit, for Mary has told her often enough. So there is really no need for Lady Harriet to entertain the seamstresses with stories of the late Duchess's stoutness at every one of Anne's dress fittings, or to comment on the Duchess's overeating at — so it seems — every other meal, or to call to mind the shocking sums she was wont to lose at gambling every time Anne has company, and calls for cards.

Lady Harriet does not play cards very often. She prefers to spend her time with such as Mr Evelyn and Lady Dorothy Grimes, and one might as well, as Mrs Jennings has it, take tea with a parcel of sermon-books. Dr Lake seems to enjoy Lady Harriet's company very much. When he calls, and Anne cannot very well be elsewhere, she offers to play the harpsichord for them: that way she need not listen to the pair of them flapping their dusty mouths about; nor will they trouble her with their questions, generally the sort which appear on first sight to have neither a right nor a wrong answer but which then turn out to have both.

Today she could wish for a louder, ruder instrument — a trumpet or a drum, something that could drown them out. She would rather not listen to talk of grieving fathers, or little dead dukes.

'Did you see him, Dr Lake? I never did, but I've heard everywhere that when he was born he looked more than likely to live, and live in good health.'

'I did,' says the chaplain, 'and he was a fine boy. Even when they opened him, even after he was dead of the fever, they found his entrails still perfectly sound.'

'So do the physicians think that his case was mismanaged?'

'Yes, indeed. I had it from Dr Scarborough's own lips that if Mrs Chambers and Mrs Manning had but put a coal leaf to the humour he had breaking out under his arm and his navel, instead of striking in it like they did, he might well have lived — and for many years at that.'

Oh for one good clash on a pair of cymbals, the blast of a cannon, a door thrown open, a cry of 'The King!' But no: there is only Lady Harriet, displaying her superior learning.

'Quo natura tendit, tendat,' she says, 'quo movet, moveat.'

'And the pity of it is,' says Dr Lake, 'that it should be this child — I don't believe the Duke ever grieved so much for any of the others.'

'No, it's true: he was distressed, always, but never like this — not even for his other sons.'

Anne comes to the end of a courant, and looks up. Dr Lake swallows whatever it was he might have been about to say, and begs her please to play on — it is charming, quite charming. So she rearranges her hands for a sombre *passacaille,* and when she resumes playing, she finds the notes are waiting for her under their keys, where they always were, and like a pack of well-trained dogs, they come out reliably when called.

ANNE ENTERS INTO HER CLOSET

According to the devotional authors, and Bishop Compton, it is written in the Gospels that Christ made his one great sacrifice to redeem the world, and, because the needs of the world shall last as long as the world itself, he established a perpetual ministry whereby this one sacrifice should be made eternally effectual as a means of atonement and expiation for all mankind. So Christ is a priest for ever in heaven, and has appointed the same ministry to be done on earth, by means of the sacramental representation of his sacrifice, in the form of Holy Communion. This coming Easter, for the first time, Anne is to participate in the sacrifice.

If she is fit to do so, she will receive Christ within her soul; however, should she communicate in an unworthy state, she will receive only the most deadly spiritual poison, the dust of the tabernacle in the waters of jealousy, that will make the belly to swell and the thigh to rot. Instead of Christ, the Devil will enter her soul and dwell there, till he returns to his dwelling of torment and takes it with him. If she is to welcome Christ and forestall the Devil, she has to prepare.

The preparation takes both outward and inward forms. Until now, Anne has attended Chapel weekly; now she is expected to go at least three times a week, to be seen, and to hear sermons written by royal preachers with her especial benefit in mind. On days when she does not attend Chapel, she prays in her closet with Dr Lake or Dr Doughty, at eight in the morning after she rises, and again at nine at night. As to how she spends the rest of her time, it is pressed upon her — by Compton, by Lake, by Doughty, by Lady Harriet — that private devotion and prayers will be more profitable, oh so much more profitable than dancing, or music, or private theatricals, or — heaven forbid — *cards*.

'Enter into your closet,' says Bishop Compton, 'and when you are in there, you must shut the door firmly against all worldly things, and *examine* yourself.'

'*Examine* myself, my Lord?' Anne asks, thinking of the catechism, and the long

Sunday mornings spent reciting it, a childish duty she would prefer to have left behind.

'Yes, Madam, as a physician might examine a body, so you must try out the condition and state of your soul.'

'But I would not examine my own body, my Lord.'

'No indeed, but the soul is another matter. For besides God, who but you can see within your soul? Its inquisition must be your act alone. You alone must search out its weaknesses and indiscretions, those secret ulcers, all those aptnesses where it is exposed to temptation —'

Compton's eyes roam over the closet she has inherited from Mary, searching out the books of love poetry, the comfortable chairs, the cornelian ring which Anne has taken off and left on the table, the ivory fan that the King has given her, all the pretty, worldly things.

'— and pray for grace, so that by finding out these diseases you may find a cure, and arm yourself against further dangers — and there will be many dangers, Madam, dangers of which you may be unaware,' he adds, allowing his gaze to drop a few inches below Anne's face, where it finds the beginnings of an impressive bosom. Anne blushes, and places her hand over the place; Compton comes to himself, and raises his eyes to a picture on the wall behind her head, as if he had only inadvertently looked for something in the wrong place, but had now — thank heaven! — found it elsewhere.

'So you see, Madam, that just as you are vigilant for your body's health, so you must be vigilant — oh how much more vigilant — over your soul's. And remember that, for all that the chief part of the labour is yours, you may seek guidance — as you would from a physician — from those of us appointed to minister physic to the soul's diseases.'

As it happens, there is no need for Anne to seek guidance: it comes to her unbidden, from all quarters, and more often than not, when she enters her closet alone, it is to shut the door against her guides, so that she might write to Mrs Cornwallis, or Mrs Churchill, or Mrs Apsley, of love, and clothes, and news from Court, and how much she won today at cards. Then all of a sudden it is the evening before the appointed day, and she finds herself on her knees in a panic, trying at once to purge her soul of a season's lusts, make an oath with herself to reply to Mary's letters, and feel charitable towards Lady Harriet.

With all this weighing upon her, Anne hardly sleeps at all that night, and as it is Communion day there is no breakfast to revive her in the morning, so she reaches the Chapel in a state of physical discomfort which anyone might forgivably mistake for penitence. She is well prepared. She speaks the responses as beautifully as she has ever spoken any line of anything secular, so that the whole Court might hear and approve her. She kneels in the proper place; the cup comes towards her; she takes one sip, and then — because, as she tries to explain later, the cup is not immediately withdrawn — she suffers a moment of terrible confusion, and takes two more. When she hears Dr Lake's sharp intake of breath, she understands at once that this was the wrong thing to have done, and that she will not now derive the slightest spiritual benefit from the Communion, the fasting, the penitence or any of the hours spent listening to the Bishop — all she can hope for, this time, is that no-one will want to tell the Duke.

'Dr Lake was most grieved to hear that you are playing cards on Sunday again,' says Anne.

'I know,' says Mary, 'because he said as much in a letter to me.'

'And to your Mrs Langford, your Mam,' says Anne Bentinck, nee Villiers.

'And to Dr Hooper,' says Betty Villiers, whom some months in Holland appear to have made sharper-tongued, and, if anything, more squinty.

Anne lowers her voice and says, 'I think he is mostly vexed that you did not choose him for your household.'

She finds herself skewered by Betty's good eye. 'My, Your Highness, you have certainly come on a great deal since we saw you last . . . I do not think your sister's soul is too much imperilled for want of Dr Lake. Not when Dr Hooper is so very — zealous.'

'He has given me some very edifying reading, Mrs Villiers. I shall pass *Of the Laws of Ecclesiastic Polity* to you when I have finished it. I know how anxious you are for improvement.'

But Betty carries on almost as if her mistress had not spoken, and addresses Anne again.

'And it is thanks to Dr Hooper, of course, that Her Highness has her Chapel instead of that over-large dining-room the Prince had furnished for her use.'

'And it is Mrs Hooper who sits behind you, Betty,' Mary hisses. 'Now, ladies, if you are ready, I shall deal.'

This is Mary's establishment, so Mary, of course, is the Bank. Anne is greatly impressed by her sister's princely person: so stately, so stout and womanly and so very, very beautiful. It is all the more impressive for being so far from what the Duke has warned Anne to expect. Ever since Mary miscarried, and even more since she began to breed again, he has been in constant fear of her riding, walking or standing too much, of her eating the wrong foods, or failing to eat the right ones, of the possible ill effects of the Dutch weather or Dutch customs or Dutch Calvinist husbands. As no written assurances can satisfy him as to Mary's condition, he has sent his wife and second daughter — very incognito, with only the three Duchesses and their closest attendants for company — to bring him back a fuller report.

He should be reassured, Anne thinks: the Duchess has said how delighted she is to find Mary in such good spirits. Anne, for her part, is astonished to see how passionately her sister can love a sullen, crooked prince. Mary has told her, in all apparent sincerity, that to see him riding off to war is the keenest pain she has ever felt.

They are playing basset this evening. Mary has dealt each player her thirteen cards, and now, one by one, they lay down their first stakes. The first card Mary turns up is the Queen of Clubs, and both the Villiers sisters, who have Clubs in their stakes, lose heavily. Mary collects her proceeds, then turns a second card: the five of Diamonds, which wins for Anne. She goes at once for seven and the go, but loses on the next card, which wins for the Bank again.

The play continues: Mary turns the cards; gold is staked, lost, won back and lost again. Anne wins, makes another bold move, and loses everything. After a little while, when the Villiers have lost nearly everything and the Bank has enriched itself at their expense, the Prince of Orange is announced, Betty swears under her breath, and the game is over.

Anne watches her sister retire with her husband, and thinks that in — what? two years? — she too could be married and the mistress of her own household, able to eat what she wants and scold her ladies and, better than anything, keep the Bank.

THE DUCHESS'S SECRETARY

The Queen and Duchess are crying into their needlework together. Anne is leafing through a new pattern-book, so that she might make a plausible show of looking for a picture to work onto a seat cover, while her two companions pretend that she can't hear them.

They have arrived back from The Hague to find the Court, and England, in uproar. All the talk is of a Master Titus Oates, and of the plot he has discovered: a hellish, Popish conspiracy to have the King murdered, the Duke put on the throne, and then with blood and fire to scourge the Kingdom Catholic. As a precautionary measure, no Catholic may now come within ten miles of London. Anne's own Mrs Farthing has come perilously close to being turned off and sent away, even though Anne knows — in her heart and in her head — that her nurse is above reproach. As is Mary Cornwallis (unless, that is, it is treason to bewitch a princess). But with the Duchess's own staff, the case has proved quite different.

She is crying for her secretary, Edward Coleman. While she was visiting her niece — her dear Lemon — in Holland, very particular accusations were made against him, and his office was searched by order of the Lord Treasurer. The correspondence between Coleman and King Louis's favourite Jesuit was more than cordial enough to send him to the scaffold.

'Oh it is beyond terrible!' the Queen is saying, through sobs, 'and now you tell me that they took your own letters to His Holiness — your most private letters! — and read them — to submit you to such a violation — it is a violation!'

Anne can hear from the Queen's voice that she is shaking. With her big eyes and rabbit teeth, she is a small sad thing that waits to be preyed upon.

'Well they found nothing in them, at least,' the Duchess says. 'Why should they? Why should I seek the death of my own dear brother-in-law?'

'Or I my husband!' the Queen cries. 'I think it is a kind of madness with these people!'

'Or the best way to power in this country,'

says the Duchess suddenly, in a harder voice that makes Anne start. She looks up to find her step-mother meeting her eyes.

'You should understand this, Anne — if you do not already, which I think you must, for you are not a stupid girl, and I know that even if you do not speak, you still listen — yes, Anne, I know, I am not stupid either — you should understand there are many who do not wish your father to be King. They would see him exiled first — or dead.'

As the Duchess has guessed, Anne did already know, but to hear it said so plainly, and in a harsh voice, out of a twisted, angry countenance, one she has never seen on her step-mother before, is such that all she can think to do is to join the others in their tears.

Fortunately, this seems to have been exactly the right thing to have done, because before the first tear has even worked its way down Anne's cheek, both face and voice have softened again.

'Oh Anne, do not cry, do not think I blame you for your education — that they took you from your father — that Compton monster! — it was the King's wish.'

'And the King is a man of good sense,' says the Queen, 'for see? Nobody has demanded to read Anne's letters.'

ANNE'S LETTERS

To Mrs Mary Cornwallis

Thank you for your letter I have kissed it a hundred times. I feared that with all the trouble there is at Court I might never see or hear from you again but thank God my poor heart is not to be quite broken yet. But I should say no more of such things. I was sorry to hear that you have caught a chill. My Danvers and also my poor unfortunate nurse always said an infusion of liquorice roots can do much good in such a case, if you wish I can have Danvers make up a bottle and have it sent to you, nothing is too much trouble for one who is ever your devoted servant. I shall pray for your good health and that I might lay eyes on you soon. Until then farewell from your most affectionate friend.

To the Princess of Orange

My dearest Mary I was so very grieved to hear of your miscarriage, I have wept so many tears on account of it myself so can scarce imagine how heavy such an affliction must have proved for you and the Prince. The Duke and Duchess are alike most affected and their talk is all of you and what must be done for your better health. I pray that this will be the end of your sorrows and that God willing you will be with child again and that time with a happier issue. It is a most kind thing in you to ask after your sisters' health when you are brought so low yourself, I am glad to say I am well and that our little Isabella thank God continues lively and strong she is grown such a pretty child and she loves to laugh and to play. Her favourite game is to watch me build her a house of cards so that she might knock it down again.

Farewell, my dear sister.

To Mrs Mary Cornwallis

Pray do not chide me for the letter you saw from me to Mrs Apsley, I know that I do call myself her husband Ziphares and she my wife Semandra but it is but a game since we read Mithridates together and it is our favourite play and you must know that Mary was used to sign her letters to Mrs Apsley your wife Mary Clorine. Believe me when I say I only use your true name not because I love you less but because no name in the world could be more beautiful to my ears or to my sight, after you and your mother left the ball last night the King even said that no man ever loved his mistress more than Anne loves her Mrs Cornwallis and everybody laughed and if I could have died for blushing I would have done I would have died gladly for your sake. There is no news except that poor Mrs Godolphin that was Margaret Blagge and Diana in Callisto has died in childbed which is sad but she is more like to go straight to heaven than anyone I can think of so that must be a comfort to her friends.

Your <u>most</u> affectionate servant,
Lady Anne

THE MARTYRDOM OF CHARLES I

Thirty years ago, on this day, Anne's grand-father, the anointed King of England, came to a most unnatural death. God suffered him to fall into the hands of wicked, lawless men, who mocked and tortured him after the manner of the tormentors of Christ, before they murdered him, and in beheading a King, they beheaded England. It was a punishment for the nation's sins, and a sin that would bring further punishment: eleven years of persecution for the people and their true Church; a plague; a fire; defeat at the hands of the Dutch; a barren Queen, and now, this Papist threat. Let nobody make the mistake of thinking that God might spare them on a whim. God is merciful, but not for nothing: they must confess their sins, they must repent of them, they must meekly acknowledge their vileness; they must weep, they must fast, they must pray . . .

. . . so the sermon goes. Seated in the royal closet, in the Chapel at Whitehall, a black veil covering her face, Anne could almost fancy herself struck by a punitive blindness. And that is just one of many torments: the fast today is complete and strict, and she has not had so much as one drop or morsel pass her lips since she woke this morning. She has had the usual fasting pain in her stomach from the first, and now she feels the usual headache approaching. This year, she has her flowers too: her body, like her soul, is working to rid itself of foul and noisome excesses. Despite all the sweet herbs she has been stuffing into her pocket, she can still smell her own blood, and she is very much afraid that the King, and all his Gentlemen of the Chapel Closet, must smell it too. The thought of this sets her face on fire. A few feet away, she hears the King irritably blowing the air out of his cheeks, and her shameful heat increases.

To console herself, she thinks of all the other matters — beside her menstruous smell — that might put the King out of temper. He hates a fast as much as she does, and he has felt compelled to order so many of them lately, every time another plot is discovered, or some Papist conflagration started, or a motion tabled in Parliament to bar her father from the Crown. Since the present trouble started, he has had guards and Esquires of the Body sleeping in the Presence Chamber every night for his protection, and he cannot stir from his privy chamber except when under guard. He hates to wall himself off from his people; he hates to have to admit that such a course might be necessary. Anne has heard him complaining to the Duke:

'That I must be always so watchful, Jamie, and everyone else so watchful about me. Dammit, it is as if I am seeing the world through your eyes, and I must say, it is a perfect Hell.'

The Duke and Duchess are elsewhere, praying after their own unfortunate fashion. Nobody told them about Anne's disgraceful first Communion, and nobody will tell them that, on this occasion, she acquits herself beautifully, and this even though one sip and one wafer are only enough to give her hunger a keener edge. She spends the rest of the day in perfect misery.

She breaks the fast at sunset, in the Presence Chamber at Whitehall, sitting under the royal canopy with the King, the Duke and their wives — it only wants Mary to remind their audience precisely who is supposed to be succeeding whom — with a full complement of carvers, sewers and cupbearers hovering behind them, and a row of decorative jellies and fruit cones on the table in front of her, to give her at least a little protection from the Court and the people, and their hungry, calculating stares.

It is at just this moment, in just this place, as old Master Erskine leans forward to fill her cup, and her eyes come to rest on the green crown of a pineapple, that a thought creeps out of some shadowy privy chamber in her heart, where it has been living and growing, all unseen, for some indeterminate time, and whispers itself to her.

'If you are ever Queen,' it says, 'you will not care to dine in public.'

She knocks the full cup back in one gulp, an act which the King notices, and applauds.

'This is what I so commend in your daughter, James,' he says, 'no gingerliness about her, no finicality — it is always a pleasure to watch her at my table — look at all those broken meats there, on her plate — I swear she has fallen to it as if she thought never to see food again!'

The Queen and the Duchess laugh. The Duke drives a forkful of veal into his mouth and says nothing. The King has come out of the fast ready to drink and laugh at his family and forget his current troubles for a spell, but the Duke has emerged from his day sullen and abstracted. He breaks his silence only to talk to the King, and then only to complain about his intolerable situation, the impudence of Parliament, the infernal busyness of Shaftesbury and his party. When he has done with his furious veal-chewing, he returns, just as furiously, to the same miserable subject.

'Enough, Jamie!' says the King. 'This — all this —' he waves his knife through the air, as if he were reaping a field of parliamentarians — 'mess will be cleared up and out of our way before too long, and then, Jamie, and then —' and now he points to Anne — 'we can set about finding a husband for your promising daughter.'

WHAT A GOOD ENGLISH PRINCESS KNOWS ABOUT THE BUSINESS OF GOVERNMENT

Almost nothing.

Only that any English King who wishes to retain his head had best rule with the consent and goodwill of his people — that is to say, with the consent and goodwill of Parliament. He might hold off ruin without its assistance, if he applies to the King of France (this being one of those things a princess knows while also knowing that she should not), but this will not serve indefinitely. He might choose to prorogue or dissolve Parliament if it vexes him too much, but even then, he cannot hope to stop up the mouths of its individual members, especially not the mouths of such as Shaftesbury, who takes his infernal busyness from the Privy Council to the Court then to Parliament and back again, and hates a Catholic like he hates the Devil, and would suffer anything before he sees one take the Crown.

ANNE AND ISABELLA

'Oh dear ladies, if you do not stop your crying, I think I must have no recourse but to find whichever quack it was said the Greenwich air was physic for melancholy and have him whipped!'

The King has his usual pack of gentlemen with him, and they laugh heartily at this; so do Sarah Churchill and Barbara Berkeley (nee Villiers), but then they were neither of them crying in the first place. Lady Harriet, ever the good courtier, says, 'Huh!' and obliges the King with a glimpse of her still-lovely throat. But Anne, who is standing next to her governess, and little Isabella, who squirms in her arms, go on weeping without the slightest interruption.

Anne cannot see how she is supposed to hinder herself from shedding tears — no, not even at the King's command — on such an evil day as this; when only moments earlier, she has watched the Duke hand the

Duchess into a tender, which is now convey-
ing them to the King's best yacht, which
vessel will take them first to visit the Princess of Orange and then on to Flanders,
where they are to make an indefinite stay.
Until three days ago, Anne was supposed to
be travelling with them, but at the last
minute, the King, as he so often does, has
exercised his infinite prerogative and
changed his mind: the princesses must be
kept safely in the bosom of the English
Court and the English Church.

The King sees at once that his wit has
failed, and tries reason.

'Anne, child, you are fourteen — you are
so nearly a woman, and surely your understanding is not so mean that you cannot
perceive the wisdom of this? How am I to
bring my more . . . tendentious subjects
round when every time they get a sniff of
your father they bark and snarl like hounds
at a covert?'

Reason also fails. The King sticks his bottom lip forward and sighs into his mous-
tache. Then he gives orders for the Ladies
Anne and Isabella to be taken back to
London in the barge. Immediately, lest they
flood his Park and drown his observatory.

Anne is settled into the seat nearest the
stern, but firmly facing the prow, so there is

no possibility of any last wistful glance backwards, that could goad her into further tears; to make quite sure, Mrs Berkeley sits on her left side, and Mrs Churchill on her right, and the two of them begin talking as soon as the barge has pulled away.

'What a poppet the Lady Isabella is become,' says Mrs Berkeley, cooing at the pretty dark child, who has fallen asleep on Lady Harriet's lap, the tears still drying on her cheeks. 'She has such a look of the Princess of Orange about her, I think, when she was this age — Lady Harriet, do you not remember?'

'Indeed I do: Her Highness was from the first a most ravishing child.'

'I did not know their Highnesses then,' says Mrs Churchill, 'but I would agree that Lady Isabella might well grow to be a beauty, and after the Princess's style.'

'Oh, look how she smiles in her sleep!' cries Mrs Berkeley. 'I do think, Your Highness, that she will be quite happy again once we reach London — and you must take some comfort from that, yes?'

'Certainly,' says Anne, dabbing at her eyes with her last dry handkerchief, 'it is always a delight to me to see her happy and smiling, and I shall be glad of her dear company, but if the King only knew what trouble this

125

was to both of us —'

Lady Harriet interrupts her. 'Your Highness, he can hardly fail to, but he must weigh your distress against many other concerns — and so must you.'

Nobody has anything to say to this, and for a few long moments there is nothing to be heard but the slapping of the oars on the water and Isabella's subdued, babyish snuffling. Then, just as it seems that Anne is about to succumb to tears again, a waterman on a nearby wherry misses a stroke, falls backwards, and lets forth a burst of profanity so ripe and so colourful that there is nothing to do but laugh instead.

'The invention of the man!' cries Mrs Berkeley. 'I do not think Rochester himself could have afforded better.'

'For all we know, he did,' says Mrs Churchill. 'Perhaps his debts are such that he must pen wit by the line, and sell it to wherrymen to pay his physician.'

The other ladies scream with laughter again, so Mrs Churchill continues on her tale of the pox-ridden Earl who must bring his verse to market, while Mrs Berkeley assists her, all the way to Whitehall.

THE ENGLISH TONGUE, ALREADY SO RICH IN INSULTS, ACQUIRES TWO MORE

Whig {from 'Whiggamore,' being an intemperate, zealous Presbyterian Scottish rebel}: one who is opposed to the succession of the Duke of York.

Tory {from 'Tory,' being a lawless Papist bandit, who runs amok in the Irish bogs}: one who is opposed to the Whigs.

Anne in Her Closet, Windsor, July, 1679

O Righteous Lord,

who hateth iniquity, I thy sinful creature cast myself at thy feet, acknowledging that I most justly deserve to be utterly abhorred and forsaken by thee; for I have drunk iniquity like water, gone on in a continual course of sin and rebellion against thee, daily committing those things thou forbiddest, and leaving undone those things thou commandest: my heart; which should be an habitation for thy Spirit, is become a cage of unclean birds, of foul and disordered affections: and out of this abundance of the heart my mouth speaketh, my hands act: so that in thought, word and deed I continually transgress against . . . o how this print hurts my eyes . . .

. . . I have first of all to beg your forgiveness for my neglect of what is due to you,

that is to say my prayers and devotions —
that this closest in my lodgings is so
wretchedly hot in daylight is I know no
proper excuse but you must know that
although I go not into my closet I keep you
always in my heart and if I dance or play
cards or stroll or ride or hunt ever so
much . . . yes, I have done all these things
and some to excess, my losses at cards
and dice this sennight I confess have been
great, but I have doubled my gifts to the
poor and hope this may serve as some
recompense . . . and I must confess also
that when I do contrive to be alone in my
closet I have used the time to write letters,
not to pray or meditate on my sins or to
give thanks

— speaking of which, I must thank you for
providing me with a friend with such
superior understanding as Mrs Churchill
has: she says that the acquittal of the
Queen's physician of treason and then the
way Mr Oates conducted himself during
this latest trial is such as to make any
person of sense wonder if they have not
given far too much credence to a dishonest and venal man and taken for Gospel

what was never more than hearsay and gossip — so she says — although I cannot think but that what he said of the Papists and their intentions was true in general. What I sincerely hope and pray for is that if Mrs Churchill is correct then maybe the tide of opinion and rumour against my father might turn again and we might once more be reunited.

And then I might see my dear Mrs Cornwallis again, who languishes with him in Flanders. As it is, the distance and sea between us does I confess break my heart almost daily — but you who know everything know this. You know what trials you have sent to me and I beg too that you might send the grace and patience to bear them — I hope that they might be a sign of your love as well as a correction to me — and I thank you for sending me such a loyal and beautiful and generous friend as Mrs Cornwallis is — I confess I sometimes do wonder if perhaps I trespass in some way in thinking on her so much, but truly her beauty is a virtue and one that you have created and in honouring it I could say I honour one of the most perfect parts of your creation . . . ?

While I am thus examining my heart and confessing my sins, I must also confess that I have spoken pertly to Lady Harriet often these past weeks, but since my uncle Hyde is made Treasury Commissioner they are both of them so puffed up, worse even than they were before — did any maid ever have such insufferable relations? . . . but I know I should bear them with patience and with gratitude for what they do for me . . .

One occasion of my speaking thus to her weighs most heavily on my heart and that is last week when we were in the Queen's apartments here. I was looking at Mr Gibbons' carvings of fruit and flowers about the door and my Lord — a certain nobleman did bow to me and ask if I did not think them miraculously lifelike, I agreed that I did and told him what I considered a droll story, about when I was very much smaller and hungry and did one morning lick a pear to see if it tasted as lifelike as it looked and was most sadly disappointed. He said he should like to repeat the experiment and the made a great show of licking it himself. It is true that I laughed very much indeed at this, but surely it was but an innocent jest so I do not see that Lady Harriet had any reason to rebuke me for being 'forward' . . .

. . . but you who know the secrets of my heart know I do not intend any forwardness by my conduct or by my conversation with the men at Court: I cannot help but laugh when they are droll and I can never hinder myself from blushing and if it is becoming or forward in me to do so, then . . . I can only pray again that my father may come home and the present trouble cease so that a husband might be found for me and then, please Lord, all this sinning that I do without designing and cannot help will be at an end . . .

. . . speaking of which, I find I must say again that if I do not spend more time on medication and prayer today or on other days it is because of the time it takes writing to my close kin overseas with whom I would otherwise have no discourse. I admit the sorrow of my father's leaving was hard to bear at first but with time I found the burden is lighter, lighter than I

ever supposed it could be — and I thank
you for this mercy.

AT THE INN FOR
EXILED PRINCES

When it becomes clear that the Duke's sojourn in Brussels — that inn for exiled princes — will not be a brief one, he sends for his carriages, his hunters and his hounds. A few months later, he requests a visit from his younger daughters, and the King agrees, on the strict condition that neither girl is at any time during her stay to enter any of the various cathedrals, churches, abbeys, convents, monasteries, oratories or shrines which have peppered the country since the Spanish laid claim.

'It is a great pity in a way,' Anne says to Mrs Berkeley one afternoon, 'for I am told they are many of them very fine indeed — and now Mrs Apsley has written and asked for an account of them, and I am sorry not to be able to oblige.'

'But she shouldn't have too much cause to complain,' says Mrs Berkeley, 'not when you are writing her such a good, long letter.'

'Oh there is enough to tell her — I have told her already about the ball — Prince Vodemont's dancing especially and of course those chocolate sweetmeats — and the park — the people here, of their manners and so forth — and although I cannot tell about the churches, I have said . . .' Anne brings the sheet she has been scrawling over up to her nose and reads:

' ". . . all the fine churches and monasteries you know I must not see so can give you no good account of them, but those things which I must needs see as their images which are in every shop and corner of the street the more I see of those fooleries and the more I hear of that religion the more I dislike it, there is a walk a little way of which if it were well kept it would be very pretty, and here's a place which they call the *coure* where they go round the streets and there is all the company every night like Hyde Park I can give you account of nothing else because I have seen no more . . ." '

'Well, as you say, if that is all you have seen, then that is all you can tell her of,' says Mrs Berkeley. 'But what opinion did you give her of the people, their manners and so forth?'

'Oh, only that they are very civil and won't

be otherwise except one is otherwise to them.'

'A fair assessment.'

'And I have told her that the streets here are clean — that is to say, cleaner than the streets in London, but not so clean as those in The Hague.'

'Yes, they are quite superlatively clean there, are they not?'

'They are, and the way my sister Orange writes about them one would think she had cleaned them all herself.'

'Your sister Orange is such a very conscientious lady. Maybe she has.'

The picture this brings to Anne's mind, of Mary sweeping a frantic path through the streets of her adoptive capital, while her husband follows with a critical look and white-gloved hand, to check her work, is enough to put her in fits of laughter; she cannot find the words to tell Mrs Berkeley why this particular jest has been so successful, but it is no matter, because the lady seems pleased enough with its effect.

It is so sweet to be alone with Mrs Berkeley, and to laugh. Anne has spent too much of her visit on show, at balls or in the places where the company reminds her of Hyde Park, and if she had not pretended to a headache today she would have had to go out with the Duchess, and Isabella, and Lady Harriet, for stiff talk in French with the stiffer Spanish nobility. She is grateful — for once — to Lady Harriet for asking her no questions and leaving her be — but then, Lady Harriet has altered her manner a little in the last few days where Anne is concerned, so that she is somewhat less like a governess and somewhat more like a courtier. Anne does not need Mrs Berkeley or Churchill to tell her why: the King is gravely ill, and until the Duke has sent back word from his incognito visit, nobody knows who might live, who might be King, and who else might be the King's daughter.

The difference in Lady Harriet is a good thing, for sure, but Anne is sorry that the Duke is not there: he had promised her at the very least one day's hunting outside the City, but this looks less likely by the day. Also he has taken Captain Churchill with him, and Captain Churchill has taken his wife Sarah, and as Sarah hopes to be confined in London, she will not be coming back to Brussels. At least Anne still has Mrs Berkeley here to make her laugh, and Mrs Cornwallis, sometimes, to gaze upon.

'It is a pity that Mrs Cornwallis has gone with the Duchess today,' Anne says, as she folds the letter, ready for posting. 'We could have spent a most pleasant afternoon here, the three of us together.'

'Can we not have almost as pleasant a time with two, Your Highness?' Mrs Berkeley reaches into her pocket, where she causes its contents to rattle enticingly.

'What? Dice, Barbara! No! When I think what you won of me yesterday . . .'

'That does not signify so very much, does it? Your Highness plays for such low stakes —'

'The Duke will not allow me to play for higher.'

'Well then . . . or would you prefer that I take up Lady Harriet's suggestion, and read to you out of *The Whole Duty of Man*?'

Anne considers this: Sunday reading on a weekday. No.

'Oh, very well then, Mrs Berkeley. Dice it is.'

THE DUKE OF YORK AND THE PRINCE OF ORANGE

Anne is not to be a king's daughter just yet; nor is England to go the way of the Spanish Netherlands. The King has rallied, and the Duke is all of a sudden back in Brussels, properly thankful for the restoration of his brother's health, and loudly victorious over the concessions he has won from him: firstly, that he and his Duchess might spend the rest of their exile in Edinburgh, where he will have the opportunity to exercise stewardship over the unruly Scots; secondly, the King has agreed that the Duke of Monmouth must likewise be sent into exile.

His nephew Monmouth is one of the Duke's favourite topics. He complains of him to whoever is compelled to listen, be it his wife, his gentlemen and grooms of the bedchamber, Spanish nobility or Flanders Jesuits. Shortly after his return, he and the Duchess accompany Anne and Isabella to The Hague. He says this is so that he might see more of them before they leave for England, but in truth he seems more interested in bending his son-in-law's ear. The instant they have all sat down to dine, he is straight to it.

'Yes,' he insists, 'the English monarchy is in danger — this is true, all too true — but not from Papists — have I not said, and more than once, that all I ever desired was the freedom to worship?'

'You have,' says the Prince of Orange, 'and — as one would expect — quite a deal more than once.'

Anne feels a sudden tautness in the air and looks up from her plate to find her older sister and step-mother have both gone very still, but the Duke carries on regardless.

'The monarchy is in danger — as I said — but it is not from Papists, who go on their way the same as before — my brother was too forgiving, I told him he would regret it — the danger is the Commonwealth party, and those Whigs — that call themselves the "Country Party" — and men of the like of Shaftesbury who compelled — nay, all but blackmailed — the King into bringing them into his Council —'

He pauses for a moment, having lost his way. The Prince takes the chance to ask his wife if her sister might perhaps like to take a waffle or two, as he sees she has already tried everything else. Anne's blush is quite excruciating. The Duke continues:

'And for their own ends these men make a property of —'

['Here he comes . . .' Anne thinks.]

'— the Duke of Monmouth, and they do this to ruin our family, and now things go on so fast, and so violently, and there are so few left about His Majesty with the will or courage to give good advice to him — I tremble to think — if His Majesty and the Lords stick to me, there might be great disorders — nay, rebellion; if he consents to what the Commons will do against me, the monarchy shall be absolutely ruined and our family with it — he shall have reduced himself to the condition of —'

[Anne waits for the inevitable arrival of another Duke.]

'— a Duke of Venice!'

Having made his point, and quite upset himself on the way, the Duke drains a glass of wine and sets about his pancake as if it were Shaftesbury. Meanwhile the Prince speaks, and with the most dreadful courtesy.

'A Duke of Venice indeed,' he says, 'or perhaps a Stadtholder of the United Provinces.'

The Duke chokes. 'Oh, of course not —

no comparison! No comparison at all! Why if anyone were master of his own house, then surely it were Your Highness.'

'And how well you do live here,' says the Duchess. 'How charmingly well. We have the most beautifully appointed lodgings here, do we not, Anne?'

Anne swallows a bite of waffle and agrees.

'Beautiful,' she says, 'and Mary has shown us such lovely things: her gardens, her porcelain collection, her paintings . . .' She feels the Prince's sardonic eye on her, and falters. 'Some lovely paintings . . . paintings of tulips . . . her tulip paintings . . .'

Everybody is relieved when Mary replies.

'Believe me, it has been a pleasure to show you how I live, how happy I am — such a pity only that the King has called you away so soon — I was in great hopes of taking you to Honselaarsdijk to show you the gardens there, so much more can be accomplished in the country than we are able to do here — I must confess to being very proud of them.'

'My wife's work does us both great credit,' says the Prince. It is the first time Anne has ever heard him praising Mary.

'But not at the expense of her health, I hope?' The Duke's voice has the anxious, pitying tone he usually adopts when talking to or about his eldest daughter. This baffles Anne, as Mary does indeed have lovely things, great quantities of lovely things, gowns and jewels, exquisitely worked wooden and silver boxes, blue-and-white porcelain vases and flowers from all corners of the earth to arrange in them, and if children could be likewise imported, commissioned, purchased, cultivated in a hothouse or grown from a bulb, no doubt she would have the best of those too.

The Prince leaves Mary to answer. 'Father, my gardens delight me, and my spirits are better for keeping them.'

The Duke then surprises everyone by taking the hint, and changes the topic, asking the Prince if he has had any good hunting about The Hague this last season. Later, when the Prince and Princess are elsewhere, he will return to another of his favourite activities: harvesting intimate news from Mary's bedchamber women, who will tell him that the Prince has given Mary no real reason to think she might be with child. When he reaches the English shores, he will write and thank his son-in-law for what has been a perfect visit.

A GAME OF OMBRE

It is the anniversary of the accession of Queen Elizabeth; the people of London are burning straw popes with the traditional merriment and customary violence. Even in St James's, with the shutters closed, Anne can still hear shouts, can still catch a whiff of smoke that is nothing to do with the fire in the chimney or the candles on the table. She won't be joining the revellers tonight. Instead, she stays in her chamber with Sarah Churchill and Barbara Berkeley and sits down to a hand of ombre.

Of the three of them, it is only Barbara who really has a mind to the game. Anne cannot hinder her thoughts from wandering out through the shutters and across the Park to the jeering, fire-maddened crowds. Sarah, meanwhile, is fast approaching her time. She has long since grown too big for all her bodices, and has taken instead to wearing a woollen waistcoat like a man. She goes about with her hair all but undone, and is never without a bottle of elder water, which she says is the only thing good for her indigestion. Her discomfort alone might be enough to put her into one of her foul humours, but she has other reasons too.

'Churchill insists he must stay with the Duke in Scotland, but surely the Duke could spare him if he wished — it is that John has some doxy in the Duchess's train — of course he denies it in his letters, but I'll not be fooled.'

'Which doxy might that be?' asked Barbara. 'My Lady Peterborough? Mrs Cornwallis? Mrs Churchill, if you could only hear yourself . . . Let us to the game. I won the bid, if you remember, and as ombre, I declare Spades are trumps.'

'Spades . . .' Anne repeats, glances at her cards for a moment, then turns to Sarah. 'My dear Mrs Churchill, my father is I am sure most grateful for your husband's support and counsel. You have been in London all this time — you have not seen how it is for him . . .'

'Your cards, Ladies? Well . . . I have the Ace of Spades! The first trick is mine.'

'Yes, Mrs Berkeley . . . but what I was going to say was . . . I travelled with my father's party as far as Hatfield House. And when we reached there, we found that Salisbury was on purpose from home, and his Lady with him, and they had left for us the most meagre amount of kindling, and food fit only for fast days — and for fasting in a pauper's house at that —'

She breaks off so that she and Sarah can consult over their cards. It is all for nothing though: Barbara wins the second trick too. Sarah and Anne pay attention for long enough for her to take the next two tricks. Then it looks as if the hand might be almost played out already, and they drift away again.

'What I was telling you,' Anne says, 'is that it was a deliberate insult — quite deliberate.'

Sarah scratches her head as she considers this: Anne has begged her many times not to stand on ceremony with her, and when they are in private as they are this evening, she rarely does.

'Deliberate, for sure,' she says, 'but he is not held in such contempt by all — you must take heart from that.'

'And speaking of hearts . . .'

They return to the cards, and are rewarded when the Queen of Hearts wins them their first trick.

'You are still like to beat us, Barbara,' says Anne.

'If I win two more of you.'

The game begins to seem interesting to everybody now, and they play the next two rounds without speaking. Anne and Sarah win both. Then a particularly loud cry goes up from the City — a triumphant shout — another Pope collapsing into cinders. Anne can almost see it as it falls; savage, murderous faces all about.

'I cannot but be unsettled,' she says, 'especially when Isabella and I must rattle around in a house that is half shut up. I could wish my step-mother had stayed to bear us company.'

'But she bears the Duke company,' says Barbara, 'and her loyalty does her credit.'

She immediately has cause to regret this observation: it sets Sarah off again.

'She is with her husband — she can see what he does. I cannot.'

'Sometimes it pains her to see, Mrs Churchill,' says Anne. 'The Duke has always had his mistresses.'

'True, Your Highness. Mrs Churchill, if this doxy did exist, would you prefer her in plain sight? Would you, really?'

'If I could see it, I could prevent it!'

'Well, if ever a lady could, Mrs Churchill, that lady would be you — but Churchill is in Scotland, and you are at St James's, with two more tricks to play for. So . . . ?'

Sarah forgets to consult Anne over their play, and throws down the Jack of Diamonds without thinking, but all the same it wins them the penultimate trick. The game hangs on the last one, the ninth.

Sarah puts down the Jack of Hearts.

Anne follows with the Ace from the same suit.

Then Barbara shows the King of Hearts, winning the final trick and with it the hand.

'And so I should,' she says, 'for I was the only one paying any attention.'

Sarah sticks her tongue out, Barbara laughs and collects her winnings. Anne calls for cakes and wine.

ANNE IS THANKFUL

O Holy, blessed and glorious Trinity, three Persons and one God, have mercy on me, a miserable sinner.

Lord, I know not what to pray for as I ought . . . I praise you for the grace you have given me, for the continuance of my good health (I have had no need of physic for the last two months at least, praise be) and that of my kin and my friends . . . I should rather say, in my sister Orange's case, for the restoration of her good health, for the word from her Court is that she is now fully out of danger. When the fits of her ague were at their height, when her death was hourly expected, I feared for her very much, especially as she was in the hands of the Prince's physicians — who you know do not bleed enough . . . You know what was in my heart then, please forgive me if I do not speak of it now, I do not think my spirit could bear it.

I must thank you too for what else is restored to us: that spring is here at last, after so long a winter — it does my heart good to find the trees in the Park in bud again, to see the first flowers in the ground when I stroll. I can look forward now to long rides in fair weather — and perhaps to hunt with my father as I was not able in Flanders — for I must thank you for his return too — for I understand the King has Parliament at bay, so for all that is said or written or printed or signed against the Duke, they can at least pass no Bills to hurt him — to hurt us, I should say — to hurt this family . . .

And thank you too for the safe return of my dear Mrs Churchill's husband, who I am sure will comfort her as I cannot for the loss of her baby Harriet, whom you have in your goodness made so perfectly happy.

THE DUCHESS'S BALL

The King is not as fond of dancing as he once was, but he does his duty, and opens the ball by dancing the brantle with the Duchess: for the *ru de vaches,* he kicks out with the vigour of a man half his age — and it is more than flattery to say so — it is the truth. All the same, he looks more than content to sit back down, and watch his brother leading out the Queen. Sitting next to the Duchess, Anne watches the lords and ladies dancing couple by couple, all in strict and dull courtly order, and while part of her is relieved that she is not to perform, as they must, on an empty floor, in front of everyone's eyes, she is in another part every bit as disappointed. If she were to perform just one of the French court dances, a brantle or a courant, with the arms held out just *so,* then it would give everybody a chance to see how fine they have grown this past year. They are no longer the awkward arms of a school-maid; they are well-turned, they are elegant, and they are more than ready to be admired.

Perhaps if the Duke of Monmouth were available, she might have danced the brantle with him. But the Duke of Monmouth is neither at Court, as Anne would wish, nor in exile, as her father was promised, but is instead making a progress through the West Country, dining in its great houses, shaking hands with its great men. The Duke is beside himself, and has talked of little else. As soon as the French dances are over, he marches straight up to Anne's Uncle Hyde, who is now First Lord of the Treasury, and begins to talk of it again.

In this interval between the last courant and the first country dance, the Court refreshes itself and puts itself at ease; now everyone can move from his place and talk to whomever he will; ladies may call for drinks; gentlemen may piss in corners. Anne has permission to dance.

First, they dance the Argeers — one of Anne's favourites: it is the prettiest tune for the guitar, with violins singing behind, and also it is danced in groups of four, so there are no unpleasant surprises as there can be when she has to make her way, peering like a mole, down a longer set. She takes her place at one corner, and Mrs Cornwallis stands at the other. Anne has Charles Montagu for her partner, the Earl of Manchester's son; he is very handsome, which she likes, and talks almost as little as she does, which she likes even better. When Montagu takes her hands in the dance, he does so too lightly, as if he were afraid he should not be touching her. Mrs Cornwallis has young John Cutts, and copes well with his wit. When he pays his compliment to Anne, it makes her blush, and besides there is something in his manner of delivering it that is so like condescension, that she feels almost slighted instead. Still, he is a good dancer: his legs look very fine indeed in their stockings, and he is tall enough that she need not look him too often in the face. When his turn comes to take her hands, he does so a little too firmly, as if he is daring her to pull away.

Argeers gives way to the Parson's Farewell. It is a slower, calmer sort of dance, of slow crossings and dignified little nods, one that is hard to perform when one is giggling as much as Mrs Cornwallis seems to be. Anne tries very hard not to meet her eyes when they cross, as the Cornwallis giggle is notoriously infectious. Despite this precaution, by the time the dance comes to an end she is all worn out with the effort of keeping her face straight, and is glad to excuse herself. Mrs Cornwallis does the same, although a little more reluctantly, and they make their way over to where Mrs Churchill and Mrs Berkeley are sitting; they are talking, as usual, behind their fans.

'What was it set you off?' Anne whispers, behind hers. 'I was almost quite undone there, and in front of the Duchess.'

'It was something Mr Cutts said to me — about what I put him in mind of when I danced — I could hardly believe it — he said —'

But now Mrs Churchill's voice cuts across her. 'Pray sit down, Your Highness, and have something to drink. You look quite done in — oh, and Mrs Cornwallis, I expect you would like to sit down too.' Two Pages of the Presence Chamber arrive with chairs; two waiters follow them, with glasses of canary in their hands. As Anne raises the glass to her lips, she notices that her gloves have retained a little of the mingled perfumes from those of the gentlemen dancers: it is one of the many reliable pleasures of a ball.

Mrs Churchill has put her fan up again.

'Your Highness,' she whispers, 'Mrs Berkeley insists that she has it on good authority that a certain cousin of hers — Her Grace of Cleveland, no less — was seen looking in at the door.'

'Barbara Castlemaine?' Anne is astonished. 'But has she not been in France with her bastards these past four years?'

'Yes, but now she is back in England.'

'But surely she would not show her face at Court? In public?'

'You see, Mrs Berkeley?' says Sarah. 'I told you it was not credible. What could she hope for here? She has her lands, she has her pension — she is long since cast off. Her Grace of Portsmouth has nothing to fear from that withered quarter. She is quite safe.'

'And yet the King did not dance the courant with her tonight.'

'Nor with Nelly Gwynne. Nor the Queen. Nor with anybody else. The King is tired — everyone saw — he danced with the Duchess of York because he had to, and then he sat down in his comfortable chair, and there he is still. He is not himself.'

Anne becomes aware that there is another lady standing in front of her. She lowers her fan and finds herself looking up at Lady Peterborough, who has come to take her back to the Duchess. She makes Anne only the most cursory reverence, but then the poor lady's husband has been excluded from the Council on suspicion of Popish plotting, her face is growing plainer and older-looking by the day, and this evening too it is melting like a candle, so it would be churlish, under the circumstances, to hold such a tiny thing against her.

ISABELLA'S SISTER

Autumn comes: Parliament must meet again, and the King sends the Duke and Duchess back to Scotland. When Anne comes to look back on the months that follow their departure, she will remember them mostly for the time she spends with Isabella. The little girl is four now, and, like the King, still recovering from a dangerous bout of illness. She has grown strong enough to find the life of an invalid tedious, so Anne puts herself, Mrs Berkeley and Mrs Churchill to work amusing her. Sarah is particularly good at this — especially during the weeks when her husband is in Scotland — and devises a game whereby two of them hide playing cards up and down the Long Gallery, while the third waits outside with Isabella, then comes in with her to search for them. They take turns as her team-mate: sometimes, when Anne is looking under cushions at one end of the Gallery, while

Sarah and Barbara are laughing together on the same settee at the other, she is tormented by the suspicion that they are merrier in each other's company than they ever are in hers, and it is at such moments she feels Mrs Cornwallis's absence most keenly. That lady has returned to Scotland with her mother and the Duchess, and so now there is no-one here with Anne — except, perhaps, Isabella — to smile at her in such a way that suggests there is nobody — truly, nobody — they would rather have before them.

Prince George Ludwig
of Hanover

Sometimes Anne likes to walk the short distance from St James's Palace to Whitehall: the Park is beautiful in all seasons, and there are always plenty of people for Mrs Churchill or Mrs Berkeley to notice and make sport of. On this particular December day, however, she is taking the carriage, and taking it with Lady Harriet. Today she must protect her gown from the dirt, her hair from the wind and her eyes from the cold air, lest it make them water. She is going to meet a prince — maybe the first of many, maybe the one and only — and his first sight of her better be the best sight that can reasonably be achieved. Anne will never rival Mary, and the likes of Mrs Churchill and Cornwallis will always shine her down, but she will do. She has the most beautiful hair.

'Such a lovely chestnut colour,' says Danvers, as she curls and pins.

'I have had five gentlemen say so only the last month,' says Anne. Others have praised her elegant dancing, her musical accomplishments, the colour in her cheeks and — the few that hear it — her beautiful speaking voice. They all know better than to praise anything else, or to send her a private note about it: Maids of Honour are fair game, but princesses, like certain stags, are for royalty alone. Poach one, and you pay the price.

Now Lady Harriet gives the much-praised hair a final tease, and urges her charge into the Guard Chamber. Anne feels the room turning towards her as she is announced; its many inhabitants shuffle back towards the walls and fold themselves; she walks through, giving the occasional nod to she-knows-not-whom, and then repeats the performance in the Presence Chamber. There is bowing and curtsying before her all the way, and much whispering behind.

The King is waiting in the Withdrawing Chamber, so she stops in the doorway, and makes, with all due ceremony, the first curtsy. There is a second curtsy to make halfway across, and a third before the throne, where the King raises her up with his own hand, and presents her to the younger man standing next to him. He is, at first blurry sight, short, fair and stoutish; he is George Ludwig of Hanover.

The short fair man takes a couple of steps forward and bows; Anne curtsies. When she rises she is looking up — a little — into a pair of blue, wide-set and slightly protuberant eyes. The Prince's face is long and serious, with a strong nose in the middle of it. He is plainly dressed, like the soldier he is. Now he speaks, in good but unmusical French: he is asking the King if he might salute his niece. The King grants his permission; then there is a tight, thickening, leery moment as the Prince leans in to kiss her; his lips on hers feel like a pair of dry, cold cushions, barely third cousins to the kinds of lips she and Mrs Cornwallis like to find in poems, but it makes no difference: the blush has already conquered her face, and settled it, before the Prince is even halfway there. The room applauds them both.

'Charming,' he says, in his odd French. 'I am charmed to meet you.'

'Thank you,' she says, remembering her line. 'It is a pleasure to meet a prince of whom I have heard so much good. Your uncle the Prince of the Rhine has been telling me about your feats on the battlefield.' His uncle is the King's cousin Rupert. Anne spent all of yesterday afternoon with him, while he praised his German nephew to her; then he composed a compliment on her behalf, and then stayed just a little longer, so that they might rehearse it together.

'I have done no more than my duty,' says the Prince. 'I for my part have heard that you play beautifully on the harpsichord and guitar, and I hope that I will be able to hear you while I am here.'

As Anne's supply of given words has now run out, she simply smiles, and inclines her head.

Later that day, she goes to visit Isabella in her chamber, as she has promised to do, to give her an account of the meeting. A succession of winter colds have weakened the child further, confining her to her rooms: she relies more and more on Anne's visits for what little entertainment she might have. Anne wishes she could tell her a more exciting tale, with a more exciting hero.

'So you did not think him handsome then?' asks Isabella, her voice gone small with disappointment.

Anne tries her best. 'He was not — *not* handsome,' she offers.

'The Prince is most distinguished-looking,' says Lady Harriet, saying as always the properest thing, 'and he carries himself like a soldier ought.'

Isabella brightens a little. 'Has he fought valiantly in the wars? Has he won many a battle?'

'I believe so,' says Anne, 'and I'm sure I could admire that in him.'

'I am certain he admired Anne,' says Lady Harriet. 'He looked very pleased indeed to have saluted her.'

Anne blushes again at the memory.

'He *kissed* you?' asks Isabella. 'He *kissed* you then? Oh, then I suppose you will be married.' She rests her head back on her pillows, looking well satisfied, as though she has arranged matters herself.

'I do not know,' says Anne. 'Perhaps.'

Lady Harriet steps in again. 'It is not certain.' She speaks carefully. 'No marriage can be arranged for your sister while your father is away.'

'That is vexatious,' says Isabella. 'That is most vexatious. Anne should be married. She should be married very soon. If a maid of her years be too long unmarried, then her seed will be retained and she will fall into a mother-fit.'

'Indeed,' says Lady Harriet, with a sharp glance at Anne. 'And where did you come by this interesting piece of knowledge?'

'In the summer,' says Isabella, 'when I heard Mrs Cornwallis reading to my sister.'

'Is that so?' Lady Harriet is looking quite steadily at Anne now, and asks her if she can recall the book.

'No,' says Anne, 'I'm afraid I cannot. We read so many.'

But Isabella is delighted to help. 'I can! I remember very well: the book was called *Aristotle's Masterpiece.*'

'Oh yes, I have heard of that — and I should like very much to see it. Your Highness, do you think you might go to your closet and fetch it for me?'

'I would be happy to,' Anne replies, 'only it is Mrs Cornwallis's own book — would you have me send to Scotland for it?'

'No thank you, Your Highness.' Later, as Anne knows perfectly well, Lady Harriet will have her closet searched. For now, she contents herself by pronouncing Isabella over-excited, and sending Anne out of the room.

The Prince stays for three more months, but gives little reason for any further excitement. Anne is perhaps a little sorry to see him leave, if she thinks about it, but when she weeps that spring, it is for Isabella.

Anne Enters into Her Cabin

O most powerful and glorious Lord God, at whose commands the winds blow, and lift up the waves of the sea, and who stillest the rage thereof . . . I know that you have sent no storm today, only some largish waves such as the Captain says are to be expected in these waters, but I wished for time alone in my cabin, and the only reason I could think of to send Danvers out was to tell her I wished to make my devotions in private — and as I would never in all my life lie about such a matter, I shall take this moment to confess my sins, and ask for grace, and offer my thanks for thy many mercies.

I confess that I have got too much in the habit of melancholy since Isabella died. It is not that I would ever question your wisdom or goodness in taking her to you and making her so happy; it is only, as Dr

Lake says, that I cannot but struggle when you test me in this way. I shall try when I arrive at Holyrood to present a cheerful countenance to my father and mother-in-law, so that I should not add to their sorrows with my own. Please help me to do this, and also to be more in charity with Lady Harriet, and to bear her strictures with more patience. Also I have been somewhat sharp with poor Danvers of late; she is my most faithful servant, and I know that this is not seemly or kind in me. Forgive me, I pray, for this, and for the excessiveness of the sorrow I feel at my being parted from Mrs Churchill: I know I should be content that she has a child and that this time the babe is strong and like to live but I find I cannot hinder myself from wishing that it did not keep her in London two more months at least. I must thank you, again, for her safe deliverance from travail and for the soundness of her daughter.

I must give thanks too, that this vessel which takes me from her returns me to my other dearest friend Mrs Cornwallis — and to my father and the Duchess. I am happy indeed that I shall be living with close kin once again: I have been too long without them. I thank you for prompting the King to give his permission for my journey, and that he has sent Parliament about its business, and that the Monmouth party are brought low, and for the love there is in the people after all, for the Crown, and the lawful succession, and for the true Church, which I pray shall never be put more in danger. Danvers says that Scotland is rotten all through with traitors and rebels against the Crown. I beseech you, keep us safe.

Scottish Gallants

August, and the sky over the Lothians is clear and blue, the breeze light and not too cold; it is the perfect day for an expedition out of Edinburgh. The journey is four miles long, and the train, it seems to Anne, is not much shorter: there is the Duke and Duchess, Anne herself, the Duchess's great friend Countess Davia of Bologna, her ladies, the Duchess's ladies, Anne's ladies, the Duke's gentlemen, and, to attend to them all, some eighty of the Scottish nobility and gentry. There are eight coaches, all quite full — some more than full — with ladies and their costumes. Their gentlemen ride alongside them; many more, with servants, follow behind. The horsemen keep the country people beyond touching distance, but there almost seems no need for this, as they have come only to clap and cheer. Yes, they are ragged and a little coarse, perhaps, but in no way hostile, and certainly nothing like savages.

They stop at a place called Polton, on the banks of the Esk, a narrow river, which runs fast and clear and is in all ways as unlike the Thames in London as any river could be. There is no brown water here, and no brown water smells. Everything looks and smells green. It is a beautiful place for a banquet — or 'treat', as the Duke of Lauderdale must have it, as he hands Anne down from her carriage. He draws the river to her attention, and the valley which he calls a glen; then the hills all around and the trees they have growing on them, and finally the buzzard circling overhead, which she pretends to exclaim at — for he can hardly, on so short an acquaintance, be expected to know about her eyes.

When he has excused himself to speak to her father, the Duchess touches Anne's arm and whispers, 'You will find the nobility here have a way of speaking about the beauties of their country as if they had commissioned them, and are looking to have their good taste commended — I think it more endearing than otherwise.' She smiles at Anne, then adds, in her proper public voice, 'See, Anne? They have set chairs down for us already. Let's sit down.'

Their hosts have spared no expense. There is very good wine to drink, jellies in their own lovely glasses, and so many different kinds of fruit, served on dishes garnished with gold fringe. It is all as fine as anything Anne might have at home (and this, she understands, is the point).

The company is good too; the ladies and gentlemen who attend the royal party, as often as not, have the French Court to thank for their excellent manners. Even the gallants are very much like those of White-hall, only when they speak it is more like singing. Anne plays the guitar for them, and they praise her neither too meanly, nor too well. The compliments they pay to Mary Cornwallis, who giggles at her side, are whispered, and probably of a different nature. Lady Harriet, who sits on Anne's other side, is almost hissing with disapproval. Anne thinks her governess unkind: if Mrs Cornwallis is to get herself a husband — as any maid would wish to — it will not be on account of the dowry her family can barely provide. It is always a pleasure to Anne to watch Mrs Cornwallis at her adventuring; it is like watching a heroine in a play, imagining a little that she is in her shoes, while knowing that, in truth, she is very safely out of them. If she could only contrive to bring Mrs Cornwallis to the true religion, she might have the pleasure of watching her frolic in the next world too.

The vision of a celestial Mrs Cornwallis is interrupted by the shrieks of her earthly counterpart, who has peach juice dribbling down her beautiful bosom. One of the young gentlemen — a Lord Robert Something or Master Jamie McSomethingElse — produces a handkerchief with a great flourish, and makes as if to come to her aid, but Lady Harriet is too quick for him.

'That is very generous, Sir, but there is no need — Mrs Cornwallis may use my handkerchief for now — and have more care for later.'

FROM LADY ANNE OF YORK TO MRS APSLEY

Edinburgh Sep the 8

My dear Semandra, I do again beg your pardon for being these two or three posts without writing to you but seriously I could not possibly help it. But now I must say something in answer to both your letters which I have received since I writ to you. In the first place I must tell you that I forgot to tell you that you should stand for me to Mrs Doylys child — pray remember me to her when you see her and then I must tell you that though you heard constantly from Pert who had a great many letters to writ and went often abroad, yet she did not go so constantly every day as I did, for I rid every day and then I was often with the Duchess and then I took a little time in my closet when I could catch it. Consider all these things well and forgive your poor Ziphares. As to what you desire to know in your other letter I do assure you I do love you dearly and not with that kind of love that I love all others who proffer themselves to be my friends. Pray therefore dear Semandra love me as well as ever, be as free with me as ever, writ me all the news you know, send me the Gazette and other printed papers that are good and forgive and believe your

ZIPHARES.

pray remember me very kindly to your Mother and tell her I will writ to her next post.

WITH THE DUCHESS

After the summer has ended, and her friend
has returned to Bologna, the Duchess, who
has been in a bright enough humour for a
while, sinks into a melancholy piety. The
hours spent at her devotions increase again,
and when she is in company her talk is all
of her lost children, of the great dangers
they might have run had they lived, of the
comfort of knowing that there are more
angels to pray for her in heaven. When her
physician tries to persuade her, for the good
of her health, to pray less and to ride out
more, she will have none of it, but then
Lady Peterborough has the good sense to
wonder aloud how much Anne would like it
if her step-mother could show her the
country round Edinburgh — such a pity
that Her Highness's frail health will not
permit this — and the Duchess decides that
perhaps she could ride again — the Duke
would not want her to neglect his daughter.

She will do her duty: she will ride with Anne.

So she rides with Anne, and talks of her children. This afternoon, they are trotting alongside the Water of Leith, towards Balerno. There are just the two of them abreast, with their ladies following at a respectful distance, and several gentlemen some little way in front, for their protection. When the Duchess speaks, there is no-one but Anne to reply.

'Truly, I should feel favoured,' she says, 'that whereas other women bear children for this world, I have given all mine to God.'

The Duke's mistress, Catherine Sedley, has given birth to a daughter this year, quite certainly his, and clearly for this world. Anne looks down at her horse's ears; they twitch in the silence, and some words occur to her.

'You might well take comfort in that,' she says.

The Duchess says, 'I do — at least I try — but I also hope that God in his great mercy will someday comfort me by giving me a male child — a male child who will live.'

Anne lifts up her eyes to the Pentland Hills, which seem to her to be on a godly scale, to have something biblical about them: if any still, small voice were to prompt her, she would catch it murmuring from that side. What is worst in her now — that she cannot, in her heart, wish her own, kind step-mother — her own father — a healthy son, or that she must now play the hypocrite, act the seeming friend?

'I too hope that God will comfort you,' she says, and nothing more.

The Duchess gives her a long, a too-long, sideways look. The red, the tell-all red, goes creeping up Anne's neck.

'Tell me,' says the Duchess, at long last, 'how are you finding your rehearsals for the play — your *Mithridates*? You are to play the King, are you not? Is it much trouble to you, to remember so large a part?'

'Not too much. I have, thank God, a good memory for such things.'

'Would you then recite a little for me now? If you please.'

A speech unfolds itself in Anne's head: a vision of Mithridates. So she begins:

'After that heavenly Sounds had charm'd
    my Ears,
Methought I saw the Spirits of my Sons,
Slain by my Jealousy of their Ambition,
Who shriek'd, he's come! our cruel Father's
    come!

176

Arm, arm, they cry'd, thro' all th'enamel'd
    Grove.
Strait had their Cries alarm'd the wounded
    Host
Of all those Romans, massacred in Asia:
I heard the empty Clank of their thin Arms,
And tender Voices cry, Lead Pompey, lead.
Strait they came on, with Chariots, Horse
    and Foot.
When I had leisure to discern their Chief,
Methought, that Pompey was my Son
    Ziphares;
Who cast his dreadful Pile, and pierc'd my
    Heart:
Then, such a Din of Death, and Swords
    and Javelin
Clatter'd about me, that I wak'd with Terror,
And found my self extended on the Floor.'

Anne has been speaking in the stage voice that Mrs Barry taught her so many years ago. The ladies have heard her clearly, and applaud. The Duchess does not join them, only she smiles, a little.

'Ziphares. Is that not the name you use to write to Mrs Apsley?'

Anne blushes again: she cannot imagine how the Duchess knows this; she would rather not imagine.

'Yes.'

'And she is your love, your Semandra?'

'Yes.'

'It is a strange affectation, this pretending to be lovers. I am not at all sure I like it, but I know it has been quite the fashion at Court — but I would never have written to the Countess Davia that way — I would not even have known the kind of words to use.'

'No.'

'Oh Anne, there is no cause to blush so. I know what a good girl you are!' Then she laughs, and it comes to Anne, too late, that her step-mother has been making sport of her. The Duchess's humours are so changeable: she cannot begin to keep up with them.

WHAT ANNE LEARNS FROM SARAH CHURCHILL

Sarah Churchill arrives from London, to be reunited with her husband and to wait on Anne. One of her first duties is to accompany her to the Grassmarket to watch the latest executions of the Covenanters. When justice is being meted out to those who would swear oaths and take up arms against their King and his Church, it is only right that royalty should be present. This is a State occasion, a public show, and Anne is there to be seen; her carriage is placed just that bit too far away from the scaffold for her to witness whatever happens on it.

Mrs Churchill, on the other hand, whose eyesight is as keen as her tongue, sees everything: the arrival of each condemned man, drawn backwards into the square on an open hurdle, so that he might be more easily spat upon; his slow, trembling progress up the ladder, on the last climb of his life; the expression he wears as he says his last words and makes his peace, before the napkin is put over his face, and he is turned off the top rung. When the last of the three malefactors' heads has been hacked off and shown to the crowd, Sarah tells the driver that Her Highness is tired, has done her duty, and must now be taken home. As she sits down, Anne sees that she is crying.

'My dear Mrs Churchill!' she exclaims.

'Is Your Highness so astonished to see me weep?'

'Not astonished, only —'

'You think me too soft-hearted, perhaps, that I should weep for the sufferings of traitors?'

'I know your heart to be good. It would grieve me if you felt you could not tell me what is in it.'

'Then I will speak plainly. To my mind — not Mr Churchill's, you understand, but to mine — only because they would not lie about their beliefs to save their skins — for that they suffered the cruellest death, for that they were tortured —'

'Tortured?' Anne thinks of Mr Foxes book, of Thomas Tomkin's sinews bursting in the candle flame. 'How?'

'You really do not know, do you? Do you ever ask questions of anyone but me?'

'The Duke does not discuss business with

ladies — and it is not our business — the Duchess talks of other matters — and I speak with Lady Harriet as little as I might.'

Besides, she does not say, she usually knows better than to ask questions — of other people, God or herself — if she suspects that she might not like the answer. It is not the least curious effect of Mrs Churchill's company that she should find herself ashamed of this.

But now she has been provoked into asking a question, and Mrs Churchill answers it, with a full account of a device she calls the Spanish Boot, its ingenious design, and its gruesome employment.

'And if that is not torture,' she finishes, 'then I do not know what else to call it.'

While Sarah has been speaking, Anne has taken her right hand out of her muff and moved it down to her pocket, and what she has found in it is both familiar and comforting.

'No,' she fumbles, 'what else, what else after all . . .'

'And now if I may, Your Highness, I would like to put a question to you.'

'Certainly you may.'

'Thank you. I know that the Duke does not discuss business with you — which is all very proper, of course — but you must know a little of it, something of where he goes and what he does?'

For a moment Anne considers withdrawing her leave for the question.

'A little,' she says, 'but only a little.'

'He must be up at the castle quite often, I imagine?'

'Yes, and often with your husband.'

Sarah scowls at this for some reason, but continues.

'And when he is at the castle, does he go to see the prisoners?'

'I do not know what he does there. It is his work, it is the business of State; I do not know what he does. Mrs Churchill, I have some comfits in my pocket. Would you care for one?'

Sarah accepts one, mercifully, and stops her mouth with it. When her teeth break the shell, the sound is like cracking bone.

THE DUCHESS'S HEALTH

O Lord, I must confess my weariness after tonight's ball, and my unwillingness to do my duty and pray before I sleep; I will not neglect this office, only forgive me if I do not say all that I ought — when I am tired all through like this, it is as if there is a fog inside my head, that not even the sincerest desire of mine to speak can penetrate.

But I must speak with you, even if it were not my duty, because I find I am troubled in my heart. Ever since I came to Scotland there has been more and more an uneasiness between myself and the Duchess. I hope I do what is right by her as her daughter-in-law, that I render her all due respect and service — certainly whatever she asks of me, I do, and I do not complain. I cannot help that I am dull company for her but I do bring Mrs Berkeley and Mrs Churchill with me when I am with her and I do not think that anyone could find them dull, so even though I do not divert her much I am sure they must.

No, I do not neglect my duty to her — in speech or in deed — but I fear that perhaps I do not always honour her in my heart — and I fear too that sometimes what is in my heart must show in my face, for at times there is that in her manner towards me that suggests this might be so. I am troubled by this tonight because she did not join in the country dancing and when I asked what the matter was, she replied that she was not yet recovered from her riding accident, but she would not meet my eye when she said so, and I do not wonder at this, because although at the time she was thrown and dragged and taken up unsensible, her wounds when examined were not so bad as had been feared, and I have seen her walking this sennight or longer without the difficulty she had before. If she does not ride now it is only because her mother wrote and begged her not to lest the next accident prove a fatal one —

— so what I am saying is, I do not think she was quite telling me the truth as the cause of her indisposition. She certainly looked out of sorts this evening, but I have to say, she seemed unwell in the way of women when they are breeding — and even in the way I have seen her before when she was with child. Indeed I am almost quite sure that she is with child, and that she is keeping the news from me on purpose, and I wonder what she thinks of me, that she should use me like this.

Lady Peterborough's Nephew

In May, the same sea that was so good to Anne and her ladies on their passage north proves treacherous against the Duke, as he sails back to Edinburgh from London, ready at last to fetch his wife and daughter home from exile. His ship strikes a sandbank; neither Catholic nor Protestant prayers can prevent it from sinking. With Colonel Churchill's help, the Duke contrives to save the strongbox with his memoirs in it, but by the time he has accomplished this vital task, it is, regrettably, too late for most of the men: over a hundred of the *Gloucester*'s company are lost, and a score of the Duke's own staff. To his great distress, his favourite hound Mumper is also among the drowned.

When the Duke brings the news to the Duchess and Anne, they are caught between thankfulness and sorrow. Another ship from the convoy, *The Happy Return,* is quite unharmed and ready to carry them home.

The Duchess, whose condition is now plain for all to see, is taken on board like a piece of delicate statuary, in a special chair worked by pulleys. Anne and the other ladies follow in the usual way — except for Lady Peterborough, who has lost her nephew in the shipwreck, and has begged that she be allowed to travel in another ship, lest she discomfort the Duchess with her excessive weeping.

Their passage is long, but not too rough; besides *The Happy Return* is a proper, big ship, a fourth-rate, steadier than the yachts they have had to travel in before. Despite this, Mary Cornwallis is sick for most of the journey; Mrs Churchill watches her contemptuously, and sometimes condescends to pass her bowl. The Duchess is sick too, but with better reason: she is sure that the child will come in August, although the doctors say September, and not a moment sooner.

Charlotte Mary is born in August, as the Duchess expected, but the doctors declare her premature, and as she lives only a few weeks, it would seem that they are correct.

What a Good English Princess Knows About Protestant Dissenters

Whereas the Papists would have the King become the puppet of Cousin Louis and his Pope, the dissenting Nonconformists would have him beheaded and replaced with another Cromwell. When a man wishes to cast a slur on a Catholic — or indeed any king of any denomination, or one of his Tory supporters — he might accuse him of the promotion of tyranny; if he seeks instead to blacken the name of a man who professes Nonconformist beliefs, or Whig ideas, or both, then he calls him Republican.

It is now the summer of 1682, and nobody gives any credence to the Popish Plots anymore: in these times the greatest threat to Crown, Church and Country comes from the wrong sort of Protestant. Any Whig who is not an outright Republican must necessarily be of Monmouth's party: in either case he will not recognise the succession that God has ordained — he would certainly have away with the Church too, if he could.

Thank heaven that Shaftesbury is in the Tower. Then thank God that, through His grace and guidance, the King has found a way to pack the Commons with Tories. And when you are done with your thanksgiving, remember to ask God to speak to the Duke in his heart, so that he will be moved to keep his promises, and always stand as Defender of the Faith, even if the Faith is not his.

The Princess and the Poet: a Romance or All-Pride and Naughty Nan: a Comedy

This is an account of what came to pass one summer, when the Court with all its pomp and gaiety took its leave of that noisome, dusty town where it usually resided, and came joyfully to the verdant woods and sweet air of Windsor. There was then at Court a Princess of the Blood, a girl of seventeen, and if she was neither among the most beautiful nor the wittiest of the maidens who graced the castle that summer, still she was not without a certain plumpish, rosy comeliness of her own, and not so lacking in wit that she was unable to appreciate it in others; she had besides a voice of quite singular charm, that the King himself had often had occasion to remark. She was destined, as princesses are, for a Marriage of State, to a prince of another realm — and, indeed, there were some who said, at seventeen, that it was somewhat irregular, and not a little unsatisfactory, that she had not been brought to such a condition long since — but, owing to a certain recent instability in the government of the Kingdom, and consequently in its relations to other Kingdoms, it was still by no means certain to which prince, of which realm, she was to be allied.

This question, of which prince, was a contentious one: her cousin Louis, King of France, was of one opinion; her cousin (and brother-in-law) Wilham, the Dutch Stadtholder, was of another; each seeking, through her alliance, to enhance his own interests, and thereby to damage his opponent's. Her father, the Duke, tended rather towards the French King's view of the matter; her uncle, the King, although properly wary of Cousin Louis's imperial ambitions, and sensible of the fear and hatred which his people felt for that Papist Despot, had been for some years, secretly, in receipt of certain monies from the French King, which had at times been all that stood between him and ruin, and knew that Louis was waiting for some sign of gratitude in return, and would not wait for ever; at the same time, he could not ignore his Protestant nephew, against whose well-drilled Dutch fleet his own had a habit of coming off worst — though, if truth be told, he had long since wearied of William's ill-tempered letters to him, and of his interference, overt and covert, in the affairs of his own Kingdom, and itched to disoblige the impertinent whelp.

The Princess, meanwhile, wished only to be married: she had had her fill of being a maid, and had no ambition to become an old one. With great longing and some jealousy, she watched young ladies of lesser degree as they were courted, wooed and won, and burned to be in their place. Whenever she could, she would retire to her closet with the dearest companion of her bosom, one Mary Cornwallis, to peruse love poetry, and romances, and certain other works of a bawdier kind — which, regrettably, this Mrs Cornwallis often had about her person, on purpose to show her royal mistress — indeed, anything which treated of that subject, of what passes between men and women when they are amorously inclined. Mrs Cornwallis was also able to oblige the Princess with tales of her own adventures, of which, since she was a very well-favoured maiden, and none too nice in her conduct, there were a great many (and if she was inclined, now and then, to exaggerate their number or their significance, given her great and sincere desire to please her audience, she can hardly be blamed).

When these two ladies were apart — even for so short a space of time as an afternoon — to prevent their passions cooling, they were wont to write each other letters in language so heated and overripe, and in every way so unfit for maidens to employ, that any scribe would blush to set it down. All the same, it might fairly have been said that the whole fervid business represented nothing more than the silly games of a pair of foolish chits barely out of the nursery, and was perfectly harmless sport, were it not for the appearance in the tale and in the game of a third player, this one a gentleman — and whether he is the villain of this tale, its hero, or merely a buffoon, I will leave the reader to decide.

The Earl of Mulgrave, having come into his inheritance at a very tender age, had, at the age of four-and-thirty, long been used to all the advantages provided by a great title and a great estate; nature had, besides this, blessed him with a handsome face and a quick wit; he was a Gentleman of the Bedchamber to the King, and — thanks to the good offices of a certain lady who was at the time great with both men — Knight of the Garter; he was a noted soldier, and had commanded an expedition for the relief of

Tangier; he was a poet, too, the author of many satires. Haughty, arrogant and quarrelsome, he was the object of many others. The Earl of Rochester himself had dubbed him 'All-Pride.' These faults of character, however, did little to prevent his being the perfect object of a young maiden's fancy. And such, for the Princess, he was.

It could be that she blushed a little deeper than usual when he made his bow to her; perhaps, when she stood up to dance with him, her eyes shone especially bright. Whatever the cause, the following facts soon became apparent to this quick-witted and gamesome gentleman: firstly, that the Princess was a charming innocent, as yet unwooed; secondly, that her eager eye had fallen on him (as well, he thought, it might); thirdly, that in Mrs Cornwallis he would find an able and most willing go-between. What his ultimate intentions might have been remains the subject of much dispute, but it is certain that it must, at the very least, have amused him to respond to the entreaties he read in the Princess's bright eyes and flushed cheeks, for he wasted little time in slipping the first of many little notes, along with a most generous gratuity, into Mrs Cornwallis's hand.

This first note made the Princess quite

giddy: she kissed it a hundred times, and then by the same hand sent her artless, rapturous reply. Always inclined more to love than to be wise, and forgetting in a moment the counsel and warning of governesses, preceptors, chaplains, step-mother and sister, she gave herself over to a correspondence which, had it fallen into malicious hands, might well have been enough to ruin her. Over the course of that hot Windsor summer, some dozen quires-worth of love-notes were exchanged, and countless more amorous looks; that most accomplished gentleman sent besides this settings for songs, which he had composed himself — he said — and which the delighted Princess spent many hours playing over and over on guitar and harpsichord until she had them by heart and had quite driven her ladies to distraction with the tedium of hearing them; and of course, he sent poems, poems in praise of her charms and virtues, poems declaring his adoration, poems lamenting the many obstacles that lay in the way of his making love to her, and, on at least one occasion, a poem to excuse his faults:

INCONSTANCY EXCUSED

I must confess I am untrue
To Gloriana's eyes;
But he that's smiled upon by you
Must all the world despise.

In winter, fires of little worth
Excite our dull desire;
But when the sun breaks kindly forth,
Those fainter flames expire.

Then blame me not for slighting now
What I did once adore;
Oh, do but this one change allow,
And I can change no more:

Fixt by your never-failing charms,
Till I with age decay,
Till languishing within your arms
I sigh my soul away.

Alas for Gloriana and her Inconstant
Admirer, this delightful scene was never to
be realised beyond the page. The lovers and
their go-between were betrayed: there were
about the Princess a tight group of ladies,
and among them were several with heads
considerably cooler, and judgement considerably keener, than that of Mrs Cornwallis,

and one of these, perhaps perceiving dangers that her mistress could not, and also perhaps seeking a means of removing from her household a lady whose company she believed could do the Princess no good, and whose foolish gabbling she feared would drown out her own, better counsel, took it upon herself to retrieve certain of the Princess's letters from her closet, and to discover them to the Duke and Duchess.

The Duke's rage, on perusal of these letters, might easily be imagined. A couple he tore at once to shreds, the rest he threw to the ground, first demanding his daughter, her so-called friend and her would-be lover be sent for at once, then changing his mind and declaring that they all be banished from his sight for he could not bear to run but the slightest danger of ever laying eyes on any one of them ever again. He lamented that the Earl, whom he had himself loved and trusted, should do him such a shabby turn as to seek to make love to his daughter — *his own daughter* — for no child of his would be married to a commoner, nor would any son-in-law of his be served a *buttered bun* on his wedding night. The Duchess, observing his condition, suggested that perhaps she had better talk to the Princess alone, and the Duke — once he had satisfied himself by kicking the discarded correspondence across the floor — agreed that this course would probably be the wisest.

The Princess was duly summoned to her step-mother's closet, where a most uncomfortable interview took place, which quite mortified both ladies, and left each with such a disagreeable impression of the other, that there could thereafter never be more than the pretence of familiarity between them. The Duchess informed her step-daughter that her Mrs Cornwallis was to be sent at once from Court, never to return, and would not, despite entreaties, discover to the Princess the name of her betrayer, only maintaining, that this nameless lady — *whoever she was* — had already proved herself a truer friend than that other, who had sought only to urge her mistress on to folly, and thereby to gain from it herself.

And as if all this were not trouble enough for the Princess, she was further discomforted, first by a letter from her sister in Holland, who showed, in her disapproval, that the news of her near-disgrace had travelled overseas, and then by the revelation that the story of thwarted love had also been spread about nearer to home, about the Court, and thence to the populace at large, to whom it had been represented in the crudest terms, in verses quite different from those with which she had been wooed:

Come all ye youths that yet are free
From Hymen's deadly snare;
Come listen all and learn of me,
And keep my words with care.

For all of you it much concerns,
That would lead quiet lives,
And have no mind to purchase horns,
Take heed of London wives.

For it's full true, though it's full sad,
There's ne'er a lass in town
But some or other lusty lad
Has blown her up and down.

And first and foremost Princely Nan
Heirs both her parents' lust,
And Mulgrave is the happy man
by whom our breed is crossed.

This happy man, meanwhile, made his submission to the King, protesting that he had been 'only ogling', but the monarch (who might well have had sympathy, in his secret heart, for any adventurous gentleman) did what he was only duty-bound to do when the virtue of his royal niece had been threatened, by stripping the hapless Mulgrave of all his Court offices, and sending him back to Tangiers, on a frigate less than seaworthy. The Earl, if truth be told, was not too sorry to have to leave Court for a while, if only because he no longer had to endure the taunts and satires of his fellow wits, who had dubbed him 'King John' for his supposed ambition, and for his foolishness, 'Numps'.

With the Earl and Mrs Cornwallis thus safely disposed of, the attention of the King and his brother turned to the fate of the Princess. They faced the difficult task of finding for her a prince who would be both Protestant and acceptable to Cousin Louis, but happily for them all, there was one prince — perhaps only one — suitable for the purpose. This was the younger brother of Louis's ally, the King of Denmark, one Prince George, a noted soldier, and twelve years' the Princess's senior. He was a large, fair man, good-natured if somewhat shy, and the Princess was delighted with him — even more so, when she was told that he would reside with her at her uncle's Court, so she need not, as her sister had, lose home and friends in exchange for a husband. The Duke was pleased to see his daughter happily settled at last; both he and the King were greatly relieved at having found a way, through her alliance, to placate Cousin Louis; Louis rejoiced to have disobliged William; William, for his part, was incensed.

PART III

His Majesty's Declaration
to All His Loving Subjects

On the 28th of July, the day of Anne's marriage to George, the King issues a Declaration, appointed to be read in all Churches and Chapels within the Kingdom, concerning the lately discovered Treasonable Conspiracy against his Sacred Person and Government.

It has been His Observation that for several years last past, a Malevolent Party has made it their business to promote Sedition by False News, Libellous Pamphlets and other wicked arts, whereby they endeavoured not only to render his Government Odious to the People, but also to incite them to a Dislike and Hatred of his own Royal Person. It was evident that the aim of this Party could only be the Ruin of the King and his Government; that even as he, by his utmost Care, manifested to all his Subjects his Zeal for the Maintenance of the Protestant Religion and his Resolution to Govern according to Law, they continued to misrepresent his actions to the People, so that the weaker Sort came to look upon them as the best Defenders of their Religion and Liberties.

Their Numbers increased, and their Boldness, so that they showed themselves in Tumults and Riots, and Unlawful and Seditious Conventicles. But it pleased God, by these their Violent Ways, to open the Eyes of His good Subjects, who easily foresaw what Trouble these Methods would produce, so that then this Fractious Party, observing that they were losing Ground daily, became Desperate, and resolved not to Trust any longer to the slow Methods of Sedition, but to betake themselves to Arms.

It is hard to imagine how men of so many different Interests and Opinions, could join in any Enterprise; but it is certain, they readily concurred in the Resolution of taking Arms to destroy the Government, even before they had Agreed what to set up in the place of it. To which purpose, Some contrived a General Insurrection in this Kingdom and likewise in Scotland; Others were conspiring to assassinate his Royal Person, and his Dearest Brother, and to massacre the Magistrates of his City of London, and his Officers of State.

It is certain, that, with so many Differences among them, if it had pleased God to permit these wicked Designs to have taken Effect, there could have been nothing in Prospect for the Kingdom but Confusion. But the Divine Providence, which has preserved the King through the whole Course of His Life, has at this time in an Extraordinary manner, showed itself in the Wonderful and Gracious Deliverance of Him and His Dearest Brother and all His Loyal Subjects from this Horrid and Damnable Conspiracy.

The Principal and main Designs of it have appeared to be as follows: about the beginning of October last, there was a Meeting of Some of the Principal Conspirators to Agree about the best means to master His Guards and to seize His Person. They found it necessary also to prepare their Friends in the Several Counties, and in Scotland to join with them.

At the same time, Some Villains were likewise carrying on that Horrid and Execrable Plot of Assassinating His Royal Person and His Dearest Brother in their Return from Newmarket at March last. The Place Appointed was the House of one Richard Rumbold, called the Rye, near Hoddesdon in the County of Hertford. It was resolved that the Forty Persons who were to be Actors in this Assassination, under the Command of the said Richard Rumbold, should hide themselves in or near the said House; And when His Coach should come over against them, then Three or Four were to shoot with Blunderbusses at the Postillion and Horses. Others were appointed to shoot into the Coach, where His Royal Person, and His Dearest Brother, were to be; Others to fire upon the Guards that should be Attending them.

And it was further resolved, that on that same Day, many Lords, and other Persons of Quality, whom they supposed favourable to their Designs, should be invited to Dine in His City of London, that they might be more ready to appear among the Citizens upon Arrival of the News. And lest His Officers of State, and the Magistrates of His said City, with the Militia thereof, and other Loyal Subjects, should be able to put some stop to their Careers, they resolved to follow this Blow with a Massacre.

But it pleased Almighty God, by His Wonderful Providence, to defeat their Counsels by the sudden Fire at Newmarket, which necessitated the return of the King and His Dearest Brother from thence before the time they had appointed.

Yet the Villains were not thereby discouraged from pursuing the same Bloody Design, but resolved to take the first Opportunity for effecting the same, wherever it might be done. And that they might be better prepared, when there should be occasion, they kept Arms always ready for that purpose; they divided the Cities of London and Westminster into Twenty Parts, from each of which they expected Five Hundred Men to be ready at the first Onset; these were to be under the Command of One Hundred Old Officers, who had been engaged in the late Rebellion.

The late Earl of Shaftesbury, who had pressed them to a Sudden Rising, which he would have had before the 17th of November last, upon finding that they would not adventure without farther Preparation, conveyed himself secretly into Holland, to avoid the danger he might be in by a Discovery.

The Party were by no means discouraged by this, however, and appointed a new Counsel of Six Persons; and they made a Treaty with Archibald Campbell, late Earl of Argyle, so that the Design might be carried on jointly in both Kingdoms. These Six then debated among themselves whether the Rising should be first in London, or in some remote parts; it was resolved at last that it should be in all parts at the same time.

And this Design was very near taking effect, but such was the Abundant Mercy of Almighty God, a Discovery was made unto the King by one of the Accomplices, on the Twelfth of June last; since which time He has used the best Means He could for the Detecting and Prevention of so Hellish a Conspiracy.

But so it has happened, that divers of the Conspirators, having notice of Warrants Issued for their Apprehension, are fled from Justice; Viz. James Duke of Monmouth, the Lord Melvin, Sir John Cochrane, Sir Thomas Armstrong, Robert Ferguson, Richard Goodenough, Francis Goodenough, Richard Rumbold, William Rumbold his brother . . . [the Declaration lists divers others].

Ford Lord Gray being apprehended, made his Escape out of the hands of a Serjeant at Arms, and Arthur late Earl of Essex, being Committed to the Tower for High Treason, killed himself.

Others have been taken and Committed to Custody, some of whom, Viz. the Lord William Russell, Thomas Walcott, William Hone, and John Rowse, have upon their Trials been Convicted, Attainted, and Executed according to Law.

This the King thought fit to make known to His Loving Subjects that they being sensible (as He is) of the Mercy of God in this Great Deliverance, may Devoutly join with Him in returning Solemn Thanks to Almighty God for the Same.

For which end He does hereby appoint the Ninth day of September next, to be observed as a day of Thanksgiving in all Churches and Chapels within this His Kingdom of England, Dominion of Wales, and Town of Berwick upon Tweed.

THE PRINCE AND PRINCESS
OF DENMARK

Anne is now Princess of Denmark, but only in name and in marriage, and her Prince is very nearly the only Dane in their Whitehall lodgings. This has not been easy to accomplish, but there are hopes that, with Lord Churchill's help, the Duke will succeed in having Von Plessen, the Prince's secretary, sent home to Copenhagen and replaced with Lady Churchill's brother-in-law, so that they might all be quite comfortably English together. The Prince, who is allowed his Lutheran religion, unimpeded in his inquiries into wine, and frequently encouraged into his new wife's bed, is not a man to complain. He is not a man to say much of anything, and as he does not seem to expect Anne to fill any silences, they go on beautifully together. It is only a few months since their wedding, and already the felicity of their marriage is a byword. Whomever she meets, whether dancing at

212

Court, or riding in the Park, or playing cards in the Duchess of Portsmouth's rooms, or watching the play at the theatre, or coming out of Chapel, asks Anne, most respectfully, how she does, and in the way their eyes flit so quickly and discreetly from her face to her middle, she perceives the question behind the question.

She has been married only a few weeks when she begins to have an inkling of an answer: tea has acquired a new, not very pleasant flavour; she feels a tenderness in her breasts when her bodice is laced, and more and more she finds herself yawning over her cards in the afternoons. There have even been a couple of occasions in Chapel, when a visiting preacher has been more than usually verbose, on which Anne has felt her eyelids beginning to droop and her head to fall forward, so that she has had to jerk it up again and make a great show of looking about her, if only to make the whispering subside. So far the only people who know that she has missed her monthly courses are herself, the Prince, Lady Churchill and of course Danvers, who has the closest care of Anne's person, and cannot have failed to have counted the weeks since she last helped her change a clout.

Anne has chosen to tell Lady Churchill

because she is her dearest friend, the favourite Lady of her newly appointed Bedchamber, and she would never scruple to tell her
anything. Strictly speaking, she should tell
her First Lady and Groom of the Stool, but
Lady Clarendon was the Duke's choice, not
hers, and Anne suffers her company only
when it cannot be avoided. As she has told
Lady Churchill, it is vexing indeed to get
rid of one Hyde aunt only to have her
replaced by another, and to be free of the
strictures and the haughtiness of the former,
only to find herself plagued with the pros-
ing of the latter, who looks like a madwoman and talks like a scholar — character-
istics which, Anne maintains, agree all too
well together.

Anne's Maids of Honour

'Truly we have all had a surfeit of your sullen faces today.' Lady Churchill is scolding the Maids of Honour. 'No doubt our company is dreadfully dull, but you might at least have the grace not to show it.'

The Maids — Mrs Drummer, Mrs Temple, Mrs Talbot, Mrs Nott — hang their pretty heads and say nothing.

'What? Silence? Is that all? If I were you I would make my submission to Her Highness.'

The Maids exchange frantic looks, then, after some silent agreement has been reached, the boldest of them, Mrs Nott, rises, curtsies to Anne and offers, 'Please forgive us, Your Highness. We are indeed weary today but we promise to try harder.' She makes a motion behind her and the others rise and curtsy in their turn.

'Oh, do sit down again,' Anne says. 'I cannot say I blame you for finding us dull today. I am sure you had expected to ride, or play cards as usual.'

She does feel a little sorry for the Maids, but she has endured two successive nights of heavy losses at the Duchess of Portsmouth's table, and is now in a penitent mood, which her household must share in. Before dinner, she heard the catechism of a couple of the as-yet-unconfirmed younger servants, a task she would usually leave to her chaplains, and now, after dinner, she, Lady Clarendon, Lady Churchill and the Maids are spending a rare afternoon at their work. Lady Churchill is prettifying a child's smock with point-lace; Lady Clarendon is working an elaborate pattern in fine gold thread onto a piece of satin, the better to adorn the binding of some enormous book or other; the Maids have been given a great, tangled pile of threads that Lady Churchill has discovered in a press, and told by her to make themselves useful and sort it through. It is a task better suited to little girls than to hopeful young ladies, and Anne cannot wonder that they should find it irksome.

'To tell you the truth,' she says, 'to work like this on such a dark afternoon is too much for my wretched eyes — they water dreadfully — and I think perhaps for their sake I should better do something else. If the Maids would have my guitar fetched, and fetch their own instruments too — they that have them — we could have a little music?'

'A delightful notion, Your Highness,' says Lady Clarendon, 'and I should particularly like to hear Mrs Temple sing again — she has such a pretty voice.'

'Then it is decided,' says Lady Churchill. 'You all heard what Her Highness asked of you — now go and do it.'

The Maids curtsy and troop out. Lady Churchill searches in her work bag for scissors, fails to find them, and breaks the thread with her teeth, which are the straightest and the whitest of any lady that Anne knows. 'Silly chits,' she says, when she is done.

'Oh I am sure we were no different,' says Anne, who is married now, with child, and all of eighteen. She takes her own work up again, and pulls it close to her face, only for the pattern to blur straight away, stinging her eyes and sending the lids into a flutter. So she sets the work down again, and turns a ring on her right hand — the newest one, a mourning ring from Frances Apsley, her Semandra. She is married now to Sir Benjamin Bathurst, Controller of the Denmarks' household, and has recently been bereaved, first of twin babes, and then of her father.

'That is a handsome ring, Your Highness,' says Lady Churchill, 'but it is a pity about the occasion of it — how did you and Lady Clarendon find Lady Bathurst yesterday?'

'As you might expect, in very low spirits. So many losses one after the other — and now her mother ill too — and you must know she has been disappointed of the hopes she had for another child — I fear she is quite overcome.'

Lady Churchill shakes her head. 'It is hard to know how to comfort her.'

'When there is such affliction as that,' Lady Clarendon says, 'comfort can come only from God. And then, if she can bear her trouble like a Christian, that will sum to her good.'

'But I think one's friends might be *some* help, Lady Clarendon, or why call them friends at all?'

'I hope I might help her,' says Anne, quickly. 'I could only wish that Lady Apsley might recover her health, and that my poor Frances might soon have a great belly again. I gather my sister has said the same in her letters.'

'So she is writing more then? Lady Bathurst was wont to complain that the

Princess had forgotten her quite.'

'When she first married the Prince, it was true, she was not a good correspondent, but now it seems . . .'

Anne glances at the door; it is closed, and there is only quiet behind it.

'. . . she would never say so, but I think she wants for company . . . the Prince . . . is much preoccupied with his armies, and other business . . .'

Lady Churchill favours the door with a glance of her own.

'. . . which he prefers to discuss with Mrs Berkeley's squinting sister . . .'

'Is that what you have heard?' Anne is whispering now.

'From Mrs Berkeley. Yes.'

'He has peculiar tastes, that — Caliban.'

'Your Highness!' cries Lady Clarendon. 'He is your brother!'

'Her brother-in-*law*. Might your cousin Monmouth find his way to The Hague? Your sister would be glad of his company — they were always good dancing partners.'

'No, he is still in Brussels . . .'

'So your Caliban-in-law will not have him yet.'

'Lady Churchill! We must pray, Your Highness, that the present troubles will pass, and then the King will be glad to have Monmouth back with him again. He loves him so well.'

'*Too* well, perhaps. But I do not think he can have him back while there are still villains enough drinking his son's health instead of his own — I heard one of the postillions say only yesterday that his brother was in a tavern where —'

A page opens the door and tells them that the Maids have returned from their errand. Anne calls for a little wine, and the conversation turns musical.

HANS IN KELDER

December comes, and brings with it a frost
so severe, that it seems like a judgement.
Trees split as if lightning-struck. All the
exotica, the plants, fish and fowl in the
gardens of the Palaces and the great houses
perish almost immediately; then the native
species follow everywhere else: the deer and
cattle perish for want of food, and the poor
for want of fuel. Even the seas are so locked
up with ice that no vessel can stir out of the
country, or in; foreign trade, like the frozen
rivers, slows to a stop. In the towns, there is
no water to be had from the pipes or en-
gines, so that the brewers, and many other
tradesmen besides, find they cannot work.

But while the cold is disastrous for so
many, there is still money to be made for
those that have the opportunity, and especially if they trade in any kind of fuel, for
fuel is become dearer than anyone could
have imagined, so dear that great contribu-

221

tions must be made in order to preserve the lives of such poor as remain. In London, sea-coal is all of a sudden so valuable that Lady Churchill says one might think that every coal merchant living had become an alchemist, and turned all his stock into gold — an analogy which, Lady Clarendon contends, does not hold together quite, for whereas men are inclined to hoard gold, they are compelled rather, on account of the extremity of the weather, to burn the sea-coal as soon as they have it. The pedantic Countess is quite correct: London is so filled with the fuliginous smoke of the sea-coal, which the cold air hinders from rising, that anyone who ventures out of his house can scarcely see, or breathe. Anne is ever fearful lest the smoke from the town should drift towards Whitehall, and smother her asthmatic Prince.

There are others, besides the coal-merchants, who are doing well out of the frost. The Thames has congealed to such a degree that a whole ox might be roasted on it without melting the ice, and there is as much and as many different kinds of trade being plied upon the water as you might find in the City proper. By the time the royal party visit, on the last day of January, there is a street running all the way across the Thames from Temple steps to South-wark; it is named Temple Street, and is considered a great wonder. Along it and around it a continual fair has risen up; there are shops selling all manner of commodities, from wine and roast beef to plate and earthenware; there are coffee houses, where you might sit down by a charcoal fire and have a dish of coffee, chocolate or tea. There are all kinds of amusements: bull- and bear-baiting, dancing and fiddling, ninepins, football; there is even a whirling-chair, or car, which is tied to a stake in the ice by a long rope, and drawn about by several strong men, as fast as they can manage. The car is full of silly girls screaming, and clinging to their sweethearts, who have purchased the ride for just that purpose.

'Look at those fellows there!' exclaims the Duchess, looking out through the glass of the carriage door. 'They are as strong as oxen. Perhaps we should have had the coachmen pull us onto the ice themselves, and let the horses rest!'

'And the watermen to help them,' says the Queen. 'They have wanted employment these past few weeks.'

Anne considers this. 'It is a good notion. I am surprised that the horses are not slipping more, and it is dreadful to think what may happen if one of them were to slip and fall — they would pull the other three down with them, and the carriage besides.'

The Duchess and the Queen exchange glances, and Anne sees that she has missed a jest again. All the same, she knows that she is right to have said what she said.

'I know that you were speaking in jest, but it is a thing that is being done — the men that are used to plying the river are dragging goods and people across by rope instead —'

'Though they swear in the usual way,' says the Duchess.

'— and I think there is good reason to worry about the horses — I am truly anxious about whether it is safe to drive them out onto the ice.'

The Queen reaches over and Anne feels, through the layers of Muscovy sable, the ghost of a reassuring pat. 'And you are truly anxious about the cold, too. And the jolting of the carriage when it goes. And whether you might have too much exercise or too little . . .'

'What Her Majesty is saying,' says the Duchess, 'is that a lady in your condition is wont to vex herself over every little thing.'

'I do know that, Ma'am — but I find all the same I cannot hinder myself from it.'

'How many months is it now?' the Queen asks. 'Five? Six?'

'Five, by my reckoning. And Dr Scarborough agrees.'

'So has he given you his speech about the apples?' asks the Duchess.

'Apples, Madam? No. Ought I not to eat them?'

'Ah, then he has not. There is a piece of wisdom from the ancients, that he likes to give to ladies with child about this time, which is that she should consider the child in her matrix as like the apple that ripens on the tree: the stem is weak in those first weeks — it has yet to establish itself fully — and weak again in the final weeks, as the apple readies itself to drop, but in between these times — and this applies to you as you are here and now — the stem is strong and firm and none but the most violent storm can loosen it.'

'I wish I had heard that speech from a physician,' says the Queen, 'but alas, I was never with child for long enough.'

They are all quiet for a moment, and in that moment there is a sadness in the carriage that agrees with the cold.

'I see I have discomforted you both — forgive me; I should not indulge myself this way.'

Now the Duchess takes a gloved hand out of her own furs and places it for a moment on the Queen's shoulder. It is not forward of her: they are old allies, old friends.

'Do not trouble yourself, Ma'am — it is so easy to fall into this kind of melancholy, especially when there is before us —' she glances at Anne — 'when ladies are everywhere and always with child.'

The Duchess has herself recently miscarried, while Catherine Sedley has presented the Duke with a healthy son.

Suddenly Anne feels herself to be obscurely, helplessly at fault. It is a tremendous relief when the carriage door opens and the King comes in, cheerful, only half cut, and ready to divert the ladies.

'Look!' he cries. 'Here is a thing you will not find every day,' and he hands the Queen a quarto sheet of Dutch paper, with a printed border and writing on it. 'You see there?' he points to the card, and reads, "Printed by G. Croom, on the ICE" — on the ice! An ingenious notion!'

'I'll say it's ingenious,' says the Duke's voice, from just outside. 'The rascal's making five pounds a day out of it.'

The King ignores him, and then passes the card to Anne, suggesting that she read it out aloud. The writing is in capital letters, so it is not too difficult:

CHARLES, KING.
JAMES, DUKE.
KATHERINE, QUEEN.
MARY, DUTCHESS.
ANN, PRINCESSE.
GEORGE, PRINCE.
HANS IN KELDER.

'Well?'

Anne is not sure what to say. 'Those are the names of our party — but who is Hans? Is there a coachman called Hans?'

The King is convulsed with laughter; the Duke too. Their wives are not.

'Hans in Kelder,' says the Queen, rather stiffly, 'is a vulgar term for —'

'Oh, my niece does not mind a good jest,' says the King. 'It is German, dear, for "Jack in the Cellar!" '

'Oh!' says Anne, and does not know whether she should laugh or blush.

ANNE'S FALL

In February the weather changes, and Anne's humour with it. She has a newfound vigour, a restlessness, which makes it seem intolerably dull to stay within doors — particularly as Lady Churchill is away in St Albans with her own family, and has sent one of Lady Sunderland's daughters to attend Anne in her place. Anne cannot for the life of her understand her friend's regard for Lady Sunderland — she is but a sly flatterer, who pretends at virtue, and like her Lord is surely governed by ambition — so she speaks as little as she can to her daughter. As for Lady Clarendon's company, it is barely tolerable, and the Maids are silly. Their company, their talk, their very presence in her rooms oppresses Anne: she has a mind to be out, in a park, and to move through it as briskly as she can — she has a mind, in other words, to ride.

Danvers and Farthing are compelled to

agree with one another: they do not think that she should; Lady Clarendon, with the greatest respect, can but question the wisdom of such a course of action; George, however, does not see why she should not, as long as he accompanies her, so they call for Griffiths, his equerry, and Ballasie, Anne's; with Lady Clarendon, and just two of her footmen to run ahead and give such persons as they might encounter sufficient notice to remove their hats, they will make a small, informal party — Anne does not care to be a gazing-stock when she goes abroad.

Anne's riding habit will not button, so Danvers has to contrive a way to pin it so as to accommodate her mistress's growing belly. This takes an age, and by the time Anne and Lady Clarendon find them, the horses and menfolk have been kicking their heels in the cold for at least half an hour. At George's insistence, she has had Dinah saddled; she is the quietest horse in her stables, a smallish mare, an ambler. When the groom brings her forward, he takes a look at Anne's riding-habited bulk and pulls the saddle-girth a little tighter, before taking a step back so that George — who will allow no-one else to assist her — can help his wife to mount.

Anne decides against Hyde Park — even though it is not yet the Season, she is sure that it must be full of company since the thaw, driving round and round the Ring and back again, just so they might see and be seen, uttering civilities to each other from out of their coaches, and hissing spite behind their hands. Besides, there is no Lady Churchill to tell her who it is who has made their reverence to her and to say if they are owed a small bow back — and she does not have much faith in Lady Clarendon's suitability for this office.

So she turns little Dinah towards St James's Park, and tells the company that they will make for the Inward Park, where they can be sure of privacy. A Princess can ride there with her party, and encounter nothing but deer and trees. She tells George that it has ever been her favourite place, and adds that it is very pleasant weather for riding. He agrees that it is, and they continue in happy, companionable silence.

But Dinah is not happy: Anne can feel the animal's unease, in her hands and even through the saddle — every gentle effort to direct her is met with a most un-Dinah-like, subtle resistance. Maybe the girth is too tight after all. But it is not trouble enough to stop. She says as much to George.

'Oh, I wish you will take care my dear,' he says.

'I *always* take care,' she snaps, and that very instant quits the saddle for the grass.

First there is only shock, then in the next instance a feeling of foolishness, then the beginnings of an awareness of pain in the parts that landed first, quickly followed by an indignant fluttering in her belly, as the child, who had been lulled by the rhythm of the ambling ride, is shocked awake. That is the important thing.

'Do not be afraid!' she calls as the party dismount and run towards her, 'it quickens — the babe quickens — the babe is not hurt.'

George reaches her first, kneels down and takes her hands.

'The fault is mine,' he moans, 'I should not have permitted.'

Nobody pays any attention to this, all knowing full well that the Prince has never permitted or forbidden his wife anything, and nor will he ever.

Then Lady Clarendon arrives, and whispers, 'Do you bleed at all, Ma'am?'

For a moment Anne is not sure what the question means. Then she understands and says, 'No, I do not — at least, I do not think so,' and then to all, 'Will somebody please help me to my feet. I think I am only bruised — nothing worse.'

George and Ballasie help Anne to her feet and straight away she proves to them that she can walk a few, stiff steps, but she must agree that she should not ride again. There is a discussion as to whether George or the equerry might lead her horse with her on it; or whether she might, despite her belly, ride pillion, but caution prevails: her chair is sent for, to carry her safely back.

When Dr Scarborough arrives, he pronounces Anne bruised but otherwise sound, orders a poultice to be made up, and makes her his speech about apples. It seems the stem is holding yet.

12TH MAY 1684

It is during Evening Prayers, halfway
through the Third Collect, as she asks God
in his great mercy to defend her from all
perils and dangers of this night, that Anne
feels the first painful little tug, somewhere
between her belly and her reins, and knows
at once that her travail has started. She
counts two more pangs as she listens to the
anthem; another during the Prayer for the
King's Majesty; one more for each of
the shorter prayers. As she leaves the
Chapel, she whispers in Lady Clarendon's
ear. By the time she reaches her lodgings, a
messenger is already on his way to Windsor,
bringing the news to the King.

George sits with her while Danvers and
Farthing prepare her chamber. The Duchess's midwife, Mrs Wilkes, arrives with her
deputy behind her, and the first thing they
do is send him away. Lady Clarendon stays
— there is no ridding oneself of the woman

— and Farthing, and Danvers. They strip Anne down to her shift and stockings, then dress her in a woollen waistcoat above the waist, with nothing else below. Mrs Wilkes orders the deputy to re-arrange the couch that Anne's women have made up, and when every last piece of linen has been removed and replaced to her satisfaction, she bids Anne lie down on it.

Mrs Wilkes is a small, almost frail-looking woman, but she has the voice of an Amazon. She puts her hands first on Anne's belly, and they feel as her voice sounds.

'The child has certainly fallen down, Your Highness — that is good to start with. Now how close together are the throws?'

'A few minutes' space — but it's not always the same.'

'Is it not? I should think then we have a long night ahead of us yet — but I shall know better when I have felt how far the mouth is opened. Pass me the oil.'

She mauls Anne with one of her oiled, Amazonian hands, not even pausing when the pain comes again. When she has withdrawn it, she holds up two fingers.

'This far only. As I thought, it will likely be a long travail — that is often the case when it's the first time. When did you last ease yourself, Ma'am?'

'Yesterday. In the morning.'

'It would be better for you were your passage not obstructed. We'll make up a clyster.'

'No! Danvers!'

But Danvers tells her to do as Mrs Wilkes asks; the deputy, who until now has barely spoken, adds that the clyster will be but little in quantity, and gently warmed. It is not too bad, when it comes, and afterwards she is allowed to eat some bread and egg yolk, and to drink a little wine.

The night, and Anne's travail, proceed together in her chamber. She measures out the time between the pangs with her feet, pacing as she has seen beasts do in the Menagerie, from the couch to the window and back again; steadily, the distance she has to walk between one pain and the next diminishes, and the pains themselves grow longer. In the smallest, darkest hour, her waters break. By the time dawn comes, she can barely draw a breath between throws, and her throat is sore from her cries. At one of the very worst times, when she feels as if her whole body is being wrung out like a sheet, she looks up to see Lady Clarendon's face before her, saying something about prayer and strength and grace, and somebody else's voice comes out of her throat.

'YOU STUPID BITCH!' it screams.

'WHY MUST YOU DRESS YOUR HAIR LIKE THAT?'

'Good, good!' says Mrs Wilkes. 'We are nearly there at last.'

She takes hold of Anne and leads her, gasping, to the couch, where the other women prop her up with pillows and almost at once the throws alter their motion through her body, pushing downwards. The oiled hand eases its way in again, and Mrs Wilkes tells her that the child's head is there. Anne is no longer crying out, but somehow a bull has got into the room, and every time her body strains, it bellows.

Dame Nature does her work; the bull bellows; the midwives urge her on; then at once it stops. Mrs Wilkes has a baby in her apron: it is tiny, and female, and very clearly dead.

ANNE GIVES THANKS IN
TUNBRIDGE WELLS

O gracious Lord, the God of the spirits of all flesh, in whose hand my time is, I praise and magnify thee, that thou hast, in love to my soul, delivered it from the pit of corruption, and restored me to health again . . . to such good health, and so soon, that I need not join the Duchess in taking the waters here, which, as I can see from her face when she sips them, is a small deliverance in itself — but I am of course thankful, as her daughter-in-law, of the good done her through the fountains that you made. I do pity her for the latest disappointment that has brought her to them, and I try every day to follow the direction in Dr Walker's sermon, to kindle devotion in myself, through consideration of your works in Tunbridge, so that I may derive profit for my soul from this place, if not for my body . . .

. . . but I ask for patience, for I am weary of my life here, since George and Lady Churchill have left, and I cannot but dwell on the loss of that blessed child, whom you have seen fit to spare from the troubles and temptations of this world. I must thank you for making her happy, and remind myself every hour of the Psalm that says I was dumb, I opened not my mouth, because thou didst it, and that it is you that has done it must silence any murmurings and grumblings in me, especially as the midwife said, you has taken the child to you so many weeks before she was delivered, that it was a miracle indeed that I had not been taken with her, that the waters had not turned foul in my womb and poisoned my blood thereby . . .

I mean in this spirit of thankfulness to give away all that I have won at cards here for the enlargement of the Chapel of Ease, that you may be glorified thereby, and though both my chaplains tell me — and every day — that card-playing is not really such an action as can be sanctified, I know that every time I win, it can only be because you have willed it so, and when I lose, I accept the loss as your correction.

Also I pray that the Duchess will soon have had a sufficiency of these waters, so that we may join the King and our husbands and the rest of the Court, and hunt perhaps in the New Forest again — though not of course if you should be so good as to make my womb fruitful once more, for I have sworn that I shall never mount a horse again if I know myself to be with child, and for this reason I beg that you might lend me the strength to hinder myself from doing what I desire when I know it will do me no good, for you who know everything know what a weak and wretched sinner I can be.

THE KING'S BODY, AND
HIS IMMORTAL SOUL

Anne has a great fondness for her sovereign uncle. He has always been kind to her, and if that kindness has come at the price of her serving as an object for his wit, then it has been a price she has never minded paying — it is only the same price that is paid by everyone else, after all.

This summer, his generosity shows itself to the fullest, when he gives her and George some of the most splendid rooms at his disposal, and for a peppercorn rent. The apartment stands alongside Henry Tudor's cockpit, from which it takes its name. It has red bricks and mullioned casements, that look out over a Royal Park — St James's this time, not Richmond, but there are days when Anne could almost fancy herself back in her old childhood home; when she has her old friends — Lady Churchill, Mrs Berkeley, Lady Bathurst — to bear her company, her idyll is almost complete, and only the Ladies Clarendon and Sunderland can spoil it.

God, like the King, is generous. He has listened to her prayers in Tunbridge, smiled on the gift of her winnings and made it so that she is with child again. The only thing she could wish for is that Lady Churchill might be less often at her own house in St Albans, but she could never prevent her going, and any unhappiness of Sarah's would surely be hers too.

Anne has learned her lesson, and stays off horseback, spending the autumn and winter shuffling quietly between the Chapel and the card table. She has the King as a model for her conduct: he has a troublesome humour in his leg, which prevents him from taking his usual walks on Constitution Hill. He passes most of his days in his laboratory, and his evenings in the Duchess of Portsmouth's apartments, listening to music. It is clear to everyone at Court that he is not quite himself, but all the same, when he falls into his first, sudden fit, it comes as a terrible shock.

The news reaches Anne almost immediately. It is the morning of Monday 2nd February, just before prayers. The King has had a convulsion while dressing; he has yet to speak or open his eyes, and there is great fear for his life; physicians and bishops are running from all corners; the Duke has rushed to his brother's side — and in a state of such amazement, Anne hears, that he arrived at the bedside wearing a slipper on one foot and a shoe on the other. The Queen is there, and beside herself. The Duchess has joined her husband.

George can barely believe it.

'*Est-il possible?* You know I was with him last night in Her Grace's rooms? He was in such good spirits — he told me how well the work on the Palace was going along in Winchester, they were to put down the lead this week — then he talked of his experiments with mercury — *so* interesting, he has been endeavouring to —'

'You should go,' says Anne. 'Get dressed, I pray you, and go, and send me word when you get there.'

Anne is dressed; she waits; she prays. The Prince of Denmark has contrived to get as far as the ante-room to the King's chamber, and his gentlemen run back and forth with news: the French ambassador has arrived; the King has been let blood, and has come out of his fit, but the effects of it hang upon him, and oppress him terribly, in body if not in spirit. According to George, the physicians are doing all that they should, in the way of cupping, blistering, purging and so on, to try to pull His Majesty out of danger. Thanks to their efforts, and the blessings of God, he rallies a little. But still, the gates to Whitehall remain closed, and there are orders sent to the ports to make certain that there are no messages despatched to the Prince of Orange, or his guest, the Duke of Monmouth.

Anne waits. Anne prays. The little notes continue to arrive: the King has had plasters put to his feet; has partaken of a little light broth and ale without hops; has complained of his throat hurting; has been let more blood. There is better news on Tuesday, when the King seems improved enough for messengers to be sent to every County, announcing that he is out of danger. Anne's prayers take on a more hopeful, thankful character. When George arrives back at the Cockpit to dine, he says that the Duke remains with the King, and Bishop Ken too. All seem in reasonable spirits.

But when Wednesday comes, it is to dash them down again. That afternoon, even as Anne gives thanks in the Chapel, where they are celebrating his deliverance, the King breaks into a cold sweat. The physicians declare him to be in danger again. George sends word from the ante-chamber that Sir

Charles Scarborough has administered Spirit of Human Skull to his patient, and that the Lord Keeper is complaining because neither Sir Charles, nor any of the other physicians, will give him any assurance — or even any clear indication — as to what the issue might be.

It is impossible for Anne to sleep that night. She calls for her chaplains, and they pray together. On Thursday morning she hears that the physicians now understand both the nature of the King's distemper, and how to treat it: he has an intermittent fever, such as he had a few years before, and they must give him Peruvian Bark. As she reads George's latest note, the bells start ringing out all over London: the new *Gazette* has been issued, but with the old news that the King is safe, and will soon be free from his distemper. Anne can follow the path of the truth through the City, in the progressive muffling of its bells.

She goes again to the Chapel, where the Court chaplains relieve each other every half hour, and lead the congregation in continual prayer. It is to be hoped that the King's soul might profit, even as his body fails, and he falls into further, more violent, convulsions. It seems they must all pray harder. The bishops assemble at his bedside again.

Bishop Ken asks the King if he is sorry for his sins, and on his word that he is, grants him absolution without the bother of confession. Much to the Bishop's frustration, the King goes on to refuse the Sacrament. He says there is time enough to consider it, but his mind is not disordered, and he cannot truly believe this.

Early that evening, at the King's request, the Duke sends everyone but the Earls of Bath and Feversham from the room — so they might take their leave of each other privately, as it is now understood by everyone that the King is dying. According to George, they wait outside for a full forty-five minutes — bishops, physicians, gentlemen of the Court, the French ambassador, speaking in shared glances, and in whispers — before they are allowed back in again, where they find the King weak, but notably serene, and ready for another sally by the royal physicians: Raleigh's Antidote to support the heart, powdered Goa stone, more Peruvian Bark, Sal Ammoniac, a stone from the stomach of an oriental goat.

Through it all, the King amazes everyone with his calmness, his courage. He gives his brother his keys, and begs God to give him a prosperous reign. He blesses his natural sons — except for the oldest, who is in The

Hague, and whose name might not be mentioned. At Bishop Ken's request he blesses his people, and asks pardon if he has done anything contrary to their interests. The Bishop urges him again to take the Sacrament; again, he refuses. He keeps refusing, but with unfailing courtesy, until noon on the Friday, when he finally, calmly dies.

From the start, amidst the groaning and the tears, there have been murmurings of priests, and of poison, and of poison and priests together. That the King would not take the Sacrament from Compton is understandable, as he is a harshly spoken man, who never tries to endear himself — but neither would he take it from Bishop Ken, whom he has always loved, and whose voice is as sweet as a nightingale's. It is not hard to guess that he has taken the Sacrament from quite another sort of cleric, such as his wife, his brother and his sister-in-law might have in attendance.

Anne can only wonder at his imperilling his own soul, when he has taken so much care to safeguard hers. Then a nasty thought steals up on her, that perhaps, on the other hand, the King must have believed that it is her soul, and Mary's, which have been placed in jeopardy — no, surely he would not do that, not unless his mind was quite disordered, and if it was, that would be the priests' doing too, or the fault of his French mistress Portsmouth — in which case, God will surely forgive him, and receive him — and Mary and Anne in due course — into heaven.

King James II's First Speech to His Privy Council, as It Was Taken Down by Heneage Finch, Printed at London by the Assigns of John Bill, Deceased, and by Henry Hills and Thomas Newcomb, and Subsequently Read to the Princess of Denmark by Her Ladyship, the Countess of Clarendon.

My Lords,

Before I enter upon any other business, I think fit to say something to you. Since it has pleased Almighty God to place me in this station, and I am now to succeed so good and gracious a king as well as so very kind a brother, I think it fit to declare to you that I will endeavour to follow his example, and most especially in that of his great clemency and tenderness to his people. I have been reported to be a man for arbitrary power, but that is not the only story which has been made of me. And I shall make it my endeavours to preserve this government both in Church and state as it is now by law established. I know the principles of the Church of England are for monarchy, and the members of it have showed themselves good and loyal subjects; therefore I shall always take care to defend and support it. I know too that the laws of England are sufficient to make the king as great a monarch as I can wish. And as I shall never depart from the just rights and prerogative of the Crown, so I shall never invade any mans property. I have often heretofore ventured my life in defence of this nation, and I shall still go as far as any man in preserving it in all its just rights and liberties.

ANNE'S RELIGION

The first act of the new King is quite unexpected: he confirms all his household officers in their places, adding only a few trusted persons, such as Lord Churchill, to their number. Despite this, the Court is instantly and utterly changed. In the space of a very few days, it has sobered up, straightened its face, buttoned its breeches and pulled its purse strings as tight as they will go. This last, says the King when Anne visits him, is both necessary and urgent.

'I would not for the world speak ill of the dead, Anne, but there was in the late King's management of his affairs such a want of — never mind, it is not for your ears — but on this subject in general — I trust you are pleased with the allowance granted you?'

'Oh yes, Sir, very pleased, and I thank you.'

'Good. Then I desire you to be a good housewife, and not overspend.'

'No, Sir.'

'I do not wish to hear that you have lost it all at cards, or dice, or from going after some other foolishness.'

'Of course not, Sir. I am very content with what I am given — and also that you have appointed the Prince to your Council. I should like to thank you for that.'

'It was only proper that we should: he is our son. And you have both your uncles back in high office where they should be — you shall be well taken care of in all respects, my dear.'

'I know that, Sir.'

'But I did not summon you to talk of your Hyde relations, Anne. As you well know, my religion —'

He stops, and looks at her.

'There's no need for you to blush and cast your eyes about like that — I have not called you here to convert you; I am no kind of monster, Anne — but I must speak to you about the Chapel.'

'I beg your pardon, Sir.'

'So. The Chapel. You must understand that just as my conscience would not permit me to enter there while I was the King's brother, neither will it permit me now that I am King.'

Anne nods.

'But at the same time I am sensible of the duty of our family with regard to . . . the Church of this country, and so I have ordered the Chapel to be kept in the same order as formerly, and — this is very much your concern — I am to give orders to this effect.'

He takes a sheet of paper from his closet desk and offers it to Anne, who takes it, and reads:

It is His Majesty's pleasure that Her Royal Highness Princess Anne of Denmark Doe sit in His Majesty's Closett at His Chappell Royal at Whitehall, upon one side of the King's Chaire, which must remaine in its place not turned: And that Noe man of what degree or quality soever, presume to come into ye clossett when Her Royal Highness is there, except the Clerke of the Clossett, or his Deputy to officiate there, And the Lord Chamberlayne and Mr Vice Chamberlayne of His Majesty's Household to stand behind the King's chaire.

'You are to be my proxy in all services, and the clergy will perform the same bowing and ceremonies to the place where you are as if I had been there in person.'

'No-one shall have reason to complain of my conduct there, Sir.'

'I know they will not. You are a good girl . . .'

'I have one request, though, Sir?'

'Yes?'

'I have observed that lately the Chapel is perhaps not in as good a condition as — there are a number of repairs that might be made — and the decorations —'

'Do what needs to be done, do not trouble me with it; it shall all be paid for.'

'Oh thank you, Sir!'

There is a discreet scratch on the door. With the King's permission, it is opened slightly, to admit two excitable spaniels, and the news that a Mr Sandford is waiting. Anne holds out her hands for the dogs, while her father addresses the servant on the other side of the door.

'Very good. I'll see him shortly.'

The door closes. One of the spaniels leaps into Anne's lap, arranges himself as best he can around her great belly, and sits down.

'Oh Anne, the poor loves — I do not know what to do with them all. My brother would have them roam all over the place, easing themselves, suckling their pups and you-know-what-else — they are sweet creatures, but there are too many, and I won't have them in the bedchamber as he did — how he slept with their snuffling, and all those infernal chiming clocks, I will never — which are these two?'

'This fellow in my lap is Louis, and the one sniffing at my shoes is Bessie.'

'Perhaps they should like to stay with you at the Cockpit?'

'Oh, I should be delighted to have them!'

'Splendid! And take a couple of the wretched clocks as well while you're about it — I know how your George admires them.'

'Thank you, Sir. He shall be so pleased.'

'And I shall be just as pleased to be rid of them. Now, I must dismiss you — there is so much trouble over precedence for the coronation, I have had to have a Commission appointed, and here is a man come to record their work.'

HER MOST GRACIOUS MAJESTY

The Commission convenes, opens a special court, hears evidence and makes its judgements, which do not please everybody. The Lord of the Manor of Fyngrith, Essex, for example, is very disappointed to hear that he does not, in the view of the court, have the right to be the Queen's Chamberlain for the day, and will thus not be entitled to her bed, furniture or any of the basins which he might otherwise have used to perform his duties. The Prince of Orange, who must on any State occasion be outranked by the Prince of Denmark, declines to attend — a pity, as he and Mary miss a very fine spectacle.

There is blue carpet spread all the way from Westminster Hall to the Abbey Choir. As the King and then the Queen process along it, they are preceded by herb-women in new and becoming costumes with deep ruffles, strewing spring flowers. The Queen, who has always — it must be owned — been a very beautiful lady, seems a goddess today. Her dress is made of white- and silver-embroidered brocade, with every seam covered by diamonds; she has a seven-yard train of purple velvet, bordered with gold lace and lined with ermine and white silk, and carried by the Duchess of Norfolk and four eldest daughters of earls; she has on her head a circlet, and over her head a canopy of cloth of gold borne by sixteen barons of the Cinque Ports. The crowd, moved both by her appearance and by the news that she has taken upon herself the liabilities of all imprisoned small debtors, weep their grateful tears.

Her conduct during the ceremony is faultless too — except for one forgivable instance, when the King's Champion, in act of throwing down the gauntlet, falls off his mount and straight onto his face, and she is observed to stifle a giggle. After the ceremony is finished, she goes straight up to George and Anne's box, and tells them that she thought, for one moment, that she might have died of laughter, in front of everyone, right there and then.

'That poor man,' Anne says, 'he could hardly help it, but it was *very* amusing.'

They laugh together, and for one lovely

moment, might believe themselves true
friends.

THE KING AND
HIS PARLIAMENT

The first Election of the new reign is a happy one, returning Tories in large numbers. Among the knights, citizens and burgesses currently shuffling into Westminster Hall and removing their hats, Anne knows there can only be a few who voted to exclude her father from the succession; but she also knows him well enough to guess that his mind will have fixed its bulldog jaws into the necks of these few, all the better to worry and worry and worry at them. From her place behind his throne, it is easy enough to tell, from the set of his shoulders, the tightening of his hands, that her guess is good.

Anne does not feel comfortable either, though in her case it is only because her part in this day of ceremony is to stand in Court dress and heavy jewels, in her heavy-bellied, sore-footed condition, in a crowded hall, and do her best, despite it all, to maintain a bland and daughterly countenance. As if to test her, the rays of sunlight which God has caused to pour through the high windows and onto His anointed, direct a small but intense portion of their early summer glory straight onto the back of her neck.

Finally, the last citizen — or is he a burgess? — has been admitted to the King's presence, and there they are in their places, the King and his Officers of State, the peers all in their robes seated on their benches, the Commons seatless and hatless, like orders of angels divinely ordained, ready to serve. There is a brief hush, the baby turns impatiently in Anne's belly, and her father directs the Lord Keeper to tell both Houses that he will defer his speaking to them until they have all taken their Oaths and the Commons have chosen their speaker, which he directs them to do that day. After this the names of receivers and triers of petitions are read, all in French, which does not take too long, considering, and then the Commons can leave, the royal party can withdraw, and Anne can think about being comfortable again. She can screw her eyes up against the sun, and not be concerned about looking disagreeable.

Anne is at home when her father makes

his speech. She is able to hear about it from her day bed, propped up with cushions behind, with her stockinged feet sticking out of the bottom of her loose, light manteau. It seems, initially, very much of a piece with his speech to the Council, assuring both Houses of his respect for the law, of the care he will have of their religion and property — but then it takes a firmer turn. In return, he says, he expects duty and kindness, particularly in what relates to the settling and continuance of his revenue. In this, they must be guided by considerations of what is just and reasonable: to call frequent Parliaments, to feed him from time to time such proportions as they shall think convenient, would be an improper method to take with him. He cautions them instead to use him well.

As he follows this with the announcement that the Duke of Argyle has landed in the West Highlands, with men from Holland and treasonous intent, he is not met with any immediate resistance, and soon receives his revenue. Certainly there is a little disquiet, a few days later, when certain members of the Commons move to have him enforce the laws against Dissenters, but with a little trouble taken — a quick summons, a sharp rebuke — they are persuaded to drop the matter.

ANNE'S DAUGHTER

This time Anne's travail is not so long, and the baby girl Mrs Wilkes catches in her apron is one that kicks and cries. She is the living proof of God's grace, and her name is Mary.

KING MONMOUTH

Baby Mary's first month of life turns out to be more than usually eventful for her kin, and for one cousin especially. As a gesture of goodwill towards her grandfather the King, her uncle Orange has sent her cousin Monmouth away from The Hague. The Duke has travelled as far as Amsterdam, where he has been meeting with other Rye House exiles, gathering sufficient men, money and arms to make an attempt on his late father's Crown.

On 11th June, when Mary is nine days old, he lands at Lyme. As his little cousin sleeps in the arms of her wet-nurse, he marches to the Market Place, where he has a proclamation read, declaring himself Head and Captain-General of the Protestant Forces of the Kingdom, and claiming that, as the late King's son born in lawful wedlock, he has a legitimate and legal right to the Crown. The so-called King James is a usurper, who started the Great Fire of London and, more recently, murdered his own brother.

Lady Churchill's father-in-law is the Member of Parliament for Lyme, so it falls to him and his son, her husband, to inform the King. Within a day, Sarah's John is marching out of London at the head of eight troops of horse guards and dragoons and five companies of foot, leaving his Lady to fret at home at St Albans, and Anne at the Cockpit to pray for his success and safety. Lord Feversham may be Commander-in-Chief over him, but nobody doubts who is truly in charge: what Lord Churchill lacks in birth, he more than makes up for in his native ability. He is like his wife in that respect.

For a couple of weeks, as Mary suckles and sleeps and soils her swaddling, the Lords Feversham and Churchill follow the Duke of Monmouth about the West Country, shadowing him as he gathers a ragtag army of hard-up clothiers, unemployed miners and disenchanted militiamen. On 27th June, the day when Anne is called into the nursery to witness what is reckoned her daughter's first smile — a grimace which the baby's governess Mrs Berkeley dismisses as wind — the two armies meet at Norton

St Philip. The next day, Anne hears the news of an indecisive battle, alarms herself with thoughts of another Civil War to come. Her private devotions double in the strength of their feeling, and treble in their length. When her confinement ends, and she goes to the Chapel to be churched and to see the baby christened, she asks that prayers be said for the King's army, for their excellent brave commanders.

Either Anne's prayers are heard, or they were superfluous, because Monmouth's troops — sceptical of their chances of victory perhaps, or despairing of the good dinner for which they joined — have already begun to desert him. There is no Civil War, just one brief, muddy rout at Sedgemoor, and the rising is over. Mrs Berkeley writes to Sarah to tell her the glad news; Anne writes to tell her that although she has no further news to add, Sarah must be so just to her as to believe that neither of her other friends who write can be half as glad of anything good that happens to her as she is, that although maybe they can express themselves better, nobody's heart she is sure is more sincere than hers.

PHYSIC

It takes five strokes of the axe, and then some further business with a knife, to excise the Duke of Monmouth from the Kingdom, but it is done now. And to make absolutely sure that there can be no resurgence of any peccant Whiggish humour, the King has sent Judge Jeffreys west, to purge whatever traces might remain. Anne is also in need of physic, so she goes again to Tunbridge Wells, this time to take the waters herself.

She commits herself to take a full course, but soon wishes she had not. For a certainty, there is nothing in Tunbridge this year but rain and tedium. Every day begins with a sodden trudge to the Springs, accompanied by Lady Clarendon, and her unsolicited lectures on the curative qualities of chalybeate, the virtues of early rising, the very interesting story of the discovery of the Wells. There, as the clouds and the Countess drizzle on unstoppably, she forces down glass after glass of wholesome nastiness, then makes the return trudge to their lodgings, for another day of dull discourse and sulphurous belching, to be accomplished within easy reach of a chamber pot, and enlivened only by the occasional lacklustre game of cards and the too-infrequent arrival of letters from Lady Churchill.

Anne writes as often as she can: to provoke an answer, to fill the weary hours, to ask how her little girl goes on, to inform the lady of her progress in the matter of securing the Windsor lodgings to which she is entitled, to complain of the weather, to complain of the tedium, to complain of her Aunt Clarendon, who grows every day more nauseating, and of her other aunt — Aunt Rochester, since her husband was granted the late poet's title — who has arrived full of peevishness about the Windsor arrangements, with no good reason at all. One Saturday, when the waters prove more than usually vitriolic, she complains about her step-mother, who has sent her a present, a watch decorated with the Queen's own face, and set with diamonds: 'I must return her most thankful acknowledgements but among friends I think one may say without being vain that the goddess might have showered down her favours on her poor Vassals with more liberality.'

There has been no repeating of the warm laughter shared on Coronation Day. When Anne writes to Lady Churchill of her suspicion that she might be again with child, she is sure to tell her not to mention this to the Queen, who asks constantly how the waters go with her, and whose questions she must always answer herself, in words most carefully counted out and chosen, so that they do only what they must do: nothing other, and nothing more. Writing these dutiful letters always leaves her with a most unpleasant, tightened-up feeling, which she has found is best relieved by writing again — in this case, plethorically — to Lady Churchill. She is at all times the perfect antidote to ceremony. If only she would not take so long to reply. If only she would come to Tunbridge in person.

At least George comes, for a spell, and is pleasant, always, to be with: she can return to wondering, with more reason than before, whether she might not be breeding again. The rain grows heavier, the walk to the Springs more slippery, and she must needs ask Lady Churchill to send for her shoemaker and bid him make a pair of wax-soled shoes, with soles to be especially thick.

July drains away. August trickles in, bringing new fears. Lady Churchill writes to tell her that the baby has soreness in her eyes. As Anne reads this, she cannot help but imagine how all the woes, large and small, that her wretched eyes have brought her will be visited on her tiny daughter. She pictures her first crying from the soreness, then a thousand handkerchiefs wiping the defluxion away again and again until the skin underneath is sore as well, then a hundred ladies scolding her for screwing up her face, a dozen doctors advancing with their noxious drops, all the panic she might ever experience, on walking into great chambers full of persons she might insult by her not recognising them, all the awkwardness that must result, the dependency on trusted friends, the fear when they are not with her, the reading headaches, the working headaches, the spectacles that pinch her nose and do not work, the whispering French Court, the poisoned aunts, the purple mourning veils — it must at all costs be prevented. She resolves that Mary should have an issue made and decides to write to the King to ask for his leave, and for him to give his commands to Mrs Berkeley. Of course it will hurt the child to feel the little bite of the lancet and to have the wax put in the wound — Anne winces as she remembers — but skilfully done, it will bring the humour out once and for all, and it is better, surely, to have a little suffering now than so much later.

It rains, it rains; the waters get no more palatable; Lady Clarendon reminds Anne daily that no physic can be effective that is not also unpleasant to the patient in some way; the Prince daily smiles on his wife, and says that although the waters might taste ever so nasty, he can see, from her looks, how well they agree with her; all the same, she does not believe herself with child; she hears nothing from the King about her Windsor lodgings; she wonders if the baby's issue might not be put off till she returns to London; Lady Churchill writes, but does not come, or say that she will; still, it rains.

Later in the month the Prince goes, but Anne has still not finished her course, so she cannot go with him yet. She is close now to having had a surfeit of Lady Clarendon's company; it takes all she has to be civil to the Countess, but just when she fears that she might dash her next glass of effective unpleasant water in that lady's face, the most welcome news comes: her uncle Clarendon is made Lord Lieutenant of Ireland and will go with his wife to Dublin. Anne's

household is purged of aunts, and this
agrees with her well.

THE REVOCATION OF THE EDICT OF NANTES

O Almighty God, King of all kings, and Governor of all things, save and deliver me, I humbly beseech you, from the hands of my enemies; abate their pride, assuage their malice, and confound their devices; that I, and the Prince, and my child and all in my household might be armed with your defence — I have in my heart today the prayer for times if war and tumults, because of this most dreadful news from France, that the King there has revoked the edict they had for near a hundred years, that the Protestants in his Kingdom should not be persecuted for their religion. To be sure this act is the Devil's work, for he has had their churches destroyed, he billets dragoons in their homes to bully them, has his priests baptise their babes in front of their faces . . . There is nothing they can do but flee, and now London is full of them telling stories that I do not wish to call to mind, for they put in my head such pictures as I swear I have never seen except in Mr Foxe's book. Such are Catholic Kings, and Catholic Kingdoms . . .

But no, no, I should not care to think ill of my own father — it feels like sinning. I hope I know what is due to him; he does not use me so ill, but I know he does not trust me quite. When I raised Lady Churchill to Lady Clarendon's old place he did not forbid me, but he would not let me have my Lady Westmoreland for my bedchamber: instead I must have Lady Anne Spencer, the Sutherlands' daughter. Of course the mother is great with the Queen and as for her father, he is a man who will do I know-not-what for the King as long he can profit from it himself . . . So my father has sent no dragoons to my house, but that he has sent one spy at least I cannot doubt. I have had it from Bishop Ken and others that he has always had spies about my sister, and now he does the same to me. And besides, Lady Anne is forever unwell, which causes much inconvenience, and extra expenditure, for when Lady Churchill is away to St Albans and she is indisposed, I cannot manage and so I expect in the end I shall have to appoint a third Lady, and pay her, and the Prince and I must struggle as it is with so paltry an allowance . . .

It is true the King is not unkind to me — but he has no kindness for my Church. He has dismissed my Lord Compton from the Privy Council because he spoke against the keeping of so great an army, and against his granting so many commissions in it to Catholics which the law says he ought not — I pray you will give the King ears to hear good counsel . . . and I pray you put it in his heart that he must have my revenues increased. I will have my Uncle Rochester speak to him — I must be thankful that there are still those that have my father's ear besides the Jesuits and Sunderland . . .

I am thankful that my child is well — she has a scabby face but the nurse tells me this is good, for all the bad is being brought out — and that the Prince has recovered from the dizziness and heaviness in his head that frightened me . . .

. . . but I am so easily affrighted, since the old King was poisoned — protect me, I beseech you — abate their pride, assuage their malice — make me please to be comfortable in my heart, and if I am, as I think, with child again, I pray you let me keep it.

ANNE'S UNCLE ROCHESTER

Here is Anne's Uncle Laurence Hyde, Earl of Rochester, great favourite of the old King, former brother-in-law and now loyal servant of the new, Lord High Treasurer, a Tory, a great man for the Church, a great man for business, and great with Hyde ambition. He has not had much to do with his niece since she got the better of his wife in the matter of the Windsor lodgings three months ago, but now he is settled comfortably in a chair in her closet, with her household accounts spread out on the desk before him, and his niece perched on the chair opposite his, wringing her hands and biting her lip, and looking to him for help. His quick mind has already taken in as much as it needs to, but he decides to let her wait a little longer before he speaks.

'You are to appoint a *third* Lady of the Bedchamber?'

'Lady Churchill must often be with her

children at St Albans, and Lady Anne is . . . well the King and Queen said I must have her, though she is always unwell with one thing or another; it is not my choice to have her in my service — so there is truly nothing for it but to take on another lady.'

'At 200 livres a year?'

'No-one will put herself forward if I offer any less.'

'Perhaps you would be better to dismiss Lady Churchill and appoint instead a lady less concerned with her nursery.'

'There can be no question of that. I cannot do without her. No.'

Rochester knows what Anne desires — what Anne needs — what is, for sure, the only conceivable solution — but he is not ready to approach that yet. He points to another item on the desk.

'This dressmaker's bill.' He reads, 'Three blue silk manteaus, all ordered together — *sixty-three pounds* for gold lace? Madam, do you mean to stage a masque?'

'Oh that is all Lady Clarendon's doing — she would insist on buying three of everything, and then took such dreadful care of all of it — Lady Churchill has charge of my wardrobe now, and will manage far better.'

'Will she also have charge of your gaming purse — Your Highness?'

Humiliation starts the blushing off, and anger does the rest.

I am the King's daughter, she thinks, and you might say it is only because your sister whored in a royal Duke's bed, and so entrapped him, but I would not care to say even in my heart what that makes you, for the Lord knows how much you and your brother have profited by it.

'I play only for the same stakes as any other lady at this Court,' she says, 'and they would have cause to complain of me if I did not.'

'Yes, I can imagine they would . . . well, it must be most vexatious to you that the Prince's revenues do not come from Denmark when they should — but I have already said to him many times at Council, that I will render him whatever assistance I can to pursue the matter.'

'He has told me, and I thank you, but as there is no knowing when the money from the Prince's estates might come, I called you here because I was in hopes that . . . that perhaps you might speak to the King for me?'

'You desire a grant to clear your debts?'

'Yes, Sir — I *require* a grant.'

'Then I must beg your pardon, Your Highness, but I cannot help you.'

Anne did not expect this — not a flat no.

'Why not, Sir?'

Rochester sighs, as if this were truly as painful to him as it were to her.

'Your Highness, you know the King's temper in relation to money matters — he is not likely to look favourably on such a request, no matter where it came from — and such a proposal, coming from me, might well do me hurt, and you no good.'

'So I cannot . . . entreat you? As your sister's child?'

'No, Your Highness — forgive me, but I cannot do it.'

'Well, then — in that case, Sir, there is nothing more to say.'

SEIGNEUR DE MONTAIGNE'S WRITINGS ON FRIENDSHIP PROVED SOUND

Anne wastes no time in complaining of her disappointment to Lady Churchill, who speaks to her Lord, who speaks to his great friend Lord Godolphin, who was married to the late, unhappy Margaret. Godolphin has the King's ear, as Sunderland and Rochester do, but as he is neither slippery nor wanting in tact, he is the perfect man for the task, and with little fuss persuades the King to make his daughter a Christmas present of 16,000 pounds.

And this is handsome proof, if ever proof were needed, that when the Seigneur de Montaigne declared that friendship, true friendship, is more to be relied upon than any tie of blood or marriage, he wrote nothing less than the truth.

The Triumph of
Squinting Betty

It is Anne's twenty-first birthday, and a year since the death of the late King. Baby Mary is seven months old now, beginning to sit up a little by herself.

'She takes so much notice of everything, Your Highness,' the nurse says. 'Just this morning, I held her up to the casement, so that she might watch the rain, and from her face you might have thought it the greatest wonder that ever was, just to see it splattering the glass!'

The baby is on Anne's lap, examining her mother's ringed fingers; from time to time she brings a jewel to her mouth and sucks on it, as if to determine the flavour. A large purple sapphire on Anne's right hand seems to please her more than the rest, and she tries her tooth on it.

'How good to hear that little tapping sound!' Anne says. 'She suffered so long, I thought the tooth was never coming.'

'So you kept saying, Your Highness,' says Lady Churchill, 'but it has. They always do.'

'And there are two more, Your Highness,' says the nurse, 'that I can feel through her gums. The red cheeks, that you feared meant a fever, were but the signs of their coming.'

'How does she like the toy the Princess sent? Does she try her gums on that?'

'Oh yes, Your Highness. She prefers it above all the others. It is the prettiest thing!'

'You will not have seen it, Lady Churchill. My sister sent from The Hague a silver rattle set with coral — the loveliest —'

'I saw it yesterday, Your Highness, when you had me go to the nursery. It is a lovely thing — almost too lovely, to have a baby dribble on.'

'Maybe . . . do you think then we ought to take it from her? Until she is older?'

'No, Madam, I do not think that at all.'

'Look — she is trying to bite my ring again! Farthing says I was used to do that when I sat with my mother. Her fingers are almost all I can recall of her.'

'My sister Frances remembers her quite well. She says she had a great deal of wit —'

'Which I know well I have none of. Never mind. Perhaps you will fare better, my love.'

She kisses the baby's delicious head once more; little Mary crows, and the baby in Anne's belly kicks — they are playing together already. This is delightful, but it is high time the older child was sent back to the nursery: Anne has that to say about her own sister, which ought not to be said in front of the nurse, who has come so recently to the family.

'She never says so in her letters to me, but Lady Bathurst reckons my sister is in very low spirits.'

'I should think she would be. The Prince has sent so many of her old people away: first there was Bishop Ken, before even the King died; now her old nurse, her chaplain, Anne Trelawney . . .'

'I don't agree, though, that Mrs Trelawney was *such* a very particular friend of hers. She would have taken her Mrs Apsley with her if she had had a choice, and Babs Villiers — she would surely have taken her over Betty — but Betty wanted to go, and Betty always seems to get what she desires.'

'Such as her Caliban. He crooked, her squinting — what a pretty pair they make.'

'It grieves me in my heart to think of my sister weeping for that Dutch Abortion. He might say he sent her people away because they were the King's spies — I expect they were, but he must have known that all along — I'm sure he did it out of spite, because she surprised him coming away from our squinting friend. And then to convince her that she was mistaken!'

'Not so much mistaken as misled, and by her oldest friends . . .'

'I know: it is enough to drive a soul mad. She could not even send Betty away when she tried: she is back in The Hague with her sister.'

'Mrs Berkeley says she has a fine diamond necklace as reward for her persistence.'

'At least my sister Orange has her own fair share of jewels. He's not mean that way.'

'No. But he has not given her a child.'

'Nor will he, I don't think.'

'Betty does not breed either. He must be either cold or incapable.'

'Or both.'

'At least my sister still has her religion — he would not have that off her. My father might try, of course, but he will never bring her round — her heart is far too good for that, thank God.'

TO THE PRINCESS OF ORANGE

The Cockpit, April 29 1686

I could never till now get any opportunity of answering your letter that I received by Dow, but before I say anything to it I must give you a thousand thanks for all the good advice you give me in it, and I desire you would still continue telling me your mind freely in this and all other things. I hope you don't doubt but that I will be ever firm to my religion, whatever happens. However, since you desire me to write freely on this subject, I must tell you that I abhor the principles of the Church of Rome as much as it is possible for any to do, and I as much value the doctrine of the Church of England. And certainly there is the greatest reason in the world to do so, for the doctrine of the Church of Rome is wicked and dangerous, and directly contrary to the Scriptures, and their ceremonies — most of them — plain, downright idolatry.

But God be thanked we were not bred up in that Communion, but are of a Church that is pious and sincere, and conformable in all its principles to the Scriptures. Our Church teaches no doctrine but what is just, holy and good, or what is profitable to salvation; and the Church of England is, without all doubt, the only true Church. Nobody has yet said anything to me about religion. The king only gave me those papers to read that were writ by the late King, and my mother, concerning which I am of your opinion: and indeed, they will do them no service, if they have not greater influence on other people than they have had on us; and I trust in God they will not.

As to what you say of taking Popish servants, I will never hence-forward. It is true I have taken on one lately, but he is in a place of no consequence, and those that put him to me did not know that he was of that religion till after he was in. I shall be sure in all things to follow your advice, and make it my chiefest case to live up to that religion in which I have been born and bred, and in which I hope God Almighty will never preserve me. I do count it a very great blessing that I am of the Church of England, and as great a misfortune that the King is not. I pray God his eyes may be opened, and I shall ever bless God for letting me be brought up in His true religion.

I have now been as free in telling you my mind as I think you can desire. I have not said so much as I would have done, if I had had more time; but I knew of this opportunity so late that I have not had time to say so much as I would; but I was unwilling to miss this not knowing when I might have any other conveniency. When we are so happy as to see one another, we shall have more time to talk of this and other matters, which is all that I can now say to my dearest sister, but that I will ever study to follow your example in all things.

The Man from Versailles

Anne has a heart every bit as sound as Mary's: she would rather die than change her religion, however much she is tempted, however much she is tried — and if the trials are to be no worse than to have the French King's envoy, de Bonrepaux, coming to talk at her in her closet, she will consider herself blessed. Their religion might be an abomination and their King a tyrant, but the French language is so pretty, and it is always a pleasure to her to hear a native speak it. He makes his compliment, very beautifully, and she bids him sit down.

'Your Highness looks very well.'

'Thank you, Sir.'

'Perhaps you and the Prince wish for a son this time?'

'That is in God's hands.'

'Of course, Your Highness. We must both know so many unfortunate persons, who have prayed in vain for a son and heir, or

288

who have wept to see the children they had return to God before they were grown.'

'Or born.'

'That brings its own sorrow.'

'It does, though I grieve less than I might have done, had I not had cause to believe her soul in heaven.'

The envoy holds up his hands and smiles. He has a charming smile.

'And if you had not been so blessed so soon afterwards — and are now to be blessed again.'

'I hope so.'

'You must think it a great pity that the Princess of Orange has not been similarly blessed.'

'Of course I do. Why would I not wish my sister happy?'

'I have no doubt that you do. And the Queen also.'

Anne feels herself colouring. 'Yes.'

'Yes. When a Queen has no child, it is a trouble not only to her husband, but to his Kingdom as well. I am sure you will agree, the late disturbance here is proof of that.'

'It certainly was.'

'But then, if it were true what the late Duke put about, that the King had owned him as his legitimate heir —'

'Which he did not!'

'No, he did not. What was it he said? "I love my son, but I would sooner —" '

' "— see him hanged than on the throne." '

'That's it! He had a pithy way with him, the old King. And — if you will excuse any slight indelicacy, Your Highness, but I would not for all the world insult you by supposing you ignorant — he was a most prolific father of natural children.'

'Well that is hardly a secret, Sir. They have always had their place at Court.'

'Quite rightly.' De Bonrepaux stops for a moment, and examines his fingernails. 'And the present King has two sons.' Now he looks Anne fully, frankly in the eye.

'Bast— natural sons.'

'But sons nonetheless — and brought up in the old religion.'

Anne can say nothing: all the words have drained out of her head, to be replaced by dreadful, incommunicable pictures. De Bonrepaux watches her, and waits, unflustered.

'You cannot suggest,' she stutters, 'you cannot . . .'

'I am not suggesting anything. Neither does my master in Versailles. Neither would the King. But I who have been so honoured — so *blessed* — as to have discoursed at length with both their Majesties on many subjects close to their hearts, I would venture — with *confidence* — the opinion that were either of the English King's legitimate children to change her religion, it would bring him the greatest joy imaginable, and would be very pleasing to my master also. So one cannot help thinking it would be a great thing, for the succession, and for the peace of this country, were that child then to take her place as heir. A great blessing indeed. Your Highness understands, of course?'

'I do.'

'The Prince must have told you that I have spoken with the Danish envoy.'

'Yes.'

'I believe he also understands.'

'I do not see why he would not.'

'Good. But I have said enough. I must thank Your Highness for such a gracious reception. I hope, Madam, that you will enjoy the gifts I brought.'

There is a small pile of slender volumes, exquisitely bound, sitting on the desk.

'They look very pretty,' she says.

'But they are all the more beautiful *inside*. The right book at the right time can work a miracle — as I believe it did for the late Duchess.'

'The King has already given me her writings on her . . . her religion.'

'He has often told me how much you are like her.'

'I know I look like her.'

'I can only imagine that he wishes at least one of her daughters might find for herself the same joy and comfort that their mother did.'

The man from Versailles takes his leave. He looks very pleased with himself.

THE VAPOURS

Of course there has from the start been a great deal of murmuring against the King's religion, and not only at the Denmarks' Court. Mutterings, whispers, anonymous verses, sharp asides. That much was only to be expected. It is quite another matter, however, to have such intolerance declaimed from the pulpit: the King's *Directions to Preachers* have made this abundantly clear, so when the Reverend John Sharp of St Giles' Cripplegate delivers, on two successive May Sundays, sermons which even the meanest of wits can only construe as anti-Catholic, the provocation must, surely, be deliberate.

Printed copies begin to circulate almost immediately. Anne is in Windsor already, but Lady Churchill is sure she knows where to get hold of a copy without too much delay, and Anne can hardly wait to hear it read. Neither, it seems, can the baby, for the little controversialist arrives, abruptly, a month before she is expected. Anne is fearful all the way through her travail — these eight-months' children so often die — but the new daughter is strong and sound, and although she is small, the general opinion is that so healthy a child cannot have come before her time.

With the King and Queen elsewhere, Anne spends the first few days of her lying-in unvisited except by her own ladies, which is how she would have it always, if she could. She need do nothing but stay in her bed in a dark, calm chamber, moving little so as not to disturb the red-lead plasters driving the milk back from her breasts, eat jellies, drink claret, sleep as often as she wishes, and have Lady Churchill read to her. It is such a great pleasure to hear Lady Churchill read: she can bring feeling to any poem, clarity to any tract; when she reads a comedy, she contrives to have a distinctively droll voice for every part, and can remember, from one sitting to the next, which voice properly belongs to which. Sometimes, if she is in a particularly impish mood, she will lend a character the voice of some real person, whom they both know, and she is so accomplished a mimic that she never has to tell Anne whose voice she has borrowed. It is always perfectly clear, and quite delicious.

Sharp's sermons arrive just before the baby's christening, but must be put away safely in Lady Churchill's own lodgings, for the King and Queen reach Windsor on the very same day. When the King is announced, Anne is sitting up in her bed — she has put aside the red-lead plasters, which never stick fast for long in any case — and eating a syllabub — it is but a light thing, and surely nothing too strong for her, when she is recovering so well. She is well, she is content, there is nothing amiss with her or her condition — until she sees, gliding in behind her father, a figure in an unmistakeable black soutane — and all at once her peace is shattered.

She cannot help herself: she jumps like a started hare, dropping her dish and spoon, spilling the contents of one all over the bedclothes and sending the other ringing to the floor; she feels her heart swell and pound and make as if to burst; her mouth falls open; nothing comes out for a moment, but by and by there is a thin wail, and then the first appalling sob.

The King is horrified. 'Oh my dear! Oh Good Lord! Where are you — Danvers! Lady Churchill!'

But they are already running into the room. Danvers retrieves the dish and spoon; Lady Churchill takes her place at the head of Anne's bed, from which vantage she favours the priest with a not-quite-insolent stare. It has its desired effect, and the King dismisses him.

'Don't take on, Anne, I pray you don't take on. I came only as your father — I did not intend — anything — I said I would never — I stand by my word to you — I . . .'

Farthing rushes in with some burnt feathers, and hands them to Lady Churchill, who holds them under Anne's nose until the sobs begin to subside. Danvers gives Anne a clean handkerchief; she buries her face in it, takes in its lavender scent, and composes herself.

'Lady Churchill . . .' the King begins to speak, and falters.

'Your Majesty, Her Highness has been recovering very well — remarkably well — from her travail, but it is still only a few days since her ordeal, and of course ladies in her condition —'

'— are frequently troubled by the vapours. Yes, of course, a windy womb — poor child.'

He comes over to the bed and puts his hand over Anne's. She allows it, as she

must, but secretly it is a great relief to feel
him take the hand away again.

THE QUEEN OF HUNGARY'S WATER

Lord, I know not what to pray for as I ought: O let thy Spirit help my infirmities, and enable me to offer up a spiritual sacrifice, acceptable to thee by Jesus Christ.

I must thank you for restoring both my girls to good health, for I have been sent word by Mrs Berkeley that although Mary was lately peevish it was only this time that she was cutting a tooth, and not a return of the sickness she is so often troubled with, and Anne Sophia goes on very well again — I thank you every hour that she has from the beginning been a healthy child, that she does not suffer as her sister does — so Dr Walgrave does not think she should be weaned yet after all, which I am glad of. I pray that you preserve them both and if it is that you must rebuke me, I beg that you will not do it through them, who must be so innocent yet of any grievous sin.

For my own sake I offer thanks that so far the waters have agreed with me again this year, that even though it is unseasonable cold in Tunbridge I am not much the worse for it, except for this queer breaking-out over my nose and cheeks. When my prayers are done, I mean to anoint my face with the Queen of Hungary's Water Mrs Churchill has sent; I beseech you in your mercy cause it to heal my face — and if this breaking-out be a sign of your displeasure, I promise to examine my heart and find out my fault as if I were preparing to communicate, and to make all proper amends . . .

I beseech you, preserve the Prince another day in good health, and my sister Orange and her Prince — and the King and Queen of course — and my good friend Lady Churchill, who I fear does not mind herself enough, for she goes up and down as much as if she were not with child. Just this sennight she has made a great journey to Althrop to see Lady Sunderland, which I must needs say according to my small understanding was a very strange undertaking for one in her condition, especially as it is so much further from Windsor or St Albans than it is to Tunbridge and I have not seen her here at all this month — and I must confess that when I do not see her, or I do not hear from her every day, I cannot but fall prey to melancholy which I know I should not, and I would not for the world cause her to do herself harm by writing to me so much every day. Truly there is no-one else for whom I feel more kindness, and in whose word and judgement I might put so much trust — for there is so much truth in her, and the world being what it is there are so few I may rely upon. I thank you for giving me this one honest friend . . .

My sister is so far away, and though I try to honour my father as the Commandment says yet it seems every day he has a stiffer neck, a harder heart . . . I was very much surprised when I heard of the four new Privy Councillors — Papist all — and I cannot help but be very sorry for it, and it makes me wonder at the King — I think Lord Sunderland whispers in his ear as his Lady does in the Queen's. I must confess that I am never easy when I am with Her Majesty, and am glad to have missed her ball at Windsor, even though there is no company agreeable to me in Tunbridge . . . Still, I must play basset with them every day. I beg thee, help me keep my countenance.

ANNE TREATS HER FATHER
LIKE A TURK

It seems an age since the King first met with his Privy Council, and assured them of his respect for English law. Although the law in regard of Catholics holding public office has suffered no change, much else has changed despite it. Parliament has not met since last November, when it opposed the King's request to appoint Catholic officers to the army. Now, by all accounts, the army in Ireland is overrun with Papists, and the English army, which the King keeps camped at Hounslow Heath — so uncomfortably close to London — seems to have every day more of the wrong sort of people in its upper ranks. Lately a sympathetic judge has ruled that His Majesty might suspend the law against employing Catholics by exercising his dispensing power, and he has been gladly dispensing not only in the army but at Court, in the universities, in the Privy Council — nowhere, it seems, is safe from his dispensing. Anne remembers how, when he was still a Duke, he was always saying that a King ought not to be ruled by Parliament; now that he is King himself he has Sutherland to encourage him in his resolve, and the Jesuits in black soutanes, and of course the Queen.

Anne would rather not have to dine with any of them, but it is unavoidable, and so here she is, at their table at Windsor again, thinking about how they have just had her old tutor Compton suspended from his office because he would not do the same to Dr Sharp, and doing her best to pretend that she cannot hear the grace said, as these days they have a Catholic priest to say it. Sometimes she can do this simply by looking another way, but on this occasion she cannot help but feel that a little extra disrespect is warranted, so she turns to Lady Rochester, who looks a little surprised, and says the first thing that comes to her.

'I do hope,' she says, 'that the meat will not be dressed in that vinegary sauce today — it does so disagree with me, even when I am not with child.'

The next day she remarks on the dryness of the summer, and the day after that she asks the Prince if his headache is quite gone. On the fourth day she compliments a lady on her gown, and on the day after that her father comes to visit.

'Do you do this on purpose or by chance?' he asks. 'I bid you, be ingenuous.'

'On purpose, Sir.'

For a moment the King looks as if he might pick something up and throw it at her, but instead he checks himself, and sighs, and his face falls so that she is almost touched to see it.

'Anne, when you do what you are doing, it is looking upon us — myself, the Queen, the Queen Dowager — none of whom to my certain knowledge have ever done you hurt — you are looking upon us as Turks, and it looks disrespectfully to me. I find by this that you have had very ill impressions made on you about my religion.'

'I can assure you, Sir, that nobody has ever opened their lips to me.'

'If you say so, then I believe you, but still I see very well what strange opinions you have of our religion.'

Anne says nothing, only turns a bracelet on her arm, remembering as she does that it was the King who gave it to her.

'Well, I will not torment you about it. I can only hope one day that God will open your eyes.'

Just as he is saying this, the Prince arrives

like a merciful angel, and the discourse takes another turn.

LADY CHURCHILL'S CHARACTER

It seems that certain people have been taking great pains to give the Princess of Orange an ill character of Lady Churchill. Anne writes back at once to vindicate her friend, and as soon as she is able, she gives Sarah a full account of what she has said.

'I told her that I believe there is nobody in the world has better notions of religion than you have. It is true that you are not so strict as some are, nor do you keep such a bustle with religion — and I said I had to confess that I think no worse of you for that, for one sees so many saints turn devils, that if one be a good Christian, the less show one makes of it the better, in my opinion.'

'Your Highness is very kind.'

'Not at all! It is only the truth — and I ventured to say the same of your Lord, that though he is a very faithful servant to the King, and the King so kind to him, yet rather than change his religion, I dare say, he will lose all his places and all that he has too!'

'And the babe is of the same opinion, Your Highness — he has just given me the most almighty kick in the ribs, and — oh, Your Highness is weeping . . .'

'Oh Lady Churchill, you cannot know — you surely cannot know — what a comfort it is to me to have friends such as you and your Lord, who I can trust will be faithful to my interests, and our religion — and now my Uncle Rochester is dismissed because he would not change his —'

'Lord Churchill does not think it was only —'

'— and my uncle Clarendon has lost *his* place too, and the King leans more and more on that knave Sunderland, just because he goes into Chapel with him, and I do believe he is wholly governed by priests and villains, and his wife —'

'Whose wife, Your Highness?'

'The Queen! I mean the Queen, who is governed herself by her confessor, and — and that flatterer your *friend* —'

'Lady Sunderland? Oh I do not think so. Forgive me, Your Highness, for saying so, but she is truly a good sort of woman — she has been so kind to me many times, and so very *very* kind to my Lord Godolphin and his boy since Margaret died — and she is not at all like to become a Papist — whatever her Lord may do.'

'Forgive you? What in the world should I ever forgive you for? For speaking the truth? No! I should ask *you* to forgive *me*, it is only that I am overcome . . .'

'It is nothing, Madam — remember, you are breeding.'

'Yes, yes, it is just that kind of humour . . . I pray we might both have boys this time — they should be such great friends if we did, such very great friends . . .'

21st January 1687

In January, Lady Churchill is delivered of a boy, christened John after his father, as healthy and beautiful a child as could be wished for. Anne sends at once to congratulate her friend, and to ask if she might visit — she would not wish to arrive unannounced and unbidden, because that might vex Lady Churchill, and the mere thought of Lady Churchill vexed is enough to make Anne's eyes to water — but her message receives the warmest reply: Lady Churchill would be delighted to see the Princess whenever it might be convenient for Her Highness to come. Anne reads the brief letter over three times, and decides to go the very next morning.

She wakes up in the best of spirits, and first gives whole-hearted thanks to God for her friend's safe delivery. Then she calls for Sarah's deputy, Lady Frescheville, and for Danvers, to come dress her. Lady Frescheville has picked out Anne's favourite manteau without being asked; when Danvers hands her the looking-glass, she sees a good, clear complexion in it. It seems that the day can only go on delightfully, but then, suddenly — just as Danvers is easing on her right shoe — Anne feels something change inside her: she does not know what, or how, only that it is nothing good.

Her Ladyship asks her what the matter is.

'I do not know, Lady Frescheville, I only — all of a sudden — Danvers, do you remember what my sister was always saying, that she had a "melancholy qualm"?'

'Yes, Her Highness's qualms, I remember them very well.'

'I never knew what on earth it was she meant, but — I don't know what it is — I think I'm having one now.'

'Your Highness is ill? Is it a pain, Madam? Do you think — shall I send the page to the stables to say they are not to send the coach round?'

'No, I think I am well enough — I only felt a little out of sorts for a moment; it can only ever do me good to see my Lady Churchill, and I *must* see the baby. I have heard so much good of him already.'

So she does go to congratulate Lady Churchill, and to see with her own eyes that the boy is indeed healthy, and beautiful, in the way of both his healthy and beautiful parents. Anne could hardly be happier, she says more than once, if she had had such a son herself. When she begins the short journey home it is with enough vicarious joy inside her to last the rest of the day, but halfway back the carriage jolts, and all at once she is like a spilled water jug, gone from full to empty in an eyeblink.

The melancholy qualm is back, attended this time by a faint dragging pain in the belly.

'Lady Frescheville,' she says quietly, 'I fear that jolt has done me some hurt. I think I should rest awhile. I will go to my chamber — you may have my dinner brought to me there.'

'Shall I have Dr Radcliffe sent for?'

'No, I do not want Dr Radcliffe.'

'Sir Charles, then?'

'No — he will only make me his speech about apples. Send for Mrs Wilkes.'

Back at the Cockpit, Anne goes straight to her chamber, one hand cupping her belly all the way; she has Danvers undress her again, back down to her shift, and put her into bed. The Prince comes in and embraces her. She weeps a little into his shoulder, then sends him out. Whatever is happening, this is no place for him.

'Danvers, bring a clout, please. I fear there is some blood.'

Danvers does as she is bid, and brings a good stack of clean linen handkerchiefs, for which there is, if anything, the greater need. Anne sobs through three of them while she waits for Mrs Wilkes to arrive.

The midwife bursts into the room before Lady Frescheville has had a chance to announce her, remarking as she does so that she never yet met a lady who helped matters by crying herself into a swoon. The woman is, as always, harsh and rude and strong enough for anything. Anne can put her faith in that.

'Pull the covers back, Mrs Danvers. I must examine Her Highness.'

Anne submits herself once more to that shrewd gaze, those Amazonian hands.

'I was told Your Highness had had some pains.'

'Some. Only since the carriage jolted.'

'Are you sure?'

Suddenly she is not at all sure.

'When did you last feel a quickening?'

'Not —' and it returns to her immediately, that morning's melancholy qualm, the exact instance of it, the understanding of its true cause, '— not since last night. No, not all

312

day!' She falls to weeping again. The midwife covers her up again, takes her hand — a firm grip.

'Your Highness, I can see that there is yet only a little blood, and you did right — you did very right — in calling me, but I must needs be truthful with you.'

Anne starts howling, but Mrs Wilkes carries on remorselessly.

'The child has fallen in your belly. I believe you will miscarry soon.'

'Will you be able to stay with me, Mrs Wilkes — until . . . ?'

'Yes, Your Highness, I shall.'

Anne has heard often that the pain of a womb forced open before its time is worse than that of childbirth, and she has two full days to learn the truth of this. The blood flows slow at first, thick and heavy, then faster, redder, until one last agonising rush, that brings out with it a four-months' child, her miscarried son. Then the Queen visits to commiserate; Anne cannot stop her.

'I grieve for you, Anne — I know only too well what you have endured.'

'I know that, Your Majesty. Are you recovered from this summer last?'

'I am not sure — I think so — but I do have hopes of conceiving again. You too. Some say, my dear, a woman miscarried of a son is half with child again already.'

'If it does not stop the womb altogether. I think that is what befell poor Mary.'

'Try not to give way to melancholy, Anne. We must all strengthen ourselves, and pray . . . And I shall try the waters at Bath — Dr Walgrave thinks they might agree with me better than Tunbridge — perhaps you might come with me, when you are well enough?'

'Thank you, Your Majesty, but I find the Tunbridge waters agree with me well enough.'

2ND AND 8TH FEBRUARY 1687

It is the cruellest season. God gives Anne only the briefest time to regain her strength — she is not even finished bleeding — before he tests her again, and harder. On the eve of her grandfather's martyrdom, as she contemplates putting on the mourning dress that will agree so well with her melancholy, Lady Frescheville scratches on her closet door, and tells her that Lady Anne's nurse, Mrs Wanley, is waiting outside, very much distressed.

Mrs Wanley is a sanguine woman, rarely put out of temper, let alone distressed, and Lady Anne a vigorous child. Before the nurse has even spoken, Anne knows that this is something terrible.

'Take me to my girl,' she says, 'and tell me what is the matter on the way. Lady Frescheville, come with us.'

They run, all three of them — it is a pity they cannot fly — and the nurse relates her story in agitated little bursts: the child was first fretful, as if in discomfort; would not suck, or eat, so the nurse thinking it was the thrush in her mouth again gave her a little physic for that — as Her Highness said before that she should — but still she would not suck, and then she watched and would not sleep all day, and now this evening she has grown all of a sudden feverish, and cries so pitifully, she must be in pain . . .

As they approach the door of the nursery, Anne hears her younger daughter's cry, and it is a cry to make the heart sink, the thin, high-pitched, insistent cry of a child grown very, very sick. The baby is lying in the arms of a very young and frightened rocker; her head is thrown back and her mouth wide open, the very picture of agony.

'Give her to me.'

The baby shows no signs of knowing her mother, only continues to scream and writhe in her arms. Anne carries her as close as she can to the nearest candle, and peers into the screaming mouth. She cannot make anything out.

'You said her mouth was sore?' she asks the nurse.

'Yes, Your Highness.'

'Lady Frescheville, have Dr Radcliffe sent for — and have Farthing come to me. Mrs

—' It is not like her, but she cannot suddenly, for the life of her, recall the woman's name. 'Madam — you have such clear skin — have you had smallpox?'

'No, Your Highness.'

'Well, I — I have the most dreadful apprehension, and I think I must nurse my child myself, and you must go —'

'Your Highness? But who will give her suck?'

'She is near weaned already! Go! I will have no-one in this nursery who has not had smallpox! So not the Prince! The Prince must not come! And you must take the Lady Mary to my chamber at once and keep her there! And get me Dr Radcliffe! And GO!'

Mrs Wanley runs out of the room, much affrighted, and the rocker after her; Mary's nurse gathers her up and follows them. Anne sinks heavily down into a chair, the baby still in her arms, and joins her tears to her child's.

'I am sorry, my love,' she whispers, 'I am so wretched — they are my sins visited on you, my backsliding, my want of respect to . . . I will pray now.

'O Almighty God, and merciful Father, to whom alone belong the issues of life and death . . .'

When Dr Radcliffe comes, he cannot confirm Anne's suspicion, but neither can he reassure her.

'There is not much one might safely give a child of such a tender age — you may use the ointment again for her sore mouth, if you wish — you might try a fomentation to draw the humour out — otherwise, Your Highness, you can only watch, and comfort the child as much as she will let you.'

He does not say, 'Pray.' He should.

'. . . look down from heaven, I humbly beseech thee, with the eyes of mercy upon this child now lying upon the bed of sickness . . .'

Before long, the baby has exhausted herself enough that she sleeps at last; Anne sponges her skin with rosewater to try and cool her, then sits with her child in her arms, watching the light from fire and candle shudder on the walls, and searching her heart for whatever sickness there might be in it, that has been answered by this sickness in her child. She wonders if she should go to Chapel tomorrow, to fast and pray with the Court, but decides that she had better fast and pray in the nursery instead.

'. . . Visit her, O Lord, with thy salvation; deliver her in the good appointed time from her bodily pain, and save her soul for thy mercies' sake: that if it should be thy pleasure to prolong her days here on earth. Prolong her days here on earth. Prolong her days here on earth. Prolong her days here on earth. Prolong her days . . .'

The baby's cries start her awake again. Farthing is pushing the shutters back: the daylight is sharp and truthful, and picks out every blister. But perhaps it is the measles? It may yet be the measles. Dr Radcliffe comes again: it is not the measles; it is smallpox and could not be anything else. Little Anne's eyes are swollen shut.

'It may be distressing for you to look upon, Your Highness, but it may be that the humour is coming out, and that is a good thing — we must do what we can to assist it, and watch, and wait.'

He will recommend no internal physic. Together, Anne and Farthing throw rosemary on the fire and stoke it up, swaddle the baby in heavy red cloth, hang the room with more; watch; bargain; plead.

'. . . If it shall be thy pleasure to prolong her days here on earth, she may live to thee, and by an instrument of thy glory, by serving thee faithfully, and doing good in her generation . . .'

The baby suffers, and grows hourly more unrecognisable. Anne watches her, fasts, keeps in mind her grandfather's martyrdom, and her own sins. When night falls, Farthing persuades her to take a little nourishment herself, and try to sleep for a while. True sleep is impossible, but she soon feels herself falling into some strange between-state, in which Farthing, walking to and fro, and the baby in her arms, cannot stay themselves for two moments together, but instead are subject to change after change, becoming Lady Frances with Catherine, Aunt Madame with Isabella, Anne's mother with Anne's lost daughter, Mary (Mary? Dead?), weeping over Anne's lost son . . . and now there is a tall man, without his wig, standing in front of her — the late King? No. She has woken up, and it is the Prince.

'George! What are you doing here? I said you were to stay away! Now you will catch the distemper — oh George!'

'Shhh, my dear — Lady Frescheville said she would come, but I said I ought to tell you myself.'

'Tell me what?'

He is crying. 'Mary has fallen sick.'

'Mary too! Send for —'

'I already did.'

Anne has little doubt that Mary's fever is from the same cause as her sister's. Still, she waits until the blisters have shown themselves before she has Mary moved back to the nursery. By then, another full day has passed, and her poor, fond dolt of a husband is complaining of a headache.

As Mary's blisters begin to push up through her skin — hard yet, like lead shot — little Anne's are turning to pustules, bursting, crusting over. Her face is pitiful to look on now: even if she recovers, Anne fears her beauty will be spoiled before it has appeared. If she recovers: she is still alive, but there is a stench coming off her now, of flesh decaying.

'. . . or else receive her into those heavenly habitations, where the souls of them that sleep in the Lord Jesus enjoy perpetual rest and felicity.'

Her affliction is so terrible to witness, it is almost a relief to Anne when at last it pleases God to take her away.

But Mary has not succumbed yet; neither has George, although he has sickened just as she feared he would. Dr Radcliffe examines him, predicts that the sickness will take a less severe course in his case, but decides that it would do him no harm to be bled. He is altogether more cautious where Mary is concerned. Anne questions, persuades, disputes, all but screams in his face, and eventually he concedes that, as she is a little bigger than her sister, he might without too much danger apply a couple of leeches to her. After some searching, they find a suitable patch of skin — it is on her leg, so sufficiently far away from her delicate nobler parts, and the pox there are just far enough apart to leave some space — and attach two of the creatures to it. Mary makes no complaint as they latch on: she is in pain enough already from the blisters, that their little bitings and barkings can make only the smallest impression. Anne and the physician watch the leeches grow fat; the next day, Mary seems a little stronger, but the day after that she succumbs.

Anne moves to the Prince's bedside. She will nurse him as she nursed their daughters. He will recover, and then they will mourn together.

'Grant this, O Lord, for thy mercies' sake, in the same thy Son our Lord Jesus Christ, who liveth and reigneth with thee and the Holy Ghost, ever one God, world without end. Amen.'

FROM THE PRINCESS OF DENMARK TO THE PRINCESS OF ORANGE

The Cockpit, March 13 1687

This letter going by sure hands, I will now venture to write my mind very freely to you, and in the first place must tell you that the satisfaction I proposed to myself of seeing you this spring has been denied me, which has been no small trouble to me as you may easily imagine; and the disappointment has been the greater because the King gave me leave when I first asked; for the night I came from Richmond, I desired him to give the Prince leave to go into Denmark, and me to go into Holland, which he granted immediately without any difficulty, but in a few days after he told me I must not go. So that it is plain he has spoke of it to somebody that persuaded him against it, and it is as certain that the body was Lord Sunderland, for the King trusts him with everything; and he going on so fiercely for the interests of the Papists, is afraid that you should be told a true character of him, and this I really believe is the reason why I was refused coming to you; though maybe he and the priests together give other reasons to the King. Therefore, since I am not to see my dear sister, I think myself obliged to tell you the truth of everything this way, that it may not be in anybody's power (if I can help it) to deceive you. And by the kindness you express in all your letters, I have reason to believe you will credit me before another, both as a sister and a friend: and that I may desire these names, I will deal as sincerely with you as 'tis possible.

You may remember I have once before ventured to tell you that I thought Lord Sunderland a very ill man, and I am more confirmed every day in this opinion. Everybody knows how often this man turned backwards and forward in the late King's time; and now, to complete all his virtues, he is working with all his might to bring in Popery. He is perpetually with the priests and stirs up the King to do things further than I believe he would of himself. Things are come to that pass now, that, if they go on much longer, I believe in a little while no Protestant will be able to live here. The King has never said a word to me about religion since the time I told you of; but I expect it every minute, and am resolved to undergo anything rather than change my religion: nay, if it should come to such extremities, I will choose to live on alms rather than change.

This worthy Lord does not go publicly to Mass, but hears it privately at a priest's chamber, and never lets anybody be there but a servant of his. So that there is nobody but a priest can say they have seen him at Mass, for to be sure his servant will turn at any time he does. Thus he thinks he carries his matters swimming, and hopes you will hear none of these things that he may always be as great as he is now.

His Lady, too, is as extaordinary in her kind, for she is a flattering, dissembling, false woman; but she has so fawning and endearing a way that she will deceive anybody at first and it is not possible to find out all her ways in a little time. She cares not at what rate she lives, but never pays anybody. She will cheat, though it be for a little. Then she has had her gallants, though it may be not as many as some other ladies have; and with all these good qualities she is a constant Church woman; so that to outward appearance one would think her a saint, and to hear her talk you would think she was a very good Protestant; but she is as much one as the other, for it is certain that her Lord does nothing without her.

By what I have said you may judge what good hands the King and Kingdom are in, and what an uneasy thing it is all good honest people, that they may seem to live civilly with this Lord and his Lady.

I had not your letter by Mr Dyckvelt till last week, but I have never ventured to speak to him, because I am not used to speak to people about business and this Lord is so much upon the watch that I am afraid of him. So I have desired my Lord Churchill (who is one that I can trust, and I am sure is a very honest man and a good Protestant) to speak to Mr Dyckvelt for me, to know what it is he has to say to me, and by the next opportunity I will answer it, for one dares not write anything by the post.

One thing there is, which I forgot to tell you about this noble Lord, which is, that it is thought if everything does not go as he would have it, that he will pick a quarrel with the Court and so retire, and by that means it is possible he will think he make his court to you.

But I have given you so just and true a character both of him and his lady that I hope it will not be in anybody's power to make you think otherways of them.

There is one thing about yourself which I can't help giving my opinion in, which is, that if the King should desire you and the Prince of Orange to come over to make him a visit I think it would be better (if you can make any handsome excuse) not to do it; for though I dare swear that the King could have no thought against either of you, yet since people can say one thing and do another, one cannot help being afraid. If either of you should come, I should be very glad to see you; but really if you or the Prince should come, I should be frightened out of my wits for fear any harm should happen to either of you.

Pray don't let anybody see this, nor don't speak of it: pray let me desire you not to take notice of what I have said to anybody except the Prince of Orange, for it is all treason that I have spoke; and the King commanded me not to say anything that I once thought of going into Holland, and I fear if he should know that it was no secret he would be angry with me. Therefore as soon as you have read this, pray burn it; for I would not that anybody the Prince of Orange and yourself should know what I have said. When I have another opportunity it is possible that I may have more to say, but for this time having written so much already I hope you will forgive me for saying no more now, but that no tongue can ever express how much my heart is yours.

Anne

THE MAN FROM THE HAGUE

There is nothing bearable in Whitehall. The air is injurious to George's health. The Cockpit's empty nursery is an open wound. The King has issued a Declaration of Indulgence, removing all impediments to office for all the Catholics he has already appointed, and to those he means to appoint. As long as Anne remains at the Cockpit, there can be no escape, from triumphant Catholics raised up and angry Hydes brought low, from the watchful eyes of Sunderlands, from the Queen's often-expressed fellow feelings, from looks that pity or gloat, and are in either case insupportable. Anne makes a brief tour, incognito, of certain London churches and their anti-Papist preachers, for her own comfort, and for the benefit of those who have eyes to see her do it, and then the Denmarks retreat to Richmond.

There the red-brick walls, the oak furniture, her old chamber greet and hold her like a child restored. It is spring in the Park again, there is a tree there that still looks like a man, the red hinds are heavy with their fawns, and Anne finds herself with child again. One prayer answered, at least. If it were not for the lack of sure hands to deliver her true thoughts to Mary, she could find no fault in the place.

Without such a pair of hands, she has to write to Mary by the regular post, and can only write to her of the company she has had, the honour the King and Queen do her in coming to dine, the progress of George's portrait, the latest Court dances, and whether or not Lords' daughters might sit with her in the Chapel Closet. Naturally there are other, more pressing subjects on which she would prefer to speak her mind; before long her impatience proves stronger than her caution, and she agrees to a meeting with Dyckvelt. She will have Lord Churchill with them, and his Lady. Churchill is such a fine, well-favoured gentleman, so softly-spoken, so gentle in his manner — Anne finds him to be a reassuring, trustworthy presence. It is one opinion she shares with her father.

They take a stroll together, Anne and Dyckvelt, the Churchills walking a short distance behind. It is a beautiful day, a perfect opportunity to show Mr Dyckvelt the Park, and to speak out of earshot. At first sight, Anne is pleasantly surprised in him: she would not have expected such pretty manners in a Dutchman, and his English has only a slight trace of that most absurd of accents.

'The Prince of Orange has charged me with offering you his sincere condolences on the loss of your children, Your Highness.'

'Thank him from me. I have received several kind letters from the Princess too.'

'He trusts, as a good Protestant, that you will find much comfort in the Word. *They that sow in tears, shall reap in joy.*'

Good English Scripture: how reassuring to hear it. She almost smiles.

'I have had that very Psalm from both my chaplains, Sir, and from my Lord Compton — and at least two bedchamber women. And you may tell the Prince and Princess —' she drops her voice, quite unnecessarily, but it is lately become a habit with her — 'that I am with child again.'

'Congratulations, Your Highness. We will all be praying that you and the Prince may see a happy outcome.'

'Thank you. I do not think I have been so well since . . . since February, but the air here is doing me much good. And the Prince too — he is much recovered from his distemper.'

'The Prince and Princess will be greatly relieved to hear of it. As your kin — and also, as your *friends*. Your Highness, I know that you have ventured to write to the Princess in very plain terms — I hope you will feel emboldened to talk plainly to me here. The Prince will always deal honestly with those he can look upon as friends, and what you say to me, you say to the Prince and Princess of Orange — and nobody else.'

They are halfway to the man-tree. Anne stops walking for a moment, and waits for the Churchills to catch up, that she might see their faces. She looks from one to the other: they smile and nod.

'I am their friend, Sir. I am sure no-one could have more kindness for my sister — and for those she loves so sincerely — than I do.'

'Or could express that kindness with such admirable simplicity, Your Highness. I must reassure you that the Prince and Princess have a kindness for you, and a great and sincere concern for your interests. Your sister, in particular, is most anxious to know whether you are well-treated here, in respect to your religion, and in other ways.'

'For myself, I have nothing to complain of. The King and Queen always profess a great kindness for me, when I need funds they are granted, and it is true that they do not trouble me about my religion . . .'

'But . . . ?'

'Last year I had a visit from Monseigneur de Bonrepaux.'

'We would expect as much. What did he say?'

'There is something he said that I cannot get out of my head, though I don't quite believe it can be true — he did not talk in a straight way, for sure —'

'These Catholic worthies do like to mystify their listeners,' Sarah mutters, but loud enough to be heard.

'He wanted me to understand that it was possible that the King — with the French King's help of course — would seek to have my sister and me put out of the succession, in favour of his . . . natural Catholic sons.'

'I am sorry to hear that, Madam, but not very much surprised. It is a very French tactic: King Louis believes that he has only to make a show of his might, and we will all bow before him. But he has been proved wrong in this more than once — and by my master. I would remind you that the Prince has risked his own life in defence of the

United Provinces, and been successful in it. He would risk it again to check French ambition — in the Low Countries . . . or anywhere else.'

'And if I may add something to that,' says Lord Churchill, 'I am certain that de Bonrepaux was only scaring you, for I do believe that the King has too much respect for the law and for the right succession to put you out in such a way. He would no more put his natural son on the throne than the late King would. The Princess of Orange will remain his heir apparent — that is why he is so anxious to convert her.'

'Well, he shall not contrive to do it,' Anne snaps. 'My sister and I are of one mind — and you may reassure her, for my part, that I am quite resolved, by the assistance of God, to suffer all extremities, even to death itself, rather than be brought to change my religion.'

'Do you fear any of these extremities?'

'I do not know so . . . as I said, the King is not ungenerous to me, and the Queen always professes a great kindness for me, but then again he would not permit me to visit my sister, which would have been such a comfort to me who has been so afflicted, and . . .'

The party stops for moment, while Lady

Churchill helps Anne to compose herself.

'Forgive me, Sir. I think that where it comes to my religion, the King would always use fair means rather than foul, but I have writ treason already, and he has shown there is a coldness in him. You must know when my cousin Monmouth was captured, the King granted him an audience but then it was only to tell him to his face that he was condemned. I do not understand how he could do that — his own brother's son . . .'

'I have heard that story, Your Highness. It is a very terrible one.'

'The King's treatment of the rebels was altogether terrible,' says Lady Churchill.

'We all know that, my dear,' her Lord says, 'but the Duke must have known what was at stake, if he failed. And for the time being at least, we can say that the King's relations with his other Protestant nephew are cordial enough — are they not, Mr Dyckvelt?'

'Yes, my Lord. The King writes often to him of the weather in England.'

'And is the Prince much interested in the weather?' Anne asks.

'The weather over the Channel, perhaps,' says Lady Churchill. Her husband bids her hush, but she adds, somewhat sulkily, that the Princess knows perfectly well what they are about, and is every bit as capable as they of remaining discreet.

'Let's hope she's more capable than you are, Sarah.'

'Oh *pish*! We are all friends here.'

'But their correspondence is not only about the weather?'

'No, Your Highness, and I'm afraid it will be less cordial by and by: the Prince does not much like your father's recent Declaration, or his choice of officers for the English troops in Holland.'

'The same as his choices here, no doubt — first one Papist, then another, then a whole mob of them.'

'Exactly. The Prince and Princess are very much of your opinion — as are many others, a good number of them within this Kingdom. Some of them are known to you — you may rely on them as friends, as you put it, "sure hands." You will always be able to write freely to your sister — and she to you.'

'But I cannot always find them — and then I am compelled to write my sister letters with nothing in them.'

'We have thought of this. In such cases, you will need to use another name to stand for the King's.'

Anne giggles. 'We do that already a little:

sometimes the Earl of Sunderland is "Roger." It is a little like when we were girls in this place, and Lady Churchill used to deliver our secret letters — do you remember?'

'Of course, Madam. Perhaps we can agree a name now, so that Mr Dyckvelt may carry it back to The Hague?'

'Yes . . . the Duke of something?'

'Better make him a plain "mister", Your Highness, such as might work in the Palace,' says Lord Churchill, 'for he can't know them all, there are so many of them.'

'Mr . . . Brown?'

'That sort of name, yes, but we could make it a little less, erm . . .'

'. . . less of a likely sham,' says his wife. 'I have it: how about "Mr Mansell"?'

'And who is this Mansell, my dear, on whom you plainly seek revenge?'

'Mr Mansell from St Alban's, who sold us pewter already cracked, and when the housekeeper complained of it, he blamed the kitchen maid, and accused 'em both of cooking up a scheme to cheat him! In the end I had to drive to his shop and deal with him myself.'

'. . . and still he trembles. Your Highness, shall we take this knave's name?'

'I can remember "Mr Mansell", Sir. Mr

Dyckvelt, is that a suitable choice?'

'Perfect, Your Highness.'

So now they have reached the man-tree, their business is done and it is time to go back.

From the Princess
of Denmark to the
Princess of Orange

Richmond, May 9 1687

When I writ to my dear sister by Sir H. Capell, I had not time to say anything to you, and being very well assured that my letter is safe in this bearer's hands, I chose rather to write my mind freely to you by him, than by Sir H. Belasyse.

I suppose you have heard of the King's sending to the University of Cambridge to make a Friar a Master of Arts, and that they refused it, at which the King was very angry and sent for the Vice-Chancellor and others of the university. Last Saturday was the day they brought in their answer to the Commissioners why they could not obey the King, upon which the Lords Commissioners have put the Vice-Chancellor out of his places. He was Head of College besides, which is also taken from him, and, the benefits of it are ordered to go to the university. By this one may easily guess what one is to hope for henceforward, since the priests have so much power with the King as to make him do things so directly against the laws of the land, and indeed contrary to his own promises. It is a melancholy prospect that all we of the Church of England have; all the sectaries may now do what they please. Every one has the free exercise of their religion, on purpose no doubt to ruin us, which I think to all impartial judges is very plain. For my own part, I expect every minute to be spoke to about my religion, and wonder very much I have heard nothing of it yet: whenever the King does speak to me, you shall be sure to have an exact account from me.

In the meantime, all I desire is that you would not believe any reports of me, whatever you may hear: but assure yourself, I will ever be firm to my principles, and neither threatenings nor promises shall ever make me change my religion, which I hope you are already very well assured of.

This last honour the King has conferred on Lord Sunderland will, I doubt not, make him drive on our destruction with more haste and eagerness than he has yet done. His Lady, too, is now in all appearance like to be a favourite with the Queen for now the Lady Rochester is dead, there is nobody to put the Queen in mind often how ill a woman Lady Sunderland is. The Queen of late has no good opinion of Lady Rochester, yet the truth she told of Lady Sunderland did certainly keep her from growing great with the Queen while she lived. But now she is dead, Lady Sunderland — what with her fawning, insinuating way, and the court her Lord makes to the Queen — is to be feared will grow in great favour; and then, no doubt, she will play the Devil, for she has no religion, though she pretends to a great deal; and so she is great, she cares not who she ruins. And to say truth, she does not want wit nor cunning, and that, with her ill nature together, may make her capable of doing a great deal of mischief. The Queen, you must know, is of a very proud, haughty humour; and though she pretends to hate all form and ceremony, yet one sees that those that make their court this way are very well thought of. She declares always that she loves sincerity and hates flattery, but when the grossest flattery in the world is said to her face, she seems exteremely well pleased with it. It is really enough to turn one's stomach to hear what things are said to her of this kind, and to see how mighty she is satisfied with it. All these ways Lady Sunderland has in perfection, to make her court to her. She is now much oftener with the Queen than she used to be.

It is a sad and very uneasy thing to be forced to live civilly and as it were freely with a woman that one knows hates one, and does all she can do to undo everybody; which she certainly does.

One thing I must say of the Queen, which is that she is the most hated in the world of all sorts of people; for everybody believes that she pressed the King to be more violent than he would be of himself; which is not unlikely, for she is a very great bigot in her way, and one may see by her that she hates all Protestants. All ladies of quality say that she is proud that they don't care to come oftener than they must needs, just out of mere duty. And indeed, she has not so great a Court as she used to have. She pretends to have a great deal of kindness to me, but I doubt it is not real, for I never see proofs of it, but rather the contrary. It is not for me to complain, and as long as she does not make the King unkind to me, I don't care what she is; but I am resolved always to pay her a great deal of respect, and make my court very much to her, that she may not have any just cause against me.

My dear sister sees now that I deal very freely with you, and tell you what I think of everything and everybody; the plainness and sincerity of what I have said will, I hope, be acceptable to you; and indeed I think myself obliged, whenever I have an opportunity, to give you an exact account of everything, because I fear there is nobody else will tell you the truth so freely, without any disguise, as I have done.

I spoke about a fortnight ago with Mr Dyckvelt, and though I did not before doubt of your kindness, yet it was a very great pleasure to me to hear so may assurances both from the Prince of Orange and yourself. Mr Russell also has given me the same assurances. If I writ whole volumes, I could never express how sensible I am both of yours and the Prince of Orange's kindness: it is what I value more than you can believe; and I hope you are but so just to me as not to doubt of the kindness I have for you which shall be lasting as my life, and ready to show itself on all occasions.

The Prince thinks of going into Denmark the end of this month, and when he is away I fancy the King will speak to me about my religion, for then he will find me more alone than yet he has done.

This bearer will come back again, I believe, in a short time, so that I shall have an answer of this by him, or if Sir H. Capell should come sooner, it will be very safe by him too.

If there be anything that I have not mentioned that you have a mind to know, or that I can do you any service of any kind here, pray let me know it, that I may show you how faithfully I will obey you in anything that lies in my power.

There are a great many books that come out every day about religion, and a great many of our side, that are very well writ. If you care to see any of them, let me know it and I will send you those that are best worth reading.

My dearest sister, farewell: this is the last opportunity I am likely to have before Mr Dyckvelt goes: whenever I know of any, you may assure yourself I will give you an account of all things that passes here.

Anne

ANNE'S FEAR

In June, the Prince sails to Denmark, and Anne removes to Hampton Court, a little further upstream, a little more distant from Whitehall and all that the King and Queen do there. She is in hourly expectation of the King's coming to speak with her about her religion, but as the days pass and he does not come, so more and more she looks upon the prospect of his visit as she might the drawing of a tooth, dreading it but at the same time wishing for it, so as to get it over with.

The King does not come in July, probably because he has more urgent business: Parliament has made it clear that it does not like his Declaration, so naturally he has had to dissolve it. Then he embarks on Progress through the West Country, to see what help might be found there. Anne is allowed to remain where she is, free to stroll in the Park and think of Elizabeth, Protestant, persecuted and ultimately triumphant, who used to hunt there. Anne would very much like to follow her example, but at the end of the month, the King issues a notice that no person, of what quality soever, may kill any animal by any means within ten miles round the Palace of Hampton Court, unless they have his particular leave, and she cannot help feeling a little persecuted by *that* — no doubt the Queen put him on to it, but then her mother has just died, so Anne does not feel that it would be quite fair to resent her too much at this time on this particular account. She sends her a very proper condolence note.

Apart from this inconvenience, the only ordeal she has to withstand is a visit from d'Adda, the Papal Nuncio, and that is more awkward than anything else. When the Prince arrives back in August, he finds Anne in reasonable health, at liberty, still Protestant, but still afraid.

She is afraid for her Church, for herself, for her Prince, but most of all for her baby. It is her one hope, her only blessing, and as long as she is carrying it, she must for its sweet life's sake stay away from anything that might fright or harm her. She will have no noxious smells about her, no over strong tastes, no extremes of hot or cold, no monsters, no deformed persons, no riotous noises, no heated arguments and as few Catholics as can be arranged. The Denmarks cannot avoid going to Windsor for a short time, to join the Court there, but leave as soon as they decently can, putting about that the Prince has a bad chest, and will find the weather at Hampton Court less cold and piercing.

It is a great relief to be back there, at first, but fear is such an excellent scent hound, and it sniffs her out again. She does not understand how it comes about, but the monstrousness of the King and Queen seems to increase in proportion with the time spent away from them, and their distance from her. She can think of nothing but their monstrousness, the monstrousness of all Catholics, and the threat to her child. Her head is full of Mr Foxe's martyrdoms, and she finds she cannot hinder herself from calling to mind a thousand times a day one illustration in particular, of an infant bursting from its burning mother's womb. The story is that it was taken out of the fire and laid on the grass, only for the bailiff to say that it should be carried back again and cast into the fire. And so was the infant baptised in his own blood, both born and died a martyr, leaving behind a spectacle wherein the whole world may see the Herodian cruelty of his graceless, Catholic tormentors.

Mrs Wilkes is Catholic, and the strength and skill of that woman, that was once such a comfort to Anne, seems now to come from a dark place, and meant for dark purposes. She must contrive a way to find another midwife, a Protestant one, without giving offence to the Queen. She will need to employ some sort of invention to bring it about. Everything in the world depends upon it.

22ND OCTOBER 1687

If it were up to Anne she would never leave, but it is not in her power: the King returns to Whitehall in October, and calls her back. Ten days later she is delivered of a stillborn son. The Protestant midwife, who is quite beyond any suspicion, says he has been dead in the womb a month already. Anne was a fool to have felt safe anywhere.

THE QUEEN IS WITH CHILD

Lord, I . . .

Lord, I must confess . . .

Lord, I cannot hinder . . .

Lord, I would die before I would curse thee to thy face, but I have come into my closet to pray and yet only the words of job come to mind: Oh that my grief were thoroughly weighed, and my calamity laid in the balances together! For now it would be heavier than the sand of the sea: therefore my words are swallowed up . . . For I have this last year had sorrows piled upon sorrows, and now the Queen is with child, and when I think of that my heart bleeds anew as if every wound it ever had were fresh . . . why must I be tormented this way? Why should she be raised up when I am so cast down? What has she done that you are so pleased with her? What have I done that you should chastise me so?

Every day I reckon up my account, and I try to number my sins, whatever they might be: that I have been disrespectful to the King — twice over, once because he is my father, and again because he is my King; that when I have sat in the Chapel Closet, I have maybe got more satisfaction than I should for being bowed to as if the King was there; that I have been too proud on those occasions, and too proud of my place in the succession, that I would so resent being put out of it; that I have loved my children too dearly, and grieved for them too loudly and too long . . . I know that they are yours; I know that I was as their wet-nurse only; I know that they are happy now. But still there are these arrows in me, and still the poison whereof drinketh up my spirit.

And whatever my sins may be, what has my dear Prince done, that you should punish him? For he too is much afflicted.

And what has the King done, and — I ask again — what has the Queen done — that you should be so gracious to them — and so gracious to the Bishop of Rome, and to my cousin Louis — that you should place this Kingdom in their hands? For you must know that the child is spoken of everywhere as a boy already. If this is indeed your Will, I can only beg you give me the grace to resign myself — if it is your Will — forgive me, Lord, but I cannot — no not even with the greatest effort — believe it ever could be.

THE KING'S VEXATION

Of all the things the late King did to vex the present one — and there were many — the passing of the Test Acts continues to gall him the most. The first makes it illegal for Catholics to hold any public office, be it civil or military; the second effectively bars them from Parliament. They have not, it is true, got in the way of his becoming King, and his Declaration of Indulgence has enabled him to suspend them for anyone he chooses to appoint, but this is not enough to satisfy him: he has desired Parliament to repeal them altogether. This Parliament has refused to do, and so he has had no choice but to dissolve it. The Kingdom is his: he should be able to order it as he sees fit.

The King has resolved to make sure that the next Parliament will prove more pliant. He needs to ensure a sympathetic majority, and for this he requires a sympathetic elec-torate.

To this end, he has ordered his Lord Lieutenants to put the following three questions to all men of substance in their respective counties:

1. In case he shall be chosen knight of the shire or burgess of a town when the King shall call a Parliament, whether he will be for taking off the penal laws and the tests.
2. Whether he will assist and contribute to the election of such members as shall be for taking them off. ·
3. Whether he will support the King's Declaration for liberty of conscience by living friendly with those of all persuasions as subjects of the same Prince and good Christians ought to do.

The Lord Lieutenants are then to take all the answers down, and give the King a full and precise account of them. Those that refuse to do so lose their places. Among these is Robert, Earl of Scarsdale, Lord Lieutenant of Derby.

Scarsdale is also Groom of the Stool to the Prince of Denmark. Following his disgrace, Anne asks the King whether he should also be removed from his place in her husband's household. The King is pleased to be asked, and replies that he shall leave it to their discretion. As Scarsdale has given neither Anne nor the Prince any reason for displeasure, they decide to retain him — then the King demands that he be dismissed, and replaced with the Earl of Huntingdon. Anne obeys, but with ill grace. Conspicuous ill grace, which anyone who knows of it is quite at liberty to report.

Of all the things the King has done to vex her, it is this act — this intrusion into her household — that galls her the most. It is her family: she should be able to order it as she sees fit.

THE QUEEN'S BELLY

There are mornings when Anne must wait on the Queen. It does not matter that they would both wish her anywhere else: it is proper, it is expected, and there is no telling what use might be made of it by certain parties, were she to stay away. So here she is, in the Queen's bedchamber, where Mrs Dawson, the Queen's Woman, is handing her the Queen's shift, so that Anne can help her on with it.

Lady Sunderland helps the Queen to ease off the old shift. Anne, who knows how little her step-mother likes to be seen naked, makes sure to leave only the shortest possible moment before dropping the clean shift over her upstretched arms and her head. It is not long enough to sneak more than a tiny glance at her belly, marking, as Anne does every time, that it seems strangely big for such an early stage of pregnancy: undoubtedly there is something in there, but it could well be a mole, or a monster, or nothing but wind. Or it could be that the Queen was already with child before she lay with the King, by the Papal Nuncio perhaps, or the King's Confessor, Father Petre.

Why not Father Petre? The King has raised him to the Privy Council, so why should the Queen not have raised him up too? And there is something grubby about the business of confession: it cannot but make priests lascivious to feel thus the privy parts of women's souls, and as for these Catholic women, why should they deny the secrets of their bodies to them, to whom they have already discovered the secrets of their souls?

Anne is careful not to meet the Queen's eyes, lest she read these pictures in her head. This is easy enough to do, as the Queen does not wish to meet her eyes either: she knows perfectly well what the rumours are; she has wept over them, and must certainly suspect Anne's part in spreading them.

They can barely look at each other. They can barely speak to each other. It falls to Lady Sunderland to fill the silence, by congratulating Anne on her own, more recent belly. She is kindly, respectful, and says everything that is proper, smiling charmingly all the while. Insufferable woman.

At last the Queen speaks, but not to Anne.

'Oh, Lady Sunderland! I feel a quickening! Come feel my belly!'

Smiling, she takes her Lady's hand, and presses it to her. Lady Sunderland nods, and they both make sure to look at Anne, whose hand the Queen has never taken to her belly, not this time, and not before. They were never on such easy terms.

From the Princess of Denmark to the Princess of Orange

The Cockpit, March 14 1688

I have now very little to say, however would not miss writing by this bearer by whom you told me I might say anything; and therefore knowing nothing else of any consequence I must tell you I can't help thinking Mansell's wife's great belly is a little suspicious. It is true indeed she is very big, but she looks better than she ever did, which is not usual: for people when they are so far gone, for the most part look very ill. Besides, it is very odd that the Bath, that all the best doctors thought would do her a great deal harm, should have so good effect so soon, as that she should prove with child from the first minute she and Mansell met, after her coming from thence. Her being so positive it will be a son, and the principles of that religion being such that they will stick at nothing, be it never so wicked, if it will promote their interest, give some cause to fear there may be foul play intended. I will do all I can to find it out, if it be so: and if I should make any discovery, you shall be sure to have an account of it.

I am very glad you don't disapprove of Lady Huntingdon, who I hope will ever deserve your good opinion whatever her Lord's behaviour may be. I must confess to you that would have hindered me from taking her if I could have met with anybody else that had been tolerable, but none having offered themselves that were at all fit, I made what haste I could to engage myself to her, for fear of having either a Papist or a spy imposed upon me.

Bentley being to go in a very little time I shall say no more at present, but end this with thanks for your kindness in giving me an account of what is passed between you and M. d'Abbeville, which I shall be sure to keep a secret. I have not heard a word of it from anybody but yourself, and you may be sure I can never have an ill opinion of my dear sister whatever I should hear, but shall be ready if ever there be occasion to justify you and to give the world that character of which you deserve.

Anne

[PS.] I think the spider would be a very good name for the noble marquess.

The Cockpit, March 20 1688

I hope you will instruct Bentley what you would have your friends to do if any alteration should come, as it is to be feared there will, especially if Mansell has a son, which I conclude he will, there being so much reason to believe it is a false belly. For, methinks, if it were not, there having been so many stories and jests made about it, she should, to convince the world, make either me or some of my friends feel her belly; but quite contrary, whenever one talks of her being with child, she looks as if she were afraid one should touch her. And whenever I happen to be in the room as she has been undressing, she has always gone into the next room to put on her smock.* These things give me so much just cause for suspicion that I believe when she is brought to bed, nobody will be convinced it is her child, except it prove a daughter. For my part, I declare I shall not, except I see the child and she parted.

Lord Rochester desires me to tell you he was much troubled to find by a letter he has lately from Mr Bentinck that you and the Prince of Orange are both so very angry with him, he never having done anything that he knows to deserve it, except his not waiting on you the last summer he was abroad, which he owns to be a very great fault and begs pardon for it and whatever else you think him guilty of, though he is very ignorant of any other crime. This I could not tell how to refuse him. Having spoken to me twice about it he seemed very much concerned, but it was in such a manner that looked rather as if it proceeded from the pitifulness of his spirit than anything else, though at the same time he assured me the concern he had was not out of

*This has happened often enough that it feels as good as true.

hopes of making any interest for the time to come, but because he would not have you nor I think him so ungrateful to our mother's memory as to do anything wilfully to displease her children.

I can't end my letter without telling you that Roger's wife plays the hypocrite more than ever, for she goes to St Martin's, morning and afternoon (for there are not people enough to see her at Whitehall Chapel) and is half an hour before other people come and half an hour after everybody is gone, at her private devotions. She runs from church to church after the famous preachers, and keeps such a clatter with her devotions that it really turns one's stomach. Sure there never was a couple as well matched as she and her good husband; for she is through-out in all her actions the greatest jade that ever was, so is he the subtillest workingest villain that is on the face of the earth.

The enclosed was to have gone by Mr Howe, but was left behind by mistake. I intended once to have sent it today by one Mr Sidney told me was a safe hand, but being sure this bearer is so, and going so soon I chose rather to keep it and send both letters together.

My dear sister, farewell; though I am not good at saying much for myself, yet believe my heart as sincere as it is possible, and assure yourself that my kindness for you and my constancy to my religion shall never end but with my life.

Anne

16 April 1688

The curtains have been pulled about Anne's bed. She lies there in the rich, reddish darkness, listening to the women talking about her. They must think she sleeps still, for they do not even trouble themselves to whisper.

'. . . could be it was a false conception,' Lady Frescheville says, 'there was so little to be seen, no-one could tell the sex this time.'

'It was early,' says Lady Churchill, back now after some months' absence, and with a new daughter of her own. 'They never can tell the sex when the miscarriage is so early.'

'And she is still so ill,' says Danvers. 'She never was so ill before. You were not here to see it, Lady Churchill — in those two days, before she lost the babe, she had a raging fever, her joints swelled, she had to be cupped twice —'

At this as if in confirmation, the wounds on Anne's back sting anew.

'And her breath was short; she was complaining of all kinds of pain,' says Lady Frescheville. 'It was terrible — and very strange withal.'

'It has been a sennight already since, and whatever ills she suffered before she would be sitting up by now, but this time she says she cannot.'

'Perhaps she might be persuaded,' Lady Churchill says. 'I do not mean she lies there on purpose — only that her spirits cannot but be dreadfully low — she needs some heart put into her.'

'The King was here again yesterday, Lady Churchill,' says another voice — Lady Huntingdon.

'Forgive me for saying so, Lady Huntingdon, but I cannot suppose that helped.'

Lady Huntingdon does not reply, though her discomfort is perfectly audible. Anne summons up as much strength as she has, and puts it into her voice.

'Lady Churchill?' she asks, sounding like a child. 'Is that Lady Churchill? Has she come from St Albans?'

The curtains open, revealing the prayed-for face.

'Yes, it is I, Your Highness. Forgive me for not having made my compliment — I thought you were asleep.'

'It *is* you. I thought perhaps I only imagined it — I have wished for you a thousand times — if you only knew —'

'Here, take my handkerchief.' Lady Churchill closes the curtains again. Then she shoos the other women out, opens the curtains, rearranges Anne's pillows, and helps her to sit up. She does not waste any time asking.

'There. Your Highness is sitting up. Do you feel any the worse for it?'

'No, thank you, and very much the better for seeing you. You look very well. What of your new girl — how does she go on?'

'She goes on extremely well, thank you, and so I am at your service — wholly.' She hands Anne a second handkerchief.

When Anne can speak again, she tells Lady Churchill that she heard what Lady Frescheville said.

'Then you heard I disagree with her. The day I pay any heed to Charlotte Frescheville is the day you'll know my wits have gone a-begging.'

'I know you dislike her, but she is not a bad sort. She does what I ask; she never keeps me waiting.'

'Oh she is reliable enough, I suppose — like a woman's months. No need to listen to her though.'

'She will not be the only one saying what she said.'

'No, she is not.'

'It was thinking that — about what people were saying — that made me want to stay a-bed so long —'

'I know.'

'— and I cannot help but call to mind what has been said of the Queen — what I have said myself — and I wonder if this is my chastisement for it.'

'But you have done nothing wrong, Your Highness.'

'But —'

'*Nothing,* you have waited on Her Majesty, you have paid her all due respect. What more could you do, in such circumstances?'

'I could have refrained from speaking against her and the King.'

Lady Churchill leans in, and whispers.

'So are you saying that you are so remorseful, it has changed your opinion of them?'

'No! No, not all. When the King visited, I could not even look at him.'

'What did he say? Did he bring a priest again?'

'No, thank God, and he said nothing to make me uncomfortable. But I knew he hoped this extremity might turn me Catholic — I could *feel* him wishing it.'

'I do not think *any* extremity could bring that about, Madam.'

'No . . . I am so dreadfully sorry, but I think I must lie down again . . .'

'Of course, Your Highness, but I believe you need nourishment too — I will have some broth fetched in a moment, and those women of yours will be scratching at the door — before they do,' and she whispers again, 'I must ask, has the Prince told you anything of the comings and goings here, while you were sick?'

'Comings and goings . . . he has mentioned some emissary from Holland . . . and he has had a visit from Bishop Compton, messages from Lord Lumley . . . but there are always messages, always visitors — what of it?'

'My Lord has not said anything to me, but I think — I think, just between the two of us, that there are fewer and fewer left who are not quite out of patience with the King — and I reckon the Prince of Orange is of their mind . . . And now you must lie down again if you need it, and I will get that broth fetched.'

ANNE IN BATH

It is a blessing indeed that the Prince of Orange has made his mind up to come, for it seems to Anne that God hardens her father's heart a little more each day. At the end of the month, as she endeavours to recover from a bout of colic which has put her flat on her back again, the King makes another Declaration of Indulgence, and orders it to be read in every church. It is plain that the prospect of a son to bring up in his own religion has made him the more determined in his purpose, and less tolerant of opposition. Anne cannot bear the thought of dining with him while he acts like this, or of dressing the Queen while her belly — her supposed belly — carries on growing, and her consequence with it. She does not want to leave her chamber and return to Court only to witness the Queen's triumph, and to be met everywhere with mockery and pity. She needs to recover her strength in peace, and Tunbridge Wells is not far enough away — she must go to Bath.

A physicians' conference is called to decide the matter. They line up at Anne's bedside — Dr Radcliffe, Sir Richard Lower, Sir Charles Scarborough — dark-coated and heavily bewigged — peer at her, have her give an account of herself, and pronounce their judgements:

Dr Radcliffe thinks her in no immediate danger; more than that, he thinks her as healthy a young woman as he has ever treated, in need of no more than good diet, air and exercise, and to stop imagining herself an invalid — but if she has a fancy for the Bath waters, he cannot see that it would do her any harm to go.

Sir Richard Lower — whom, if truth be told, Anne has always liked more — disagrees, and is urgent that she must go to Bath.

Sir Charles Scarborough — the most senior, the Queen's physician, and there at the King's suggestion — agrees that the Bath waters would do Her Highness good, but she must take a course of physic to prepare herself first. A lengthy one.

Sir Richard is vexed to be overruled, and saves face by prescribing Anne a steel diet. Not only is she still no nearer Bath, but she now has twice a day to take a condensed, powdered spoonful of the sort of stuff that makes the Tunbridge waters so unpleasant. It is no good: she calls another conference, without Sir Charles, and they are this time unanimous in their opinion that Anne must go, and take a six-week course. On 24th May, finally, she is able to leave, and anyone who thinks it odd of her to go away for such a long time without first seeing the Queen safely delivered, must content themselves with the explanation that her health requires it. The King has.

Bath is as far from London and as difficult to reach as Anne could wish. The journey takes five days by coach, and there is no way in or out of Bath that is not slow, steep and difficult. The smell of the place precedes the sight of it; by some distance, and the view when it finally comes is scarcely more pleasant: it is a mean-looking town, congested and dirty. Tunbridge would certainly have been more convenient in every respect — except that it is an easy drive from London.

At least the streets are easily avoided. The Denmarks lodge with Dr Pierce at Abbey House, and from here they can walk straight out onto the galleries around the baths, where the Sergeant of the Baths pays his compliment to them, and will summon guides to assist them to bathe. The lodgings are comfortable, and the doctor has a confidence in the waters which is most infectious. He procures a pint for Anne almost as soon as she arrives, and she finds them more than foul enough to do her good. A six-week course of drinking and bathing, he says, should ensure that her next child will be carried to perfection.

Dr Pierce chooses the Cross Bath for Anne's treatment. He says it will not heat her blood too much, and reminds her how well it worked in the Queen's case. Anne would rather not be reminded of the Queen, so it is unfortunate that she must look every time upon the Cross in the centre of the bath, which has been decorated in the Queen's honour, painted all over with saints and cupids, and the Este eagles. If it were not for the sight of the Cross, the whispering and staring from the Gallery, and the strong smell of eggs, the bathing would be pleasant enough. Three or four times a week, she is first dressed in a vast shift of fine yellow canvas, with enormous sleeves, that fills up in the water so that it takes the shape of an upended pudding bowl, and gives her at least a modicum of privacy. Two of the women guides help her into the water, which would be strong enough to tumble her down if they did not, and then two men guides clear a way for her as they lead her to her stone seat under an arch set into the wall, where she sits up to her neck and can enjoy an easy, pleasant talk with her favourite guide — another Anne — whose own growing belly she takes as a sign of the waters' good effects.

Over the next few weeks, while she bathes and the Prince plies Dr Pierce with questions about the particular properties of the waters, and does his best to discover what sort of wines are to be had in Bath, the news coming from London makes Anne gladder every day to be where she is. The Archbishop of Canterbury, along with seven other bishops, has refused to have the Declaration of Indulgence read. They have presented the King with a petition, asking to be excused and giving their reasons why; for this, he has summoned them before the Privy Council, which has accused them of seditious libel and had them sent to the Tower, where they are now awaiting trial. Their petition was printed and broadcast all over London, and crowds came down to the river to shout their support for them on their way to their captivity.

Anne reads this in letters from her friends,

who urge her in the same letters to return to London — she should not be away at such a time: she is reluctant at first, but they make a compelling case, and she is already preparing to leave, when Colonel Oglethorp arrives from Court with a message from the King: the Queen has given birth to a son — and not in July at Windsor, as had been expected and planned, but a month early, in St James's. In that same bedchamber with the ruelle, where Anne once hid, and surprised a necessary woman as she came in from the backstairs. Anne remembers it well: the girl was carrying a chamber pot on that occasion, but there are other objects that can be carried up and down the backstairs — warming-pans, for example, such as have hot bricks or coals in — though one might hide something else in one, if one was so inclined. And then convey that something to Mrs Wilkes, waiting at the foot of the bed — cunning Mrs Wilkes, with her large and clever hands.

Colonel Oglethorp says he has seen the baby, in the flesh, with his own eyes. Well, it is certain enough that a baby has been produced — but where from?

London has a certain skittishness about it, in the way that fairs do just before the brawling starts. On one side are the Papists of the King's Court, all puffed up by the supposed birth or a supposed heir, and growing every day more insolent; on the other side, and far more numerous, are all the people who cannot or will not believe, muttering, publishing, preaching, versifying, swapping tales of changelings and warming-pans, passing about maps of St James's Palace to show how easily the trick was done, sharing pictures of the Queen pinning a cushion to her shift or doing unspeakable things with priests — because the King and Queen between them, as everyone must know by now, are fit only to produce a race of ninnies. There are far more bonfires lit for the bishops' acquittal than there were for the birth of the Prince.

Anne does her best to steer a course

through all this, dissembling where she must, but letting her opinions be known where she can. On 8th July she joins a large congregation at the Chapel Royal to hear a sermon preached on Exodus 14:13:

And Moses said to the people, Fear ye not, stand still, and see the salvation of the Lord, which he will shew to you to day: for the Egyptians whom ye have seen to day, ye shall see them again no more for ever.

It is very plain to everybody who are the people, and who the Egyptians. Did God not harden Pharaoh's heart, in order to destroy him? Anne fears not: she stands still, and sees salvation coming: the people are all of a mind, which is heartening; the King has accepted her physicians' latest recommendation, that she leave for Tunbridge Wells; Lord Churchill has told her that a letter of invitation has been sent to the Prince of Orange, that the army is packed already with his supporters, and that when the time and the weather are right, he will come. Salvation is coming.

And when it comes, Anne will be ready. Before she leaves, she gives instructions for extensive refurbishments to the Chapel

Royal and orders a back staircase to be built at the Cockpit — for how can anyone plot without backstairs? She also has a little work to do for Mary, so she summons Mrs Dawson.

FROM THE PRINCESS OF DENMARK TO THE PRINCESS OF ORANGE

The Cockpit, July 24, 1688

I received yesterday yours of the 19th, by which I find you are not satisfied with the account I have given you in my last letter; but I hope you will forgive my being no more particular, when you consider, that not being upon the place, all I could know must be from others; and having been but a few days in town, I had not time to inquire so narrowly into things, as I have since; but before I say any more, I can't help telling you I am very sorry you should think I would be negligent in letting you know things of any consequence. For though I am generally lazy, and it is true indeed, when I write by the post, for the most part, I make those letters very short, not daring to tell you any news by it, and being very ill at invention, yet I hope you will forgive my being lazy when I write such letters, since I have never missed any opportunity of giving you all the intelligence I am able; and pray be not so unjust to believe I can think the doing anything you desire, any trouble; for certainly I would do a great deal more for you, if it lay in my power, than the answering your questions, which I shall do now as exactly you desire.

1. I never heard anybody say they felt the child stir; but I am told Lady Sunderland and Madam Mazarin say they felt it at the beginning. Mrs Dawson tells me she has seen it stir, but never felt it.
2. I never saw any milk; but Mrs Dawson says she has seen it upon her smock, and that it began to run at the same time it used to do of her other children.
3. For what they call restringing draughts, I saw her drink two of them; and I don't doubt but she drank them frequently and publicly before her going to the Bath. Dr Waldgrave was very earnest with Sir Charles Scarbrough, to

be for her going thither; but he was so fierce against it, that there was another consultation of doctors called, Sir Charles Scarbrough, Dr Waldgrave, Wetherby, Brady, and Brown. After that there was only Sir Charles Scarbrough and Dr Waldgrave (and for this first I believe he knew but little), excepting once when she was to be let blood, and when she was to have gone to Windsor. Then some of the others were called in to give their opinions.

4. All I can say in this article is, that once in discourse, Mrs Bromley told Mrs Robarts, one day Roger's daughter came into the room, when Mrs Mansell was putting off her clouts, and she was very angry at it, because she did not care to be seen when she was shifting.

5. She fell in labour about eight o'clock.

6. She sent for the King at that time, who had been up a quarter of an hour, having lain with her that night, and was then dressing.

7. As soon as the King came he sent for the Queen Dowager and all

the council. After that, it was known all over St James's.

8. Most of the other men, I suppose, that were there, was at the King's rising.

9. They came into the room presently after the Queen Dowager came, which is about half an hour before she was brought to bed.

10. There was no screen. She was brought to bed in the bed she lay in all night, and in the great bed-chamber, as she was of her last child.

11. The feet curtains of the bed were drawn, and the two sides were open. When she was in great pain, the King called in haste for my Lord Chancellor, who came up to the bedside to show he was there; upon which the rest of the privy councillors did the same thing. Then the Queen desired the King to hide her face with his head and periwig, which he did, for she said she could not be brought to bed and have so many men look on her; for all the council stood close to the bed's feet, and Lord Chancellor upon the step.

12. As soon as the child was born, the midwife cut the navel-string, because the after-burthen did not follow quickly; and the she gave it to Mrs Labaudie, who, as she was going by the bedside, across the step, to carry it into the little bed-chamber, the King stopped her, and said to the privy councillors, that they were witnesses there was a child born, and bid them follow it into the next room and see what it was, which they all did; for till after they came out again, it was not declared what it was; but the midwife had only given a sign that it was a son, which is what had been done before.

13. When the Queen Dowager first came into the room she went up to the bedside, but after that stood all the while by the clock. There was in the room Lord Chancellor, Lord President, Lord Privy Seal, the two Lord Chamberlains, Lord Middleton, Lord Craven, Lord Huntingdon, Lord Powis, Lord Dover, Lord Peterborough, Lord Melfort, Lord Dartmouth, Sir John Ernley, Lord

Preston, Sir Nicholas Butler, Duke of Beaufort, Lord Berkeley, Lord Moray, Lord Castlemaine; these were of the council; and for the others, there was Lord Feversham, Lord Arran, Sir Stephen Fox, and Mr Griffin, besides pages of the backstairs and priests. The women that were there were Lady Peterborough, Lady Belasys, Lady Arran, Lady Tyrconnel, Lady Roscommon, Lady Sophia Buckley, Lady Fingall, Madam Mazarin, Madam Bouillon, Lady Powis, Lady Strickland, Lady Ceary, Mrs Crane, two of the Queen Dowager's Portugueses, Mrs Bromley, Mrs Dawson, Mrs Waldgrave, Lady Wentworth, and Mrs Turine. All these stood as near as they could. Lady Belasys gave the midwife the receiver, and Mrs Dawson stood behind a Dutch chair that the midwife sat upon to do her work. All the time the child was parted, I do not hear of anybody that held the Queen except the King, and he was upon the bed by her all the while.

14. I don't hear that any ladies were

sent for but the Queen's own, and they were called presently after the Queen Dowager. She came a quarter after nine. Where she stood, and at what time she was sent for, I have already told you.

15. Her labour never used to be so long.

16. I never heard what you say of the child's limbs. As for seeing it dressed or undressed, they avoid it as much as they can. By all I have seen and heard, sometimes they refuse almost everybody to see it; that is, when they say it is not well; and methinks there is always a mystery in it, for one does not know whether it be really sick, and they fear one should know it, or whether it is well, and they would have one think it is sick, as the other children used to be. In short, it is not very clear anything they do; and for the servants, from the highest to the lowest, they are all Papist.

17. The Queen forbid Lady Powis to bring the child to her before any company; but that, they say, she used to do her other children. I

dined there the other day, when it was said it had been very ill of a looseness, and it really looked so; yet when she came from prayers she went to dinner without seeing it, and after that played at comet, and did not go to it till she was put out of the pool.

18. I believe none of the bedchamber women have any credit with the Queen but Mrs Turine; but they say Mrs Bromley has an interest with the King.

I am going to Tunbridge; but if I was to stay here I could not watch the child, for it is to be at Richmond. Lady Churchill does not go with me at first, and as long as she stays here I am sure she will do all in her power to give you and I an account if anything happens that is worth knowing.

I have done my endeavour to inform myself of everything, for I have spoke with Mrs Dawson, and asked her all the questions I could think of: for not being in the room when the Queen was brought to bed, one must inquire of somebody that was there; and I thought she could tell me as much as anybody, and be less likely to speak of it; and I took all the care I could, when I spoke to her, to do it in such a manner that I might know everything; and in case she should betray me, that the King and Queen might not be angry with me.

It was she that told me what I have said in the 5, 6, 7, 9, 12, 13, 14 and 15th articles. She told me, besides that when she came to the Queen, she found Mrs Turine and the midwife with her. All that she says seems very clear; but one does not know what to think; for methinks it is wonderful if it is no cheat, that they never took no pains to convince me of it.

I hope I have answered your letter as fully as you desire; if there be anything else you would know, pray tell me by the first safe hand, and you shall always find me very diligent in obeying you, and showing by my actions how real and sincere my kindness is.

One thing I had forgot, which is, that the last time she was brought to bed, the reason of her being delivered in the great bed was because she was catched; and this time, Mrs Dawson says, though the pallet was up, the Queen would not go into it because the quilts were not aired.

Anne

THE PARABLE OF
THE TEN VIRGINS

The Prince of Wales is ill. Anne sends
Colonel Sands, her most trustworthy
equerry, from Tunbridge Wells to Richmond
to enquire after the child's health, and bring
her back a full report. He returns with the
strangest story: when he reached Richmond,
he says, he came into a room, where he saw
a child dead or dying in its cradle, with the
nurse, Mrs Labadie, weeping beside it. He
peeped into the cradle to see for himself if
the child breathed, and found it quite still.
When he had his audience, he noticed that
the Queen's eyes were red with weeping.
The King asked him if he had seen the
child, whereupon it occurred to the Colonel
that it might well be dangerous to say
anything that showed he knew the child was
dead, so said he had not. Then a table was
laid, and some Irish army officers tried to
get him to drink too much, which, he says,
he politely refused to do, after which he was

taken to see the Prince — only the child he
saw this time was a plump, lusty infant, and
seemingly several months old.

Could it be that a child so sick he might
be taken for dead could be revived so
quickly? Or did Colonel Sands see two different infants? It seems reasonable to Anne
to suppose that, if they can bring in one
false Prince, then they could just as easily
find another. Bishop Compton himself has
said it is his belief that several babies have
been acquired and kept, just in case they
were needed, and that he has heard that a
busy intriguing Papist woman had tried to
buy some bricklayer's child, to be held in
reserve in this way.

Anne has no reason not to trust the word
of Bishop Compton — and she must trust
him; she depends on him more than she
ever did, for now they are plotting together,
and it will be the Bishop's task to escort her
and Lady Churchill safely out of London, if
That Time Comes. While Anne and George
sit quietly in Tunbridge Wells, out of the
way, Compton and Lord Churchill are busy
on their behalf, and they have ensured good
support for her cause: the Duke of Or-
monde is with them, and Lord Scarsdale,
and Colonel Berkeley, her Master of the
Horse; her uncle Clarendon's son, Lord

Cornbury, will come in on their side, along with another of Anne's cousins, the Duke of Grafton, who is the late King's son. And should her resolve ever weaken, another man of the Church, Dean Tillotson, is with her in Tunbridge Wells to help her shore it up again. It is Anne's opinion that he preaches the Gospel better than any man alive.

The sermon he preaches before her at Tunbridge Wells is as fine an example of his work as she has ever heard. He takes as his text the Parable of the Ten Virgins, who were to meet the bridegroom and escort him to the marriage, lighting the way with their lamps; five were wise, and took oil in their vessels with their lamps; five were foolish, and kept no oil in reserve, so that when the bridegroom came, late and all of a sudden, they had no oil left to keep their lamps alight, and the wise virgins had no surplus to share with them, and so because they were unprepared they were late, and because they were late the door was shut in their faces — and so will the unprepared be denied admittance to the Kingdom of Heaven.

The good Christian is like to a wise virgin, who keeps herself in a state of readiness for that death and judgement which may come at any moment, and the only way to do this is by constant vigilance, the thwarting of her vicious inclinations, the curing of her evil and corrupt affections, the due care and government of her unruly appetites and passions, the sincere endeavour and constant practice of all holiness and virtue in her life. This is the hard way, the right way. The Catholics, who seek to do this the easy way, through the external and little observances, superstitious practices, and insolent attempts to bargain with God, are like to foolish virgins. They believe that grace, like oil, can be transferred from one soul to another: they are wrong — we must all prepare ourselves, or suffer the proper consequences. And by the way, in denying the possibility of salvation to anyone who does not follow the Bishop of Rome, they demonstrate that their Church is a most unchristian one, and founded on schism.

'For God's sake,' he says, 'since in this hour of temptation, when our religion is in apparent hazard, we pretend to love it to that degree to be contented to part with anything for it —'

(Her liberty? Her life? Her father?)

'Let us resolve to practise it; and to testify our love to it in the same way that our Saviour would have us to show our love to

Him, by keeping his Commandments.'

An infelicitous phrase, that last one — Anne must remember to ask the Dean about how she is to honour her father — but she can do that later; for now, her heart is full, so she will gird up the loins of her mind, summon all her forces, and put on the whole Armour of God.

Anne's Uncle Clarendon

Lord, I find I cannot sleep this night, so I had better pray instead. It is very uneasy to me to be telling lies, and I cannot say that it was a good thing I did, to put it about that I am with child, when I am quite certain I am not — but believe me when I say that in telling this one great untruth, and saying that I dare not stir from home lest I miscarry, I am sure to prevent the telling of a thousand others. When I waited on the King and Queen at Windsor, I had to dissemble so that I thought I should get ill of it. I had the King on one hand — now that it is plain to him that the Prince of Orange must come soon, he must talk for hours and hours together of that and nothing else, and all the time thinking that we are the two of us of the same mind — how he can think this of me I do not know, but then he has never had eyes to see what he will not see. And on the other hand the

Queen, all reproachful because I had not visited her for weeks before, and complaining that Mary does not ask how the child does in her letters, and telling me how much better he has gone on since they found him the wet-nurse at Richmond, and being sure I must be thankful too . . . I hope, Lord, you will forgive me, if I say that I would sooner jump out the window than face them every day . . .

And then if it had not been for the tale of my being with child I do not know what I would have done when the King summoned me to swear before the Council that I knew the Queen to be breeding. I could hardly swear about the birth like all the others, since I was not there, which is a thing that lately I am heartily glad of. I will own it was out of kindness that the King said I should not be summoned if it would be only to save one child at the expense of another — but he still would not quite spare me from being caught up in the business. I must confess it was the greatest mortification imaginable to have the whole Privy Council on my doorstep with the supposed evidence, and I am at the best of times so tongue-tied, so I know I can only thank you for putting the words in my mouth to tell them I have so much duty to the King, that his word must be more to me than all the depositions.

I did hope to satisfy him with that, but now he has sent me his own copy of the Prince of Orange's Declaration, and he desires me I am sure to declare outright that I oppose it, but that would be a lie too far for me. Still I can hardly prevent my father from visiting me here and expressing concern about my condition, and I must own I do pity him a little: he is now endeavouring too late to appease the people, sacking Catholics and appointing Protestants, but he can satisfy no-one of his sincerity in this — and I say this even though he has dismissed Sunderland, whose wife as it turns out has been writing all along to her old lover Sidney and the words in the invitation to the Prince were Sidney's own I'm told. So it is plain she has been plotting against the King and Queen and sending intelligence to the other party — I have always said of her that she is a false woman and now it is proved, but it seems we have been of the same opinion in some matters all this time. I do not know what I am supposed to think of her now, but I cannot like her . . .

I beg you send a wind to blow the Prince and his ships into an English harbour soon, for I am so full of apprehension every day I wonder that I do not burst . . . and in the meantime give me strength not to give myself away to my uncle Clarendon, who is here almost every day, putting a thousand questions to me to find out what I know and where I stand and if I lie. And then he must needs press me to speak to the King, and this when he knows the King does not love I should meddle in anything, and even if that were not the case the Papists would not let him veer from the path they have set him on. With all of this my uncle does make me so ill at ease in my own chamber I could almost wish I had gone to the wretched meeting after all . . . I do not understand why he should be so loyal to the King, when he has been so humiliated. I have truly been quite sorry for my uncle . . . I pray you might open his eyes, and show him what is the right course in this matter: he is I think as good a Protestant as any of us.

I must confess I do not know what my brother Orange means to do once he has arrived, but I have no reason to think it will not be all to the good, and then I might be my true and honest self again.

HIS MAJESTY BLEEDS
AT THE NOSE

One day in early November, Lady Churchill comes into Anne's closet to tell her that their prayers have been answered: an obliging Protestant wind has blown the Prince of Orange and his troops all the way to Torbay; they are camped at Exeter. The King has responded by raising Lord Churchill to the position of Lieutenant General and has sent him and the rest of the army to Salisbury. Sarah talks calmly enough about this, but when she helps Anne on with her clothes, her hands are shaking. Anne is privately glad that her own husband is at Whitehall still, though she wishes that the King would go, and take her uncle Clarendon with him: he is at the Cockpit again, trying to persuade her to remonstrate with the King, even though it is too late, and would never have done any good, and even if it would have done — and this is what of all things she cannot say — *she never wished to.* She never knows what to say to him on the subject, and he never changes it —

— at least until Lord Cornbury becomes the first officer to defect to the Prince of Orange, and then Anne can comfort him with the notion that there is at least nothing exceptional in his child's disloyalty: as people in general are so apprehensive of Popery, it will surely not be too long before many more of the army do the same. She does not tell him that the Prince of Orange has said as much to her in a letter, and that is why she is so sure.

A few days later, the King takes leave of her. He begs her have a care of herself, and to try and comfort the Queen, if she can, if her condition will allow it; he seems exhausted, anxious, grey-faced, old. She feels a kind of revulsion for him, half-fearful, half-contemptuous. Now poor George will have to bear him company all the way to Salisbury — she can only hope that he will find wine enough to help him tolerate it.

As soon as they are safely gone, she replies to the Prince of Orange:

Having on all occasions given you and my sister all imaginable assurances of the great friendship and kindness I have for you both, I hope it is not necessary for me to repeat anything of that kind, and on the subject you have now written to me I shall not trouble you with many compliments, only in short assure you that you have my wishes for your good success in this so just an undertaking, and I hope the Prince will soon be with you to let you see his readiness to join with you, who I am sure will do you all the service that lies in his power. He went yesterday with the King towards Salisbury, intending to go from there to you as soon as his friends thought it proper. I am not yet certain if I shall continue here or remove into the City; that shall depend on the advice my friends will give me, but wherever I am I shall be ready to show you how much I am your humble servant.

It is the King's nose that decides the matter. Salisbury does not at all agree with it: it bleeds after he arrives; when he receives news of the risings in the North of England, it bleeds again. He loses heart, and starts back for London with his army. The next day Lord Churchill defects, and the Duke of Grafton, and Colonel Berkeley. Orders arrive for guards to be placed at Lady Churchills lodgings, but they are none too strict in their work, thank God, and make no attempt to stop her visiting Anne, or Mrs Berkeley, or anyone else. When further orders come, for Lady Churchill and Mrs Berkeley to be taken into custody, Anne appeals to the Lord Chamberlain, who, for her sake, agrees to do nothing about it yet. By the time the news of George's defection arrives, along with an order for the Queen to have Anne secured in her lodgings, Sarah has already contrived to visit Bishop Compton and they have made the necessary plans. There are guards waiting outside the Cockpit, and it is time for Anne to make use of the new backstairs.

Lady Churchill, has, with great patience and kindness, helped her compose a letter to the Queen, to be found after she is gone:

Madam.

I beg your pardon if I am so deeply affected with the surprising news of the Prince's being gone, as not to be able to see you, but to leave this paper to express my humble duty to the King and yourself; and to let you know that I am gone to absent myself to avoid the King's displeasures which I am not able to bear, either against the Prince or myself. And

I shall stay at so great a distance as not to return before I hear the happy news of a reconcilement: and, as I am confident the Prince did not leave the King with any other design than to use all possible means for his preservation, so I hope you will do me the justice to believe that I am uncapable of following him for any other end. Never was anyone in such an unhappy condition, so divided between duty and affection to a father and a husband; and therefore I know not what I must do, but to follow one and preserve the other. I see the general feeling of the nobility and gentry who avow to have no other end than to prevail with the King to secure their religion, which they saw so much in danger by the violent counsels of the priests; who to promote their own religion, did not care to what dangers they exposed the King. I am fully persuaded that the Prince of Orange designs the King's safety and preservation, and hope all things may be composed without more bloodshed, by the calling a Parliament.

God grant a happy end to these troubles, that the King's reign may be prosperous, and that I may shortly meet you in

perfect peace and safety; till when, let
me beg you to continue the same favourable opinion that you have hitherto had
of your most obedient daughter and servant.

That night, when the clock strikes one,
unhappy Anne, divided between duty and
affection, in pursuit of the King's safety and
preservation, the security of the English
religion, the avoidance of bloodshed, reconcilement and a happy end to present troubles, and carrying her best pair of shoes so
as not to wake Danvers — sleeping all
unawares in the ante-room — tiptoes from
her chamber into the little room where she
has her close-stool, and from there steps
onto the backstairs.

As she emerges onto them, everything
strikes her at once: the stairs are shabby and
need painting; it is raining heavily; two
ladies in hoods are waiting at the foot. They
do not dare speak, of course, but as she
reaches them, they put their hoods back for
a moment and she sees that they are indeed,
thank God, Lady Churchill and Mrs Berkeley. Anne puts her shoes on, her silk-lined
slippers with the red heels. Lady Churchill
whispers that, with all due respect, they
were a bad choice and the mud will ruin

them, Mrs Berkeley covers Anne up in a heavy cloak and hood, and the three of them set off together into the sodden dark.

When they have taken their first few squelching steps, a gentleman comes forward to meet them: Lord Dorset, First Lord of the Bedchamber to the late King, here to assist at the ruin of the present one. He makes a practised bow, and whispers that there is a Hackney coach waiting; he will escort them to it. The rain falls harder; the mud grows stickier. Anne's feet sink in deeper with every step, and the squelching noises grow louder and more ridiculous. Anne cannot hold her laughter in anymore: it whoops out of her, at a dangerous volume, so that her companions gather round her sssshhhing. It is too late, though: now she has lost a shoe — her beautiful shoe! — in the mud. Lady Churchill retrieves it, tutting, while Lord Dorset whips off one of his long gloves and gently pulls it over her stockinged royal foot. Then she takes hold of his arm and hops, whoops, hops the rest of the way to the coach.

They are taken to Bishop Compton's lodgings, where they eat. Sarah holds up half the muddy shoe in one hand and the snapped-off muddy heel in the other, so that Anne can laugh even more at it. Then the ladies change into the travelling clothes that Lady Churchill has had discreetly delivered there. The Bishop dresses himself up as a soldier, complete with jackboots and broadsword, and looks more comfortable in that than he ever has in his episcopal robes; Anne is lifted onto his horse behind him, and then for the rest of the night and part of the morning, she rides pillion behind her old tutor, until they reach Waltham Forest, and Lord Dorset's house. From there they travel, in stages, to Nottingham.

Finally, Anne can give up the role of Dutiful Daughter, the one it has oppressed her so much to have to play, and she is giddy with relief. Her spirits are so high that by the time they reach Nottingham they have made her feverish, and she has to take to her bed for a few days. She has Dr Radcliffe sent for, but he will not come: instead, he sends a message to say that he will not come to attend a rebel Princess. It sobers Anne up a little, to be rebuked like that — as Lady Churchill says, Radcliffe is a man so fitted by nature for medicine, that he has given his patient physick without even meaning to.

When she leaves her chamber, she finds a house filled with noblemen, gentlemen, yeomen and militia. They are, for the most part, gallant, excitable, and intoxicatingly at her service. They are greatly moved to hear of her sufferings, her courage, her daring escape; she is, for once in her life, almost eloquent, and very comely with it. They are more than delighted to follow her to Leicester, gathering more troops as they go. The good, common, Protestant people line the roads and cheer her. She is almost Good Queen Bess.

Almost. She is taken to task again in Leicester, in front of Bishop Compton and the Earl of Devonshire and everyone. She has had such a good notion: Queen Elizabeth, she is sure, in her time, had given her blessing to a league for defending the monarch against malicious Papists — why not form one to defend the Prince of Orange? Her new followers are very keen. Bishop Compton is prepared to consider it, and to draw up the articles of association. A meeting is called at an inn. It is very well attended, and Anne's hopes are high — but then the Earl of Chesterfield stands up to speak. He has known Anne since childhood, and has already reminded her several times that he has served her father, and hinted that, under such circumstances, and in his opinion, it might well become Her Highness to look a little less pleased with herself.

He is here, he says, to protect the Princess, but he does not care to be summoned to public conferences without having first been consulted privately — regarding the matter in hand, if he had been so consulted, he would have refused to have anything to do with it. He is for the Prince of Orange, but he will not join any murder, and he is sure that the Prince — whom he has known for many years — would never approve of one.

And that is that.

Anne suffers through a few tetric days, but then the extraordinary messages start to come: the Prince of Orange has entered London; the Queen and her baby have fled to France; her father has fled, and his army have been disbanded. When she is told of this, the whole room hushes about her, and she knows they are all watching her now, waiting to see how she deports herself, if it is fitting — but in this moment, though she suspects she ought not, she finds she can do nothing at all but smile. Feeling utterly at a loss, and having eaten already, she calls for cards.

■ ■ ■ ■

PART IV

■ ■ ■ ■

There's Mary the daughter,
There's Willy the cheater,
There's Geordie the drinker,
There's Annie the eater.
                              — Jacobite rhyme

The Throne Is Vacant

It is January 1689, and Anne could almost think that nothing has changed: here she is back at home in the Cockpit, with another growing belly, being scolded by her uncle Clarendon.

'. . . and I was disappointed to hear of your conduct when the news was brought you — *most* disappointed. I am told that when it would have most become you to show some remorse or some pity at least, instead you continued merry as ever — and called for cards! *Cards,* Madam!'

'What would you have had me do, Sir? It has never been easy to me to dissemble.'

'Is that so? Then what were you doing all these months past?'

'I did only what I thought was best.'

'And you did not think it best to tell me what your design was?'

Anne cannot think of an answer.

'And so now you are gone silent again —

that was ever your refuge, wasn't it? With
your father, with the Queen — and now
with your own uncle. You have hurt us,
Anne — the King more than anybody. I
believe it was your defection that took the
heart out of him — and I am not the only
one who thinks so. Did you have no thought
for his sufferings, that day, when you smiled
and you called for your cards?'

'I admit I was glad that day — but it was
only that there was so little bloodshed. The
King has fled, but he is alive; my sister's
husband and mine, are unharmed. Should I
not be grateful for that, at least?'

'So you have what you wanted: your father
is defeated, your brother Orange is come.
What do you suppose will happen now?'

'Would you care for a comfit, Sir?'

'No, I would not — I desire an answer.'

Anne would like a comfit. She takes one
and crunches it as slowly as she can, looking at the floor as she does so. She feels very
stupid, and ten years old.

'I understood — I was assured that — I
was assured . . .'

'You were assured — of what?'

'. . . that the Prince was coming here in
defence of the Protestant religion, and the
laws of England, which were in peril, and
that when he came here there could be a

free Parliament summoned — which is a thing we had not had for too long under the King.'

She looks at her uncle Clarendon: will he at last be satisfied?

No.

'It is true that we have a Parliament, and now that the King has fled, they have decided to declare the throne vacant.'

'I know that, Sir.'

'Someone else must fill it.'

Anne thinks she knows the answer. For as long as she can remember, she has drawn comfort from the succession, and from her place in it. Like the Lord's Prayer, the catechism, or the rules of precedence at Court, it is a thing that sticks securely in her memory, ready to be brought out and rehearsed in times of strain:

Charles [deceased]
James
Mary
Anne
Anne's unborn child

'Mary,' she says.

'No — or at least not alone.'

And Anne, who has only just bitten into her second comfit, nearly chokes.

ANNE'S ABDICATION

William, Anne, the Lords, the Commons and the People are in easy agreement about one matter: that there should be no more Papists on the English throne, by law, ever again, and no Papist consorts either. James Stuart has broken laws, violated rights, attempted to extirpate the Protestant religion, prosecuted worthy prelates, obstructed Parliament, appropriated funds it had not granted, and kept an army without its consent. And since it has pleased Almighty God to make His Highness the Prince of Orange the Glorious Instrument of delivering the Kingdom from Popery and Arbitrary Power, it is clear that the Lord agrees too.

Other questions are less easily settled. The Lords cannot quite share the Commons' enthusiasm for the declaration of a vacant throne — perhaps, they suggest, James should remain King, while his daughter and son-in-law exercise power as regents? The

Commons will have none of this; neither will the rabble surging about the Parliament building, calling for the pair to be crowned. They will have William — that Glorious Instrument — and Mary, for the succession's sake, and the Protestant religion, their English laws and their English liberties. And William will accept no power dependent on the will of a woman, so William must be crowned in his own right, and rule in both their names.

Distasteful as it is to Anne to find herself subject to her sister's Dutch Caliban, she is prepared to consent to this. What she finds she cannot consent to is the proposal that the succession be re-arranged thus:

William and Mary

Mary for Life after William's decease/ William for Life after Mary's decease

The heirs of Mary's body

In default of these, Anne

Anne's heirs

In default of these, William's heirs by a later wife

Nobody has ever spoken to Anne of such a thing. It would be to the prejudice of herself and her children. She cannot, she will not consent to it.

Neither will George, and he tells several peers as much; Lord Clarendon makes Anne's feelings known to a few more, and Lady Churchill makes herself busier on Anne's behalf than either gentleman could ever manage. Her persistence is remarkable, her own belly no hindrance at all — but it is all in vain. On 6th February the House of Lords agree to the double-bottomed monarchy and to the new succession. Lady Churchill has a word with Dean Tillotson, and brings him to speak to her mistress.

'There it is, Your Highness,' he says. 'The matter is decided. I would advise you as your friend to accept with good grace. I do not believe there is anything you could do now to alter it.'

'But Dean, I do not understand it. Why does my sister put aside her rights like this?'

'Is it truly so hard to understand? You are such a good wife yourself — would you expect your husband to live as his own wife's subject?'

'That would be against the natural order of things,' says Lady Churchill, 'would it not, Sir?' She is addressing the Prince, who starts, swallows a mouthful of claret, and begs her pardon.

'The Dean was saying, Sir, that no man could be expected to live as his own wife's subject.'

'No, I should have thought not . . .' says the Prince. 'You are speaking of the Prince of Orange? No, not he . . . what was it he said . . . ?'

' "I will not be my wife's Gentleman Usher," ' says Lady Churchill.

'Oh yes, that was it — very good!'

Anne makes a furious little noise at the back of her throat. The spaniels sitting at her feet cower a little.

'I beg your pardon, my dear, but I have to agree with the Dean: we must live with this settlement. And I am sure our interests won't be forgotten. Did the Prince not wait on us as soon as we came back?'

'That was no more than he ought to have done. And I cannot think that the gratitude he expressed was all that sincere!'

She is still angry, but it is now tempered with remorse at having frightened her dogs; she picks up the one closest to her and weeps quietly into its fur. The room watches her.

'I simply do not understand it,' she says at last.

'As I said, Madam, your sister —'

'*No,* Dean — not my sister — *him.* What does *he* want with the English throne?'

It is Lady Churchill who replies.

'He is the ruler of a small country, Madam, with a great enemy. He requires English troops, English ships, English funds, and our alliances with —'

The Dean interrupts her: 'And it is all for the good of the Protestant religion, Your Highness.'

'Very well then, very well — but *Parliament* to choose the King? That is in God's gift, not *Parliament's.*'

'In *principle,* Your Highness, but, with the greatest respect to Your Person —'

This time Lady Churchill interrupts the Dean: 'I would venture to say, events have proved that if a King of England — even an anointed King — should try to rule without their consent, he won't be doing it for long.'

AND WHAT IS
EVEN WORSE . . .

. . . is that, since there can be from this time on no Catholics on the throne, in default of any heirs from Mary, William or Anne, the Crown of England must pass to the next Protestant along in the line of succession — and what with the lamentable habit the Stuarts have had of being or becoming or marrying Catholics, there is no Protestant nearer than Sophia, Electress of Hanover, and as she is very likely too old to outlive all three of them, the more plausible prospect is her son, George. That would be George of Hanover — short, fat George, of the dry lips and protuberant eyes, who can command not a word of English, and whose French is surely no better than Anne's — depressing the throne of England with his graceless, German behind. No, it must not come to that.

ANNE'S SISTER

The cry has gone up at Greenwich. Anne, who can see nothing yet, gazes faithfully into the fog. She is listening out for the sound of oars moving through water, but hears only her brother-in-law, wheezing next to her. By the quickening of his breath, she knows that he has caught a glimpse of Mary; until this moment, Anne has never thought that he could be moved by anything, and despite herself, she is touched.

Mary's delight at seeing her husband is less subtly expressed, but no less touching for that. A little comical too: Mary is wrapped in furs, and when she embraces William it looks for a moment as if he has been seized by a great, tearful bear. Then the Mary-bear lets him go and comes for Anne. She smells astonishingly sweet, and the pearls that dig into Anne's cheek feel as big as quail's eggs. Queenly pearls.

Then she stands back, and her eyes move

straight down to Anne's belly.

'You look well, Sister,' she says.

'You too.'

They smile at each other; they embrace again; neither sister says *I almost did not know you.*

LORD DEVONSHIRE'S LEAVINGS

O Lord I am ashamed and blush to lift up my face to thee; I am supposed to receive the Sacrament tomorrow morning, but as I have read over the Catalogue of Sins in The Whole Duty, I have found more and more which I must own, and I fear I could never achieve repentance enough to make myself fit to receive in so short a time — and when I try to repent, I find that my mind wanders and my heart is stubborn — I am afraid sometimes, when I cannot sleep, that it is my heart and not the late King's that has been hardened all this time, and the thought fills me with such terror . . .

When I used my father as I did, I believed myself justified in it — I even rejoiced, and was chastised by others for it, and I own I resented their chastisement — I believed then that it was your Will that the King should be checked, and Providence that brought the Prince of Orange here — the King, I should say, to whom I now owe respect and obedience, and to my sister the Queen, as I once did to my father. But I am sorry to say, that if I ever had any certainty that my condition and that of the country and the Church should be bettered by their coming, I cannot find it in myself anymore.

If I hoped for gratitude from the people, I have not got it . . . Lady Churchill — the Countess of Marlborough, I should say — has shown me the verses written on me and my sister. They say we are like Lear's daughters, or Tullia driving her chariot over the body of her sire, and one verse — I cannot get it out of my head, I could wish that such unpleasant things did not stick in there so:

To be but half a Hyde is a digrace
From which no royal seed can purge its
    race.
Mixed with such mud the clearest streams
    must be,
Like Jordan's sacred flood, lost in the
    Sodom Sea,
Ambition, folly, insolence and pride

Proves it too well you're on the surer side.

Not that I can look to the Hydes for any comfort — my uncles have made non-jurors of themselves, that is to say they believe my father is still King in law, and so will not swear any oath to be loyal to William and Mary. There are many good men of the Church who agree with them, and that is a great hurt to me and to my sister. The Archbishop would not crown them. Now all these clerics must lose their places, and I am sorry to see it. Of all things I desired the good of the Church, and it is a great trouble to me to see it divided. I do not believe the new King cares for it any more than the old — he has had Parliament pass an Act so that Dissenters might hold office; I cannot think that is right. I cannot suppose that it is pleasing to you . . . It cannot be pleasing to any good Englishman to see all those Dutchmen taking English places, striding about as if they had bought and sold us, looking down their noses, calling their lodgings squalid and the Court noisome.

As for the Court, it is but another thing for which the King has no proper regard. He takes himself off to Hampton, pleading his health, snubbing the very people to whom he should be most grateful. He leaves my sister behind to smile and be gracious to everyone, when everyone knows already there is no profit for them in speaking to her alone: she will do nothing and grant nothing unless her husband says she might. To be sure she will do nothing for me . . .

It is the greatest sorrow to me, it is the poison in my soul that I fear must make me most unfit to receive your mercy, that so soon after her return there should be such a want of charity between the Queen and me. I do not understand it. When we dine together, the King can barely say a civil word to me or my husband — he does not scruple to hide his contempt for us — and yet she prattles on in that way of hers as if nothing were amiss. Certainly I would not expect her to rebuke the King before us, but she might well without fear say something in private, and I cannot help but think that if she does not, it can only be because she is secretly of the same mind as him about us — and I keep re-membering how when we were children she never did think much of me, and how she was always trying to school me to make me better.

We are not children anymore. I have endured so much for her sake — I do believe I put myself in danger for them both — I let them put me out of the succession — and I am repaid with contempt. It is true that they gave me the Duchess of Portsmouth's old lodgings, but when I asked for the rooms next to them, which I would need for my family, that the Duke of Devonshire had, and I said he might have the Cockpit in their place which I thought a very reasonable thing to suggest — no, a generous thing — but then my sister said only if the Duke agreed. Naturally I was compelled to tell her that in that case I would stay where I was and use the new lodgings for a nursery, for I could hardly be expected to take the Duke of Devonshire's leavings. So I have only a paltry few rooms for a nursery: I did ask for Richmond, which everyone knows is most suitable for children, but no, I may not have that either — it is let to some of the Villiers family, who it seems are more to her than I am — and I cannot help noticing, by the by, that when I wait on her with my ladies, she would sooner talk to Mrs

Berkeley than to me: it seems I have not wit enough for either of them.

Lady Marlborough, I thank heaven, still stands my friend. In the matter of the revenues due to the Prince and me, she gives me such good advice, is so solicitous for my interests, and it is at her suggestion that we have persuaded Parliament to take a hand in the matter — for, as Lady Marlborough told me herself, the King has said that he wonders how I could possibly spend 30,000 pounds a year, let alone any more. When I find that he has granted me none of the estates that were the late King's, I have every reason to suppose that if it were left to him and the Queen, the Prince and I should be burning rush lights and wearing nothing but wool and linen, while we watch them building new houses for themselves at Hampton Court and at Kensington, as if they did not have palaces enough.

I cannot talk to my sister. I cannot talk to her. We are scarcely ever alone together and when we are we know not what to say to each other: there are too many things that cannot be said. A few days after she was first in England I was in the Queen's closet with her at Whitehall, she was unpacking her things, her porcelain, that blue-and-white Dutch ware — she has so much of it, I swear I have never seen so much! — and she took out a vase, a tall one with spouts all the way up it, for displaying tulips I suppose — but then she stopped, and said it had been a present from our father. I could say nothing to this, and she said nothing more; only she put it aside, and we did not look at each other, and I have not seen it in her closet since.

Even to think of my father puts me in terror, lest I should have to face him again. That he should have landed in Ireland on the day of the coronation seems such an ill omen — and then — oh, I can hardly bear to call it to mind — that morning, as I dressed, I received such a letter from him, and I know — though she will not speak of it — that my sister received a like one, for the Earl of Nottingham told me. So now we are both of us told, that the curses of an angry father will fall on us, as well as those of a God who commands obedience to parents.

I had Mrs Dawson with me when the letter came, so I asked her, again, if the Prince of Wales was indeed my brother and she said, yes he was the son of the late King and Queen, as surely as I am the daughter of the late Duchess, and this was only to speak what she knows, for she was the first person to hold us both in her arms.

Every time I see the King and Queen, I am reminded of what it is that I have done, and then I am afraid, I am beyond all expression afraid.

PEAS

William and Mary, Anne and George are dining together at Hampton Court. George is drinking, placidly; William is eating, morosely; Mary is telling Anne of her plans to make the English people more serious in their devotions, and Anne is yearning, with all her heart, and with that peculiar intensity of a lady in her condition, for the dish of peas sitting on the table, just in front of the King. She is willing him to look up, so that she might catch his eye and ask for the dish to be passed to her, but he is staring steadfastly at his plate, and when he speaks, speaks only to his old friend Bentinck, Earl of Portland, who stands behind him.

'It has pained me very much to see how lightly religion is taken at Court,' says Mary.

'I am very serious in my religion,' says Anne, without taking her eyes off the peas.

'Of course I was not speaking of *you*, Sister, but I have noticed, since my return, how seldom one sees the Court ladies at Chapel, and when they do attend, how they dress as if they were at a theatre, and whisper behind their fans, and try to catch the eye of the preacher if they think him handsome — and do the like with other gentlemen too.'

'I know,' says Anne, 'but what can you do about it?'

'Set them a good example. They have lacked one for too long; they have grown used to monarchs who either smile at their levity, or pray elsewhere.'

'We can both do that. I have always attended very publicly, since I was married.'

William reaches for the dish of peas.

'I am so glad we are of a mind in this, Anne. I was used to live so quietly in Holland, reading and writing — I was used to pray four times a day, and I miss it —'

Anne can hardly breathe for wondering what he will do. Now would be the time to ask, but she cannot do it.

'— at least since I have been back here at Hampton, I have been able to compose some new prayers, and also some pious —'

William takes up his fork, begins to shovel the peas into his mouth.

'— ejaculations . . . Anne?'

A horrific scene is unfolding at the head

of the table, and Anne cannot withdraw her gaze from it. She knows that Mary has taken it in, and understood, and will not say anything to it.

'Also since I have been here I have had so many thoughts about the gardens, I am in great hopes that we can make them as lovely as Het Loo — perhaps finer. I have Sir Christopher Wren coming to speak to me, and when he does I shall take a walk with him — you would be welcome to join us — Anne?'

It is too late. William has eaten all the peas, and Anne has turned an unhappy, furious shade of red. He will have everything, this Dutch Abortion. It is quite clear that he will not willingly yield her a single pea or a single shilling, and that Mary will say nothing to it. They have no real kindness for her, so there is no point in appealing to it.

So Anne continues to pay all imaginable respect to the King and Queen, waits on her sister every day, and has the matter of her revenue raised in Parliament. She says nothing of it to her sister; perhaps they might contrive just to knot fringes together and leave the unpleasant business to others — they are neither of them fitted for it.

Then one evening Mary takes her to one side.

'These proceedings in Parliament,' she hisses. 'What is the meaning of them?'

Mary looks especially tall when angry, but all the same Anne has never been afraid of her and the crown makes no difference.

'I heard my friends had a mind to make me some settlement,' she says.

'Pray what friends have you but the King and me?'

Mary almost spits; Anne stands her ground. Call this a Man if you must, Sister, but I have made up my mind, and I will not change it: Tree it is; Tree, Tree, *Tree* . . .

Anne Is Delivered in State

Anne wakes abruptly, soaking wet, and suddenly in pain, as if her travail has started midway through this time. As soon as she is able to speak, she calls for Danvers. There is a scuffle outside the room, of several people rising and whispering, grabbing shoes and candlesticks, opening doors, and then her bed-curtains are wrenched open and it is Danvers and Farthing, jostling for a glimpse of their mistress, and talking together.

'Have the Queen fetched,' she tells them, 'it is time.'

She hopes there is no more she need say, for she cannot speak again. When the pain releases her, Danvers tells her that a State Room is being prepared; the Queen will be there, and they will take Anne presently.

'A State Room? Oh yes — oh Lord, I wish I did not have to.'

But it must be a State Room. The whole

of Hampton Court will be rousing itself around them: the King, the Court Officers, the Officers of State; this birth must have its proper audience. And there will be no Sarah for this performance, to inspire her, to steady her nerves, for Lady Marlborough is herself confined, and somewhere else. She has never been more grateful for Danvers and Farthing, supporting her as she makes her way across the Palace, stumbling from pain to pain.

Mary is already there, in a loose manteau, her hair half-dressed; she has a book in her hands.

'Dear Sister, I came as soon as I could.' She holds up the book. 'I have found out some pray —' She stops mid-word, goes utterly still: she has never seen Anne in the midst of travail before.

Now Sister, Anne thinks, let me tell you something.

When the throw has spent itself, she says, 'Yes, I am in pain, but it is no worse than usual, and I believe it will not be long this time.'

Mary's eyes are full of tears. 'How women suffer . . . may we at least make good use of it, that it might bring us closer to God.'

'That is well said, Your Majesty,' says Danvers, as she buttons a waistcoat over Anne's smock. 'Now Her Highness must lie down. The midwife must examine her.' She takes one of Anne's arms; Mary, quite unnecessarily, takes the other, and together they lead her to the bed.

The midwife is a brisk, local woman, smaller than Mrs Wilkes but no less commanding. She confirms what Anne already knows: that it will not be long.

'Need we do anymore now?' Mary asks. 'Will you stay on the bed, Anne?'

'No, Sister, I prefer to walk the room.'

'Then I will keep pace with you.'

It is no use to Anne, to have the Queen walking next to her, asking how she does, offering her pious reflections, but Mary seems to derive some good from it, and Anne cannot find it in her heart to begrudge her. She indulges Mary in this way until the throws start pushing downward, and it is time to stop walking, grab a bedpost and wonder at how great a noise comes out of her without her willing it at all. The midwife says something to her — heaven knows what — and then her hands are prised off the bedpost and four or maybe six arms are hauling her onto the bed.

Now the doors of the State Room are flung open and the King and Court surge through them. George runs to the bedside, takes hold of her shoulders. The King is saying something to the midwife.

'Presently, Your Majesty,' she says. 'I see the head — bear down, Your Highness, bear down!'

Anne closes her eyes tight. She has no desire to see the King's face at any time, and especially not at this one. She does what she is told; she bears down; she lets out a scream that silences the room and into that silence a baby cries.

'A boy,' the King says. 'Very good.'

THE NOISE OF FOREIGN WARS

The boy is christened William, after the King and created Duke of Gloucester. The Court pronounces him a 'brave, lively-like boy', but it seems the infant himself disagrees, because for the first few days he will not feed. While Anne prays, and tries to steel herself for the worst, Mrs Berkeley, Farthing and Danvers decide between them that the wet-nurse's nipples are too large, and have her sacked. Mrs Wanley is brought in to replace her, with happy results. Anne gives thanks, the Court rejoices, and Master Purcell, organist at the Chapel Royal, composes an ode in celebration of His Highness's birth.

The piece is called *The noise of foreign wars.* There is very little mention of the child in it, but a great deal about jealousies and fears, wrangles, complaints, discord, battalions and the like. Still, the harpsichord part is very pretty, and Anne means to learn it when she can. She will welcome the distraction if and when George goes to Ireland with the King, there to meet her father in the field.

That could not truly be called a foreign war, and neither could the rebellions in Scotland, but there can be no denying that, since the Crown of England and the Stadtholdership of the United Provinces have been brought together in the person of the King, there can be no easy distinction drawn between what is England's business and what is Holland's. First the United Provinces declared war on France; then England signed a Treaty with the United Provinces, over the fitting out of fleets; then England declared war on France. Now Anne's father has landed in Ireland, to fight, with French assistance, for his old Crown.

And then, in the midst of all this, it looks very likely that there will be a war between Denmark and Sweden. William steps in: the United Provinces are now allied with the Empire against France, and he cannot allow the Emperor to be distracted by a war on his northern borders. He succeeds in negotiating a settlement, which includes, among other terms, an undertaking that the lands of George, Prince of Denmark will be surrendered to Sweden; the Prince will of course be compensated for the revenues lost. George signs the release at once: he can desire no better security, he says, than the assurances His Majesty has given him.

MRS PACK

What is it God requires of Anne? What does she have to do to keep her babies from the fire? She has appointed Mrs Wanley wet-nurse, she has had the family removed to Craven House, where they might all benefit from the good air of the Kensington gravel pits, she has secured the best lodgings at Whitehall for his nursery, she has given thanks — has she not always given thanks? — and for the last few weeks he has thrived, but now here is Mrs Wanley to wait on her in her chamber again, distressed as she was on that most terrible of days, and weeping for her newest charge.

'Such a strong convulsion fit, Your Highness — I do not think I have ever seen one so bad — and he is listless now, he will not suck, he will scarcely even cry.'

When Anne reaches the nursery, she finds her son in the arms of a weeping rocker, and fitting again. She takes the child up herself, and has the doctor sent for. It takes an age before Dr Radcliffe can be found, and by the time he arrives William has suffered — Anne keeps count — two more convulsions.

'They are almost continuous,' she says. 'What is the cause of them, Doctor? What can you do?'

'I can only answer one question at a time, Madam. As to the cause: I do not know — he is feverish — it may be measles, or the smallpox — do not take on, I did not say it was, only that it might be, and I was about to add, that I do not think it either. The case does not look good, I am afraid, but you must try a change of milk — that would be your best chance — the only chance, I should think.'

Mrs Wanley's face crumples, and she runs from the nursery.

'Oh dear,' says Mrs Berkeley, 'there was no need for that: she will keep her place as bedchamber woman.'

'Find another wet-nurse,' the doctor says. 'Any other physician will say the same.'

For the next few days, Craven House is full of doctors concurring with Radcliffe, and nursing mothers, whose own babies must be no older than one month, competing for the chance to provide the better milk the doctors recommend. At first, a Mrs Ogle, the wife of one of the Prince's footmen, seems the ideal candidate, but she has scarcely been installed before Mrs Berkeley is looking at her askance. She has a dishonest air about her, this Mrs Ogle, and sure enough, when Mrs Berkeley checks the parish register, it turns out that her milk is nowhere near as fresh as she has claimed. And so the Duke, who has not ceased fitting, is dragged away from yet another breast.

New candidates are called in, and a notice sent out, offering a reward to anyone who can discover a remedy. The Prince walks about the rooms of Craven House, casting his eye over the countrywomen who line the walls in their dozens, searching for whatever it could be in this one's face or that one's figure that might signify the capacity to supply exceptional nourishment. He catches sight of one particular woman. She is a big lass, vigorous-looking, who stares back at him in a way that he ought to find insolent.

'You there — what is your name?'

'I am Mrs Pack, of Kingston Wick. Sir.'

'Mrs Pack. Very good. Now go to the nursery and feed my son.'

She does as she is told. Within the day, the baby's fever has gone and his convulsions have ceased. Mrs Pack is not a prepossessing woman; she is plain, and dirty; her manners are coarse, and she is every bit as insolent as she appears — she is a Quaker, as it happens, and they are quite notorious for it. Nobody in the household likes her, but she is the instrument of God's mercy, so she must have whatever she desires to eat and drink and never be crossed. Fear the Lord, fear Mrs Pack.

PERSONS NOT AT EASE

With her son out of danger, Anne returns to London, where she employs the better part of her energy and ingenuity in finding ways to avoid being alone with Mary. The Queen herself makes this a little easier than it might have been, by never staying too long in the same place: when she is not at Whitehall, she is at Hampton Court or at Kensington, outpacing Sir Christopher on long walks through the grounds, checking the progress of the new buildings, finding reasons to put off the hour when she must retire to Holland House, where she and the King are temporarily but most inconveniently housed.

When Anne and Mary find themselves obliged to talk to each other, the building works provide a safe topic of conversation, ready for them to take up when Mary has finished asking after the Duke. He goes on very well now; he takes the air every day;

she has received another good report of him. Well, that is good to know. It is. Good.

Mary's new buildings do not always go on so well as Anne's son. A workman is killed when the roof falls in at Kensington; not long afterwards two carpenters working at Hampton Court are crushed beneath a collapsing wall. According to Mrs Berkeley, the only lady at Court still on intimate terms with both sisters, Mary blames herself.

'I have heard her say she has been too impatient,' says Mrs Berkeley, 'she has demanded too much of the workers, and now she is humbled for it — she sees the hand of God in this.'

Anne all but snorts into her tea cup. 'How very like my sister: some other poor wretched woman loses a husband, and she says the chastisement is meant for her. I can believe she thought the same when my child was ill.'

'And she rejoiced to see him well again,' says Mrs Berkeley. 'Should she not be concerned about her own sister's child?'

'That was not what Her Highness meant,' says Lady Marlborough. 'It is only that the Queen —'

'Only that the Queen *what,* Lady Marlborough?'

Lady Marlborough drums her fingers on the tea table. 'In the matter of Her Highness's revenue —'

'Oh Lady Marlborough, *please*! Have you not exhausted the subject?'

'No, because the subject is far from being exhausted.'

'Mrs Berkeley, I must say I am so grateful to Lady Marlborough — if it were not for her efforts, her zeal on my behalf, I am sure the matter had been dropped. That it is now to be brought before Parliament is all owing to her work. If only *certain others* possessed that sincere concern for my interests that she has . . .'

'Have you a handkerchief, Your Highness — if not, I shall — ah, you do. If you refer to the Queen, I can tell you how truly grieved she is that there should be a breach between you. I have often heard her express the greatest kindness and affection for her dear sister.'

'But when she sees me, she can barely speak to me.'

'With respect, Your Highness, it has been suggested that you are taking pains to ensure that she hardly sees you at all.'

'But can you blame Her Highness, Mrs Berkeley? The Queen may speak of this great kindness and affection, but do we see

the tokens of it?'

'The Queen longs for kindness from her sister every bit as much as Your Highness longs for kindness from the Queen.'

'But what has Her Highness done, pray, that is so unkind?'

'For her own part, nothing, *of course,* but — and I believe I would be at fault if I did not say this, Your Highness — it could be said — by some — it *is* being said — it could well *appear* to some that Her Highness makes parties against her own sister and brother-in-law, and in doing so, provides ample opportunity for those who might seek to make a property of her, to oppose the King and Queen, and promote certain other interests.'

'But I only want what is mine by right!' Anne cries. 'Must I be dependent on the King and Queen for every penny? Must I be impoverished?'

'Of course not, Your Highness. We will see what Parliament decides.'

'And until then, Lady Marlborough, may we *please* talk of something else?'

The matter comes before Parliament, and is debated with some heat. There are Members who think Anne's request unseasonable: there are wars to be fought, taxes are high, and the King's own revenue not yet

settled. Others desire to know why it is not seasonable that the Prince and Princess, and the Duke of Gloucester should have meat, drink and clothes.

Another argument is put to the House, concerning the possible danger inherent in making the heir to the throne financially independent of its occupier. The House is reminded that when Charles V, in his will, gave great portions to his children, Cardinal Guimeni said, 'If you provide thus, your son may set up for himself.' To which Anne's friends respond that the greatest part of disturbance is usually for persons not at their ease: let the Princess be at ease.

It begins to look as if the matter may go against the King. The next morning, he sends the Earl of Shrewsbury to talk to the Earl of Marlborough, then to his Lady, and when that proves useless, to her mistress. It feels almost as awkward as having the King himself in front of her, in her own home. Anne cannot look at him.

'The King is prepared to settle your debts, Your Highness,' he begins. 'In addition, he will see that you are provided with 50,000 pounds a year — any more, notwithstanding his very sincere gratitude towards Your Highness, being impossible at such a time as this — but on condition that you accept it as being in his gift, and at his discretion.'

For him to dangle before me and take away, Anne thinks. She colours, fidgets with the half-knotted fringe in her lap. She does not know what to say. She has to say something.

'I beg your pardon, my Lord, but I have met with so little encouragement from the King that I can expect no kindness from him and so I think I must stick to my friends in Parliament.'

'And is that your answer, Your Highness?'

'Yes. Thank you. You may go, Sir.'

That afternoon, the Comptroller of the Royal Household announces in the Commons that the King accepts that Parliament might vote the Princess of Denmark her allowance, and moves to have it set at 50,000 pounds a year. The House agrees.

Anne has her revenue. She arrives at Court that evening feeling triumphant, vindicated, *justified* — but not for long. Mary summons her immediately, but not to reconcile.

'Why did you tell my Lord Shrewsbury that the King has been unkind to you?'

'I did not say that exactly — I said I could expect no kindness from him.'

'And how is that different? Look at me, Sister — I *hate* it when you will not look at me — in what way has he been unkind to you, that you should say such a thing?'

Anne hates her sister's face when she is angry — she will not look at it. She is sure she must have a thousand possible answers to Mary's question, but flustered as she is, she finds she can call nothing to mind but a dish of peas — and she can hardly seek to placate the Queen with peas.

'I —' she begins, her blush deepening, 'it is not that —'

'Tell me one thing in which he has not been kind to you: *one thing!*'

Peas, Anne thinks, and stands helplessly, mutely, before her sister, touching her fan to her mouth.

'So there is nothing, then — and yet you could not bring yourself to speak to him, or me, of a matter that concerned you so much — you must instead be complaining to your *friends,* and letting them drag business that should have been private in front of Parliament for everyone to have his say on, making out to the whole world that we are unkind to you? Do you not see what a want of respect you have shown to us both? And how unkind *you* have been to *me?*'

Me . . . me me me me me . . . 'I never meant to be unkind to you, Your Majesty.'

'But you *were.*'

'I said I did not mean to be, and indeed I

did not.'

They part ill friends. The King himself visits Anne just before New Year, has her hold her curtsy until she near capsizes — it is an unpleasant habit of his — refuses to take any refreshment, and announces to the portion of empty space just above and to the right of her head that he considers it an ungenerous thing to fall out with a woman.

'I have no desire,' he says, 'to live on ill terms with you. You have your allowance. We shall put this business behind us. The Queen has been most upset — it is no small trouble to me to see the Queen upset — you will be friends again, I trust.'

'I will, Your Majesty.'

In truth she does not think it likely, but she can hardly say so to the King.

ANNE IN LENT

O Lord, once more I am preparing to receive the Sacrament, and more than ever I read over the Catalogue of Sins and I blush, for here is the fourth Sunday in Lent, and though I have forsworn sweet-meats all these weeks — and this year without a lapse, for which I must thank the grace you have given me — I still find I have neglected that repentance, which should have been my proper duty. I have not assigned any set times for humiliation and confession — as Mary says she does — but instead have considered my sins here and there when I might, and so I fear I may not have considered them deeply enough to beget contrition.

Mary . . . I suppose it might be said we have trespassed against each other, that we ought to confess our sins to each other, and forgive. She has always said that I am stubborn, but I for my part find her every bit as stiff-necked, and if I have pride, so does she. I would rather be in charity with her than otherwise, but if I have not once sought to be alone with her these past months since my settlement was granted me, it is only because whenever I go to Court she never looks upon me or speak to me as if she were truly pleased to have me there. Besides I fear what might be said if the chance arose: she has already said what cannot be unsaid, such words as have hurt me, and which I find I cannot forget. She believes, I know, I should show more gratitude to her and the King — perhaps I should — but for what ought I to be grateful? What have they ever given me willingly?

I do not want to hurt her. I know she will be angry that I am to take the Sacrament in my own Chapel today, and not at White-hall. Lady Marlborough has chided me for this: she says we should take every opportunity to show ourselves united, when there has been such a public quarrel, but as I said to her, Mary has seen fit to change the order of service at Whitehall, a thing which is not pleasing to me, or to any good Churchman, or surely to you, who must desire peace in your Church above all things. I cannot understand why she seeks to make alterations to that which already had within it all things necessary to salvation, and which was always the greatest comfort in times of greatest trial. The Church is the rock on which I stand — why must she move the very ground underneath me? They will not have stringed instruments in the Chapel anymore, which all my life I did rejoice to hear, and think it such a great pity they are gone. They have tried — the King and Queen and their friends — they have even tried to change the litany so that Nonconformists might approve it. In doing so they have put the Church in danger, and I thank Christ that they have failed. But still, as I feared the non-jurors are all turned out of their posts; the Church is divided in a way which must give you pain, as it pains me.

So no: I will not take the Sacrament with Mary today. And I will not go to hear the weekday sermons they have in Whitehall now: there was no need for them. My sister I fear changes services as she changes palaces — all for her own satisfaction, and only because she and the King believe nothing good enough that they have not had the ordering of themselves. And if I have expressed such an opinion to certain people it is only because of my sincere beliefs in this matter — and if in doing so I have murmured against my sister and my Queen and been disloyal then truly I repent of that — or at least I will endeavour to.

It may be that I have something to reproach myself for in my conduct towards my sister — I do own it, I do — but I hope that I have not failed as a mistress or as a friend, for I am sure nobody ever had more kindness for anybody than I have for Lady Marlborough. It is thanks to her efforts that at last I have my revenue settled — or rather, most it, for I do not think 50,000 pounds quite enough to keep me comfortable, although 'tis sufficient to keep me from embarrassment for the time being. It is my desire that Lady Marlborough should accept from me a thousand pounds a year, as an earnest of my good will and gratitude. But I do not wish her ever to mention of it to me, for I should be ashamed to have any notice taken of such a thing from one that deserves more than I shall ever be able to return. (Also it is a relief to me to be able to settle the gambling debts I have run up with respect to Lady Marlborough, for it has been a great mortification to me to have been unable to do so before.)

Have mercy upon me, O God, after thy great goodness; according to the multitude of thy mercies, do away my offences; make me a clean heart, O God, and renew a right spirit within me — and if it is that I must be chastised again — as I fear I may deserve — I beg you in your mercy to allow me to bear the affliction in my own person, that my innocent child should not be put in danger again on my account, and I beg you to preserve the lives of the Prince and my Father in Ireland — and the King's, of course — for they shall meet in battle soon, and if I am with child again as I suspect I am, please spare this child as you were pleased to spare my boy. I offer you my contrite heart. Amen.

CHINTZ

It can only have been a few weeks since Anne was last in the Queen's Gallery at Kensington, but it seems in that time to have become twice as cluttered. There are new cabinets and new shelves, all of them supporting great, teetering piles of porcelain and Delftware; Anne has to watch her feet, lest she trip over a velvet dog-bed, and her headdress (they have since Mary arrived grown tall, like Dutch gables) in case it gets tangled in a hanging bird cage. She has to make her way round the forest of chairs and embroidery frames Mary has permanently set up, so that neither she nor her Maids of Honour might ever waste a moment in idleness. Two or three Maids are working at the frames when Anne arrives, and are themselves somewhat overfurnished, with long, wide lappets dangling from the sides of their headdresses, lace sprouting abundantly from their elbows, and huge bows jostling each other up and down their stomachers. Not that Anne herself is any more plainly dressed: her sister has set the fashion, and she cannot but keep up with it.

The Maids very properly stand up and curtsy when they see it is Anne approaching with all proper ceremony, the Lord Chamberlain at her side, and Lady Frescheville behind. When they reach the end of the Gallery, the Lord Chamberlain knocks on the door to the Queen's apartments, and announces Anne; a Lady of the Bedchamber opens it, and shows her through. Lady Frescheville stays behind in the Gallery. There is no-one in the bedchamber but the King standing, Anne curtsying, and, reclining somewhere behind new chintz bedhangings, the Queen.

The King must be in a gentler temper today, because he does not leave Anne to hold her curtsy for more than an instant, but shows her to a chair at the Queen's bedside.

'We are glad to see you here,' he says. 'We were very pleased when you asked to wait on us. The Queen has wished you might come since she first fell ill.'

'Thank you, Your Majesty. I do not think anybody — save yourself, of course — could be more concerned for Her Majesty's well-being than I — and I have prayed to God a thousand times for Your Majesty's recovery.'

Mary smiles, and holds her arms up so that the sisters might embrace. She looks a little feverish, tired, but truly not so ill that one might fear for her.

'Please, dear Anne — we are quite private — there is no need for "Your Majesty" here.'

Mary's speaks in a tiny, scratched voice. It makes Anne wince to hear it.

'Does your throat still pain you, Sister?'

'Yes, very much; it has grown worse by degrees, and — I am so glad you are here, for I do fear I might die soon, and I must endeavour to set my affairs in order, and I could not bear to leave this world with such a coldness between us.'

'Mary, I do not believe you are dying!'

'Neither do I,' says the King. 'Perhaps you might persuade her of that, for I cannot.'

'Whatever happens, it will be God's will, and I need to know that when I am gone, things will not go too badly between you.'

Anne meets the King's eye and sees that he does not know how to answer this any better than she does: they are neither of them accomplished liars. Happily, Mary spares them the trouble.

'I expect God will take of it,' she says.

'And if you should live, my dear,' says the

King, 'which I have every confidence you will, you will need your sister's friendship when I am in Ireland.'

Mary takes Anne's hand and grips it hard. 'Oh Sister, I am so afraid — I will have my Council to advise me — but I am so unfit for business, so unfit . . .'

'Mary, I have never known you do anything badly — you, who are in all things so diligent . . . And I must say I will be in need of friendship too, with the Prince gone.'

This is greeted with complete silence. Anne decides to leave the subject to one side, and to say what she has come to say.

'I must not delay more in saying — to both your Majesties — that I have come today not only to see how the Queen does, but also to ask pardon of both of you for all that has passed, and to beg that you might see fit to forget anything I might have done to displease you.'

The King only nods, but the Queen holds out her arms again, and a single, pretty tear falls down her cheek.

'Pass it all over, Anne — say nothing of it — only please be assured, dear Sister, always, that I will ever be ready to show you any kindness I can — whatever you need.'

Anne knows that she had far better not say what she is about to say, here, at this moment, and yet she finds she cannot hinder herself from saying it. Perhaps she is possessed.

'Then you now have a fair opportunity to do so, Sister, for I would be grateful if you and the King would consent to make up my revenue from the Privy Purse — I should be quite comfortable, I think, with 20,000 pounds more.'

At once Mary lets go of Anne's shoulders. The look of disappointment on her face is near intolerable, but Anne has started now, and she must carry her point.

'It was the Speaker of the House, M— Your Majesty, who suggested it, and I have spoken also to Lord Rochester, and he agreed that this would be best.'

'And my Lady Marlborough?' Mary asks. 'What did she have to say to it? A great deal, I daresay.'

'You look tired, my love,' says the King, and to Anne: 'The Queen is tired.'

It is the strangest thing, but the Gallery seems even more cluttered on the way out.

CAMPDEN HOUSE

As the Duke of Gloucester approaches his first birthday, and it looks every day more likely that he will live beyond it, Anne and Mary suspend their quarrel for a few days and look for a larger, more permanent home for his growing household. Their fancy alights upon Campden House, one of those red-brick merchants' homes that aspire to be castles, all covered in turrets and chimneys and studded with coats of arms. It is a good size, not too far from Kensington Palace; it has an avenue of elms and a fine shrubbery. The rent is outrageous, but Anne takes it anyway. If it pleases God, she will give birth again come winter, and there will be room enough for that child too.

Before then, she must endure a summer without George, who has followed the King, at his own expense, to Ireland. In his own coach, too, for the King will not have him in his. The King does not care to talk to

George. He does not care to talk to anyone save his old friend Portland and his pretty page, Keppel. George is thoroughly snubbed in Ireland. He is fighting alongside William when they defeat the late King's army on the banks of the Boyne, but there is no mention of this in the *Gazette*. When couriers leave for England they do so without waiting for his letters, so Anne has to ask the Secretary of State, Lord Nottingham, to intervene so that she can hear the news from her husband. Anne cannot help but observe that Mary seems to have taken but little interest in the matter herself.

'But did you mention it to her?' asks Barbara. She is Lady Fitzharding now, and in mourning for her father-in-law, the late Viscount: it is a very uncomfortable thing, to have to wear black in summer. They have had the drawing-room windows opened at Campden House this evening, but the air is unmoving, and warm as soup, so it makes no difference.

'No. It is impossible to speak to my sister about anything that matters — we dine, we play cards, we talk of the Duke and the weather and how her gardens do and that is that.'

'With respect, Your Highness, the Queen has a great deal on her mind, and I am sure she does not wish to bother you with all the business she is dealing with.'

'Well, I know full well she does not trust me with it.'

'But do you truly desire to hear of it? The petitions, the warrants, the naval commissions, the letters patent — are they what interest you, truly?'

'No. I did not think they interested my sister either, but all of a sudden she has taken to interfering in things she was meant to leave to the Council.'

'It is hardly interfering when it is all done in her name — and by all accounts, she acquits herself very well.'

'My sister-so-diligent? Of course she does.'

'Your *Highness*!'

'Oh, you think I am unkind, I know, but there is a want of kindness on her part too — you would think, with our husbands away, and our father — you would think we could comfort each other — but we cannot. She does not care for me, or my husband, or my friends.'

'Am I not your friend? I find her kind enough.'

'You know who I mean.'

Lady Fitzharding smiles. There is a rumbling sound in the distance. Anne starts.

'Surely those are not guns? The French

were in the West but weeks ago — do you think . . . ?'

'No! It is thunder, and very welcome, if it brings an end to this heat.'

Lady Fitzharding must have God's ear, for out of nowhere there is a gust of wind to stir the elm trees, and in an instant the room is cooler. A moment later the lightning comes. Footmen and pages rush in and close the casements, just in time for the deluge to start.

'We must go to the nursery, Lady Fitzharding. I think my boy might be frighted.'

But it is only his mother who is frighted. Gloucester is sitting on a carpet the Queen has sent over from Kensington for him, striking a silver rattle against the leg of Mrs Pack's chair, and crowing at every thunder-clap.

'He looks perfectly content, Your Highness,' says Lady Fitzharding.

'He's in a merry pin,' says Mrs Pack. 'The louder the thunder gets, the more he likes it.'

'A born soldier,' says Lady Fitzharding. 'His uncle will be proud.'

'Not any time soon,' says Anne. 'Past his first birthday and he is barely crawling.'

At the sound of his mother's voice,

Gloucester looks up from his work. 'Y'ighness!' he cries, and holds his arms out.

'Dearest! Do you want to play with your mama's pearls again?'

Anne picks her son up and, as she expects, he at once seizes hold of the pearls she wears about her neck, and proceeds to examine them with a serious air, as if he were checking them for flaws. Then he pulls at the string hard, watching Anne's face, laughing at her grimace.

'Ow! Why does he do that?'

'To see you pull that face, Your Highness,' says Mrs Pack. 'It is *very* comical.'

'You are insolent!' snaps Lady Fitzharding. 'You must beg Her Highness's pardon.'

'No, no, not at all . . . I daresay it *is* comical . . . Mrs Pack, that rattle there —' Anne points to the silver toy on the carpet — 'was that another gift from Her Majesty? It looks familiar, but I cannot remember its arriving.'

'I found it when we were moving from Craven House, Madam. It was in a cupboard.'

'Now I remember: it is the rattle my sister sent from Holland, that Lady Mary used to play with.'

For a moment no-one speaks. There is no sound but the rain, and the clinking of

Anne's pearls against each other as the Duke continues his investigations.

'Mrs Pack will have it put away if you wish, Your Highness.'

Anne looks at the rattle, and then at her son, now rubbing the pearls against his face. Ever since his illness at Hampton Court he has had a small issue kept open on his head, to try to take off the watery humours that swell his head and cannot but make him giddy — she cannot boast of his beauty, or of his good health, but he is lively enough when he is well, and with it content, and she would have him stay that way. 'No, it was meant for a child to play with — let him have it if he wishes.'

Abruptly, the Duke lets the pearls go. 'Down,' he says. Anne puts him back on the carpet, where he takes Lady Mary's rattle up again. He strikes it hard on the floor, and as if in obedience to him, the rain falls harder, on Campden House where his mother shudders at it, on the Tower where his great-uncle Lord Clarendon has been committed for his loyalty to his grandfather, on Whitehall Palace where his aunt the Queen, and his governess's sister Betty both await the King's return, and on the Cockpit, where his good friend Lady Marlborough prepares to give birth, and her Lord readies himself to travel to Ireland, and finish what the King has started.

14TH OCTOBER 1690

The King and the Prince are home, the latter quite unharmed, and the former merely grazed upon the shoulder. The late King has suffered another nosebleed and fled once more to France, where he is safe — humiliated, but safe. Anne is relieved. So is her friend Lady Marlborough, recently delivered of a second son, who expects any day the return of her own victorious husband; the lady is also glad of the news that her sister, Lady Tyrconnell, wife of the late King's General, has herself reached France unharmed.

There is so much to be thankful for, and the King has appointed Sunday, 19th October, as the day when everyone will show it. Anne's visits to the Queen have grown ever more strained, and she is wondering whether she might not plead her condition in order to excuse herself from a Whitehall service, with all the ceremonies performed as Mary would have them; it is almost certain that the King and Queen will find a way to insult George again, either there or at dinner, and Anne fears she might show her displeasure somehow, in front of all the world, and then more harm will be done all round than if she had stayed away as she wishes to. On the Monday before the service she retires to Campden House to think about it, and very early on Tuesday morning, two months before time, the birth pains start.

It is not to be expected that a seven-months' child will be strong, but some do live. The household prays, and the child, a daughter, is delivered alive. She is a little pale doll of a thing, with a feeble cry like a kitten. Anne has her chaplain sent for as soon as the navel-string is tied. Within the hour, she has been baptised Mary, after the Queen, and before the morning is out she is dead. God has seen fit to punish Anne by granting her wish: she will not be expected to give thanks at Whitehall.

THE QUEEN'S LADIES

The following January, the King departs for the Netherlands, to lead the English army against the French. Mary is alone again. Anne must wait on her every day. As for respect, she hopes she behaves towards her sister with as much as is possible. Lady Marlborough will keep chiding her for not being pleasant enough to the Queen, but the truth is, Anne says, that she does not have it in her to feign an affection she does not feel, and she cannot — no, not if it were to save her soul — make court to any lady she has no very great inclination for. The dissembling she had to do during her father's reign was surely enough for a lifetime. She will not dissemble with her sister. Not with Mary.

But duty is duty, and they must be seen to be friends. Anne waits on her sister. They play every night together at comet or basset, at the Queen's apartments, where Mary keeps the Bank. On Anne's birthday, the Queen condescends to play cards at the Cockpit instead, and afterwards, in Anne's honour, she holds a dance in her own drawing-room. All in all, they endeavour to give the Court as little as possible to whisper about, but all the world knows which lady it is takes first place in Anne's heart, for she cannot hide that either. She offers Lady Marlborough her 1,000 pounds a year, and after some discussion with Lord Godolphin, Lady Marlborough accepts.

The Queen may disapprove, but Anne thinks it must be out of jealousy, for Mary has no lady she might truly call a friend: it has been a long time since Lady Bathurst was her 'husband', her Aurelia, and her husband's position in Anne's household makes it impossible for the Queen to renew their former closeness; Lady Fitzharding moves easily between the sisters' Courts, but is not quite trusted in either; her sister Anne, Lady Bentinck, died when she was still in Holland; her older sister, Betty, has never been any kind of friend to the Queen. Mary is fond of one of her Ladies of the Bedchamber, Lady Dorset, a sweet and conspicuously virtuous young matron, but otherwise, it seems to Anne, all of Mary's real friends are bishops.

On the night of the fire at Whitehall, however, there are no bishops available — indeed, it seems that there are no gentlemen of any kind in the Palace, for when Anne and George find Mary by the Privy Garden sundial, where she is watching the Stone Gallery burning down, there are no men in sight. Lady Dorset stands at the Queen's side; Lady Scarborough comes forward to greet them; Betty Villiers is there too, keeping herself at a tactful distance.

'The Princess, Your Majesty,' says Lady Scarborough.

Mary turns to see them. Her face is orange on one side, lit up by the blaze, and grey as death on the other.

'It began in your boy's lodgings,' she says. 'An accident, I'm told — a maid left a candle burning when she should not, but of course when I was told the news I must confess I did think about — other causes.'

'O Good Lord! Well we must thank heaven he is safe at Campden House!'

'I have heard no reports of anyone hurt,' says Mary. 'That is a great blessing, at least.'

'You seem very calm, Sister.'

Mary shrugs.

'You heard the blast — the men have blown up the Earl of Portland's lodgings so the fire will not spread to the rest of the

Palace. I have been heartily frighted, yes, but — all these lodgings burning there, you remember who lived in them? The Duchess of Portsmouth, all those other lewd creatures, and I always thought them ugly buildings, unhealthy — the King never liked them either — he will not grieve to hear they've been consumed.'

She laughs, a little uncertainly.

'Portland will not be very pleased,' says Anne, and smiles.

'He'll have new lodgings. So will your son. Did you keep much of value there? You'll have lost it all.'

She says nothing about compensation.

'Most of my boy's possessions are with him at Campden. We did not keep much here.'

'I'm glad to hear it.'

They stand there for a moment, the three of them — Mary, Anne, George — and watch as the old, lascivious, filthy Whitehall their uncle played in burns away. Then there is a shout of, 'Her Majesty! There she is!' and the guards that have been so noticeably absent find their Queen and run, belatedly, to defend her.

'I am quite unharmed, as you see,' she tells them. 'My Ladies and I will be taking refuge at Arlington House till we're told 'tis safe to return. And here is our escort —'

She breaks off, puts her hand over her mouth, and laughs, not half-heartedly this time, but wildly, as Anne has not heard her laugh for years. The escort is one Master Fuller, and he has just fallen face first into a patch of nettles. He recovers very gallantly, dusting off his coat, and making his compliment, even as his face is swelling up; it is an honour, he says, to have been the man who has made the Queen so pleasant.

Still laughing, the Queen takes her leave of Anne, and leaves for Arlington House, trailing ladies and guards behind her. George decides to accompany her part of the way, an offer she does not rebuff. When he comes back to the Cockpit he tells Anne that the Queen was pursued all the way through St James's Park by Sir John Fenwick and Colonel Oglethorpe, the Jacobite knaves, shouting after her that the fire was but a forecast of just, eternal punishment.

ANNE DINES AT HOLYWELL

This afternoon Anne dines in paradise, otherwise known as Holywell House. She has George sitting on one side of her, and Sarah on the other. Later, she will have the pleasure of playing with Lady Marlborough's pretty children; her pleasure for the moment is all in a dish of trout caught from the Marlboroughs' own stream, and served up in a creamy sauce with all kinds of flavour in it.

'Can you guess?' Lady Marlborough asks.

'Anchovies, certainly.'

'Yes.'

'Horseradish, thyme . . . lemon peel?'

'Very good, Your Highness. And those first two from my garden.'

'You are so fortunate, Lady Marlborough. We have nothing as good to eat in town. I would rather live as you do here — but I have a sister I must wait on.'

'Though I imagine she is much taken up

with business, with the King away?'

'Indeed, but there is plenty of time left over for her — her knotting and fretting!'

'Yes, I can just see her now.' Sarah takes up her fork and weaves it tightly back and forth as if it were a knotting shuttle. 'And hear her too: "Fret, fret, blabber, blabber, knot, knot, Lady Fret how charming, your children Lady Blabber, fret, fret, knot, the King, when I was in Holland, last night at cards, the gardens at Kensington, fret, knot, fret, knot, most exquisite straight from China, fret . . ." '

'Oh *stop it,* I pray you — you have made the poor Prince choke on his wine!'

'I beg your pardon, Your Highness.'

'No, no, no, Lady Marlborough — you have the Queen to a nicety, that's all.'

'Then I fear that was treasonable.'

'Not to us. You may say what you wish before the Prince and me. Especially since this latest insult.'

'Are you so very sorry, my dear, to have your husband with you when the Queen and Lady Marlborough do not?'

'Of course not, George! But for the Queen to *forbid* you to go to the wars — *forbid* you — and all your belongings hauled off the ship — as if you were but a schoolboy run away to sea! I'm sure no Prince was ever used so.'

George shrugs. 'And yet when I told the King of my design, he embraced me — I took it for consent.'

'*Anybody* would. And why should you not have gone? Surely all the world would expect you to?'

'Your Highnesses —' Lady Marlborough looks as if she must say something, but then she hesitates.

'Go on, I pray you.'

'Very well. I did not tell you this before, but the Queen asked me for help in this. Her request was that I persuade His Highness that he should not go, but that I should do so as if I were only giving him my own thoughts on the matter — so you would not think she had interfered. Of course I said I would not do it.'

'Your loyalty does you credit — my Mrs Freeman.'

'Mrs Morley, I am at your service.'

'These are the names you told me of, Anne? That you use in letters? Very droll — I like them.'

'It is only good sense to use pseudonyms,' says Lady Marlborough. 'Between Holywell and the Cockpit, who knows? A dozen hands might open them, and two dozen eyes peruse.'

'There is that, but what pleases me so much, George, is that it removes that distance between us, that comes from our different places in the world — I do believe I could do without my rank and all that comes with it, if it meant I could enjoy our friendship the more.'

'Your High— dear Mrs Morley, would you care for some peas?'

FROM THE PRINCESS OF DENMARK TO THE KING

Tunbridge, August 2, 1691

I hope you will pardon me for giving you this trouble, but I can't help seconding the request the Prince has now made to you to remember your promise of a Garter for my Lord Marlborough. You cannot certainly bestow it upon anyone that has been more serviceable to you in the late revolution nor that has ventured their lives for you as he has done ever since your coming to the Crown. But if people won't think these merits enough, I can't believe anybody will be so unreasonable to be dissatisfied when 'tis known you are pleased to give it to him on the Prince's account and mine. I am sure I shall ever look upon it as a mark of your favour to us. I will not trouble you with any ceremony, because I know

483

you don't care for it.

Anne

Anne's Non-Naturals

O merciful and righteous Lord, the God of health and of sickness, of life and of death, I must own that my great abuse of those many days of strength and welfare which you have afforded me, has most justly deserved this present visitation. I have much time at home and here at Tunbridge to meditate and search my heart, for though my fever is gone, there are still days when I am so lame I cannot go without limping. We have two companies of foot guards stationed here with us, but poor fellows, they can do nothing but kick their heels outside my lodgings, for I scarcely go abroad.

Dr Radcliffe says it is most likely the gout — though the joints are not inflamed quite as he would expect in such a case. When I felt the pain first I was much reminded of what I suffered after I last miscarried, before the late King went away — that was as if I was burning on the inside — the most terrible torment — and what I have now is that same pain in little: little fires in my legs, that burn me if I am so foolish as to move too much. Perhaps that is how your displeasure feels . . . and if so, I must accept there is no mending my legs until you give me grace to mend my soul, and I pray for that grace this day, that I might search my sins out, and repent of them.

It is intemperance that Dr Radcliffe thinks me guilty of: I have indulged myself too much at the table, he says; now there is such an excess of blood in my body, that nature cannot manage it in the usual fashion, but is pushed to this extreme remedy, this gouty attack on my joints. He does not think it is wise to purge, but I trust very much in the waters here: I have some brought me fresh every morning — and while the effects may render me still less capable of venturing out, I am satisfied in them, for they are the signs that the waters are working well with me again.

The doctor's preferred remedy, of course, is temperance. He says I ought to pay proper attention to my 'non-naturals', as he calls them. Less meat and drink, of course; I should neither sleep nor watch too much; I should have a care of the passions of my mind, not fright myself over every little thing; I should stay where the air is good. Most of all, he believes I do not exercise enough. I do love to exercise, I do love to ride, but in my present state I cannot without great pain mount a horse — I have ordered a caleche to be made for me, so I might hunt in that — though Sir Benjamin says I can scarce bear the expense. Whatever I require, he says there is not the money for: the King and Queen never would give me that twenty thousands more — and of course I cannot help but worry over that, and other matters.

I cannot but be concerned with the health of those whom I love, and there is always much to be concerned about — I am forever on the rack over the condition of my poor boy; I fear he will always be sickly: there is the watery humour in his head, he is often suffering with fevers and not so long ago he was quite ill of a looseness though through it all his temper was good. He can at last cross a room by himself but I do not think he shall be able to go abroad with leading-strings, he is so clumsy and so heedless. I was advised against carrying him with me to Tunbridge, but he must always be with me in my thoughts — I am his mother. Permit me to commend him, Lord, as I do daily, to your blessing and protection.

Let me this day commend to you my Lady Marlborough, who is here not only to attend me but also to take the waters herself, for she is not this summer as strong as she is usually and it is a great trouble to me to see her suffering. She complains of the vapours and of headaches which she says are like a weight on her eyes. 'Tis plain to me that the headaches are caused by her excessive reading — Seneca and the like, which she says is to improve her mind but she has already such a sound understanding that I cannot see the good of it — what is in Seneca that can make her manage her household better, or raise her children, or be a better friend to me? Yes, I confess I am jealous of Seneca — and of Lady Fitzharding, who I am sure draws my Lady Marlborough away from me whenever she can to play cards and laugh together, but when she is with me does nothing but put a sullen face on and complain. I should repent of my jealous temper, but Lady Fitzharding does not treat me as she ought, and I wish she might repent of that. But I do not mind her so much as I do the state of Lady Marlborough's house, for I fear much it might cause her to resign her post, and without her I do not know how I will go on. I beg you, do not suffer anymore or anything to take her from me.

My Lord Godolphin is with us, and also takes the waters. I pray that they will do him good, because he is vexed daily by the Treasury business that comes to him here, much of which he says might be carried on just as well in his absence as if he were there himself. Lady Marlborough says it is the peculiar predicament of men as reliable and able as he, to find themselves so burdened by those who trust no-one else. That the King and Queen trust him I have no doubt. The late King trusted him too — and it is true that he took no part in the revolution. He is a prudent man. He gives good advice. We play cards together every day. If he were to resign his post, I do believe I would have no real friends left in Council.

I would do what is prudent; I would also do what is right. When I was in Tunbridge that other summer, and His Grace the Archbishop — the Dean, he was then — preached on the Ten Virgins — I did truly believe that it was both prudent and right to join with my sister and my husband against my father. I was in better health then than I am now — though I must beg your forgiveness for having dissembled about that, because I thought it expedient. I lied, and in dishonouring my father I broke a Commandment, and these are the fruit of it: fires in my joints, a sickly son, another dead daughter, a near-empty purse and between my sister and I a coldness that must pain us both.

I put aside my rights for the King and Queen, and we have not asked them for much in return, the Prince and I. The Prince has given up his lands and received this month but meagre compensation — and even then no money, but only the promise of it. And to our letters requesting the Garter for my Lord Marlborough we have received no reply, and I do not believe we ever shall.

That the King and Queen neither like nor

trust my friends the Marlboroughs is clear enough. The King will not give him the commands that he is more than fit for; the Queen will barely speak a civil word to my friend — for all that she is not above trying to use her influence with me if she thinks it in her interests to do so. . . . I can only regard their unkindness to our friends as further unkindness to us . . .

While we have been in Tunbridge, Lady Marlborough has told me that her Lord has written to my father to beg his pardon; Lord Godolphin has written to him too. I understand that half the country has done the same. For myself, I do not feel safe as I had hoped I would: the Jacobites are defeated in Ireland, but threaten to rise in Scotland; my own uncle Clarendon is a prisoner in his own house; no-one knows how the war may go in the Low Countries. The Queen is afraid, she jumps at the slightest thing; now her Lady Dorset has died there is no company at Court might render her less splenetic.

I beg you give me the grace to know where my duty lies, to tell what is danger-ous from what is safe, for my own sake, and for the Prince's, and for that of my sister whom I do love even though she is unkind, and of my true friends, and my household, and most of all my boy.

Amen.

THE REFORMATION
OF MANNERS

'I think I'm ready, Lady Marlborough —
the duckett, please.'

Sarah passes the cloth to Anne, and gathers up her mistress's skirts. Anne rubs her
thumb over the duckett for a moment: it
feels rough, unkind; far too unkind for its
delicate office.

'Your Highness? Are we to stand like this
in your stool closet all evening? There's no
sense in putting it off.'

'I beg your pardon. I'm a coward, I know.
Very well then —' She grimaces, wipes the
cloth over her privy parts and at once,
without glancing at it, hands it back to Lady
Marlborough.

'Well? Tell me what it is.'

'Wait — I must get a candle . . . Ah, I
thought so! 'Tis good news: no sign of Lady
Charlotte — if you were with child before,
then you are still.'

'Let me see. Are you certain? Are you sure

there is no blood? What about that dark patch there?'

'That is nothing. Only — only *moisture,* Your Highness. Of course, I can keep the duckett by me till daylight if you are not sure.'

'No, no! I would not have you sleep with my soiled ducketts! It is just — I thought I felt some — when one has miscarried so many times, one always fears . . .'

'I know, I know . . . Well, let's drink to the health of this child. Did you say anything to the Prince?'

'No. I would not have him frighted without cause.'

Danvers is waiting outside the closet door. Sarah tells her that there is no need to alarm herself, and to answer the scratch on the bedchamber door.

'It is Lady Fitzharding, Your Highness.'

'Come in, Babs! Sit down with us! We are to drink to the health of my unborn — Danvers, ask for some wine — no — brandy — and cakes with it.'

'Brandy? Is that not a touch strong? Would the Queen not consider the drinking of brandy by ladies in the evening to be a disorderly practice?'

Anne frowns. 'I know she would not do it herself, but . . .'

'I do not think Lady Marlborough is serious, Your Highness. She is talking of the King and Queen's attempts to promote a reformation of the manners of their subjects.'

'Oh, I see! Well, as we are merely to drink a toast in my chamber, and not in the street —'

'— and will not at the same time indulge in any profane cursing, swearing, profanation of the Lord's Day, or any other lewd, enormous or disorderly practice, I think we may proceed without fear of dishonouring God, bringing curses upon the nation — or, worse than that, upsetting your sister.'

'The Queen's intent is only for the nation's good.'

'Yes, Lady Fitzharding, it is, but I fear the nation will only laugh at her — and do so on the Lord's Day, too.'

'My sister was used to laugh more herself,' says Anne.

'She still does.'

'With you perhaps, Lady Fitzharding — not with me.'

A footman comes in with the brandy and cakes. Anne tells him to set them down upon the table: she will serve her friends herself. She pours for Sarah, then for Barbara, then for herself. They drink a toast to the child.

'And to the King and Queen?'

'Of course, Lady Fitzharding, though I think, so as not to offend, we should call the liquor "cold tea" this time.'

'Yes, let's — and would you like a measure more of cold tea to make the loyal toast?'

With all due respect, they toast the King and Queen.

'This reformation of manners business,' Anne says, 'is all the Dutch influence. They look down upon us, they call us lewd — I heard that Bentinck sent his eldest daughter back to Holland; he said he would not have her "debauched" by remaining in England! Imagine!'

'And this from a wooden fellow who can barely utter a civil word.'

'He and the King are of a kind. All coldness. I have heard the King strikes his servants with his cane when he is vexed — the Prince and I would never treat our family so. How is that a good example?'

'It is a dreadful example!' Sarah slams her glass down on the table: she is working up to one of her rants. 'He has no gratitude, no proper feeling for anyone who is not a countryman! He is King of England, yet we have Dutchmen all over Court, Dutch Officers of State, and *so* many Dutch generals, when there are Englishmen twice as capable!'

'And one Englishman in particular,' says Lady Fitzharding, 'who, I'm told, has made his feelings known in Parliament — and among his army friends.'

'My husband is very popular in the army,' says Sarah, 'and so he should be. *They* know his true worth at least. And is it such a terrible notion, that Englishmen only should fill English places?'

'Not to an Englishman, but the King might see it differently. Would you not, if you were in his place, wish to have your old friends by you?'

'Is this how he thinks? Is this what Betty tells you? Will he not accept an Englishman's oath? It is insulting. Does he not believe my husband can be trusted?'

Lady Fitzharding says nothing, only contemplates her empty glass; Sarah scowls; Anne breaks the silence to offer more cold tea.

From the Princess of Denmark to King James, Written with the Assistance of the Earl and Countess of Marlborough

The Cockpit, December 1, 1691

I have been very desirous of some safe opportunity to make you a sincere and humble offer of my duty and submission to you, and to beg that you will be assured that I am both truly concerned for the misfortune of your condition and sensible, as I ought to be, of my own unhappiness. As to what you may think I have contributed to it, if wishes could recall what is past, I had long since redeemed my fault. I am sensible it would have been a great relief to me if I could have found means to acquaint you earlier with my repentant thoughts, but I hope they may find the advantage of coming late, of being less suspected of insincerity than perhaps they would have been at any time before.

It will be a great addition to the ease I propose to my own mind by this plain confession if I am so happy as to find that it brings any real satisfaction to yours, and that you are as indulgent and easy to receive my humble submission as I am to make them, in a free, disinterested acknowledgement of my fault, for no other end but to deserve and receive your pardon.

I have had a great mind to beg you to make one compliment for me, but fearing the expressions which would be properest for me to make use of might be perhaps the least convenient for a letter, I must content myself at present with hoping the bearer will make a compliment for me to the Queen.

Anne

ANNE AND HER SISTER MARY

After all that has passed between them, all Anne desires from Mary is that she leave her be, but she is not to have even this most meagre satisfaction. The Queen has summoned her to her presence; they are in her closet, with the door shut, alone. Anne makes her compliment dutifully.

'Oh don't "Your Majesty" me, Anne! We are quite alone. Do sit down.'

Anne eases herself, stiffly, bulkily, into a chair.

'Look at the pair of us, Anne — both grown so stout.'

'I am with child.'

'You are *always* with child. The Prince gives you no time to recover; it's disastrous for your health — can he not leave you alone for a while after this one?'

'I am sensible of your concern, Sister, but I don't care to be left alone. We prefer to share a bed.'

'So I've heard — as if you were paupers with no choice about it — very odd. But then, I find your household arrangements odd altogether.'

'I don't understand you, Sister. What do you mean?'

'Mrs Pack, for example.'

'What of her?'

'She is dirty, and her manners are appalling. I do not think her a suitable person to attend upon the Duke.'

'We owe Mrs Pack a great debt.'

'Yes, but, he has been weaned so long, surely you have redeemed it by now?'

'She is a perfectly capable dry-nurse, and my boy loves her.'

'I suppose he loves Jenkin Lewis too.'

'Oh, I do believe he prefers Jenkin Lewis to any other soul on earth! What is wrong with Master Lewis?'

'He is another very capable servant, I'm sure, but should he be such a close companion to the boy? The child is talking more and more now — and sounding more and more Welsh with it.'

'Lewis only ever speaks English with him.'

'Well it's some strange variety.'

'But if you only saw them together, Mary. Such good friends. And Master Lewis is no booby, you know — he is Lord Fitzharding's protégé; he gives him the run of his library. You only see my boy when you summon him here — you cannot know how we care for him.'

'No, I suppose I would know nothing of child-rearing.'

'*Mary,* I did not mean to —'

'But Lady Marlborough gives you all kinds of advice, I expect.'

'Yes, she does.'

'And not only about the boy.'

'Sister, I do not know what you mean.'

'Did she advise you that she needed an annuity?'

'It is up to me what I do with my own income.'

'That income was given to you so that you might run your household, not make presents to your favourites.'

'It is up to me what I do with my own income.'

'You should not have given her that money.'

'It is up to me —'

'Oh *stop it,* Anne — stop saying the same thing over and over, it is enough to try a saint's patience when you do that.'

So Anne says nothing at all. She will not look at Mary either.

'Well, even if you will not speak, you can

at least listen. I see the influence that woman has over you, and I am truly appalled by it — the King is too. We had hoped that in time your infatuation would wear itself out — heaven knows you forgot about Mrs Cornwallis quickly enough — if she were a more trustworthy person, we could smile on it, but we have good reason to doubt her loyalty to us — and her Lord's even more.'

'I don't know what you mean.'

'Oh *don't* you? Do you know what is meant by "Caliban"? Or how about "the Dutch Abortion"? No, you need not bother protesting — your blushing gives you away.'

'I do not wish to pick quarrels, Mary.'

'Is that what you think this is, Anne? "Picking quarrels"? We are not in the nursery anymore. I am the Queen, and my husband is the King, and you are our heir, and there are those who will seek to make a property of you just as there were those that made a property of our poor cousin Monmouth!'

'What has that to do with my Lady Marlborough and me?'

'And now you pretend to be stupid — of course! You never change. Listen: this is what you will do: you will cancel that annuity —'

'No.'

'I beg your pardon?'

'No. It is up to me what I do with my own income.'

'If you do not cancel the annuity, we will take half of your income away.'

'You cannot. It is not in your power. Parliament granted it to me.'

'Then I ask you as your sister.'

'No.'

'Then you do not love me.'

'*Mary.* Don't cry, please — I'll cry too.'

'Only because I have vexed you. You don't care.'

'Mary —'

'You are dismissed.'

'*Mary.*'

'Leave my presence.'

All Anne can do is to make a deplorable curtsy, and obey.

THE EARL OF MARLBOROUGH'S DISMISSAL

Next morning, the Earl of Marlborough, who is a Gentleman of the Bedchamber to the present King as he was to the last, takes his turn in waiting upon his master. The King accepts his shirt from him in absolute silence, but then he always does, so it is a shock to the Earl, only a little later on, when Nottingham calls upon him to give him the news that he is dismissed — from the bedchamber, from Court, from the army, from everything. There is no reason given by the King or Queen, so the Court tries to find out its own: Marlborough has been stirring up trouble in the army; the most compromising letters between him and King James have been discovered to the King; he has, through carelessness and his wife's family connections with the Court in exile, caused damaging intelligence to reach the French; he has been caught taking excessive bribes and has been extorting money at every opportunity from officers under his command.

'It is all lies,' says Anne to Godolphin, through tears, 'because surely the only true reason is that the King and Queen have no real friends in England and so they must needs deprive me of mine.'

A letter arrives at the Cockpit, unsigned, in an unknown hand. Its author, as a friend and well-wisher, desires to beg Anne to have a care of what she says before Lady Fitzharding: remember, the letter says, she is Lord Portland and Betty Villiers' sister, and Anne may depend upon it that these two are not ignorant of what is said and done in her lodgings; it is for Anne to judge whether they make not their Court at her expense, by exposing her and preserving the King, as they take it. Anne must know that she is but an honourable prisoner, being in the hands of the Dutch Guard, and if any violence were to be offered, what could her friends possibly do for her then? The King and Queen have been told that not a day has passed since Lord Marlborough's being out, that Anne has not shed tears. Without a doubt, the Earl will be arrested as soon as the present Parliament is up, and if Anne does not part with his Lady of her own accord, she will be obliged to it. Lady Fitzharding is not sincere in her concern, and she is the confidant of poor, deluded Lady Marlborough. Should Anne slight this advice, the writer wishes she may not have leave to repent it. And by the way, it has been taken great notice of Lord Godolphin's being at Lord Marlborough's lodging so late the night he was turned out.

Anne cannot take such a letter as absolute proof of Lady Fitzharding's treachery, so she does not confront her, though it seems reasonable enough to have a care of what she says in that lady's presence from now on, and to encourage Sarah to do the same. She cannot take seriously any suggestion that violence might be offered her — Mary, even at her most unkind, would never, ever countenance such an act — but the other evil the letter warns her to expect, that she will be made to part with Lady Marlborough, seems all too likely an eventuality, and one that she resolves to do all in her power to prevent. William and Mary must understand that she simply will not tolerate any such interference in her own household: the Prince may have relinquished Lord Scarsdale when the late King ordered him to do, but that was all part of their pretended obedience to her father, and there were good reasons for it. Her sister and brother-in-law will have her sincere obedience, or no obedience at all.

Here is the perfect opportunity for Anne to prove, once and for all, that Lady Marlborough could have no greater friend. The dismissal of her husband has come as a great shock to Sarah, and Anne must comfort her, put heart into her, refuse her offers of resignation, lest she run away to St Albans for good, and never come to town again. Mrs Freeman has done nothing wrong; Mrs Freeman is indispensable to Anne's happiness; Mrs Freeman should not on any account relinquish any of those duties which she performs so much more capably than any other lady Mrs Morley has ever employed; Mrs Freeman is Mrs Morley's most faithful and trusted Lady, and esteemed friend, and as such she will accompany her mistress to Court.

As they make their progress through the Palace that evening, from the gate to the door of the drawing-room, the same scene plays out again and again: the Princess of Denmark is announced; the room bows and curtsies; then it sees Lady Marlborough; there is the briefest silence, and then a great wave breaks, of exclamations, laughter and, here and there, applause. At the final door, opened by an astonished Gentleman Usher, Anne feels Sarah hesitate: she has to take her hand and all but drag her in.

The drawing-room silence is instant and complete, and, save for the odd uneasy titter, does not seem likely to break. The Lord Chamberlain conducts them to the table where Mary has been playing basset. She sits with her gaze fixed on Anne, her face a perfect mask, while the eyes of the Court flit from one sister to the other and back again. Anne and Sarah make their curtsies, their compliments. Mary accepts these, allows them both to kiss her hand, but after that she turns away and takes her cards up, makes some inconsequential remark to the lady next to her, and carries on as if they were not there. The chatter starts up again. They stay long enough for Anne to exchange a few words with one or two ladies, just to show that she is not ashamed, but the Queen does not invite either of them to sit down, so it is no hardship to be leaving early.

FROM THE QUEEN TO THE PRINCESS OF DENMARK

Kensington, February 5, 1692

Having something to say to you which I know will not be very pleasing, I choose rather to write it first, being unwilling to surprise you, though I think what I am going to tell you should not, if you give yourself time to think, that never any body was suffered to live at Court in Lord Marlborough's circumstances. I need not repeat the cause he has given the King to do what he has done, nor his unwillingness at all times to come to extremities, though people do deserve it.

I hope you do me the justice to believe it is much against my will that I now tell you that, after this, it is very unfit that Lady Marlborough should stay with you, since that gives her husband so just a pretence of being where he should not. I think I might have expected you should have spoke to me of it; and the King and I, both believing it, made us stay thus long. But seeing you so far from it that you brought Lady Marlborough hither last night, makes us resolve to put it off no longer, but tell you she must not stay, and that I have all the reason imaginable to look upon your bringing her as the strangest thing that ever was done. Nor could all my kindness for you (which is always ready to turn all you do the best way), at any other time, have hindered me from showing you so that moment, but I considered your condition, and that made me master myself so far as not to take notice of it then.

But now I must tell you, it was very unkind in a sister, would have been very uncivil in an equal; and I need not say I have more to claim, which, though my kindness would never make me exact, yet, when I see the use you would make of it, I must tell you I know what is due to me, and expect to have it from you. 'Tis upon that account I tell you plainly, Lady Marlborough must not continue with you, in the circumstances her Lord is.

I know this will be uneasy to you, and I am sorry for it, for I have all the real kindness imaginable for you; and as I ever have, so will always do my part to live with you as sisters ought; that is, not only like so near relations, but like friends, and as such I did think to write to you. For I would have made myself believe your kindness for her made you at first forget what you should have for the King and me, and resolved to put you in mind of it myself, neither of us being willing to come to harsher ways; but the sight of Lady Marlborough having changed my thoughts, does naturally alter my style. And since by that I see how little you seem to consider what, even in common civility, you owe us, I have told it you plainly, but, withal, assure you that, let me have never so much reason to take any thing ill of you, my kindness is so great that I can pass over most things, and live with you as becomes us. And I desire to do so merely from that motive, for I do love you as my sister, and nothing but yourself can make me do otherwise; and that is the reason I choose to write this rather than tell it to you, that you may overcome your first thoughts. And when you have well considered, you will find that, though the thing be hard (which I again assure you I am sorry for), yet it is not unreasonable, but what has ever been practised, and what yourself would do were you Queen in my place.

I will end this with once more desiring you to consider the matter impartially, and take time for it. I do not desire an answer presently, because I would not have you give a rash one. I shall come to your drawing-room tomorrow before you play, because you know why I cannot make one. At some other time we shall reason the business calmly, which I will willingly do, or any thing else that may show it shall never be my fault if we do not live kindly together. Nor will I ever be other, by choice, than Your truly loving and affectionate sister, M. R.

FROM THE PRINCESS OF DENMARK TO THE QUEEN

The Cockpit, February 6, 1692

Your Majesty was in the right to think your letter would be very surprising to me. For you must needs be sensible enough of the kindness I have for my Lady Marlborough to know that a command from you to part with her must be the greatest mortification in the world to me, and indeed of such a nature as I might well have hoped your kindness to me would have always prevented. I am satisfied she cannot have been guilty of any fault to you. And it would be extremely to her advantage if I could repeat every word that ever she said to me of you in her whole life. I confess it is no small addition to my trouble to find the want of Your Majesty's kindness to me upon this occasion, since I am sure I have always endeavoured to deserve it by all the actions of my life.

Your care of my present condition is extremely obliging. And if you would be pleased to add to it so far as upon my account to recall your serve command (as I must beg leave to call it so in a matter so tender to me and so little reasonable, as I think, to be imposed upon me, that you would scarce require it from the meanest of your subjects) I should ever acknowledge it as a very agreeable mark of your kindness to me. And I must as freely own that as I think this proceeding can be for no other intent than to give me a very sensible mortification, so there is no misery that I cannot readily resolve to suffer rather than the thoughts of parting with her. If after all this that I have said, I must still find myself so unhappy as to be farther pressed in this matter, yet Your Majesty may be assured that as my past actions have given the greatest testimony of my respect both for the King and you, so it shall always be my endeavour, wherever I am, to preserve it carefully for the time to come, as becomes

Your Majesty's very affectionate sister and servant.

SYON HOUSE

Lord, I wish it were in my power to understand why you have seen fit to harden my sister's heart against me in this way. There is ever the suspicion in my heart, especially when I wake at night, or am lame for some days together, or fear to lose another child, that my sins must weigh heavily indeed, for why else would you afflict me so? For certainly whatever the King and Queen do to me is only what you have suffered them to do; but, for the life of me, with my mean understanding, all I can ever think is that she is jealous of the great jewel you have given me in Lady Marlborough's friendship, and that he — he is still angry that he was bested over the matter of my revenue and, knave that he is, he means out of revenge to make the Prince and me uncomfortable in any way he can.

But I shall not be parted from my friend,

516

for I could no more part with my own soul. It is a great sorrow to me that the Queen will not understand this: she has refused to listen to my entreaties; she has refused to listen to my Uncle Rochester — not that he would ever plead my case in any manner sincere enough to damage his own interest with King and Queen. Indeed it is every day clearer to me that it is not to my own kin that I can look for true friendship in this world. My loyalty must, in all conscience, lie with those who have proved most loyal to me, however prejudicial it might be to my own interest, so if the King sees fit to banish Lady Marlborough from Whitehall, then I sincerely believe I have no choice but to leave with her — and might not the kindness the Duke of Somerset has shown in leasing us Syon House be taken as a sign of your blessing?

It is indeed a mercy to have such a place of refuge in these times. Isleworth promises to be very pretty come spring, and there is that about the Park that puts me in mind of Richmond, where we were all of us so content . . . I do believe Mary was content then, and though she might have reproached me for this or that offence she was never unkind. I cannot help but suppose it is the King's influence that makes her so unkind to me now. I visited her before I left, in some hopes she might relent a little, but I might just as well have made my compliment to a statue. When the Lord Chamberlain did not show me out, it was the sign of what was to come, for these days the Prince and I are treated like the meanest nobodies. Our guard has been taken away, so I was forced to travel here by chair without any proper attendance; when the Prince went to London, the guard at St James's did not present arms to him as they were supposed to — and I cannot doubt but that they showed such Dutch breeding on Dutch orders, especially since last week, when the Prince took leave of the King before he went abroad again — as was only proper — and came back to Syon to tell me he had barely been taken notice of.

All these humiliations, these petty slights are what the King and Queen hope to vex us with, but they shall be confounded, for they only strengthen my resolve, and are proof to me that to deny such a pair of monsters the satisfaction they seek is no sin, be they King and Queen of all the world. And moreover, when I see how they conduct themselves in this matter, and note how little I am daunted by it, it comes to me that what I suffer at their hands may not after all be chastisement at yours, but rather a trial of my heart and my faith, that they might both be proven in the fire, and pray I might be found unto praise and honour when my time comes.

And I pray also that you will not suffer Lady Marlborough to have any more of the cruel thoughts she has of abandoning me. Every day she offers to resign, every other day she begs me to let her go, and then I weep, for I do swear I had rather live in a cottage with her than reign empress of all the world without her.

Anne is on the rack again and this time it is worse. The pangs are fierce and so irregular that she cannot prepare herself as she has grown used to doing; worse than that, is the way they spread themselves into burning girdles all the way around her middle and then go crawling up and down her spine. If she is to die in travail, then surely it will be this time. She sends Sir Benjamin Bathurst to present her humble duty to the Queen, and to tell her how much worse she is than usual, but when he comes back it is only to tell her that the Queen would not see him, and had no answer to give.

She cannot complain of lack of assistance: she has Lady Marlborough with her, Danvers, Farthing, two good midwives of the Parish of Isleworth, and, of less value but still present, a pair of vapid Lady Charlottes — Frescheville and Beverwaert — but for all their combined skill, experience, willingness, duty, love and prayers, there is nothing, nothing they can do to help their mistress. She is lost to the pain. She rocks on all fours and cries out to God. When the chief midwife has examined her for the fourth time in an hour, she calls her deputy over. Anne hears their voices conferring together; then Lady Marlborough joins them. She kneels in front of Anne, takes her face gently in her hands, and tells her that she must be patient a little longer yet, for it is clear that the child is not offering itself in such a posture as that it may find a passage forth without assistance, and they need a man-wife to come. They are sending for Sir Hugh Chamberlen.

'No! None of him! He will bring a crochet! He will bring a hook! He will kill my child!'

In her agitation, Anne has shaken the last few pins from her hair; it hangs in her face, heavy with sweat and tears. Sarah, the Good Mother, smoothes it back.

'No, he has an instrument of his own, that God willing might save the child. Dear Mrs Morley, you will need to trust him.'

Anne closes her eyes and submits, to Sarah, to the midwives, to God and to the pain. Soon there is a great noise at the chamber door. It is Sir Hugh. He has come like a fiend in a nightmare, with quite inhuman speed. He is an unimpressive-looking man, old and crooked, but he has a great air about him, of majesty almost. His assistant walks in behind him, carrying a gilded box, which he sets down, with some ceremony, upon the table. Then Sir Hugh issues his orders: Her Highness is to be moved on to the bed, and then the other women are to clear the room — *all* of them. Anne hopes that Sarah might disobey, but even she does not dare. Anne is left alone on the bed, with her pain and her trapped child and these two alarming men. Sir Hugh tells her that it is best that she does not see what he does, and then his assistant blindfolds her.

There are first the most extraordinary, unexpected noises — rattling and the ringing of bells — and almost straight after the most extraordinary, unexpected pain, the most violent pulling and tearing, as if she has been turned into a hart, and Sir Hugh is the huntsman, dividing flesh from flesh, even as she breathes. She offers her soul to God, but in the next instant the torture stops. The blindfold comes off, and Sir Hugh tells her that she has had a boy. The women may come back into the room, and then she must send for her chaplain.

UNKINDNESS

Mary stands at the foot of Anne's bed. She is righteously, majestically tall, her head-dress pointing up to heaven. She has brought a sweet, clean fragrance into the chamber, rose and frangipani. Anne is on her back, brought down to the earth again, where the smells are very different.

'Your Majesty,' she says. The headdress tilts in acknowledgement, then its wearer sits down. Anne holds a hand out. Mary does not take it. She has a speech ready.

'Sister, I have made the first step, by coming to you, and I now expect you should make the next by removing my Lady Marlborough.'

Anne cannot look at Mary and speak at the same time. She redirects her eyes onto the comfortably blurred faces of the Queen's Ladies, Scarborough and Derby, who are standing behind her, and now she can make her answer. There can only ever be one answer.

'Your Majesty, I have never in my life disobeyed you, except in this, and if it is all you have come to speak about then I think you'd better have spared yourself the trouble.'

Before she has even finished, Mary has risen up without another word, and gone away. Lady Derby turns and follows her. Only Lady Scarborough has kindness enough to inquire after Anne's health and offer her condolences on the loss of the child, before she too has to leave.

Mary is all out of patience with Anne, all out of charity. A little less than a fortnight after her visit, an order is put out forbidding anyone at Court from waiting on Anne, and the last of her guards are taken away.

LADY MARLBOROUGH'S MISFORTUNES

May arrives. A Jacobite fleet is poised for invasion, and Anne is running a fever, which is caused by the Queen's unkindness. She does not have Sarah with her, because the Earl of Marlborough has been arrested on suspicion of High Treason and sent to the Tower, and so his wife must spend all the time she has in London, waiting at Whitehall to be granted permission to see him, and working for his release. Since they have arrested him on the word of some scoundrel who claims to have found a compromising letter in a flower-pot at the home of the Bishop of Rochester, and have no other evidence, they will have to grant him bail before too long, but Anne cannot help but fear that, in the meantime, her dear Mrs Freeman will wear herself out. When she sees her, all too briefly, she is in a most dismal way; she is tearful and will not take any food or any physic that Anne can offer;

she will talk of nothing but her husband's case. Most painful to Anne is that little sliver of spleen she detects in her friend's manner towards her, that might suggest she considers her to blame for this misfortune.

Of course Anne would do anything in her power to help her friend, but what might that be now, when she is forbidden the Court, when the Queen rejects her attempts to send her compliments, when she cannot even climb the stairs unaided? She cannot eat her dinner without her face flushing afterwards, so that she can barely put her head down to write her letters. She cannot see well enough to do her needlework and her hands are too stiff to play her instruments. The laudanum she takes for her pains fogs her mind and then she cannot remember the simplest things: the rules of whist or ombre, the words of her evening prayers. Her sleep is broken by melancholy dreams of her lost infants, seven — or is it eight of them? — piled up in their tiny coffins in the Abbey, her own growing race of ninnies.

Sometimes she feels she must be the most contemptible creature alive; at other times, when she reads over the unreasonable letters Mary has sent her, or looks into Lady Marlborough's unjustly stricken face, she feels only outrage. They are neither of them being treated as they deserve. In her own household she is greeted with insolence and ingratitude. Lady Fitzharding is avoiding Lady Marlborough, which much increases her distress, and with it her mistress's. One of the Prince's servants, a Mr Maul, who only gained his place in the household because Lady Marlborough helped him to it, tries to prevail upon the Prince to dismiss that lady, then shows his resentment at his failure by waiting upon them at table in as unpleasant a manner as he can, slamming the meat in front of them and hurrying it away again, without a glance or a word. Anne, to vex him, lingers that bit longer over dinner. And yet it is not at all like her to make work hard for her servants: formerly her first thought was always to send them to dinner as soon as possible, so that they might be easy. She would always prefer to be kind; she does not know herself.

News comes that the Jacobite fleet has been defeated. Anne does not bother to send her sister any compliment on her victory; neither does George trouble to pay his in person. They could not offer them with much sincerity; neither do they suppose that the Queen would accept them. Never mind: if Mary will not relent towards them, they can at least hope, now the immediate threat is passed, that the Marlboroughs' condition will improve.

It does, but not before it pleases God to worsen it. Their youngest child, their son Charles, is taken gravely ill. Sarah rushes from London to St Albans, in hopes that he might be saved, but nothing can be done. Knowing well what Sarah suffers, and not wishing to inflame further the grief she must already feel, Anne forbears from saying too much on the subject, but makes an offer to visit whenever Sarah will have her. She is now able to go up and down stairs so if dear Mrs Freeman will only give her leave she can come any time . . . but Sarah does not ask for her, and when the Earl is released in June they retire to St Albans, there to grieve in private.

THE DUKE OF GLOUCESTER'S BIRTHDAY

The issue on little William's head is kept
open, but more in hope than for any other
reason, for it has not prevented his head
from becoming oversized; neither has it
reduced the frequency of his illnesses. Every
time she hears he is ill again, the Queen
sends messengers to see how he does and if
Anne is there, they walk straight past her as
if she were any rocker. It is no help to her
to be the Queen's nephew's mother.

On the other hand, it does no hurt to William to be her estranged sister's son. He has
retained his guard, and receives every
courtesy due to his rank. The Queen sometimes has him brought to her when he is
well. She gives him the most lavish presents, and makes sure that every one of them
is mentioned in the *Gazette.* Her latest gift
to him, for his third birthday, is a miniature
tool set, with every piece carved in ivory.
Anne and George are staying with him at

Campden House when it arrives. However angry Anne may be with Mary, she cannot help but acknowledge the perfection of the gift, and share a little of her son's very obvious pleasure in it.

'How clever of the Queen,' she says to him, 'to know that you wish to be a carpenter.'

'I think Lewis must have wrote a letter,' he says. He only sounds a little bit Welsh. 'He told her which tools were best. He knows about tools and he taught me so now I know as well.'

'Then you both have the advantage of me, for I am afraid I do not know anything about them at all.'

'Do you not? Never mind, Mama, I will teach you. Come and sit with me at my table.'

Anne does as she is told. Her boy takes the tools up one by one and passes them to her, naming them as he does so.

'This is a hatchet. This is a handsaw. This is a brace and this is its bit. This is a hammer. This is a mortise chisel — now, this looks a bit the same but it is not, because actually it is a paring chisel. This —'

'Wait! Wait, my darling! Your mama is not clever like you, she cannot take in so much new knowledge at such speed! Before we go on, I must see if I have this correctly: now this — this is a brace?'

'No, no, no, Mama — it is the bit! The bit!' He sighs and shakes his head. 'I am afraid you are not being such a good scholar today. I do not think you listen. You will not learn, you know, if you do not listen.'

'I beg your pardon.'

'I will not punish you, but there is no good teaching you today. Instead I must mend this table which is not suitable.'

'May I stay and watch?'

'Yes, but you must not talk.'

'Very well, but that will be a trouble to me, for I do love to talk with you. I wish I could bring you with me to Bath.'

'I said no talk, Mama. No talk.'

Letter from the Earl of Nottingham, Secretary of State, to the Mayor of Bath

Whitehall, 30th August 1692

The Queen has been informed that yourself and your Brethren have attended the Princess to the Same Respect of Ceremony, as has been usually paid to the Royal Family. Perhaps you may not have heard the occasion Her Majesty has had to be displeased with the Princess, and therefore I am commanded to acquaint you that you are not for the Future to pay Her Highness any such Respect or Ceremony, without leave from Her Majesty who does not doubt of receiving from you and your Brethren this public mark of your Duty.

Your most humble servant
Nottingham

ANNE IS PARDONED

Dear Lord, I find once more I must beg your forgiveness for the neglect of my private devotions these past months. In truth this move to Berkeley House has been far more troublesome that I ever could have imagined; Lady Berkeley has so drawn matters out with her demands and complaints and being always so generally unreasonable and out of temper that we almost changed our minds and took a house in Hampstead instead, but at last she has decided to be satisfied with what she has at the Cockpit and to permit us — permit us, mind! — to use the rooms we need here for our household. So now all is installed, although it does still smell of paint, which in some parts of the house is strong enough to make one nauseous — but I am here for the winter, and I thank you, and I shall forbear from complaining more.

Grant me I pray the grace to bear my troubles patiently. I cannot help but find it a most melancholy thing to be on this other side of St James's Park, looking across at the Palace that was once my home, but where I cannot now go except on the most unreasonable conditions — and since the King and Queen must know that I will never accept them, whatever they say to the contrary, they have as good as banished me. We have but little company here to divert us: only my Lord Shrewsbury comes to play cards, but he is out of office, so he knows it can do him no hurt. Also I am honoured — if that is the word — with visits from the likes of Lord Ailesbury and his Lady and others of the Jacobite party; I know what hopes they have of me and I fear they will be disappointed in them. My father will ever remain a Papist and I have no more respect for that religion and no more desire to see England and the Church under siege from it than I ever did. I know which is the true Church and I will never be swayed from it, not even if I were to undergo a million tortures.

I did not write to the late King because I wanted him back but because he is my father, and I knew very well how I had wronged him and I desired more than anything to beg his pardon for it. His letter which I have lately had by my Lord Marlborough is the greatest comfort to me, for he says in it that he understands how truly penitent I am, and he has given me his pardon, and expressed sincere satisfaction at what he says is my return to my duty.

Of course he also says how he would desire me to deserve his forgiveness by my future actions, and as I do not know what to say to that I have not written back, though he has offered his pardon to Marlborough too, and says he will trust him to send him back any letters on my behalf. I do not know what to say, and in truth now that an invasion seems so much more unlikely than it did, I am no longer plagued with fears of punishment at my father's hands. Of your forgiveness, Lord, I know I can never be sure. For the mercies you have already shown me I am truly thankful; I beg that you will grant me the grace to deserve more, so that you will not be compelled to chastise me too much in the days to come.

In Bed with the Denmarks

There is some small disturbance going on outside Berkeley House: drunken shouts, running feet, the watchman's bell ringing. It is enough to wake both the Denmarks, who have been sleeping together in Anne's bed-chamber, according to their peculiar habit.

'Did you hear what hour it is, my dear?'

'No, George. He was not telling the hour — he was after some rogue or other.'

'Again? That is the third night together. It was not like this at Syon.'

'No, but we could not stay there, and we must make the best of it . . . anyway I think I will have watched more than slept tonight, even without the noise.'

'Why is that? Is it your pains?'

'They are not so bad — and I've not seen any blood since yesterday. I have taken the new medicine again and I swear it is doing me more good than anything.'

'That medicine. I am of Mrs Freeman's

mind — you should tell your doctors about it. Heaven knows what is in it.'

'Why should I? They would only tell me not to just because they did not think of it themselves, and you are as desirous of children as I am, so why should you not want me to try a thing I've heard so much good of? I am sure it can do me no harm. If the child is weak I hope it may strengthen it, and if it be loosened it will not stop it for many days.'

'As you wish, my dear.'

'It is not my pains that keep me awake. It is that letter — I cannot forbear from thinking about it and whenever I do, I get so mightily vexed.'

'You mean the one I had out of my own country? But I have already said: we are of a mind that it is none of my brother's business, and I will write to tell him so. Why must you keep troubling yourself about it?'

'Because of Caliban — 'tis plain he is behind it — why else would your brother ask us to reconcile with them? What business is it of his?'

'As I said, none. And I will tell him so. Stop troubling yourself.'

'It is none, but to be sure Caliban will endeavour by all ways that can be thought on to make us yield rather than make one step towards it himself —'

'True, but —'

'— and if I — if we — ever make the least step, may I — we — be as great a slave as he would make us if it were in his power!'

'We are not about to be slaves, my love. Put it out of your mind.'

'I only wish I could, but you know how it is with me and such ugly matters: they get inside my head, and then I never can be rid of them.'

23RD MARCH 1693

The patent medicine Anne has been taking does not work quite as well as advertised, for when spring arrives her pains come back with it. They wake her rudely every morning; sometimes they attack her knees and ankles, sometimes her hips — sometimes, for a change, her wrists and hands — wherever they are, she is mightily on the rack.

On those days when she has been sleeping alone and wakes too early for George to be disturbed, she calls Danvers to help her out of her bed and into her easy chair, where she might arrange herself comfortably enough to try and sleep a little longer. She will dream, and start awake, and then dream a little again, until it is time for chocolate, and for prayers. One morning, she is startled out of a most agreeable dream of walking with Sarah through the orchards at Holywell by a catching in her limbs: they have woken by themselves, and without her will or leave, they are dancing a lively jig, such as Anne has not been able to do on her own account for a good many months, if not years already. After a short space the dancing stops, leaving Anne very much frighted. As soon as she can, she writes to Sarah to ask her to send Dr Radcliffe. She is glad that none of her women were in the room, for had they been, they would quite certainly have told other women in other households, who would tell their mistresses, who would then tell their friends, who would tell it to malicious people, who would then spread a rumour abroad that she has got fits.

When Dr Radcliffe comes, Anne makes a tearful confession of her secret medicine-taking, for which he scolds her, because he is certain that it is the cause of her limbs convulsing, since she has never been afflicted in that way before. He has the bottle brought to him, so that he may destroy it himself, and says he will have Anne's apothecary make up some pills for her out of rue and castor, to prevent further convulsions. He cannot promise Anne that the child has not been harmed by her foolish actions. And so the old, melancholy qualms come back, and before the week is out she has miscar-

ried and then there is another dead daughter
to bury.

WHAT A GOOD
ENGLISH PRINCE KNOWS
ABOUT WARFARE

As soon as Anne has recovered sufficiently to go abroad, she makes a visit to her son at Campden House. She arrives to find him exercising his troops in the gardens. Lady Fitzharding is watching proceedings from a chair at the top of the front steps. She cedes the chair to Anne at once, and orders another.

'So these are the Duke's Horse Guards, that I have heard so much of.'

'Yes, Your Highness.'

'What are those weapons they are carrying? Surely not —'

'Only wooden swords — they can do no harm with those. And they wear paper caps.'

William has had his troops line up, and is walking up and down in front of them. He stops in front of one boy, who at once salutes, and straightens his hat.

'It is a pity we could not sit a little closer, Your Highness, so that you could hear how

His Highness talks to his men — it is a near-perfect imitation of the King!'

Anne laughs. 'These days, when my son speaks, more often than not, it is the King's words I hear. "Soldiering is better than carpentry, Madam, and a thing most fit for princes." '

'His Highness so loves to wait on the King. It is very hard to settle him when he comes back: His Majesty has a way of speaking to him as if he were a man already, and he does not care to be a boy again after that.'

'Perhaps it is just as well then, that His Majesty only comes back into England when he desires more funds for his war.'

Lady Fitzharding says nothing. Anne recalls how close her son's governess is to the Queen, and wishes, too late, that she had bitten her tongue.

'Who is that who walks behind my boy?'

'His Aides-de-Camp, Madam. The boy is young George Lawrence, and the man, of course, is Lewis.'

'Lewis is such a very good friend to William.'

'Indeed, he is, but he is not His Highness's tutor, and he is wont to forget that.'

'Does it do so much harm, that Jenkin Lewis should tell him what he knows of —

of fortification and Caesar and the like, when that is the stuff His Highness most loves to speak of?'

'There might well be no harm, Your Highness, except that he pretends to teach him mathematics and such things, which are more properly left to Reverend Pratt, and then I have Pratt complain to me that His Highness will not listen to him, and tells him that, in his opinion, Lewis is the better tutor!'

Anne laughs. 'He will come about. It is only that Lewis is such an old friend to my boy, and Reverend Pratt so newly arrived here. I do not think any worse of my boy that he is so loyal to his friends.'

The troops disperse, and William comes over to make his compliment to his mother. Anne cannot help noticing how unsteady he is on his feet still, and when she sees how the other boys — fine, strong fellows all — can run and jump about, there is that familiar little bite in her heart. For all his soldierly ambition, her son still refuses to go up and down stairs by himself.

When William makes his bow, he stumbles a little, and reaches for Lewis's arm, to steady himself again.

'There is no need to look like that, Mother — I am perfectly well, only that was not one of my best bows. Lewis, why are women so easily frighted?'

Lady Fitzharding scolds William for showing his mother so little respect, and tells Lewis to take him off and change him into clean clothes, so that he might appear to his mother properly attired, and with the like manners.

' "Women are easily frighted," ' Anne repeats. 'I do believe I have heard the King say just that.'

'Perhaps he had it from Lewis. He depends too much on him. Did you see how quickly His Highness grabbed his arm, when he had barely stumbled?'

'Who else's arm would he have grabbed, when it was Lewis who stood behind him? I am sure he depends every bit as much on his nurses, his footmen . . .'

'He seems to regard Lewis and his footmen as his private guard: last time the surgeons came to blister him, he called for them to come and fight the scoundrels off!'

When William returns, with two of his footmen, he makes a perfect bow, and waits very properly to be given permission to sit.

'I am told that you are having all manner of lessons now,' Anne says. 'What has Master Pratt been teaching you?'

'Master Pratt has taught me Mathematics

and History and Greek and other such things — though he does not know as much about war as Lewis does. Lewis told me only today that it need not matter that the King lost at Neerwinden, or that the navy did at Lagos. Lewis says that when the war is won the country will forget all the losses and all the expense and honour the King as they should. It is true that the King is not strong, but that does not matter because a General's best weapon is his mind.'

'Very true,' says Lady Fitzharding, 'but now you must tell your mother what Master Pratt has taught you.'

LIKENESSES

Somehow, the Sunderlands are back. He has the King's ear and she has renewed her friendship with Anne's Lady Marlborough. Lady Sunderland is in good health and can easily visit Holywell, a piece of good fortune which Anne has too much reason to envy. On a very good day she might stir out of doors, to visit the theatre or pay a call on one of the few ladies who are prepared to take the risk of receiving her; on a rarer sort of day she is able to go hunting with the Prince, but with him on horseback and her in a caleche with a dull Lady Charlotte, it does not give her the pleasure that it used to, and only serves to remind her, painfully, of all the vigour she has lost. There are many more days that are spent lying on a day bed, praying that a groom or footman will scratch on the chamber door, and bring in a letter from St Alban's. If no letter comes, Anne re-reads old ones, or writes another one herself, to ask again how Mrs Freeman does, and to ask what service Anne might render her, what are her commands?

Sarah must need something from Anne: she is having a terrible summer. Her mother has been struck down with a fit of apoplexy, and there can be no hope of her life. She has been moved from her own house in St Alban's to Holywell, so that her daughter can nurse her herself, which she insists on doing night and day, barely sleeping or eating. Anne is in pain for her friend, and frightened for her health, which is the most precious thing in the world, and ought never to be neglected. She sends Sarah the milk of an ass she keeps at St James's, and implores her to drink it to cool her blood, which she is certain must be heated and disordered from so much watching and sitting up. She sends her own doctors to Holywell. She offers more than once to accompany them in her coach, but Sarah never gives her leave, and she knows better than to risk her anger by going without it. She prays to God, that he might permit her to take Sarah's afflictions upon herself (she is not sure if it is truly the action of a good Protestant to do this, but if she does not ask her chaplains, they can never tell her it is not) and God obliges by sending her pain, and sparing Sarah's health, although he cannot spare her mother or her conscience. Mrs Jennings dies in late July; Lady Marlborough remembers how she once had her mother thrown from Court, and is full of self-reproaches.

Anne remembers so little of her own mother, that when she first comes upon her likeness in one of the lesser-used chambers at Berkeley House, she does not at first realise whose it is. She has to call Danvers, to ask if the picture is any good.

'It is very like, Your Highness — by the looks of it, it was done after the painting Mr Lely did of her, when you were small.'

'I truly cannot tell whether it is like her or no. I only remember her hands.'

'She had fine hands, very like your own.'

'But one cannot see them in this picture — only one arm, and a great deal too much bosom —'

'That was the fashion then.'

'— and her double chin. I do believe I resemble her in stoutness now.'

'Your hair is the same colour.'

'Perhaps . . .'

It is a shame that Lely is so long dead. Anne admires his Windsor Beauties very much, and if he were still alive she would surely pay him whatever he asked to have a

549

picture of Sarah after that same style. But any picture of Sarah is better than none, and Anne hopes she will sit for Closterman, so that he might paint a likeness that Anne can keep by her always, for the pleasure and comfort it will give her, to look upon the image of her friend.

21st January 1694

When Anne miscarries of another dead child, her affliction this time is so great as to cause her to fall ill of an ague. The Queen has enough affection and kindness for her to send to enquire how she does when she is at her worst, but, despite the hopes this raises in some quarters, there is no reconciliation when she recovers.

GLOUCESTER'S PROGRESS OR THE MAKING OF A SOLDIER

If any reader wonders why he should trouble himself to peruse an account of the character and deeds of a Prince who was, at the time these events took place, no more than five years old, then this author can do no more and no better than beg him to be patient, for the answer will soon be discovered in the course of reading it, so that before long he will find himself obliged to own that William, Duke of Gloucester, even at such a tender age, was already proving himself to be a wise leader, courageous soldier, loyal patriot, and in all, one of the brightest stars that ever shone in that great constellation of warlike English heroes.

He spoke early, and was wise for his years. He had already been well-schooled in the civility, patience and condescension required of princes, as observed by two of his father's Danish countrymen, who came to enquire of him, if he had any commands for their master, the King of Denmark. The Prince responded very properly by saying, 'My duty to the King of Denmark. And tell him I love him.' When asked if he would be visiting their country with his father, his face was seen to take on an intense, purposeful expression, and he replied, 'No, but I will go to France.' For all his courtly manners, Gloucester was, first and last, a soldier.

It can thus easily be imagined, how much he was vexed by those around him who refused to recognise this truth: his nurses and his governess, forever watching and warning him and asking him if he were not perhaps too hot, too cold, or bilious and then pronouncing him bound or loose or feverish or tired; the physicians, who pulled silly grave faces, prescribed their foul medicines and set surgeons upon him with cups and knives; and chief of them all, his mother, who took fright at everything he did, and supposed him to be the merest baby.

He resolved to prove himself to all of them, and took whatever chances came his way. In the spring of 1694, his governess Lady Fitzharding decided that it was time for him to be breeched, and a tailor, Mr Hughes, was summoned. He arrived on Easter Sunday, bearing a fine suit of clothes for the Duke: a coat, waistcoat and breeches, all brocaded in white and silver, with silver buttons. Gloucester thought the coat and breeches very fine indeed, but his suspicions were aroused by the waistcoat, for this was boned just like the stiff coats he had always been made to wear; they were supposed to give him a good carriage, but they only prevented him from moving as he wished, and it made him wonder if the handsome new clothes he was shown, and the tailor that brought them, were not merely parts of some cunning, womanly plot to keep him a baby forever. If so, he would see that it came to nothing. He took himself to his Presence Chamber, which he had all fitted out for military exercise, and consulted with his men.

A plan was quickly agreed upon. Gloucester sent for the tailor, and as soon as this unfortunate man arrived, he gave his men the command — 'Put him on the wooden horse!' — then stood back as they charged. They did their best to haul Mr Hughes onto the horse, and might have succeeded, were it not for the intervention of Gloucester's aide-de-camp, Jenkin Lewis, who stepped in and explained to His Highness that the boning of the waistcoat was not to be laid at the tailor's door, for he had only done what he was told to do by others; that the offending garment might well be altered, and that Mr Hughes must be forgiven. Gloucester granted the man his pardon, most graciously.

Of course there were defeats as well as victories. Gloucester was a bold, vigorous and courageous boy, but sometimes even the bravest hearts can fail, and so it would be that when the Duke had to go up or downstairs, he would find himself unequal to the task alone, by reason of the giddy feeling it always gave him in his head, and so he would insist on having at least one of his footmen to support him on his climb or his descent. In his protestations the Duke was being utterly truthful, because, as we have seen, he was more inclined to deny his infirmities than to make a show of them, but his physicians could find no explanation for his giddiness, and so they concluded that Gloucester's refusal to assay the staircase was just that — a refusal, occasioned not by ill health but by indulgence, coddling and the too-tender ministrations of too many nurses. It was not treatment that was required, but punishment.

Gloucester had never yet been beaten — his mother would not hear of it — but as a sickly woman, she was forced to depend greatly on her physicians' judgement, and inclined, more often than not, to think it sound. And so she made her tearful concession: for once, the rod would not be spared. She went with her husband to wait upon their son, and, while she watched, he showed Gloucester the birch and asked him, so would he now go up the stairs by himself? Gloucester refused. His father repeated the question; Gloucester refused again. There was no choice then but to go through with the beating; son, mother and father all wept, and the Duke from that day went up and downstairs by himself.

Our hero was very much loved, not only by his parents, but also by his mother's sister, the Queen, and by the King. Certain misunderstandings between the sisters had led, most unfortunately, to his mother's being forbidden the Court and denied the honours that would usually be due to one of her rank, but this treatment was not extended to her blameless son, so Gloucester was summoned to see the Queen from time to time, and they would talk together and she would give him presents. On one occasion she offered him a beautiful bird to take home. It was a red and green parrot, of the kind girls posed with when they sat for their portraits, and not at all the thing for a soldier — the Duke did not wish to take the bird home, but he could see what a handsome gift it was, and was truly sensible of the affection and kindness the Queen showed in offering it to him, so, showing the tact that was so remarkable for one of his tender years, he simply bowed to the Queen and said, 'I will not deprive you of it, Madam.'

Gloucester could not but be aware that his mother and his aunt would neither see nor speak to each other; he did not understand why this should be so, and it troubled and bewildered him. What troubled him still more was the withdrawal of his mother's guard, for it grieved him to see her so unprotected; he and his own troops would do what they could, of course, but even though they had been promoted out of their paper hats and into proper red caps, with fine plumes to them, and had added muskets to their swords, and though it wounded him to admit it, it was clear that, in the face of any threat from grown men bearing real arms, they could not do very much. What they could do — and this was a notion which came to the Duke's parents, once they could be certain that he understood matters well enough to feel wounded on their behalf — was perhaps provide an op-

portunity to bring the two households together.

He was by now an accomplished General,
well able to command his men, of which
there were nearly ninety; he was proud of
this army, and the King and Queen very
fond of him, so his father ventured to
request that they might honour Gloucester
by receiving him and his troops for a formal
inspection. The request was granted and a
date set. The Duke spared no effort in
preparation: his men must be exercised
whenever possible, his cannons and pasteboard fortification in the best possible
condition. It was a pity that in paying such
diligent attention to his men and materials
he neglected his own health, for as the day
neared, he grew restless, then agitated,
became afflicted with an ague, and was
forced to retire, most reluctantly, to his bed.

His grief and chagrin at this turn of events
can scarce be imagined, and his sufferings
were all the greater because his mother
thought it best to summon a man who had
supposedly cured the late King Charles of
an ague and to suffer him to administer to
her son his own medicine, which was made
of brandy and saffron, and only caused him
to vomit. It is a testament to his strength, of
body as well as character, that despite the

depredations of both the sickness and its cure, Gloucester soon mended, and was ready, on the appointed day, to lead his troops to Kensington.

The expedition met with great success. Gloucester led his army, in two companies, over the short distance from Campden House to Kensington Palace, drums beating as they marched. They paraded in front of the Palace, while the King and Queen stood and watched, with all proper seriousness. Afterwards the King praised both the General and his well-drilled troops, singling out the drummers for their fine performance. He had twenty guineas divided up among the boys, and gave William Gardner, the very best of the drummers, two gold pieces; he told his nephew that he would visit him at Campden House the next day, for a second inspection.

When these formal proceedings were over, Gloucester was able to make his speech to the Queen. Without preamble, he said, 'My Mamma once had guards — now she has none.' The Queen did not reply. The King paid his visit, gave his nephew leave to salute him with his cannon and gracefully accepted the compliment which Lady Fitzharding had insisted her charge should rehearse. The two generals talked a while together, first about swords and guns, and then about horses; when Gloucester lamented that one of his four cannon had broken, the King offered to send him another. Greatly moved by this generosity, the Duke offered the King both his companies to accompany him when next he went to Flanders. He added that he hoped the King would conquer Ireland as well as France, and the whole world.

It was Gloucester's finest moment. He had proved himself a true soldier, and nobody thought for a moment that it was his fault that the guards were not restored, or that the King did not, in the event, remember to send that cannon.

MARY CONSUMED

Lord, the new Archbishop just taken his leave, and I have desired my women to let me sit alone in my closet awhile, for although the Prince will wish to hear what was said, my heart is too full yet for me to speak a word aloud. It has come, this death, like a thief in the night — we could none of us have guessed the hour, or to which house . . . For I have been so unwell this year, and my poor boy, and all the world knows the King was never in good health — I could have believed that any of us might quit this world in an instant — but Mary? Never.

My comfort is that she always watched for your coming — even when we were children she never for one moment neglected to love or fear you. I know she will have been as prepared as any soul could be for you to receive her, and what the Archbishop told me of her conduct and conversation during her sickness convinces me that my sister died as a good Christian should: that when he told her the end was coming, she said she thanked you that she had always carried this in her mind — that she had nothing then to do but to look up to you and submit to your will; then she took her final Communion, and bid her bishops pray for her when she could pray no more.

I cannot then doubt but that she has gone to a happier place, but I hope I may be allowed to grieve a little without your thinking me rebellious, for her suffering in her last days were so dreadful; I who have seen with my own eyes my children die of that distemper cannot help but imagine with horror and pity all her agonies, and to think that she spent full ten days on that rack . . . I pray you will forgive me if I say that if you had to cut her down so young, I could wish that you had done the thing more cleanly. Of course that is a wicked thing to think, and I must beg your pardon for it. I know you must chastise me for it, as you have done for all my many faults.

But oh, it grieves me that I was not allowed

to see her, that when I last saw her there was such a want of kindness between us, that there never was any real opportunities for us to mend matters. It is true that she hurt me, that she said and did things I still cannot help but think she should not have, but if I had by some chance been given foreknowledge of how little time there was, I hope I would have found some way to appease her, without . . . without giving her that impossible thing that she would insist upon.

I am sorry that in the midst of our quarrel I thought and said so many things of her that were unkind, and allowed myself almost to forget how much I loved her . . . now she is gone I find it is as painful to me to recollect all those instances of kindness and affection and companionship as it is to recall our quarrel — no, more painful, because they make me all the more sensible of my want of charity to her, that can never now be mended. All I have to console myself with on that head, is that when I sent Lady Fitzharding to tell the Queen for my concern, she sent back her thanks — by then she could say no more.

The King wrote to me to tell that I could

see her when she was well enough . . . perhaps if she had recovered we could have reconciled — what a torment it is to imagine that now! As for the King, he has astonished everyone with how deeply he has been affected. I have been told by several people that during those ten days there were occasions when his reason was feared for, and even his life, he was so much disordered. I never imagined that man could feel so much, or how much he loved her — they say he could not support himself, but had to be carried almost to her bedside.

And now he has sent the Archbishop to say he would have me wait on him, so it seems I shall be received at Court again, and all the world must know it. There were even a few who did not wait until their Queen was dead before they sent their compliments — that was the clearest sign I had that there was no hope, so I could hardly rejoice at it. Then when she was gone my Lords Marlborough and Godolphin told me I should write him my condolences, and so I did though Lady Marlborough did not wish it, but I had to tell her I do not have the heart to prolong the quarrel more, and it seems he does not either . . .

So I will go and be received, when my health and my condition permit — for now I have both a bad hip and a great belly, I find I cannot walk at all, but I thank you now for softening his heart, even though I am mightily sorry for the cause of it — and if I say I am sorry, I do not mean that I do not submit to your will, for I do, and always shall.

Amen.

PART V

ANNE AT THIRTY

Anne and Sarah are sitting together in Anne's chamber at Berkeley House, knotting fringes. They are both making far too many mistakes, Anne because she is tired, and Sarah because it is dull work, and she has had a surfeit of it.

'I am sure I am mightily grateful to be receiving company again,' says Anne, 'but I am all the more glad when they have all gone, and it is just the two of us. Too much company tires me; it always did.'

'It was a squeeze, wasn't it?'

'There were far too many people. Lord Carnarvon was quite put out — did you hear what he said when he'd pushed his way through?'

'No. What?'

'He said he hoped I would remember that he came to wait upon me, when none of that company did.'

'What, does he think you ought to pay him

in gold for his visits?'

'Well, I could not even if I wished to: Sir Benjamin does nothing but tell me I have no funds.'

'My Lord Carnarvon must think you have the King's ear — which you certainly should.'

'It should be obvious to him that I don't. Nobody has it now but Shrewsbury and Keppel — even our Betty is put aside, which is a thing I never thought to see.'

She hopes by mentioning Betty's name to divert Sarah, but Sarah's blood is up. Again.

'But you are his *heir,* Your Highness.'

'He receives me cordially enough, he has given me the late Queen's jewels, I have my guard back — and he has been most civil to you, and permitted your Lord to kiss his hand again — and that last to me is more —'

'Oh never mind that! He receives *you* with no more ceremony than he does any other lady, and not nearly often enough! He ought to see to it that you are kept informed of business — indeed, it would be most improper if you were not Regent next time he goes abroad.'

'It would be an ugly thing indeed if he did not offer it me, but I must confess I feel myself unfit . . . and my health . . . my condition . . .'

'He will not leave till May — you will have been delivered of the child by then.'

'Yes, but I cannot do it — I have been ignorant my whole life of . . . I cannot.'

'Ignorance can be remedied, Your Highness.'

'You know I cannot read so well — with my eyes.'

'Then I will read to you.'

Anne shakes her head.

'The Prince — the Prince must be Regent — or on the Council, he may act on my behalf. I am unfit.'

'But — forgive me — do you intend still to be "unfit" when you are Queen?'

Anne has begun to twist her fringe-work this way and that in her hands; she becomes aware that it has grown damp with sweat, and lets it drop into her lap.

'Your Highness?'

'I am put in mind of something my late sister once said to me — I had forgotten it till now — she said that anyone who envied her the Crown was a fool.'

'Then I must beg pardon for asking what I know is an impertinent question, but did you envy it?'

'Sometimes — but mostly, I did not envy it — truly I did not — and I do not envy the King's position now, although it is true he is a foreigner and should not properly have it. I only ever desired what was due to me in mine.'

UGLY THINGS

Anne does not get what is due to her position. She is not invited to be Regent; George is not asked to serve as one of the Lords Justice during William's absences. The Irish lands, that were her father's, and that she should have had long since, are given to Betty Villiers, who has been married off and made Countess of Orkney. The King has announced that she should take over the Duke of Leeds' lodgings in St James's, but not in such a way as to cause the Duke to make haste over it.

Was there ever in all of history a princess so shabbily used, or so little respected? If it were not for the Marlboroughs, Lord Godolphin and — for she must own it — the Earl of Sunderland, then surely she would be as little regarded in this Kingdom as any country squire's wife. Her own physician will not come away from a party to see her, and sends back word that her distemper is nothing but the vapours, that she would be as healthy as any other woman alive, if only she would believe it. If this were not humiliation enough, Dr Radcliffe must then spread this opinion about Court and town, along with another, shared by many, that Anne's belly is but a false conception. Anne dismisses him. She does not reinstate him when he turns out to be correct. She takes her husband, her son and her stubborn bulk to Windsor for the summer, and wonders when God will be done with this chastisement.

God must think better of the King, for although he has but lately taken his wife, he has now granted him a great victory at Namur. Lady Marlborough does not think that he deserves Anne's congratulations, but her Lord and friends overrule her. Anne duly sends a respectful note, to which the King does not reply. It is as Lady Marlborough says: she will never get her due from Caliban.

THE GOOD HOPE

In one respect it hardly matters that Anne makes so mean a figure: the Duke of Gloucester is Prince of Wales in all but name, and the King loves him.

Every day he seems less of a baby and more of a Prince. Now that Mrs Pack is dead — and not before he has learned to detest her as much as everyone else — there is no-one to tell him otherwise. When he hears Anne fret over him, he likes to show her how steady he is on his feet now, and to remind her how infrequent his fevers have become. It is not for her to keep him by her as if he were a girl, he says: she should only hear his catechism, and let him go.

'Perhaps it is only because you are so often ill yourself, that you fear so much for me,' he says. 'But you should not. You should not fear, and you should not weep so much either.'

The cutler has made for him at his request

a basket-hilted sword — a proper one, not wooden — and he carries it whenever he can. He has a Huguenot tutor, M. Hautecourt, whose only task is to teach him about fortification. He has lately acquired some new interests to place alongside soldiering: he has grown to enjoy his lessons with Mr Pratt, and has also taken to sea-faring. They have had a ship made for him, complete with masts and guns, from the toy-makers in Cannon Street. It is called *The Good Hope;* he boards it daily with his men, who are more often sailors than soldiers now.

By the summer of his sixth birthday, he is considered strong enough to come for the first time to Windsor. Within two days of his arrival, he brings his mother a full report of a battle he has fought in St George's Hall, with the Bathurst boys and young Lord Churchill, who were visiting from Eton College. The stairs and the balcony were a castle, which the boys from Eton had to defend from Gloucester's army. The castle men were allowed one sortie before they were routed. He tells Anne that it was a very hotly fought battle, with many casualties; Gloucester was himself bruised a little when Peter Bathurst charged into him.

'But I did not stop fighting because of

that,' he says. 'I only stopped because the fighting was over and it was time for Atty to blow the wind back into the dead with her pipe.'

Gloucester has not yet been allowed to learn to ride, but he is permitted to follow a hunt in his coach, wearing boots and spurs as if he were on horseback. When Anne asks him afterwards if he does not think the crying of the hounds the most glorious sound that ever was, he owns that he still prefers the sound of cannon firing, and of drums, but the baying hounds are almost as good.

At the end of the chase, a buck is driven out in front of his coach, and he watches as its throat is cut by one of his father's pages. One page puts his hand into the wound, rides up to Gloucester and smears his face with blood. When this is done, Gloucester smears blood over Lewis, then Lord Churchill and lastly the Bathursts. The next day there is another hunt, this time to celebrate his birthday, and he is responsible for dividing the slaughtered buck between the nobler members of the household. He does very well, except that he forgets to put aside a portion for Lady Fitzharding, and when she teases him about this, he weeps like any three-year-old. Anne assures him that he has done very well indeed, and he soon

577

recovers his composure.

Having spent his first Windsor summer in good health, Gloucester returns to Campden House, where he is judged strong enough to begin lessons in boxing and fencing. There is talk of his receiving the Garter soon: one of his boy drummers, Harry Scull, has even been dreaming of his investiture, and the prescience of his visions is confirmed that winter, when Lord Stafford dies, leaving a vacancy in the Order. The King sends Bishop Burnet to bring the news.

'Does the thought of the Garter make you glad?' he asks.

'I am gladder of the King's favour to me,' says Gloucester, without any need of a prompt.

The King shows his favour by summoning Gloucester at once to Kensington, where he ties the Order, with the emblem of St George on it, around his nephew's neck himself.

'And when he did so,' he tells his mother, 'I felt myself grow strong enough to slay a dragon.'

18th February 1696

O merciful God, I pray that I may always fully and entirely resign myself to your disposal, so that whatsoever state I am, I may be therein content. Lord, grant I may never look with murmuring on my own condition, nor with envy on other men's . . . Forgive your servant: I meant to read Allestree's 'Collect for Contentedness' all through, for his words are such that cannot be improved upon, least of all by one who has so mean stock of them as I, but I find I cannot finish — my eyes hurt, and they are full of tears besides. It is the condition of other women I must endeavour not to envy, for again you have suffered me, in your wisdom and mercy, to be delivered of another dead child, a daughter. As I have found before, so I find again that among the evils I am subject to when these calamities happen is the envy I feel for more fortunate women — for

Lady Marlborough even — who have their quivers full of living healthy children. Besides knowing it is a sin it pains me more than I could ever express that such ugly feelings should have those I love as their object . . . Please I beg you grant me the grace to overcome them, for I desire above all things not to be so tormented.

I must instead study to be thankful, ever thankful — for the blessings you have given me: that I may come now to Court again, and the Court come to me; for my lodgings at St James's and Windsor; that although I am sick often you have seen fit to preserve my life so that I might yet have a living child again; for the friendship of the Marlboroughs and my Lord Godolphin; most of all for the preservation of the life of my poor boy, for the liveliness and the wit that he has, and for the love the King bears him.

I know full well it is for my boy's sake that His Majesty receives me, for he always keeps me waiting when I go, and would surely not see me at all if he could do so without its being murmured about . . . I flatter myself that I behave towards him with all the duty, respect, meekness and submission that I owe to him as King, and I pray that I may continue to do so, for I must own I was used to lose my temper with the late Queen over such matters, and I cannot but regret it a little now that our quarrels can never be made up in this world.

I should thank you too for the preservation of the King's life, that by your grace and mercy the late plot to murder him was found out and prevented, and the invasion that was to come with it — I am in truth mightily grateful for this, as I can hardly bear to think what would have become of all us poor Protestant English if my father had been restored . . .

But he is my father still, and I have written to him to ask him to give his blessing for me to have the Crown after the present King, if I were to arrange for some restitution afterwards, but I have no hopes of his agreement or of his true forgiveness on such terms.

Everyone in the King's service is now to take the Oath of Association that says I shall succeed my brother-in-law, so it looks as if it shall come to pass — should you suffer me to outlive him. I must confess that I cannot always hinder myself from thinking upon this prospect with some satisfaction, both for my own sake and my poor boy's — and I wonder if it is not this — this ambition, this pride, this desire for a Crown that can only come to me through the death of one whose life I should wish to be preserved — I wonder if it is not this ambition, that I can hardly speak of — I wonder if it is not on account of this that you have so many times chastised me.

Gluttony, lust, envy, wrath, covetousness . . . as Anne's sins are multiplied, so are the curses that strike her womb. She knows very well that she has a plethoric constitution, so ought not to gorge on rich foods when she is with child and her body cannot discharge the excess blood in the usual way; the excess humour that results from this overindulgence can offend the body and cause abortion. She knows this, but she cannot help her eating. She has also been told many times that she and the Prince ought to refrain from venereal embraces when she has a child already in the womb, as the dangers attendant on this are twofold: firstly, there is always the possibility, especially in the earlier and later months (remember the apples?), that the bands which fasten the child to the womb might be fatally loosened; secondly — and it appears that this is what has happened in this case

583

— there is the possibility that the womb, which should remain closed, might come to open in the fervour of libidinous congress, so as to admit the seed which delights it so much, resulting in the conception of a second child, the presence of which will then overburden the womb, causing it to miscarry. The midwives and the physicians alike tend towards this latter explanation, as there were quite certainly two unripe children expelled in the twenty-four hours of Anne's travail, one of seven months' growth, and the other, as far as could be judged, of no more than two or three.

ANNE DANCES

The King has arrived back for the winter, weary, ill and foul-tempered. Anne is to host a ball at St James's to celebrate his birthday: she knows perfectly well that he does not wish it, but they both know that there must be a celebration of some kind, and that she must be the hostess. She will have to sit up next to him: the Court will dance towards the pair of them, and keep their sharp eyes on them while they do. Everybody will be looking at her, noting how stout her figure has become, how red and mottled her complexion. She can do nothing about either of these — and heaven only knows, she has tried — but her hair is still pretty, so she can have that dressed as well as she can, with the late Queen's beautiful jewels in it, and take care that no-one should find any fault with her dress.

Of course somebody will, since the generality of the world disapprove of every

585

fashion they did not bring up themselves. She would very much prefer to wear a manteau to the ball, for she is so often stiff enough in her movements without the further strictures of a gown, but when she asks Lady Fitzharding for her opinion on the matter, she replies with an air as if she did not think it respect enough for a ball. Anne writes to Sarah to ask her if she agrees that she will not be thought fine enough in a manteau, but Sarah is of the same mind as Lady Fitzharding, so she resigns herself to an evening of stately discomfort.

The pleasant discovery, the blessing of the ball, is that she is well that day, quite free of pain, and even able to dance herself. She and the Prince dance a minuet together by themselves, and are applauded as much as if they had lost none of their old grace. Later on, she dances the Parson's Farewell with Lord Marlborough, who is a delight as a partner, slim and graceful as any man half his age. He has lately been accused of plotting with the Jacobites again, but as his accuser is Sir John Fenwick, who all the world knows is a scoundrel, one who would say anything to save his own skin, nobody at Court gives the story much credit. If Marlborough himself is troubled, you would never know it from his dancing.

Anne does not dance with the King. The King does not dance with anybody. He prefers to spend the evening scowling. He does not at all desire to be in such a noisy, crowded room as this, and he would have everyone know it. Anne, who has chosen the musicians herself, and taken the greatest care over everything, expected all along to be offended by him, and she is. It comes to her, with no little pain, that she need never have fretted so much over her dress, for tomorrow nobody will be talking about anything except the King's being out of temper.

She is quite correct in her assumption. The King's ill humour is the chief topic of discussion the next day, and the rest of that week and even for a few weeks more, until it gets about that Anne has been suffering from convulsion fits again, and there is that to chew over instead.

In the three wintery months that have passed between the King's birthday and Anne's, events have moved with a spring-like quickness. Marlborough's accuser, Sir John Fenwick, has been discredited before all of Parliament and soon after deprived of his life; as a result, the Kingdom has been well rid not only of one of its worse trouble-makers but also of one of its most uncivil men, whose tormenting of the late Queen as she fled from her burning home has never been forgotten, least of all by the King. It must be said, however, that the excision of this latest malignancy has not been ac-complished without a serious cost to the body as a whole. Sir John was so very liberal with his accusations as to provide certain persons with the perfect opportunity to settle old scores, a chance which they seized at: now Godolphin is out of government, and Shrewsbury is in it only in name.

The King's humour is in no way improved by any of this. He spent the anniversary of his late wife's death shut up all alone, and the rest of the winter trying to cure his spleen with drink. During the day, he has barely uttered a word to anyone, not even to Portland — perhaps especially not to Portland, whom his new favourite Keppel is bent on driving away. Most nights, the King has been closeted up with Keppel, drinking beer and talking Dutch. It is regrettable, his dependence on this young man, who seems to think of little else but his own dissolute pleasures, and is impudent to boot. When Anne hears that the King has made him Earl of Albemarle, she is properly disgusted.

But still, give the King his due: he is not entirely neglectful of his duty to his sister: he will host the celebrations for her thirty-second birthday, in Whitehall. She is with child again, so no-one will persuade her out of a manteau this time, but Gloucester is to come with her, and she means to make a splendid figure of him. He is seven and a half, and his looks have improved considerably. He is tall for his age, with his father's Danish colouring and a long, handsome face, which everyone says is so reminiscent of the late Queen's; fair as he is, it looks even more like his grandfather's, but nobody will say that aloud.

On the day of her birthday, she has him dressed in a new suit of white satin, which she has had made on purpose to set off the pale blue of his Star and Garter. She has also had some of the late Queen's jewels reset for him to wear: his suit is buttoned, clasped and sewn all over with diamonds; there are gems in his sword-hilt, and the George he wears around his neck is made of rubies, emeralds and yet more diamonds. The whole assemblage is topped off with a white periwig large enough to fit a grown man — for though his head is a handsome one, it is still noticeably large.

Someone — who knows who? — has given the King sound advice, for he has chosen to have Anne's favourite play put on at White-hall. It is Mr Congreve's *Love for Love,* surely the wittiest comedy that was ever written by anyone: all the characters — except the boobies — speak like the Ladies Fitzharding and Marlborough on their most sparkling form, as Anne would wish to speak herself, but never could; the one called Scandal, that is the friend of the hero, reminds her of Lady Marlborough most of all, because of all the truth in him.

After the play is finished, the King comes over, in his stiff way, to exchange compliments with them. He says what he must to Anne and George, and then takes a long, thoughtful look at Gloucester.

'You are very fine,' he says.

Anne waits for her boy to make one of his charming, courtly replies, but he only stares at his uncle, opening his mouth and shutting it again.

'All the finer for you, Sir,' says Anne at last, before her face can flush any more. Gloucester bows, silently.

'It is all right,' she whispers to him, 'you may speak. Say something to the King, William.' But he only bows again; the King nods, and moves away. Anne is disappointed, as much with herself as with her son: she ought not to have forgotten what it is like at Court when one is only young, and small, and burdened with too many jewels.

25TH MARCH 1697

Another stillborn daughter. It comes to
Anne, in the sad days afterwards, that grief
and gout might well be cousins of a kind:
both wax and wane, both have that way of
leaving one alone for a space only to come
back again more viciously, seeking out new
places to attack, and though it is quite true
that either one alone might render life
unbearable, neither of itself can end it.

THE PEACE OF RYSWICK

It is a late afternoon in autumn. The Windsor stable hands are picking the year's first yellowing leaves out of Anne's caleche. Anne has a dish of fresh plums next to her chair; she has chosen them over apples today, even though she knows that apples are better for strengthening a baby — for as she said to Danvers only this morning, there can surely be no harm in indulging such an innocent fancy, and she can always eat more apples tomorrow.

'These are delicious,' she says to George. 'I think indeed they may be the finest that I ever ate. Do try one!'

'Thank you, my dear, but I do not think it will go at all well with this wine.'

'Oh I pray you, just *one* — it would so increase my pleasure to know it was shared.'

'Oh very well, then.' He takes one, eats it in two bites. 'That was good — very sweet, not too soft — but so remarkably fine? I'm not so sure — I think your sense is sharpened by your condition, dear.'

'I think you ate it too quickly to judge of it. Never mind. I'll not force another on you — but I wonder should I have some sent to Holywell?'

'They have their own orchard at Holywell.'

'But not like this — and the gift might prompt Mrs Freeman to write — I have not heard from her these last five days.'

'She will not have forgotten you.'

'But if there is something amiss? If she is ill?'

'Why should she be? She seemed in excellent health all the time we were in Tunbridge.'

'My Lord Godolphin not so much. It is a blessing in disguise, really, that he should be kept away from business for a space — working for Mr Caliban would shake the strongest constitution, and his is not.'

'Our Mrs Freeman will enjoy having him at Holywell — they are very fond of one another, are they not? Do you suppose — ?'

'No, I do not suppose! Mrs Freeman would be quite incapable of such a thing!'

'But he is quite certainly in love with her.'

'Of course,' says Anne to George, and to herself, 'Could anyone not be?'

Anne has been agitated for a little while,

chewing over the dearth of letters from Holywell, but talking about Lady Marlborough is the next best thing to hearing from her, and has lifted her spirits again. She selects another plum, and there is a scratch on the door. There are still no letters from Holywell, but a courier has arrived from Holland, to tell them that France has signed a treaty with the Allies. Louis has recognised William as King: there will be no more attempts to force the old King back up on them. It is surely the most welcome news imaginable: they give the courier a handsome present to take away, and several dozen plums.

2ND DECEMBER 1697

It was surely a mistake, to rejoice so much in her father's discomfiture. Anne's gout returns: by mid-October, she is a perfect cripple. In December she miscarries of two more sons. The King has persisted in his resolve to give her father's Irish lands to Squinting Betty. He will not change his mind, and now he has taken 35,000 of the 50,000 pounds Parliament granted for setting up a household for her boy — her only boy. Anne is like Foresight in *Love for Love,* for all her affairs go backwards.

WHITEHALL BURNS

Of course it was a Dutch maidservant who started the fire, for as Anne has often had cause to observe, the people of that country have no regard for what they have neither thought up nor made themselves. This particular lass, being no exception, left sheets drying unattended over a brazier in Colonel Stanley's lodgings — a piece of neglect which she must surely have known was forbidden — so that in the natural course of things the unwatched sheets caught fire, and then the hangings that were in the room, and then the Colonel's bed, and soon after that the rest of his lodgings, and the timbers in his roof, and then those of his neighbour's roof, and so and so on through the old, wooden Palace until the whole southern side was ablaze.

It being early January, the Thames was frozen, and there was precious little water for the pumps; nor were buckets much use, for nobody could get near enough to the flames to throw the water on them. Soon the fire had made so great a havoc that they were forced to blow some buildings up to try to confine it, but all they were able to accomplish by this means was to send great pieces of burning timber flying in all directions, thus spreading the fire into parts of the Palace it might otherwise have spared. All this while, the Palace residents were running back and forth into the fire and out again, desperate to save their belongings, while the servants were doing the same with hangings, paintings, archives — any number of treasures. Despite their efforts, any number were lost, some to looters. It was a scene of destruction and confusion as had not been seen in London since the great conflagration that happened when Anne was but an infant.

She has spent two days in her rooms at St James's, watching the flames rise and fall, and worrying about the effect of the smoke on George's lungs. Now the fire is over, and nothing has been spared but the Banqueting House, which the King has taken great care to protect, and a few other smaller buildings. One of them is the Cockpit, but she will not now be able to return to it, as it will be needed for government offices. There will be no more Whitehall drawing-rooms, no more Whitehall balls; the State Rooms where she was introduced to foreign princes, the bedchambers where she was at one time wont to avoid her step-mother's gaze and at a later time her sister's, the Chapel where she almost sat in her father's place and felt such dangerous pride, the Hall where she and Mary once stepped so carefully onto the stage and said their lines — all gone. So much gone.

GLOUCESTER IS TAKEN OUT
OF THE HANDS OF WOMEN

The Duke is eight years old and it is time, the King says, that he was given his own household, and put into men's hands. No more governess, no more nurseries with clucking nannies in them, no more paper hats or wooden horses, no more pasteboard forts — and no place for Jenkin Lewis, for even though he is a man, he is not a gentleman, and only gentlemen are fit to wait on heirs presumptive. Gloucester seems no more moved by this loss than his mother was by the loss, so many years ago, of her Mrs Cornwallis; perhaps his heart has grown to be like hers, with its hidden backstairs and dusty chambers out of sight.

He is moved out of Campden House and into his own set of rooms in St James's Palace. The King appoints Lord Marlborough as his Governor, which pleases Anne very much, but then chooses Bishop Burnet to be his Preceptor, which does not. Burnet professes an austere kind of religion, which was always more to Mary's taste than hers; moreover, she finds his discourse hard to follow. But she must bear with the appointment, as once her own father was forced to accept Bishop Compton's. He is the King's choice, and that is that. She tells Gloucester that he must be good for the Bishop.

The King's high-handedness in this matter is no more than she expected: it seems to Anne that he humiliates her as a matter of course. She is given almost no say in the choice of servants for her son's new household, yet she is compelled to pay for the plate and furniture for his rooms out of her own funds. It is a fortunate thing indeed that Marlborough has contrived to make a friend of Albermarle, who may sometimes choose to speak for her to the King — if it were not for this, who would take care of her interests now?

Her other consolation is her son, and all the good reports she has of him. She wonders if perhaps she was wrong to have trusted Burnet so little, for Gloucester thrives under his tutelage. Every quarter, five of the King's ministers come to St James's or Windsor to examine him on his progress, and every quarter they pronounce themselves amazed.

Sometimes Gloucester tries to explain what he has learned to her, but she finds she cannot even pretend to follow him. On one of her visits, he chides her for it.

'It saddens me to say so, Madam, but I fear you are not a very apt pupil. It concerns me that you should be so unlearned, when you are to have the Crown. Do you think I should ask the King to appoint you a tutor as well?'

'Well, it saddens *me* to say *this*,' she says to George later, 'but I fear that the King would not think it worth the effort.'

COIN

The war just ended has cost the Kingdom every penny that it has — and then more than that. Vast sums, so vast that a Bank of England had to be established in order to raise them — a very Dutch notion, and surely such a thing as was never thought of in the country before. Now that the war is over, Parliament is trying to send the Dutch Guard home, but the Dutch King remains, with every year growing sicker and sourer, and no more generous to Anne after the Peace of Ryswick than he was before.

But it is not only the King's unkindness that has been making a beggar of Anne. Lady Marlborough, always so quick to sniff out incompetence or dishonesty in others, has been looking over her mistress's accounts, and has discovered Sir Benjamin to be quite certainly guilty of the first fault, and possibly of the second too. He has failed entirely to make those investments which would have protected the Princess from the effects of the devaluation two years' since; he has lost her a good deal of money through these errors. This by itself would be reason enough, Lady Marlborough says, to sack him, even if he had then not shown himself to be a knave as well as a fool, by claiming to have lost more. She shows Anne what she has found, and alas, it is all as she says it is, but, for dear Semandra's sake, Anne keeps Sir Benjamin on. Lady Marlborough sees to it that the accounts are undone and redone correctly, and Anne hopes that this will be the end of it.

Of course it is not. The summer after the Whitehall fire, Sir Benjamin brings Anne some bills to look over. Mindful of what Lady Marlborough has said to her on the subject of carelessness and being too easy, Anne puts on her least disappointing spectacles and takes a seat by a window, where she examines the bills closely and discovers, among other faults, that the expenses of oil and vinegar are somewhat extravagant. She is sure that there must be some cheat, and tells Sir Benjamin that she will speak to Hapgood, her Yeoman of the Wine Cellar.

The next day, she has the Prince sit with her, for support, and calls Hapgood in. He arrives promptly and makes his compliment, seeming a little bewildered but not at all afraid.

'I have called you here —' Anne begins, and then hesitates — she wishes Lady Marlborough were with her, and could do this in her place. She tries to imagine how that lady would conduct herself, then clears her throat, and starts again. 'I have summoned you to explain something to me — that is, why it should be that these expenses, of oil and vinegar, should be so great. I do not understand why you have not taken more care with the management of my cellar.'

'Your Highness,' he says, 'I am sorry that you have had reason to find fault with me — I thought I was taking all the care I could, but I shall try to do better. I hope you can forgive me.'

Anne's first impulse is to assure him that of course she forgives him, then offer him a comfit and send him away, but she knows it will not do — she summons her absent friend's spirit again.

'I might well forgive you, as long as you can give me a full account of the matter. I must point out to you, that as you did not buy your place, you can have no manner of pretence for cheating me.'

'Your Highness, no man could be more grateful than I for the place you have given me, and I have never cheated you in anything.'

'I should hope not. I say again: your place was my gift; you can have no reason to cheat me.'

'Your Highness, once more, I am sincerely grateful and I never would cheat you in anything, and will from now on be more careful in all that I do in your service . . . But perhaps I should say . . .'

'What, Hapgood?'

'Though I was put in by Your Highness, I did give Sir Benjamin a hundred pound when I came.'

'Good Lord!' The Prince is moved to speak. 'Why were you such a fool?'

'It was only — it was only that I was desirous of living a quiet life, and Sir Benjamin told me himself of the Dutch cook, who was raised to be Master Cook here, and the new cook who came in were to give him money, because he had been obliged to return a handsome present to Mr Pasmore when he was turned out, and so between the two cooks and myself, he expected something towards the making up of the sum he had lost.'

The Dutch cook, when he is called, tells her that he has paid all of two hundred pounds for his quiet life — and others have had to pay too. When she summons Sir Benjamin and tells him what she knows, he claims never to have asked for the money — it was only offered to him, so that he might give it to Mr Pasmore — he never would tell Anne a lie. On this occasion it is not difficult to put on a stern voice. She tells him that his story sounds unlikely, rejects his offer to question the servants on the matter himself, and insists that he return their money to them. Sir Benjamin gives her assurances of his sincerity and fair dealing that she thinks must sound false even to his own ears, and then she lets him go. She can barely stand to look at him, but she does not turn him out. Poor Frances has done nothing to deserve this trouble, to be married to a dishonest man, who oppresses poor people.

It has been a most grubby and distressing business. Thank heaven for Lady Marlborough: she may say that she has done no more than her duty, but Anne knows that such a great service as she has done can only come out of great kindness, true friendship, real love. The Marlboroughs' oldest daughter, Lady Harriet, has this spring been married to Lord Godolphin's son — poor, pious Margaret's child — and Anne, to express her own love, her own kindness, her own friendship for all parties, was moved to offer something towards Lady Harriet's portion — just her poor mite, just 10,000 pounds. Lady Marlborough — always so good — tried to refuse half of it at first, but has been persuaded instead to accept the disputed half as a present for Lady Anne when she marries. Lady Marlborough is fortunate in having so many healthy, beautiful daughters. Anne has taken to giving balls on Mondays and it has been both a pain and a pleasure, watching other women's daughters dance. Perhaps the child Anne is carrying now will be a daughter. It would not be too much, would it, to ask for two living children? Even Mary Beatrice has two now.

15TH SEPTEMBER 1698

Lord, God — my Father in Heaven, for what reason has it pleased you to empty me of another life? No lady I'm sure could have taken more care of herself or her child than I did — all those months I kept to my chamber, I took of the powders the Swedish ambassadress commended to me, and the spa waters that I know have wrought so well for other ladies. You must know that I prayed — but for all that I have come to expect calamities, so that when my son grew still in my womb it was as if I were watching a tragedy that I had seen put on before: always there is that tiny hope that it might end differently this time, yet one is none too surprised when it comes to the same bad end.

I have had Dr Pratt and Bishop Burnet at my bedside, telling me that I should not seek to know why, that this is all part of your design, but I must confess I cannot help but question: what is your purpose in this? What is it that I have done or said or thought, that you should chastise me so much and so harshly? And sometimes I even wonder why it is that I should remain in this world, when so many I have loved have left it. I remember every one of my children — the particular time they were with me, the different ways they had of quickening — and I cannot think it a sin that I should hold them in my heart in this way. I cannot believe you would judge me for that.

If you are indeed punishing me, I know full well what it is for and I have always known. I have wondered often if you have not hardened my heart like you did Pharaoh's, as it was all part of your design for the freeing of the Israelites from bondage, and so was the slaying of his first born; I do believe what I did, I did to free this country from Papist tyranny, but I had to break a Commandment to do it, and we have all suffered for it — myself, my poor sister, who for all her faults — her unkindness and ingratitude — was I believe as good and sincere a servant of yours as ever lived. Do you also punish me for my

610

disobedience to her? Would you have had me betray a friend who has always been so good and loyal to me? Surely that would have been at least as much of a sin: Lady Marlborough is a member of my household and as such is in my care — that I understand, that I am sure of.

She and her Lord have been my consolation through all these trials — and do not begrudge me that, I beg you. I had hoped she would be with me more now that he is made Privy Councillor, but it has not been so. Still she has shown her goodness by sending her cousin Hill to be my bedchamber woman and she is so capable, so kind, so discreet, so thoroughly pleasant a young woman that I am sure Lady Marlborough must have done herself a hurt in parting with her. I am thankful for both of them, for the Prince who loves me and is always so kind — for my boy too, of course. I pray you preserve his life — and as for his mother, let her pray also that you might make her at ease in the next world, for she knows she must not expect it long together in this one.

ANNE'S BEDCHAMBER WOMAN

Kind, quiet, plain Abigail Hill — Anne has every day more reason to be thankful for her. Before she has been a few months in Anne's service, she seems to understand the needs of her mistress's heart and person as thoroughly as if she had spent a lifetime waiting on her. She has a way of knowing, without being told, when Anne is in pain, and will appear by her side, discreetly whispering, is Her Highness uncomfortable? Would she like assistance to move to another chair? To her bed? Does she require some of the medicine that Dr Lower prescribed? Some laudanum, perhaps? Some more cold tea? Her touch is as gentle as her voice, and Anne will have no-one else to put ointment on her gouty limbs, or to change her bandages.

Hill is a better nurse than poor Danvers, and better company than any Lady Charlotte. She plays the harpsichord beautifully, and is a fine mimic too. Her impersonation of Lady Marlborough is a marvel — so wonderfully exact in tone and gesture that Anne is almost moved to write to Sarah and tell her about it, but something tells her she had better not. She would never want her Mrs Freeman to think she was in any danger of being replaced. Even though Anne sees her so seldom, that would be unthinkable.

'I am writing again to your cousin, Hill,' she says. 'Shall I write that you send her your compliments?'

'Yes, thank you, Your Highness. *Always*. I take it you have received a reply from my Lady?'

'Yes — and it pains me to say so, but — and you must not tell anyone, Hill — I fear we are at odds.'

'Your Highness and her Ladyship? Forgive me, but I cannot believe it.'

'Tell me, Hill, when you were with the family at Holywell, did you ever have cause to meet the Sunderlands?'

'Yes, often — Lady Marlborough was even kind enough to introduce me to them. And I have accompanied her Ladyship to Althorp more than once.'

'I see. And what did you make of them?'

'I found my Lady Sunderland to be a very

pleasant lady.'

'Oh, she is certainly charming. And what of *him*?'

'I did not have so much to do with the Earl, Your Highness.'

'What of their son? Lord Charles Spencer — have you seen him?'

'I cannot recall.'

'Well, if you had, you would recall a young man with no more genteelness than a porter, with a face all over smallpox scars, and so *Whiggish* withal he would have Parliament in the King's place — indeed no King at all — and *this* is the man Lady Marlborough would marry Lady Anne to. I cannot like it.'

'I am sorry, Your Highness.'

'And I know I have displeased Lady Marlborough by saying so, but I cannot but think it would be a most dreadful mistake, and if I tell her so it is only out of the greatest respect and kindness that I have for her.'

'I am sure no-one could ever have had more kindness for anyone than you have for her Ladyship, Your Highness.'

'Why that is just what I am always saying to her, Hill! How well you know me!'

'You flatter me, Your Highness.'

'Dear Hill — I shall tell you something else — but of course you will know that I have missed my courses for two months now.'

'I did notice, Your Highness, and I was pleased at it. If I may ask — are you feeling well with it?'

'As well as I ever do. You will take good care of me, won't you Hill?'

'Of course, Your Highness. It will be my pleasure.'

THIS LATEST MORTIFICATION

For much of the time, Anne and William are able to avoid each other, and thus remain cordial. She spends her summers in Windsor; he spends his in Holland, at Het Loo, looking out over his late wife's finest garden. When they are compelled to be nearer each other, they have bad health on both sides as a ready excuse for neither waiting nor receiving: Anne has her perpetual childbearing and her worsening gout, William has his failing lungs and swollen legs. It seems that Anne might outlive him after all, and that will be her Sunshine Day.

This afternoon, however, is the King's birthday, so she must sit next to him at the dining table at Kensington Palace, listening to his disgusting eating noises. He has served her a fresh morsel of resentment to gag upon, for here is the poor Prince, whose brother the King of Denmark has only recently died, compelled — as she has also been — to put off his mourning and attend the King, all in bright colours, and in full view. It is too humiliating — worse than that, it is *unkind.*

And it is as it always is when they dine with the King: the Prince puts himself out to engage the King in conversation, the King rebuffs him, and it breaks Anne's heart. She has learned to arm herself against William's baleful stare, but George is still put as much out of countenance by it as she once was, when she sat at a table in Holland, gabbling about tulips.

'Sire,' George begins. Oh dear. 'I did mean to tell you, I have lately finished another model ship — I thought you might do me the honour of taking it for your closet in Kensington — it is one of your Dutch fleet, the Vreekheed.'

'It is pronounced "Vrijheid", and thank you but no: I have quite enough models for my closet.'

'Our son will be delighted to have it,' says Anne. 'He is *always* delighted by your *beautiful* models.'

'Gloucester will do more than build models,' says the King. 'Such a great understanding already — a natural admiral.'

Anne decides to overlook the fresh insult to her husband. She swallows down all the

617

things she would like to say, and says thank you instead. She would like to ask the King if he ever means to hand over the rest of the money that Parliament granted for her son's household; she would like to ask when her husband is to be paid back for the lands he surrendered ten years ago; she would like to ask him why he must always be so uncivil, and unpleasant, and inhospitable to all but his Dutch friends — but they dine in public today, the Court leans in on all sides, and even if they were alone, and she did dare raise such questions, no possible good could come of it.

Then the King surprises her, and everybody else. He speaks, unbidden, to her.

'Madam, I have a request to make of you: it has long been on my mind that we have had no drawing-rooms here since the late Queen died, and for a long time I did not think it right that we should have any, but now I think differently — we shall hold them again every week — with cards, and so forth — and Madam, you will be the hostess. You must preside.'

'It will be an honour, Sir,' says Anne. From now on she will do her duty every week, and every week she will hate it, though it will become a little less excruciating after the drink is served.

Sometimes Anne has an apprehension that she is to be disappointed again, and in such cases she is able to arm herself a little, but this is a calamity of the crueller, more unexpected kind. She dines, she prays, she spends a pleasant evening at cards, then she retires, and two hours later is delivered of a stillborn son. Her seventeenth delivery, her eighteenth child — or nineteenth, depending on the reckoning.

From the Princess of Denmark to the Countess of Marlborough, in Gratitude for Her Lord's Good Offices in Securing a Repayment for the Prince

St James's Palace, February 15, 1700

I was once going to endeavour to thank your Lord myself for what was done last night concerning the Prince's business, it being wholly owing to your and his kindness, or else I am sure it would never have been brought to any effect but I dearst not do it, for fear of not being able to express the true sense of my poor heart, and therefore I must desire my dear Mrs Freeman to say a great deal both for Mr Morley and myself and though we are poor in words, be so just as to believe we are truly sensible and most faithfully yours, and as for your faithful Morley she is more if it be possible than ever, my dear dear Mrs Freeman's.

THE DUKE'S ELEVENTH BIRTHDAY

Gloucester's birthday feast is over for another year: the fireworks are spent, the bells have finished pealing, gardeners are snuffing out the lanterns that have blazed so prettily in the trees, and servants are moving through the Great Hall, clearing away what remains of the banquet. It is time for Anne, George and Gloucester to retire.

'And far too late for you, I think,' she says to her son, 'for you look quite worn out!'

'It will do him no harm,' says George, 'and he enjoyed himself — you did enjoy yourself, son, did you not?'

'Very much, Sir. It has been a wonderful day: only the presence of the King could have made it better. I wish he would not spend every summer in Holland — he always misses my birthday.'

There are many things Anne might wish to say, but she knows better than to say them, especially when Bishop Burnet stands at her elbow. It is the Bishop who breaks the silence.

'But Your Highness must surely wish the King to be well, and these summers in Holland have a most restorative effect on him. We must all be grateful for that.'

'I suppose we must. But I do wish that, if he could not remain here, he might sometimes take me with him.'

'When you are older, perhaps. For now, you must try to be patient: I do believe you are old enough to understand how melancholy His Majesty finds his English palaces, since the Queen departed them.'

Gloucester nods. 'Yes, I understand that, and besides he has no wars to fight, and his Dutch Guards are all gone, and now Parliament has taken almost all his army away, and he has told me himself, that a General without an army is a miserable creature.'

'I am sure he will send for you when he returns,' says Anne, 'and then you may have more discourse with him. Now have your Gentlemen take you to bed.'

'Very well, Mama. In truth, I am perfectly content to retire, for I find I am afflicted a *little* with a headache — but it is only a *little* headache, Mama — so I am certain that a good night's sleep will cure it.'

30TH JULY 1700

'Your Highness? Your Highness, are you asleep?'

Anne opens her eyes and sees three women standing dismally by her bed: Danvers, Hill, one of the Ladies Charlotte. This is not good.

'Hill? Why do you stand like that? Is there bad news?'

Hill looks at the other two, as if to beg their pardon for what she is about to say. 'It is Gloucester, Madam — he is taken ill.'

Anne stirs herself at once with a vigour she thought never to have again.

'Then do not stand there! Dress me! Dress me straight away!'

The women move then, but not nearly fast enough: no, Anne does not care which shoes are brought, she does not wish her hair to be dressed, and must they be so nice over every little thing? No, she will not wait for a chair with short poles — Danvers and Hill must walk either side of her so she might lean upon them, and that way they will reach Gloucester's rooms the quicker.

George is already in his son's chamber. His face, his demeanour, are a study in dismay. Not so Gloucester's: he looks peevish, almost angry. He beckons Anne over and whispers into her ear.

'Mother, they wish to bleed me, but it is all nonsense — I am only tired after yesterday, so that accounts for the headache and the fever, and my sore throat is surely from talking to so many people, and if I feel sick it is only because I was such a glutton at the feast — tell them they must not bleed me.'

Anne puts her hand to his forehead, which feels to her as it often did in Campden House days, hot and moist.

'Darling, you must forgive me — I know it is always tempting to be one's own physician, but it is better to heed the proper ones.'

It is a pity that the chief physician on duty should be the Catholic Dr Harris, but the King thinks highly of him, and the King is very critical when it comes to physicians. Anne is attending to her son, who has burst into tears, but the man is set on taking her aside, so she gives her place to George, and goes to talk to him.

'I am sorry, Your Highness, but I must tell you what I have told the Prince already, which is to say I fear this is a lapse of that illness that we had thought long outgrown.'

'I thought as much.' She lowers her voice. 'Is my boy in danger?'

'We must pray he is not. We shall watch him today and if the fever has not abated by tomorrow, then he must be bled.'

They bleed him the following morning, and although he is weak, he bears it with fortitude. At first it appears to have succeeded admirably, for the Duke's blood is instantly cooled. He is able to take a little nourishment, to talk quite reasonably with his parents and his tutor, and to sleep comfortably. It seems there might be no need to pray after all, except to give thanks, but then the evening comes, and the fever rises again. For a little while his condition is as bad as it was, and then it is worse: the Duke is talking gibberish, and he no longer knows anyone.

Desperate now, Anne sends for Dr Radcliffe. He bursts into the chamber in his old, rude fashion, neglecting to make any compliment to her and demanding to know what remedies have been tried.

'You let blood!' he shouts. 'Then you have destroyed him — and you may finish him, for I will not prescribe.'

He tries to leave, but Anne begs him not to, and because he is not entirely devoid of pity, and she weeps so very much, he stays. He has the surgeon apply blisters. The fever rises again. They have eight physicians in the chamber with them now, and Bishop Burnet, and Dr Pratt, and Compton. The Duke is thrown in and out of sleep; he tosses himself this way and that in the bed, and cries, and now and then he shouts. The doctors pour potions down him, order him to be blistered, or cupped, and in between times they argue. The clergy encourage Anne to pray. Since Dr Radcliffe arrived, her composure has amazed everybody, but by Sunday she has borne too much, and she falls into a swoon. Radcliffe sends her out.

It is not for him to keep her out. She returns on Monday. Dr Harris approaches her and tells her that there is hope today: His Highness's breathing seems to have eased a bit, and his pulse is mending. Anne looks at Radcliffe: he shrugs.

'I have told Dr Harris we might apply more blisters,' he says. 'We can do no more harm to him now.'

She does not ask Dr Radcliffe what he means by this, but she nods to Dr Harris.

So the boy is blistered, then they watch again for a short while, then his breathing turns convulsive, he cannot swallow anymore, his speech grows ever wilder, his cries more piteous, his movements more violent. Anne keeps hold of his hand. She is quite composed again: it is quite clear now that they are coming to the end. It is what God has all along intended, and no less than she deserves.

SETTLEMENT

George meets Sarah at the door of Anne's chamber. He has the look of a man who has not slept for days together, who has spent the time weeping instead.

'We thought she was with child again,' he says, 'but we were wrong, and now she has a fever, her heart is quite broken, she will see nobody —'

'In that case, Your Highness, I ought not —'

'— except for me, and you. She has been asking for you — no physician, no divine — only for you, Madam. Only you.' The Prince shuffles off in the direction of his chamber, where the bottles will be lined up and waiting.

There is only one candle lit in the chamber: it is as dark as if it had been burrowed out of the earth; there is a strong smell, composed mostly of unwashed linen and brandy, but with a touch of blood in there, and with it a tincture of sickness. It forces on Sarah the remembrance of other rooms, in which she has watched a parent or a child die, or lain by herself and grieved. She knows what it is to be in Anne's condition — she pities her sincerely — but she does not mean to join her in it. She is here to be of use, and they will both feel better for her usefulness.

The figure on the bed is still, and snoring a little — she sleeps: good. Somebody — Hill or Danvers — has been filling her up with cold tea, so they might all have a break from her weeping. Sarah creeps nearer, and spies a book open on the little table by the bedside, next to the candle. She sits down in the chair beside it and takes a look at what sort of stuff her mistress and her Prince have been reading: *The Christian's Defence Against the Fears of Death.* All very well, but in Anne's place she would prefer to resort to the stoics. Perhaps she will read a little Seneca to her, made into English — Anne has always liked to be read to.

Sarah replaces the book. She notices that there are three bottles on the table and takes them up one by one, squinting at the labels with her short-sighted eyes: laudanum — as always; spa water — it would be better taken at the source, but Anne is in no condition

629

to travel; the third one has no label, so she takes off the stopper and has a sniff, but she cannot identify the contents — well, there are always new doctors and new concoctions, and this must be another of those.

She leans over the bed to see her mistress better, and the sight of her brings out the usual mix of humours: tenderness and kindness on the one hand, impatience and vexation on the other. She has always been sensibly touched by the Princess's loyalty, her generosity, her sincere desire to put ceremony aside so as to be a better friend; she has always been exasperated by her stubbornness, frustrated by the dullness of her conversation, and driven to distraction by her demanding, repetitious letters. It shames her a little to own it, but whenever she hears that the gout has gone to the Princess's hand, she cannot but feel relieved that it will stay the letters for a while.

So, Anne is not with child after all. Looking at the body stretched out upon the bed, so broken and so monstrously swelled, Sarah cannot see that any living child could ever come out of it now. They had better settle the succession on her German cousins, and soon. But let Anne please outlive the Dutchman — let her survive him long enough for Sarah and her Lord to achieve what only they can achieve.

The snores cease abruptly and Anne's eyes open. They brighten when she sees that Sarah is there, but a moment later they are full of tears.

'O, dear Mrs Freeman! Mrs Freeman!'

'Sshh . . .' Sarah leans forward and embraces her. 'Ssshhh . . .'

'O Mrs Freeman, how unfortunate is your poor Morley now, see how the Lord chastises me now, how harshly am I punished!'

'No, Mrs Morley! Not punished — only unfortunate — your goodness has ever been —'

'But — do you not see? I must think that I am punished, for otherwise there is no sense in it — my children, my sufferings — and to lose the sense of it is to lose all reason.'

'I am sure your chaplains have told you, it is not for us to find out the sense — to go a-hunting for the sense is the best way to lose reason that I know.'

'Then I shall try — I shall try to leave aside that question — but there still remains another.'

'And what is that?'

'How shall I bear my life, Mrs Freeman? How shall I bear it?'

Historical Note

Anne outlived her brother-in-law, and came to the throne in 1702. She died in 1714, aged 49. As she left no children, she was succeeded by her distant — but Protestant — cousin, George of Hanover.

The employees of Thorndike Press hope you have enjoyed this Large Print book. All our Thorndike, Wheeler, and Kennebec Large Print titles are designed for easy reading, and all our books are made to last. Other Thorndike Press Large Print books are available at your library, through selected bookstores, or directly from us.

For information about titles, please call:
  (800) 223-1244

or visit our Web site at:
  http://gale.cengage.com/thorndike

To share your comments, please write:
  Publisher
  Thorndike Press
  10 Water St., Suite 310
  Waterville, ME 04901